The Sheriff Gets His Girl

JANE POLLER

VINCI BOOKS

Dedicated to my husband, you are freaking amazing and I love you more every day. Thanks for making my life a real Happily Ever After.

Vinci Books

vinci-books.com

Published by Vinci Books Ltd in 2026

1

Copyright © Jane Poller 2021

The author has asserted their moral right to be identified as the author of this work in accordance with the Copyright, Designs and Patents Act 1988. This work is a work of fiction. Names, characters, places and incidents are the product of the author's imagination or are used fictitiously. Any resemblance to actual persons, living or dead, places and incidents is entirely coincidental.

All rights reserved. No part of this publication may be copied, reproduced, distributed, stored in any retrieval system, or transmitted in any form or by any means, including photocopying, recording, or other electronic or mechanical methods, nor used as a source for any form of machine learning including AI datasets, without the prior written permission of the publisher.

The publisher and the author have made every effort to obtain permissions for any third party material used in this book and to comply with copyright law. Any queries in this respect should be brought to the attention of the publisher and any omissions will be corrected in future editions.

A CIP catalogue record for this book is available from the British Library.

Paperback ISBN: 9781036707941

By Jane Poller

Crimson Creek

The Soldier Gets His Girl
The Sheriff Gets His Girl
The Songwriter Gets His Girl
The Surgeon Gets His Girl
The Mechanic Gets His Girl
The Ranger Gets His Girl
The Cowboy Gets His Girl
The Convict Gets His Girl

Chapter One

Beginning of October

When the bakery doorbell dinged at precisely 6:02am, Maryanne smiled, adjusted her bra to showcase the girls, pulled down her v-neck t-shirt to maximize cleavage, and walked through the swinging door to the front of the shop.

She sucked in a breath and almost fanned herself. Gunner never failed to disappoint. He was wearing the short sleeve uniform shirt today, which made his biceps bulge and strain against the thin material as he spun his cowboy hat in one hand.

The light from the floor to ceiling front windows shone on his light brown hair, making his natural golden highlights stand out. It was getting a little long, and her fingers itched to run through it.

Even when they were teens, he maintained that high and tight military haircut that she was so familiar with as an Army brat. He kept it longer on top now than he did back then. His jeans were pressed, and his black boots shone with military precision, not a speck of dirt on them.

Shaking herself out of her trance, she grinned. "Morning, Gunner. What can I get you?"

His strong jaw clenched before he smiled tightly and stepped up to the counter, setting his hat down and sending a shiver up her spine.

"Usual."

His growl made her heart skip a beat. His voice was rough and dark, just like all her deepest fantasies about him.

"I thought you might want to try something different this morning. Different could be fun," she sing-songed, waving a hand below her breasts before moving it over the goods under the glass. His eyes narrowed as she crossed her arms and leaned on the counter, pushing her double treats on display.

His eyes gleamed with a predatory heat. He didn't let it shine through very often. She let her shoulders dip a bit more, making him suck in a deep breath.

"Just the usual."

You'd think she'd be used to his rejection by now. He'd been shooting her down almost daily for two years. Still, she refused to give up on Gunner.

Pasting on a coy smile, she cooed, "Are you sure I couldn't tempt you into something else this morning?"

He shook his head, remaining silent, his face stony and expressionless, just like always. Even when they were kids and she'd come to Crimson Creek to visit her grandmother for the summer, he maintained that stoic expression. No matter how hard she tried, she couldn't shake him up.

She sighed and straightened, turning to grab a to-go bag and bending into the display case to fetch his order.

"Suit yourself. Maybe tomorrow. I'm experimenting

with a pumpkin spice this month. You'll have to tell me what you think, alright? I'll throw in one of those, along with the apple one. But fair warning: next month, the normal bear claws will switch to cinnamon apple. You okay with that?"

She stood to place the box on the counter and caught his gaze zeroed in on her cleavage. His eyes shot to hers in surprise before he cleared his throat, shifted on his feet, and glanced away. The pink tinge on his tanned cheeks was the most adorable thing she'd ever seen.

"Yes."

Smiling wide, she arranged his treats in the small box. "Cool, let me grab the rest of these. How's everything over at the station?"

"Fine."

She tried a different tactic. "How's your mom and dad?"

"Good."

She rolled her eyes and sighed as she stepped to the cash register. "One of these days, Gunner, you're going to actually talk to me, and it's going to be amazing."

Catching his green hazel eyes, she saw them darken as he clenched his jaw. Then he blinked and relaxed his shoulders with a visible shrug.

"Nothing to talk about."

Turning to make his coffee, she sighed. "Darlin', if you ever want to work on your people skills, I'm here. I'll have you making small talk with the best of them."

"I saw you yesterday morning. Nothing has happened since then."

Her heart fluttered. "Wow. Two sentences in a row? That's a record."

She glanced over her shoulder and winked. His cheeks blushed again as he looked away.

Was he starting to thaw out? She wondered if he talked more at work. Or when he arrested someone. She could always try to get herself arrested so he'd have to recite her rights. It'd be worth it to hear his voice.

She finished his coffee and tried to pass it to him. He glanced at her outstretched hand but waved for her to put it on the counter as he pulled out his wallet.

Swallowing the knot of rejection in her throat, she rang up his total and grabbed the cash he'd tossed down as he picked up his breakfast and walked out.

It hadn't escaped her that he refused to touch her yet again. He'd kept well out of her reach since her first day back in town nearly two years ago. He'd pulled her over and their hands had met over her license.

She watched his ass as he crossed the street, and a dreamy sigh escaped her lips. She glanced out the front window at the rising sun, not realizing she'd crossed to the front of the store so she could watch him walk across the street and down the block to the police station.

The purples and pinks in the sky reminded her of when she'd escaped back home two years ago. Like today, it had soothed her confused and tired heart.

She'd always used her smile when she was a kid—and later, her generous curves—to get what she wanted. She'd smiled and things just fell into place. When she'd gone to Colorado for Culinary Arts school, her smile and curves had bitten her in the ass, though.

She'd opened an edible bakery with her then boyfriend. She shivered because two years later, he still gave her nightmares. She'd come home to lick her wounds and start over.

Her little red convertible had been packed so high with

The Sheriff Gets His Girl

her brightly colored suitcases and boxes that she couldn't even see out her side or rearview mirrors. That was when she'd seen the flashing lights in her driver's side mirror.

She gripped the steering wheel, knuckles turning white as she pulled over onto the side of the little two-lane highway, the anxiety climbed higher in her tense shoulders.

Shit. Her heart felt like it was going to race away when she remembered the pot stashed in her bags. Please, God, don't let them search the car.

She watched with wide eyes as the cop swaggered up to her window. There was something familiar about that walk, but with his cowboy hat, aviator sunglasses, uniform shirt, jeans, and boots, he could be anybody. Anybody who had bulging biceps and thighs, that is.

Shaking her head to free herself from staring at his body, she pushed the button to roll down her window.

"Ma'am. Do you know how fast you were going?"

"No, officer. Was I speeding?" Her heart was definitely speeding at that deep, growly voice. It sent goosebumps along her arms.

"Yes, ma'am. Speed limit through here is only fifty-five. You were doing seventy-one. License and registration, please."

She swallowed hard. "I'll need to unbuckle to reach the glove box. Probably need to shift my bag over too. Is that alright?"

"Sure."

He crossed his arms, making his biceps bulge and her eyes pop behind her sunglasses. The dude's massive muscles were barely contained in his uniform shirt. Her mouth watered as she caught sight of a piece of tattoo barely hidden by his shirt sleeve.

Slowly, she unbuckled and got on her knees to reach over her luggage set. She opened the glove box but could feel his eyes on her ass.

She wiggled a little extra as she found the paper and shut the glove box, then slid back to her seat. With any luck, her ass would get her out of the ticket.

"Here's the registration, Officer."

His fingers brushed against hers when he took the paper from her. The slight contact was like lightning up her arm. It left her breathless, and she snatched her arm back. It'd been years since she'd felt this zing.

Taking a deep breath, she reached for her purse and license. When she handed it over, she grazed his hand again, trying to replicate the effect. Would it work?

Hot damn, it did.

The lightning went straight to her core, making it pulse with need. She only reacted to one person like this. His hand jerked when she let go of the license, and he walked toward his vehicle.

Frowning, she leaned her head out the window. Was it him? She hadn't seen him in nearly a decade.

"Gunner? Is that you?"

He'd only gotten three steps when he turned halfway, his body in profile glowing in the setting sun. She'd always crushed on him when she'd stay with her grandma in the summers, but holy shit. He'd grown up and filled out that uniform perfectly.

Slowly, he reached up, making his biceps strain from the muscle, and took his sunglasses off. She could almost hear her vagina howling for him. The brightest hazel green eyes she'd ever seen flashed in the afternoon light, flecks of gold drawing her in like always.

Her heart spasmed with joy. It was Gunner, all right. The first boy she'd ever crushed on and her first kiss.

Well, maybe. She wasn't sure if it had happened or not, but in her heart, she counted it.

She whipped off her own sunglasses and grinned.

"It is you, all grown up now. What's it been? Ten years?"

"About that."

One side of his mouth tipped up, drawing her gaze to his lips. She licked hers, wanting a taste of him.

"That's too damn long. Being a cop suits you." *She gave her best flirty smile.* *"And that uniform... damn, Gunner. Not sure I've seen a sexier cop in my life."*

Her laugh bubbled up when his cheeks turned pink, and he narrowed his eyes at her, putting his hands on his hips.

"Are you... flirting with me? To get out of a ticket?"

"Oh, am I getting a ticket?" She raised her eyebrows and flicked a hand to her chest in mock surprise. "No! Say it ain't so!"

He barked out a surprised laugh and shook his head.

"Let me run your license and see if you'll be getting that ticket. Hang tight."

She watched him walk away in her driver's side mirror. His ass in those jeans made her mouth go dry, so she reached for her soda.

He'd always acted cool and aloof when she was in town for the summers. She wasn't even in town yet, and she'd gotten him to laugh. That was new. Maybe he'd lightened up in the past few years.

When they were kids, he'd not paid any attention to her at all. He was always scowling and only laughed when his brothers were around. When they were all hanging out at summer barbecues or the city pool, he'd laugh and joke around with the group.

But by the time he was a senior in high school, it'd been painfully obvious—to her, at least—that he was keeping her at arm's length. And she had no idea why.

It hurt though, to think he'd laugh, joke, and talk with everyone else, but not her. What was wrong with her, anyway? Was she not interesting enough? Pretty enough?

She'd developed the traditional boobs and ass of her Latina heritage pretty early, but the more she tried to get him to notice, the more distance he put between them.

Then he'd started dating that Justine girl. Maryanne bit her nail as she watched him walk in the mirror. Justine had been the tall, blond cheerleader while he was captain of the football team. Maryanne had always felt inferior around girls like that.

She shook off the thoughts and leaned an elbow out the window as he squared up to it. "So, what's the verdict?"

"No ticket. Just a warning."

"Yes!" She hit the steering wheel and bounced on the seat. "Thank God! I cannot afford a ticket right now. Man, this is some welcome home."

He grinned, handing her license and registration back. She grabbed them slowly, holding his fingers for a few seconds longer than necessary. Her breath caught as she stared up at him, his hazel eyes burning a hole in the newly erected wall around her heart.

"No problem. Just slow down. Welcome home, Maryanne. It's good to see you." His voice spoke straight to her core and made her quiver. A quick glance revealed no ring. Hallelujah, he wasn't married.

He turned and quickly strode back to his SUV, lights still flashing.

The image from the past and present merged in her mind. Same uniform, jeans, boots, and cowboy hat. Same swagger and ass she just wanted to bite into.

The bakery door pushed open beside her, bringing her back to the present. She'd been staring aimlessly at the police station and hadn't even noticed Holly walking from the other direction.

"Morning, Maryanne. How's it going? Oh, I love your Halloween decorations! How'd you get the front window decorated so fast?"

Holly flicked her dyed silver braid over her shoulder. Holly had been in a car accident which caused a miscarriage and her husband's death two years ago. Last year, she'd moved to Crimson Creek, Texas, to join her brother and get a fresh start on life.

Holly's orange yoga shirt was loose over her black yoga pants, and she was sweaty from her morning session.

"Morning, Holly. I came in last night when I couldn't sleep. How was sunrise yoga? Did you have a big crowd?"

Maryanne asked as she bustled back behind the counter to make Holly's favorite fruit smoothie.

Maryanne didn't just have baked goods. She also had smoothies, milkshakes, cappuccinos, coffees, and more. She catered to her customers year-round. And with the addition of the CBD infused drinks and treats, business was booming.

Only a few years younger than Maryanne, Holly had moved to Crimson Creek with her brother last year. They both owned shops on Main Street and had quickly become friends.

"We had about half a dozen. Not bad for our second Saturday. What are you up to today?"

Maryanne handed over the smoothie and swiped her friend's card.

"Well, normally I'd be wrapping up about nine to take Cody to his soccer game, but Mom's taking all three of my nephews for the weekend."

Her sister, Cindy, worked at the hospital on the weekends, which meant Maryanne normally watched her nephews after closing early on Saturday.

"Wait, you have a free weekend? You're kidding me!"

"Nope. Want to have a girl's night? Unofficial, of course, since my sister is still working at the hospital. Maybe you and Lola can hang out? I need to dye my hair for the Halloween season."

"Tired of the purple highlights already? What are you going for next?"

"Orange," Maryanne said with a grin. She tightened her high ponytail and then leaned on the counter. Holly regularly came over to dye each other's hair: Holly's silver to match her grief, Maryanne's streaked with colors to match the holidays.

Holly had only been in town a year, but she and Lola

were best friends already. Maryanne and Cindy grew up with Lola, always hanging out with her in the summers when they visited Crimson Creek.

"Why don't we go to the Electric Cowboy? Lola's been pushing me to get out and have some fun."

"Sure, that sounds great. I haven't been in years."

Chapter Two

October

"Wow, this place is packed! Is it always like this?" Maryanne asked Lola as she paid her cover charge and followed them into the bar on the outskirts of town. The L shape of the barn gave a view of both the bar and stage as she entered.

People mingled around on the dance floor in front of the stage. Orange Halloween lights draped the ceiling around the stage where a band was already playing. She couldn't see who it was, but they sounded good and she couldn't wait to dance.

Although the Electric Cowboy was legendary, Maryanne's busy schedule had kept her from the club over the last two years.

"Pretty much." Lola, the tallest of their group at six feet, glanced over the crowd and pointed to the side. "Let's grab some food first. Come on."

They walked past the bar and through the saloon doors into a back room. There were pool tables in the middle of the large space, with booths along the edges. The vibe was good here, relaxing and fun, and Maryanne instantly loved it.

They drew stares from the guys playing pool. Maryanne knew they were a striking group. Lola's dark auburn hair was pulled back in a ponytail. With her freckles and bright blue eyes, she was fresh-faced and all-natural. She wore her favorite plaid pearl snap shirt tied in a knot just above her belly button, tight jeans, and cowboy boots.

Holly was around five feet but with her dyed silver hair and blue eyes, she looked like a little fairy girl, ethereal, calm, smiling, and fragile in her petiteness.

She may have been a few years younger than Maryanne, but the tight purple dress and kitten heels definitely showed her as a woman in her twenties.

Maryanne was between the two on height, but she'd played up her other assets. Her orange sequined shirt was a deep v-cut nearly to her belly button, showing off her generous cleavage. Her favorite four-inch black heels did wonders for her legs and rounded ass.

They sauntered over to an empty booth and a waitress came and took their order. When she walked off, a loud, bushy-bearded man stumbled to their table, pool stick still in his hand.

"Hey, ladies. Wanna play a game of pool?" He smelled of cheap booze and cigarettes.

Maryanne flicked her black hair over her shoulder and smiled politely. "Maybe later, hot stuff. We need food first."

She turned to face her friends sitting on the opposite side of her as the man shrugged and wandered back to his game.

Holly laughed, covering her mouth with her hand. "You tell him, Maryanne."

Just then, the band in the main room started up a new song. The upbeat tempo seeped into her soul, making her body sway in her seat.

"Oh, I can't wait to get out on that dance floor." Lola tapped her fingers on the table in time to the muted music. "I really need to let loose a little. Mama's been driving me up the wall."

"Is she feeling any better?" Holly asked.

"Not really. Her cancer treatments are exhausting, but that's been going on for a while now."

Maryanne felt her heart constrict the more Lola talked about her mom.

The entire conversation reminded her of when her grandma passed away almost two years ago. She'd blown into town after her nasty breakup with nowhere to stay.

She'd moved in with 'Buela for a few weeks... only to find out that Hospice was already coming in to help. Mom and Cindy hadn't even known about Hospice.

She'd held on for another six months before passing away. It was hard to see her wither away slowly like that, and to hear that Lola's mom wasn't doing well...

The topic caused all three of them to fall silent until the waitress delivered their food and broke the tension.

"Perfect. Greasy food is just what I need on my weekend off." Maryanne popped a loaded French fry into her mouth. She needed to relax. Her CBD hadn't been as effective lately, and she didn't want to break out the last of her pot stash from Colorado. Maybe dancing would help.

"When are you going to hire someone to help at the bakery?" Lola asked as they ate.

Maryanne snorted. "Who says I need to?"

Lola rolled her eyes and dipped a fry into ketchup. "You haven't taken a day off all year, Maryanne, and it's the beginning of October. You're going to burn out if you don't get help."

"Nah, that's why we do girl's night on Thursdays, remember? To help us all meditate and de-stress and shit. Besides, I take off early on Saturdays for soccer games this time of year, and Sunday's we're closed."

"Taking off early isn't the same as taking a day off per week," Lola scolded. "And you still have all the church stuff to do on Sunday's, even if you're not in the bakery."

"Well, it's a good thing we're here tonight. I miss karaoke and dancing with my Colorado friends. Now, let's drain this pitcher of margaritas and hit that dance floor. The band is calling my name." Maryanne reached for her drink.

"It's the Williams' boys. They're pretty good, right? They play most weekends here. You should join them, Maryanne. Maybe you could do a duet with Gunner."

Maryanne nearly spit out her drink. "Wait, they're still playing? I thought they outgrew that years ago."

Lola grinned. "Nope. They're regulars here. Gunner says it helps keep the trouble away to have a cop as the lead singer at the bar. It's good, clean fun and none of that funny business you get at the bars down in Fort Worth or even over in Denton."

Maryanne drained her margarita, the strawberry tart on her tongue, and poured them all another round. She could feel the flush in her cheeks already, but hopefully her friends assumed it was alcohol related. Her thoughts naturally drifted to Gunner.

"I don't know that I've seen him out of uniform in the two years I've been back."

Holly tapped her chin. "I've seen him around the

grocery store a few times this year, but you're right. He's usually in uniform."

"And a mighty fine uniform it is, isn't it?" Maryanne sighed as she played with her straw.

"I love the short-sleeved one. I always want to push it up to see what that tattoo is." Lola wiggled her brows.

"But his biceps are so damn big, there's no way you could push his sleeve up even a little!" Holly smirked, making them all laugh.

"I never saw him as the tattoo type, but I guess the Marines changed him." Maryanne sipped her drink, wishing her mouth was wrapped around him.

"I didn't realize he was in the Marines. How long ago?" Holly ate the last fry and wiped her fingers on the napkin.

Lola shrugged, "A few years, right after high school. His girlfriend, Justine, wasn't happy that he'd enlisted, but he promised he'd stay faithful. Oh, I didn't tell y'all what happened did I? So, you know how Granny is friends with Mrs. Williams, right?"

Holly and Maryanne nodded, so Lola continued.

"Granny said that Mrs. Williams was so happy she was dancing in her kitchen last week because Justine moved back home."

"Because they're going to get back together?" Maryanne asked, a weight pressing on her chest.

Lola shook her head. "Nope, she was dancing because Justine and Gunner are officially over."

A lump formed in Maryanne's throat as she asked, "How does she know they're over?"

"Justine ran into Mrs. Williams with her new boyfriend and was so excited to move back home with him. Apparently, Justine didn't even realize that Gunner was waiting for her." Lola's brows waggled, and Maryanne's heart ached for Gunner. He was probably devastated.

"Oh no, poor Gunner," Holly said. "He's such a good man. I hope he wins as sheriff."

Maryanne sat, dumbfounded as a new realization sank in. Perhaps Gunner had blown her off the past two years because of some misguided loyalty to his old ex-girlfriend. What did that mean now that he was free?

"Based on what Granny and Mrs. Williams said, I don't know if they were broken up, had expectations to get back together, or even if he's been faithful this whole time. Justine certainly hasn't, but I don't think Gunner's dated anyone, especially not since he moved home after the Marines." Lola's brows drew together as she reached for her drink.

Maryanne thought back to his visits to the shop the past few days. He wasn't keeping his eyes firmly on the floor or on the menu as much as last year. Her heart sped up at the thought that maybe she could finally win him over.

"We have to go dancing," Maryanne said, before chugging the last of her margarita.

Holly arched a brow. "Duh, that's why we're here."

"No, I mean right now. Come on!" Maryanne pulled them out of the seats and swaggered out the saloon doors onto the loud dance floor.

"Hey, I thought y'all were gonna play pool with us!" the older bearded man called.

Maryanne poked her head back in the door to say, "Maybe later. We want to dance!" Then she turned and headed toward the dance floor, with Holly and Lola trailing behind.

Chapter Three

October

What the ever-living fuck was she doing here? She was going to get roofied if she kept dancing like that with every Tom, Dick, and Harry in the place.

Gunner watched Maryanne wrap her arms around some cowboy, who pulled her flush against him. Gunner's breath caught and his eyes narrowed. Her shiny orange shirt was like a beacon of light that pulled his gaze. But if he were honest, it wasn't the bright shirt that drew his attention. It was her.

They danced in front of the stage as if to taunt him. Her black jeans had rips in them, revealing a tantalizing amount of tanned skin.

And God, those black, fuck-me heels... He was a sucker for those, and she wore them all the time. Seeing her strutting around in those heels had him thinking about bending her over the end of a bed, wearing those heels and nothing else.

He sang the words to *Chicken Fried*, his mind on autopilot, not even registering the words coming out of his mouth. After four more songs, his brother, Landry, elbowed him out of the way, whispering in his ear, "Take a break. You're shit tonight."

Normally, he'd punch Landry and keep going, but he couldn't see Maryanne anymore. Landry had distracted him, and now she was gone. His heart rate increased just thinking about her running off with some random guy. He slowly hopped off the stage and walked to the bar. It wasn't his place to say who she went home with. She was just a girl from his childhood whom he saw every morning at the bakery.

He circled to the back room and looked through the saloon doors. She laughed around a pool table with half a dozen guys, and he let out a sigh.

He refused to analyze why it felt better to be closer to her. Instead, he focused on her flirting. Flirting with guys that weren't him. Gritting his teeth, he sucked in a breath of stale beer and sweat.

What was wrong with him? He'd seen her around town at different festivals, barbecues, and functions. It didn't make sense why he was jealous more so now than last year. She always flirted with everyone.

Still, he wanted to make sure she didn't do something stupid and get herself hurt. He turned and grabbed a beer from the bar, then slipped inside and sat at a booth in the dimly lit corner.

Of course, she was reigning court like some sort of damn queen. She slid the blue chalk around the tip of the pool stick, her flirty smile playing around her lips.

Gunner knew he wasn't the only one getting hard as she handled the end of it almost sensuously. Two of the guys near her were joking and flirting back, while a few of the others were talking with Lola and Holly.

The light shone off the orange streaks in Maryanne's jet-black hair. She had it pulled halfway back in some sort of clip while the rest hung down her back. He wanted to wrap his fist in it.

A familiar blond slid into the booth across from him, pulling his gaze to her shining blue eyes. "Hey, Gunner. How's it been going? Haven't seen you around the past few weeks. Are you still mad?"

He grunted, then glanced around the room to make sure Maryanne was still playing pool before looking back at Justine.

"I'm alright. Wasn't totally unexpected but it would've been nice if you would've officially broken things off years ago. I'm not a fan of sitting in limbo."

"Yeah, our communication wasn't that great, was it? When you went to boot camp, we wrote all those letters. I thought I'd explained it then."

Justine's lip pouted out, making his gut twist. Her lips would never be as luscious as Maryanne's.

Maryanne's called to him like a siren. Justine paled in comparison, but he'd only realized that the past few weeks she'd been home.

"That was ten years ago, Justine. And I came home six years ago. When I left the Marines, you said we were still on for the plan."

He narrowed his eyes at her. Why had he once thought she was the perfect woman? She was far from it. Sure, she was pretty in that All-American way, but she did nothing for him. There was no emotion except emptiness now.

She arched a brow. "Why didn't you ever call me? We talked like twice a week, then even that slowed down. It's been years since we talked even once a week. Surely you saw this coming?"

"I thought you were just busy with finals or something. How the hell was I supposed to know you were moving on?"

He clenched his jaw and leaned back in his seat. Okay, so the emptiness had some anger in it. He didn't like being taken for a fool.

"Are we going to be all right? I mean, I don't want to cause problems in town or anything. I just want us both to be happy."

She reached forward and tried to hold his hand. He jerked it back and grabbed his beer to drink, his gaze wandering over to Maryanne as he swallowed.

He didn't want to touch Justine or anyone else. He'd not been celibate throughout the years since he'd moved home. Officially, they had broken up. Unofficially, they'd both agreed to pick back up when the time was right. So, when he'd moved home, he'd waited, minus the occasional one-night stand here or there.

He couldn't remember the last time he'd been with a woman. He glanced from Maryanne's luscious lips to Justine's bright pink ones and back again. The thought of Justine's thin lips revolted him.

But Maryanne's cherry red ones called to him...

He lost his train of thought as Maryanne bent over the table, her shirt hanging open as she lined up her shot. He and half the room had an open view right down her shirt to the magnificent breasts swinging inside.

She was braless. Now those, he wanted to touch.

Good God, what was wrong with him? Touching Maryanne would be like setting a gas station on fire. One touch and they'd both go up in flames. It'd almost happened before.

He didn't stop drinking his beer until it was gone. Then he dragged his eyes back to Justine with a sigh. It was time to cut the anchor.

"It'll be okay, Justine. I didn't tell anyone I was waiting for you because we did break up. I've had hook-ups here and there, but I guess I was just sort of in a limbo state, expecting you to come back and pick up where we left off."

"It's good to get it all out in the open and cleared up, right?" She bit her nail. He could feel her knee tapping under the table, clearly uncomfortable.

He nodded. "Yeah, I may be disappointed, but we'll be alright, Justine."

"This won't cause any problems with my business?"

Her worried frown didn't mar her pretty features. She was still beautiful, but the fact that she was more concerned about her business than him put the nail on the coffin of their relationship.

He arched a brow. "Nope, and it won't impact my future running for sheriff, right?"

"Right." Her smile of relief was fleeting.

They sat in silence a moment longer, his gaze roaming around the room. She cleared her throat, then slid out of the booth.

"Well, I guess I'll see you around then. Bye, Gunner."

She waved as she walked past him and out the door. The swinging of the door sent a little burst of air around him. Maryanne's deep chuckle echoed throughout the room, the sound going straight to his cock. He couldn't take his eyes off her, Justine already forgotten.

The sparkle in her warm, chocolate brown eyes said she was up to something. He'd seen that mischievous look so many times when they were kids. She placed her palm on one of the guy's chests as she laughed.

Rage washed over him, narrowing his vision down to just her and that guy. He wanted to march over there and haul her over his shoulder like some kind of Viking raider.

He'd almost done just that right after he'd graduated high school.

She was a few years younger. Every summer, she'd come to Crimson Creek to stay with her grandma. No matter where she moved to with her dad in the Army, she always came to Crimson Creek for the summer.

He'd watched out for her since she was ten, and he'd saved her from drowning at the city pool. She'd hung out with his younger brothers more, but no matter what scrape they got into, Gunner was always there to bail her out.

Maryanne brought out a completely different side of him, a protective caveman side that he didn't know how to handle.

The summer after he'd graduated, Parker and Landry had thrown a massive end of school year party out at his parents' sale barn on the back of their property.

He knew Maryanne had goaded them into it, claiming it would be a good way to send him off to basic training. But really, she just wanted to party.

She'd danced all night with every single guy there. He'd tried to guard the kegs and keep the other kids from over drinking. He knew he couldn't keep them all from drinking, but he'd be damn sure no one got alcohol poisoning.

Maryanne was one of a handful that he'd had to put his foot down with. He'd stood there, refusing to move or let her have a refill. Arms crossed to keep from rubbing his hand along her smooth stomach in the crop top she wore, he'd stared at her when she argued, yelled, and even flirted to get another drink.

"You're not the boss of me."

She'd stood on her tippy toes to wave a finger under his nose. Even then, he'd been freakishly tall, making him feel like an outsider. The top of her head had barely come up to his shoulder, which was frustrating because it made the cinnamon and vanilla scent of her shampoo overwhelm him every time they were in the same room.

The party had gone on around them as she tried to smile and get her way. He'd held firm, his face stony and silent as she'd talked.

It was his only defense against her; he knew if he gave in even once, she'd wind him around her finger like a whipped puppy.

It wasn't until someone had accidentally bumped into her from behind and thrown her flush against him that she'd stopped running her mouth.

He'd caught her around the waist to steady her, making her gasp, the sound shooting straight to his semi-hard cock. The feel of her in his arms for the first time quickly changed that to a full-fledged woody. His heart raced and his skin prickled where his hands rested on her generous hips.

He'd stared down at her with his hazel gaze burning in the barn's light. Time seemed to stand still as they stood in each other's arms. His heartbeat pounded in tandem with hers and the music.

Only a few seconds passed since she'd been tossed against him. His fingers bit into the silky-smooth skin at her waist, and he swung her around and pushed her up against the wall.

His lips ravaged hers. They were lush, thick, and soft. Her tongue tasted like apple pie moonshine, heady, potent, and a brand on his soul. Her perky breasts pressed against him, making him groan.

He needed to taste them. Fuck, this was so much more powerful of a need than any he'd ever experienced before.

He'd roughly broken the kiss, stepping back so fast that she lost her footing. She slid along the wall to the ground, and before he could reach out and grab her, she'd blacked out.

He'd picked her up, bridal style, and wove through the party to his truck. Then he'd taken her to her grandmas to sleep it off.

When he'd placed her on the couch on the sun porch, the streetlight had fallen on her face, making her look like an angel.

The need to have her had clawed at him, creeping up his chest and threatening to close off his throat. It had been getting harder and harder to talk to her each summer without reaching out to touch her, claim her, pin her.

She was wild. She wanted nothing but a fun time, and when he was with her, he wanted that, too. But he couldn't let her derail his plans. First on the agenda was the Marines.

He'd walked away that night, every step like lead trying to anchor him to her.

After avoiding her all the following week, he'd convinced himself their kiss had been a mistake, a fluke, a bump in the road to achieving his goals.

With those goals fresh in his mind, he'd gotten back together with his ex-girlfriend, Justine, then had shipped to boot camp a week after that.

He'd relived that kiss over and over while in basic training. It took months before he could convince his heart that it wasn't real and to let go. Surely something as wonderful as that had been a figment of his imagination.

As an adult, he realized it had been the best kiss of his life. Every morning when he looked at her over the counter at the bakery, he wondered if her lips had been that soft and lush.

Staring at her now, bent over that pool table, he wondered if her pussy would be that soft and lush.

Gunner shook his head. He couldn't afford thoughts like that. He had to stop protecting her because she wasn't his to protect, no matter what his body said about the matter.

He slid out of the booth with his empty beer and through the saloon door to the main dance hall. It was too much; he couldn't take seeing more of her flirting.

The Sheriff Gets His Girl

He handed over his empty beer, then went to the restroom. Why was she even here tonight? She'd not come to the bar in two years.

Well, at least not on the nights when he and his brothers played. He had to let go of whatever it was pulling him to her.

She was a big girl. She didn't need him watching over her or whatever it was he was doing. No, he'd go back to the stage and do his job: sing and watch the crowd for trouble.

He forced himself to do just that, smiling and singing and laughing with the crowd until two am closing time.

When he grabbed beers for his brothers, he ran into Lola. He figured out that Maryanne had driven them all tonight, which was a relief. She wasn't likely to get drunk and go home with someone then.

But no one knew that when he left, he drove down Main Street to make sure her little red car was parked and safely out behind her second-floor apartment. And no one knew the sense of relief he felt to see it was the only vehicle in the parking lot.

Chapter Four

Mid-October

God, she couldn't wait for girls' night tonight. The new social media campaign she was doing for the fall season was drawing in even more customers, which meant she was busier than ever.

Then she was watching her nephews in the afternoons until her sister got off work. She loved her life, but it was exhausting.

Tonight, they were baking at Kendall and Holly's house. Her sister, Cindy, had promised tons of goodies for the bake sale that weekend to raise funds for her son Cody's middle school soccer team.

As the resident confectioner in town, Maryanne was organizing most of it.

She enjoyed being in charge, but she didn't like to ask for help. It made her feel weak to rely on someone else, and she didn't want to be burned like she had with her ex, Barry.

The Sheriff Gets His Girl

He might be why she hadn't hired someone to help at the bakery. Barry had helped her get started with her shop in Colorado, and it had ended in disaster. But after two years, she was making it just fine on her own.

Lola grumbled under her breath as she scrubbed the dishes hard enough to peel the protective coating off.

"Then he just pushed me out of the way and started changing the tire. Like I was some sort of helpless little female."

Lola had been griping about Holly's brother, Kendall, for the past ten minutes. He was the best doctor in Crimson Creek and smokin' hot. Maryanne had flirted with him a few times, but they had no chemistry.

Lola, however, was a different story. She and Kendall argued over everything and had apparently had a run in earlier in the week.

"That's intense washing there. You scrubbing Kendall from your mind?"

Maryanne teased as she leaned over the sink to wash her hands too. Cindy came up on the other side of Lola. Both sisters leaned in, crowding Lola as they peered at her face.

Lola frowned even deeper, then flicked the water on her hands into their faces. They squealed, and Cindy jumped back. But Maryanne grabbed the faucet, a sneaky grin pulling at her lips as she sprayed Lola in the face.

Maryanne's heart jumped. It'd been ages since she'd done something ridiculously unexpected like that. And it felt so good! Like she was herself again. Not even going to the bar last weekend had given her such joy and freedom.

"Wha—" Lola squealed, water dripping from her face, mouth hanging open in surprise.

Maryanne dropped the faucet and stepped back, mouth pulling wide and hands up in the air. She backed away slowly, as if from an angry dog, but she wasn't afraid. Her heart was racing from the sheer fun of it.

"There, there, girl. It's okay." Maryanne whispered soothingly with a grin.

Lola's blue eyes blazed as water dripped from her chin. Cindy grabbed her side, leaning over the counter as she laughed.

"Oh, you laugh, do you?" Lola lunged for the faucet and whipped it at Cindy and Holly. They both screeched and lunged towards Lola.

Each grabbed one of Lola's arms. The faucet was still on and whipping around the kitchen. Maryanne was laughing too hard to move. Cindy and Holly struggled to keep Lola from breaking free, laughter ringing through the room and blending with Lola's ranting.

The banging of a door made them freeze.

They glanced at the entryway, and Maryanne's heart skipped a beat as she saw Gunner standing just to the side of the open doorway, his face blank of expression as always. But seeing him in jeans, green t-shirt, and his leather jacket?

Damn, he made her mouth water.

Holly's brother, Kendall, stood just inside the house, his jaw dropped in amazement. Behind him crowded a bunch of tall hunks in jeans.

"Hey, man, let us in."

Kendall, Gunner, and the guys crowded into the kitchen, staring in amazement.

Kendall raced to the faucet, shutting it off. Gunner stood off to the side and took his jacket off. Maryanne couldn't tear her eyes from his bulging biceps.

"What the hell is going on here?" Kendall's face shone red as he growled. Lola shook off Cindy's hands and crossed her arms.

"What's it look like, Ken doll? We were just washing up."

"That's not how you clean up!" He roared, waving his hands around at the mess. Water was dripping from the cabinets, the drawers, and even the oven behind them.

Holly rolled her eyes at her brother's yelling, making Cindy grin. They all ignored Kendall and Lola as they started whispering and gesturing furiously at each other. Maryanne snapped her gaze from Gunner and tossed Cindy and Holly rags to wipe up the counters. Her hands were clammy at being in the same room as him. Most of the guys went to the dining table to look over the baked goods.

"Holly, can we help clean up? Will work for cookies." Parker, Gunner's youngest brother, took the dish towel from Holly and winked.

"Of course!" Holly beamed.

"Only if you donate to the bake sale." Cindy countered, as she wiped off the counter.

Maryanne set down her rag to pick up the flour to take to the pantry, eying Gunner as he stalked towards her. The predatory look in his eyes sent a shiver up her spine. He was like a lion, always watching, waiting, and observing, except he never pounced.

There was something in the way he moved tonight that made her nervous. Her chest ached when he neared.

She hadn't seen him outside of the bakery or outside of his uniform in the two years she'd been home. She'd barely looked at him at the bar, refusing to make eye contact or let him distract her from having a good time.

Now, he was so close. Without a counter separating them, she felt like it was open season on hunt Maryanne... the smell of his cologne as he neared swept over her, making her core clench in response. That cedar and pine combination reminded her of Autumn bonfires when she was a teenager.

She smiled up at him as she picked up the bags of flour, then brushed past him. Her breast slid along his bicep, and her nipples hardened under her thin t-shirt as she walked to the pantry. Gunner grabbed the baking soda and sugar and followed her.

She lifted the flour and reached up to slide the bags on the top shelf. Feeling his body heat behind her, she turned in the tight space and froze.

He was so close. This was her chance. Maybe if she flirted now, in this tight space, he'd kiss her again. Then she'd know if the kiss from high school was real, or if she'd just imagined it.

He pushed closer, sliding the rest of the ingredients onto the shelf behind her. Her heart raced, as it always did when he was near. Had he ever been this close before? Not since that first kiss in high school.

She glanced up into his hazel eyes and blinked in the dim light shining into the unlit pantry, unable to read his expression. His face was in the shadows, his back to the pantry door.

"Hey there, handsome. Tight fit in here, huh?" She licked her lips, tasting her ruby red cherry flavored lipstick that she never went without. She saw his head dip as he shifted on his feet. Was he looking at her lips? They tingled like he was staring at them.

"Tight fit like your ass in those jeans," he growled, moving his hands to either side of the shelf beside her hips. He blocked her in. A flash of triumph leapt in her chest, and she blinked in shock. He'd not only spoken but said something suggestive.

What had changed in him? Was it just the proximity

pulling them together at last? Two years of flirting with him over the bakery counter every morning? She'd finally gotten a response, and she wouldn't waste it.

She leaned forward, pressing her chest to his. He sucked in a breath as she placed a hand on his bicep and slid it slowly up around his neck. She inched closer, tilting her head.

"I've got a tight fit somewhere else, too. You're always welcome to try it out."

He growled and dipped his head, making her stomach flip in anticipation. Their lips met softly, gently at first.

But the pressure built rapidly until she gasped. He swept his tongue inside, and she lost all control. Her head spun when she closed her eyes and leaned into him. Her body molded itself to his, her soft curves cradling the hard planes of his muscular chest.

Something clicked in the back of her mind, shooting joy throughout her entire body like a flash of lightning in her veins. A vital puzzle piece that had been lost was finally found. Her whole body was throwing a party to celebrate.

His hand snuck around her waist and down over her ass. He grabbed it with both hands and pulled her harder against him.

It brought his thick erection into the v of her legs, and she moaned. Blinding need swept over her, so she wrapped both arms around his neck to deepen the kiss.

Laughter from the dining room broke through the lusty haze in her mind. They both pulled back with a gasp. Wrenching herself out of his arms, she held herself up with the shelves behind her and sucked in a breath.

Holy shit. This second kiss was just as mind blowing as the first, *which had really happened.*

She thought she'd imagined it in her drunken state, but

no. What they had was real and unlike anything she'd ever experienced with anyone else.

His eyes glowed in the soft light of the pantry.

She licked her lips, eyes still wide as she panted. "Well, guess I didn't imagine that kiss in high school then, huh?"

He wiped a hand down his face as his breathing evened out. "Nope. It was real." God, the growl of his voice made her toes curl.

Her nostrils flared wide, taking in the delicious scent of him. "Did you get me home that night?"

He nodded.

"Thanks for that." An awkward silence descended as she stared at him.

She held the smile on her lips, but her heart was racing fast at the idea of him turning her down again. This could be her one chance at her teenage crush.

"Do you—do you want to get out of here?"

Somehow, tonight felt different from when she flirted at the bakery. She forced herself to take deep breaths, trying and failing to slow down her heart rate.

"I don't have time for the distraction of a girlfriend." His voice was like sandpaper on her skin.

She shrugged, masking the ache of rejection. "Who said anything about a girlfriend? I'm not looking to be tied down either."

"Good. I'm running for sheriff in the next few years, and there's a lot on my plate right now."

Her spine straightened as she arched a brow. "Well, don't let me stop you. I was just looking for some fun. Besides, I don't even know if you're any good."

He snorted. "Oh, I'm good. The best you'll ever have, little girl."

She narrowed her eyes. He'd called her that when they were in school.

"I'm not a little girl anymore, in case you couldn't tell. If you're down to play, let's go. If not... well, I'm heading home anyway."

She flipped her long ponytail over her shoulder and ducked under his arm and out the pantry.

Everyone sat around the dining table, talking and flirting. The kitchen was clean, so she grabbed her purse from the couch and walked out the door, texting her sister goodbye.

She didn't want to deal with the goodbyes and putting a forced smile on her face when her stomach was in knots over Gunner's kiss and rejection.

Just when it seemed like he'd finally take her up on her offer and fulfill a decade of fantasies, her hopes were dashed on the ground. It would inevitably be another lonely night dreaming of him.

She glanced over her shoulder when she walked to her car, and the last of her hope died. He didn't follow her.

Her heart fell as she got into her little red car and started the engine. Grinding her teeth, she put it in reverse, and glanced out her driver's mirror as she began to back up. When the passenger door opened, she slammed on the brakes, whipping her head around.

Gunner slid in, his jeans stretching over his ass and the leather seats. Her heart skipped a beat as she froze, staring at him in the soft light from Holly and Kendall's front porch.

"One night," he said gruffly as he shut the door.

She grinned like the cat who ate the canary as she backed up and drove home.

Chapter Five

Mid-October

She parked behind the pharmacy and got out of her car. While Gunner was getting out, she quickly wiped her sweaty hands on her jeans.

She didn't know what had made him change his mind but now that it was finally happening, she was nervous. Maybe she'd built him up to be something he wasn't. That's what girls did with their teenage crushes, right?

As they walked to the outside stairs to her second-floor apartment, she wanted to ask him so many questions—the main one being why now, after all these years, was he finally giving in? But she didn't want to jinx it. He could still change his mind.

She led him up the stairs and unlocked her door, closing it behind him. The scent of cedar and pine swept over her as they walked down the short entry hall to the open concept living, dining, and kitchen. The smell made her shoulders relax and her core clench in anticipation.

Glancing around, she waved at her space. "Welcome to my home. Make yourself comfortable. Would you like something to drink?"

He shook his head as he stood near the kitchen table. "No, thanks."

She turned into the kitchen and slipped past him to open the fridge. "I have some pastries. No bear claws, though. Would you like some—"

"No. No food," he growled from right behind her.

She spun to face him as he closed the refrigerator door. He pressed himself flush against her, pushing her into the cabinets and making her nipples harden painfully against his chest.

When she gasped, he swept his mouth down to hers. He led her on a dance of ecstasy as they kissed, getting deeper, hotter, wilder. Her panties quickly became as wet as her mouth.

Her hands roamed up his biceps. Somewhere it registered that he'd taken off his black leather jacket. She slid her palms under the sleeves of his shirt and moaned.

His skin was like fire, sending a flash of heat down her entire body. She craved skin to skin contact. Grabbing the hem of his shirt, she pulled it up.

He leaned back and threw the shirt over his shoulder.

"Holy hell," she whispered in awe. The tattoo on his shoulder stretched across one pectoral and down toward his nipple. She traced it with one finger, causing him to suck in a breath. It looked like skin had been ripped back to reveal gears and mechanical parts.

"Why this tattoo?" she whispered, afraid to meet his eyes as she traced it slowly, the emotions already hitting her in waves.

"The Marines... they said I was a robot, unfeeling and unafraid."

She glanced up, unable to avoid his gaze any longer, craving a peek into the soul he kept hidden so well.

The predatory green shone in the soft light, making her insides twist. She wanted to be owned by him, by this lion who kept his emotions on such tight rein. It would be glorious to see him lose control and let those emotions roar.

"You're not a robot," she whispered, sliding her hand up his neck and pulling him down for a kiss.

Taking control, she swept her tongue into his mouth this time. It made him growl and slam his hips into hers, pressing her ass into the counter behind her. He reached his hands down, lifting her into his arms. She had no choice but to wrap her legs around him as he stormed into her bedroom and fell back onto the bed.

She bounced on top of him, her knees landing softly on either side of his hips. The motion pushed her pussy onto his cock, frustratingly separated by their jeans. His hands slid under her t-shirt, pulling it up and over her head before she'd even taken a breath.

"God, these breasts drive me wild."

He palmed each and flicked her hard nipples through the purple lace. There was a bolt of electricity that shot straight from her nipples down to her clit, making her grind on him as he teased. She reached behind her and unhooked the bra, pulling it off with a flourish.

When he moaned, he palmed her breasts. She smiled widely and rocked her hips. Placing her hands on his chest, she lifted her body and then slid back down slowly, pushing her breasts together and riding him.

Once, twice. On the third time, he released her nipples, gripped her hips, and flipped her onto her back.

Sliding off the bed, he stood up and demanded, "Pants off. Now."

The order sent a thrill up her spine. She lifted her hips and slid her jeans and panties both down, kicking off her heels. When she looked up, he was standing beside the bed as naked as she.

Her heart sped up as he slid his hand up his cock and back down, his eyes devouring her. Good God, he was big. Not so much long—probably just over average length—but he was wide. His meaty palm barely wrapped around it.

"Condom?" he asked, gazing at her laying on the bed. She shivered at the deep tone of his voice, like he was barely restraining himself.

"I'm on birth control and the last test came back clean. So it's up to you."

She slid her fingers over her left breast in a wide circle. His gaze zeroed in on her hand as the circles got tighter and tighter until she reached her nipple.

When she pinched it, her hips lifted slightly from the bed, and she gasped. It seemed to snap him out of his trance because he grabbed her knees and pulled her to the edge of the bed.

Kneeling, he pushed her legs as wide as they'd go and held her still. She tried to sit up to see him better, but before she could even lift her head, his mouth was sucking on her clit.

She screamed. His five o'clock shadow raked along her pussy, driving her higher and higher so fast her head spun. She couldn't catch her breath.

Then he added a finger and spun his tongue in a circle around her clit. She bucked against his mouth, but couldn't get much leverage with as wide as he had her knees. She needed to climb closer.

"So close," she gasped. He slid his finger out, then crossed two fingers and slid them inside.

It pushed her over the edge, and she cried out as her pussy locked down on his fingers and pulsed wildly. The intensity left her breathless, panting for air as he eased back and slipped out. The emptiness consumed her, but she'd barely opened her eyes when she felt him grab her knees again.

He pushed them over his forearms as the head of his cock lined up with her soaking pussy. She grabbed her breasts, palming and kneading them as his eyes captured hers. He paused for what felt like an eternity as they gazed at each other. She tilted her hips up, trying to draw him inside.

Finally, he pressed the head in, making her gasp as he stretched her. She might be a flirt, but it'd actually been a while since she'd had sex.

This went beyond just sex, though. This was the missing puzzle piece. When he finally was seated to the hilt, she realized it felt like coming home. Exhilarating, like she could just be free to be herself.

"Maryanne... I don't know that I can—"

"Gunner, just fuck me already."

She clenched around him and lifted her hips to meet his. He groaned, pulled out to the tip, then slammed back into her. She gasped, arching her back, which made him pause.

"Again," she demanded, glancing back at her sex god with his bulging biceps. She captured his eyes, his predatory gaze now having taken control. He slid his hands down to grip her ass, her knees still over his forearms, as he slammed back in.

They set a furious pace, her soft moans mixing with his.

The scent of sex filled the air and mixed with his cedar and pine cologne.

He slid his hands around her hips and up to her breasts, dislodging her own hands. She reached to the side and gripped the sheets. His hands felt way better than hers, anyway.

When he pinched her nipples, her orgasm came fast, loud, and hard. She screamed his name as she spasmed around him, making him groan and lean forward.

He captured a nipple in his mouth. Her orgasm continued as he grunted and came to a stop. She felt him gush inside her, his dick growing impossibly wider and making her gasp as her own orgasm just kept going.

Lapping softly at her nipple, he soothed the hard peak with his tongue. She whimpered as her entire body floated back to earth. Her eyes closed to savor the rightness of him in her arms.

When he started to slip out, she opened her eyes slowly. The emptiness when he stopped touching her was truly consuming now, and she didn't want him to leave. He looked around, then walked into her bathroom, shutting the door behind him.

Frowning, she sat up and reached for a tissue from the box on her nightstand. She cleaned up, threw the tissue in the little trash can, and pulled back the covers before crawling into bed. She'd just laid down and pulled the covers up when he came out of the bathroom.

Spying him in his jeans, she felt a stab of disappointment rip through her heart. She hadn't even noticed him grab his clothes.

"You're not staying? If you let me take a nap, I can go for round two."

She pushed up onto an elbow, her hair tumbling down

her back. The movement dislodged the sheet, exposing one of her breasts. He froze, staring at her. Then he shuffled slowly toward her, leaned down, and took her nipple into his mouth.

She gasped, slowly rolling onto her back, only to have him break contact and sit on the edge of the bed. He pulled on his socks and boots and let the silence stretch.

Was this it, then? Wham, bam, thank you ma'am? She wasn't sure what she'd expected, but him leaving so abruptly wasn't part of it.

When he was done, he reached out a hand and brushed the hair away from her face. It was gentle and made her feel... cherished. He leaned in and kissed her softly. Her heart slammed into her chest, and the unexpected tenderness brought tears to her eyes.

He pulled back and stood up. "Have to work tomorrow. Maybe next time." Backing toward the bedroom door, he smiled, and her stomach fluttered.

Her heart tripped a beat. Next time? There'd be a next time? Oh, thank God. It was great sex, short but intense, but with him rushing out she was afraid it hadn't been as good for him.

She laid in bed, listening as he shuffled out of her apartment and shut the front door behind him.

She reached over into her nightstand and pulled out her CBD. Dropping a vial full under her tongue, she laid back down as she thought about what had just happened.

They'd agreed to no relationship. Before they'd left Holly's, he'd said it would just be a one time thing. But then he'd said next time too, so maybe this would turn into a fuck buddy situation?

She could live with that. If that's all he could give, then

she'd take it. She drifted off to one of the deepest sleeps she'd had in years.

Chapter Six

Halloween

Gunner moved the last of the trash cans around the barn as more people showed up. His mom always threw the after-trick-or-treat party. Adults only, but some of his earliest memories were sneaking out here and watching the adults laugh and have fun.

It seemed like he was always on the sidelines of those parties. Even in high school, he'd never really joined in the fun of the parties his friends threw.

He'd always been the one watching out for everyone else, making sure no one drank too much or burned down the barn.

As he walked into the barn, he saw his brothers tuning up their instruments. They played at the Electric Cowboy on most weekends, but he only filled in as a singer when his work schedule allowed. Thankfully, he had tonight off work.

He strode over to join them. Landry strummed his guitar, adjusting the strings. Glancing up, he grinned his lopsided smile, his light brown hair falling into his eyes. He was dressed as a pirate, with a fake earring and eye patch above one eye.

Gunner snorted, "You're the sorriest pirate I've seen in a while."

Landry laughed, Gunner once again envying his lighthearted brother. "And what are you supposed to be exactly?"

Gunner pulled on the edge of his leather jacket and jerked his chin.

"Take your pick. It's a leather jacket, tons of hair gel, a white tee, and jeans."

Parker tuned his own guitar and smirked.

"You could be a few different things in that getup. Whatever you are, I bet Mom loves it."

Gunner grinned. "Yep. She called me a Greaser."

They all laughed just as their mom walked up. Ava Williams was dressed as a 1920s flapper girl, her long hair pinned under to appear cropped. She may be past fifty, but you'd never guess.

She was tall, fit and muscular from working the ranch, but somehow, she didn't look weathered at all. She still looked fresh, young, and energetic.

"We were just talking about you." Landry grinned. She smiled at him because that's what everyone did around Landry.

"Good things, I hope? Y'all about ready to get this party started?"

She glanced at each of them, so they all nodded and took their places. Gunner hopped up the two steps to the stage they'd brought in and patted the mic.

"Happy Halloween, y'all! It's officially ten o'clock and time for the adults to play!" Gunner said into the mic as a surge of the crowd descended on the dance floor of the cattle barn. They kicked off the night with some up-tempo songs, going from country to hip-hop to classic rock and back again.

His eyes scanned the crowd as he sang, watching for trouble as always. This was mainly why he played in the band at the bar on the weekends: one, to bond with his brothers, and two, to keep things from escalating.

After two hours, they closed out the night exactly at midnight with their mom and dad's favorite slow song. It was tradition to play *Forever and Ever, Amen*.

Soon their parents would sneak off to God-knows-where, leaving Hunter, Landry, Parker, and Gunner to lock up the barn and send the caterers on home.

People started trickling out to the parking lot as Landry and Parker moved the instruments to the trucks. Gunner joined Hunter in herding people out.

He went outside, waving to folks who thanked him for the fun and packed up the giant Jenga game into the box.

Then he went around the back of the barn to the tack room, where they stored the Halloween decorations. He heard a crash and a soft yell inside.

Setting down the box quietly, he slowly eased the doorknob so it wouldn't creak.

"I told you, no. Why are you even here? How did you find me?" A woman's voice, high and panicked, echoed in the small room. His heart skipped a beat. Was that Maryanne?

"You think I wouldn't eventually track you down?"

A deep voice rang out, making Gunner think of when he was a kid and a classmate had laughed while plucking the feathers off an injured bird. He ground his jaw, his body already preparing for a fight. But he had to do this smart.

Gunner pushed open the door slowly and slipped inside along the wall.

He froze as his eyes adjusted to the near total darkness. An overwhelming need to protect her washed over him, making him feel both hot and cold at the same time.

He shook, trying to hold himself still and not step between the two yet. The need to hit the man slammed through his body, warring with his mind that screamed to wait and see what he could arrest the bastard for.

"I didn't think it'd be worth it to you. We're done, Barry. We were done long before I left."

"I've moved down to Dallas. You were right. It's a gold mine here in the South." A cruel chuckle rent the air, causing the hairs on the back of Gunner's neck to stand up.

"Leave, Barry. I don't care what you do, as long as you're not doing it here. Get out of my town."

Her furious whisper was as tight as the clenched fists at her side. The shelf behind her had fallen, but instead of an injured bird, she looked ready to swing at the guy.

He eased the door open with his boot, bringing more light inside the dim room.

"There you are Maryanne. I've been looking for—oh, hello. Didn't see you." Gunner stepped forward, moving slightly between the two.

The man turned as Gunner entered the room fully. The light revealed a very lanky man with a Superman t-shirt. His black beard was trimmed neatly, but the tousled hair on his head looked unkempt. The man reeked of cheap cologne, and Gunner tried not to cough.

He smiled, but the hair on Gunner's neck raised even more in response.

"Nice to meet you. I was just leaving. See you around,

Mary." He smirked as he nodded and walked out. When he was gone, Gunner turned to Maryanne.

She was paler than normal and shaking, her fists still clenched at her sides as she stared out the door.

"You know that guy?" The cop in him demanded he find out how much of a threat he was. Maryanne's head jerked as if she just realized he was there. She spun around, avoiding his gaze as she dropped and started picking up the knickknacks that had fallen from the shelf.

"From Colorado, yeah," she mumbled. She sounded tired, defeated and her shoulders were slumped. It wasn't a tone of voice he'd ever heard her use before. She was always confident, sassy, and in charge.

He pulled her up by the arm slowly, turning her to face him.

"Is he trouble?" He rubbed his hands softly up and down her arms until she finally looked into his eyes.

Her forehead wrinkled in worry as she slowly shook her head. "I—I don't know."

She looked so lost as she stared at him. All he wanted was to wrap her up in his arms and keep her safe. He knew he couldn't do the latter—that was a slippery slope he wasn't ready for—but he'd damn well do the former. Pulling her to him slowly, he lowered his mouth to hers.

He'd not stopped thinking of their one-night stand. Every waking moment, she'd tormented his daydreams. At night, he imagined holding her in his arms, hearing her moan and scream.

She moaned into his mouth now, and he pulled back sharply. Still holding her, he stared into her face as her eyes fluttered open. Her brows were perfectly arched, her makeup heavy for the party, but it just highlighted the perfection of her face.

Dressed as a sexy witch, her high cheekbones sparkled in the faint light. He found great satisfaction in seeing her red lipstick smudged. She was usually so perfectly put together.

He wanted her shields lowered again. He knew that was what her clothes and makeup were. They'd been her defense mechanism since high school. He wanted to see her free, spread out under him and crying his name again.

"Maryanne... I know we said one night. But—maybe—" he stuttered as the most beautiful smile broke out on her face.

Her smile always made him breathless. Was it any wonder he couldn't seem to talk around her and always clammed up?

"Always open for you, tough guy." She winked, and the vulnerable look left her face. "Can you give me a lift home? I've already told Cindy and Andy I'd find a ride."

He nodded, going back to grab the Jenga box and put it away. She helped him clean up the fire pit, grabbing the leftover s'more supplies.

Her mischievous grin lit her face as she waved them at him. "Can I take these home?"

He shrugged and nodded, barely registering the question as he thought about her sweet mouth and all he wanted to do with her. She'd always been up for trying anything when they were kids.

She was the fun one, the one who never turned down a dare. She'd always been able to sweet talk his younger brothers, Landry and Parker, into doing some ridiculous things.

That was back before she started wearing high heels and red lipstick every day. He watched her hips sway as they walked to his truck, and he opened the door for her. He grabbed one of her pigtail braids and pulled her lips to his for a deep kiss.

When they were kids, she'd been quite the tomboy, always rounding the others up to get into some trouble. But it'd been a while since he'd seen her in pigtail braids. He broke the kiss with a smile, closing the door and rounding the cab to hop in the truck.

For as long as he could remember, she had always blindsided him. She was still doing it, with every glance, every kiss, every smile.

He never saw it coming and still didn't. Back then, he'd be off working the horses or practicing at summer football camp. Next thing he'd know, he'd have to go bail his brothers and Maryanne out of jail or rescue them from down the river.

She was the reason he'd spent so much time at the jail when he was in high school... she and his little brother, Chase, who was still in prison. Without her influence, he probably wouldn't have watched the cops so closely or become one himself.

Why did his life dreams always circle back to her?

Chapter Seven

He held her hand as he drove them into town and pulled behind the pharmacy. She walked up the stairs to her apartment, his eyes riveted on her swaying hips and too short witch's dress. Was she even wearing underwear? His mouth salivated as she unlocked the door and walked through the kitchen.

"I'll be right back. Make yourself comfortable." She waved over her shoulder and walked into the bedroom.

He turned, glancing over the open plan living and kitchen combo. There was an orange couch, a red shag rug in front of it. The side tables were some kind of sleek, modern design.

A TV hung on the wall opposite a large, colorful tapestry that mirrored the tile backsplash in the kitchen. The dining table and chairs were a bright purple.

It was fun and bright, just like her. He spied a pan of brownies on top of the oven and grabbed one. When she came out of the bedroom, he got a glimpse of her costume for the first time in full light.

The witch's dress had some sort of bustier that accentuated her tiny waist and pushed her breasts up. She had cleavage for days, and he reached out to trace a finger down it. She froze at the caress, her eyes locked on his glowing with anticipation.

"Do you want a beer or anything?" She licked her lips, her voice shaky. Was she nervous?

He shook his head, and as always remained silent.

She smiled and turned to the fridge to take out a wine cooler. "I need a drink. You'll be happy to note that I did not get tipsy at the party. I've grown up a lot since we were in high school."

She bent over and her very short skirt rode up her thighs. He could barely see a purple something underneath. His brain short-circuited until she turned with her drinks in her hand.

He snorted at her drink selection. "Obviously not by much. I don't think grown-ups drink those."

She grinned at him saucily and shrugged; the movement made her breasts bounce as she twisted the cap and drank. He saw her throat work as she swallowed, and his cock hardened. He imagined her mouth wrapped around it.

He ate another brownie to distract himself from touching her. When she finished guzzling her wine cooler, she glanced at him and froze.

"Did you... did you just—how many did you eat?" She looked worried.

"Um, three?"

She closed her eyes, then took a deep breath. "Um, do you work tomorrow?"

"No, why? Want me to stay the night?" The thought more than excited him.

As he reached for a brownie on the plate, she quickly

snatched it away and gave him a playful scowl. "I'll let you stay the night if you stop eating all my brownies," she said as she pulled out a Ziploc bag and bagged up the rest of the brownies.

He rolled his eyes and tried to focus on the present, but his mind kept wandering back to the last time he had been in her apartment. His body warmed and his fingers tingled with the need to touch her.

He shrugged, his tongue turning thick as he swallowed the last bite. "Fine, I'll take that drink now, though."

She turned quickly and bent over to grab him a beer from the fridge. "I have some cupcakes. If I'd known you were coming over, I would've grabbed a few bear claws."

Her words went in one ear and out the other. Her ass was just too tempting and made his cock twitch. He eased up behind her and couldn't resist sliding his hands up the outside of her thighs. Her black high-heeled boots came up above her knees. As he skimmed his fingers up to her ass, he groaned.

She squirmed, rocking back against his crotch as she held onto the refrigerator door. He pulled her to the side until she was leaning her forearms on the counter.

She sat the beer down on the counter, and he kicked the fridge door shut. He palmed her ass, pushing her skirt up and sliding her thong down to the floor.

When he slid a finger down her slit, her moan rocked through his body, making him crave more. He gently pushed her feet wider apart with one boot.

With better access, he slowly slid one finger inside, the scent hitting his nostrils and making his mouth water. God, she was so tight and wet, like she was made just to drive him wild.

He kneaded her ass before rounding his hand to the

front. She bucked her hips hard against him. She was so wet, and he couldn't wait to plunge inside. He shook as he held himself back.

Fumbling with his other hand, he finally got his jeans unbuttoned and freed himself. He wrapped a hand around his throbbing cock, rubbing circles on her dripping pussy.

Soon she was moaning and pushing back against him. He pushed the tip in and out, keeping time with the circles on her clit.

But then she squeezed, locking down on his cock so hard he growled. He couldn't hold back anymore. He slammed inside, gripped her hips, and pumped in and out.

They were messy, loud, and rough. Every squeal and moan drew him higher, her muscles clenching on him until he was gasping for breath. Her orgasm came without warning, her body tensing up under his hands and squeezing him, pushing him to the edge. The room was spinning around them, and too quickly, he groaned as he came inside her.

They were both panting, his head resting on her back, her head resting on her arms on the counter as her spasms slowed around his cock. How had he stayed away from her for weeks?

After their breathing slowed, he pulled out and handed her a napkin from the kitchen table. He cleaned himself off and pulled up his pants, opened the beer and guzzled it down.

She went to the bathroom, her ass swaying, making him want to follow her, but he didn't want to seem too clingy. Besides, he was still thirsty.

He grabbed another beer from the fridge. It might have been the sex, but he hadn't felt this good in a very long time, if ever. Thinking back over the night, he couldn't remember if he'd eaten dinner.

The brownies should have been enough, but the one beer had hit him hard. Everything was fuzzy and soft. His body felt loose and free.

He frowned at his empty second beer. Barefoot but still in the costume, she came out of the bathroom and looked at him nervously, shifting from foot to foot.

He grinned. The normal inhibitions that tied his tongue around her loosened. His heart and body felt so light and happy.

"You're so fuckalicious."

Holy shit, where had that come from? He'd never talked like that before, much less around Maryanne. She always left him speechless.

She laughed, the sound shooting joy through his heart. He loved to hear her laugh.

"You're not so bad yourself. Gotta admit, though—that was the best kitchen sex I've ever had. What about you?"

He couldn't stop the grin that spread across his face.

"Best kitchen sex, or best sex ever? Told you I'd be the best you'd ever have."

She laughed again as she grabbed the bag of brownies and went to sit on the couch. He grabbed another beer and a wine cooler, following her to the couch and handing hers over. With her short dress and her legs pulled up under her, he could almost see her bare pussy from his side of the couch.

He glanced at the beer in his hand. Was this three? Why was he so thirsty? The bag of brownies caught his eye on the coffee table, and he reached for it. But she snapped it up and held it away from him, sticking her tongue out at him.

"No more for you. I need to catch up, though. Hey!

Let's play never have I ever. That'll give you time to recover for round two." She winked at him.

He kicked off his boots, put his feet on the coffee table and turned so his back was in the couch's corner. He wanted to see her and that pussy better.

Her black hair was streaked with orange this month. Pulled back into French braided pigtails and tied right behind her ears, the rest of her long hair flowed down over her shoulders. He leaned forward and flicked one pigtail behind her so he could see the cleavage of her costume too.

"There. Now I can see you while we talk."

He loved her hair. It always made him want to wrap his fist around it and expose her throat. His cock twitched at the thought of licking and sucking on that delectable neck of hers.

"Okay, but the game? Never have I ever used a fake ID."

"I haven't either. Hello? Cop here?"

She quirked her lips, leaned forward and touched his knee, making his cock twitch. It was the same as always, that little zap that shot from her fingertips through his body, making the hairs on his neck stand up.

He couldn't believe he'd lasted ten years from that first kiss before he'd gotten another one, before he'd felt her hands on him a few weeks ago.

Now that he had? He craved her touch like a fish craves water. It was necessary, essential, that he be around her, kiss her, in her. His need to be with her worried him.

He'd been incredibly careful to avoid touching her these past two years, but when he'd seen her in Kendall and Holly's kitchen, something in him had snapped.

In his mind's eye, he'd seen a flash of her in the kitchen

baking cookies, a herd of kids and dogs running around as she laughed.

He hadn't been able to shake that image. Her smile, full of joy and so carefree, had lit the same reaction within his heart. It burned now, threatening to consume him.

It was scary as fuck, which is why he'd avoided her the past few weeks. He felt kind of bad about it, but she didn't seem to have missed him.

She twisted a piece of her hair around a finger. "So maybe we should play a different game. Where's the craziest place you've ever hooked up?"

She leaned in closer to him. He curled his arm along the back of the couch and ran his fingers along her shoulder, pushing down the little lace capped sleeves of her dress.

"I don't know. Didn't get any crazy opportunities while in the Marines and since coming home... Well, cops have to obey all the rules, including those against indecent exposure." He ran his finger down along her collarbone.

Her jaw dropped. "You—at least tell me you've done it outside?"

"Nope. Never have I ever had sex outside."

She groaned and rolled her eyes. "I walked right into that one."

"Yep, now drink up." She ate another brownie and took a long sip of her drink. Then she leaned forward and kissed him.

His brain took a second to catch on to all the sensations —her breasts pressed against him, her hands on his thigh creeping higher, her soft lips molding to his.

He wrapped an arm around her and pulled her onto his lap, but she broke the kiss with a giggle. She hopped up; her smile lit up her face as she held out her hand. "Come on, I have an idea." She tugged him out the door.

They tiptoed down the stairs and across the street. It was hard to walk down the stairs; it seemed like he was walking in slow motion. He didn't feel drunk, but it was something similar. Why was he feeling like this? She tugged on his hand as they reached the sidewalk.

"Sh." She peered around the corner. "You don't want the cops to find us."

He squeezed her hand softly. "I am the cops, honey. And where are we going? When did I buy white shoes?"

He frowned at his feet. His shoes were awfully thin. He could feel the cracks in the sidewalk through them as they walked.

Something wasn't right. She was obviously up to something. He just hoped it wasn't breaking any rules. Wait, why would she be concerned about the cops finding them?

"We're not doing anything illegal, are we, M?"

"Sh! No, it's not illegal. Not exactly."

He glanced up to ask what that meant, but they were at the park in between the courthouse on Main Street and the Baptist Church.

They followed the sidewalk to the walking path. The city lamps on the corners barely provided enough light to walk through the trees.

He was supposed to ask her something, but he couldn't remember what it was. Why was he so forgetful?

"Ow! The sidewalk is eating my feet!" He wriggled his toes. They felt like they were being poked by tiny needles. He lifted his foot and shook it.

She smirked. "It's not eating your toes. It's the rocks, silly. There. See the pond?"

She pointed to the very center of the park. The pond was shaped like a U with a little gazebo on the peninsula. Peninsula. That was a funny word. Peninsula.

She pulled him toward it and into the grass, but they stopped at the bottom of the U. The grass felt much better on his toes.

"How do we get over there?" He squeezed her hand, staring at the gazebo on the other side. She turned and grinned at him.

"We swim." She pulled her dress off over her head. His head swam as the pale light from the moon illuminated her soft curves.

"Damn it, M, you weren't wearing a bra this whole time?"

His cock jumped in his pants, and his mouth went dry. He wanted to taste her.

"Hurry. It's kinda cold this late at night."

She shivered, tugging his t-shirt over his head. He quickly shucked his jeans and socks—socks! Those were socks, not shoes! Where the hell were his shoes?

He shook his head. Those beers had hit him hard. Everything was in slow motion and foggy. She grabbed his hand as he stepped out of his jeans, and they plunged into the pond.

She squealed at the coldness of the water. He slapped a hand over her mouth and pulled her back flush against his front.

"Quick! Sink down. If the cops heard you, they'll be here any minute."

He kept his voice low and nipped her ear lobe. He didn't know why they needed to avoid the cops, but she was a smart girl. If she said they needed to, then he'd make sure they did.

They sank down into the pond, the water making her slippery against him but not impacting his cock at all. It pressed against her while he pulled them deeper, his arm wrapped around her waist. When they got to the gazebo on the other side, he was still standing in the pond.

"I think we're safe. No one's coming yet." She glanced around, looking for whoever.

He growled in her ear, nipping the soft spot on her neck. "Someone's about to come."

He spun her around in his arms so they were face to face and grabbed her ass, lifting and impaling her with a gasp, pressing her back up against the concrete base of the gazebo. The mud between his toes was sinking him lower, but the water barely reached his shoulders.

The buoyancy gave an added layer to their lovemaking. He slammed into her as she panted. In the back of his foggy mind, he hoped he didn't scrape her back on the gazebo. He felt like he was going to ram a hole through to the concrete behind her.

"Yes, Gunner, yes!"

Her soft gasps shot straight through to his heart. But when her fingernails dug into his arms, he felt it as a shot of electricity straight to his cock. She squeezed him like a vise, making him gasp.

Then she bit him on the shoulder. It pushed him over the edge. They came together, her squeezing and him pulsing. It was like their hearts had synced into one. He held her up, her legs and arms wrapped around him in the best hug he'd ever had.

She giggled. "I think that checks that off your bucket list, huh? Can't say you haven't had sex outside now."

He grinned, carrying her through the water as it got shallower and over to the bank. Still locked together, he walked into the gazebo. It was open air, with rails on the bottom half to keep kids from falling into the pond.

He sat on the bench inside, keeping her firmly impaled

on his cock. Feeling himself twitch, he grinned at her and lunged his hips up.

She gasped. The sounds she made drove him wild until all he could think about was making her come. So he started them on that path, surprised that he was ready to go again. No other woman revved him up so fast.

He felt so free and knew it was her. She made him feel so much lighter, like the weight of his responsibilities had just disappeared. Fully present in the moment, he focused on just the two of them and the fire burning through his veins.

He pushed up, holding her by the hips and setting the rhythm. She leaned back and placed her palms on his knees.

"Maryanne, God, your tits—" he gasped as she bounced on him. His mouth watered, wanting to pull her dusky nipple into his mouth. And why not? He leaned forward and caught one, rolling it between his teeth.

She clenched with a gasp. He groaned as she squeezed him hard. He pushed higher into her, over and over, never releasing her nipple. She grabbed the back of his head with one hand and pushed him closer to the edge.

He growled, gripping her hips tight as he held her still against him. As he pulsed and came inside her, she ground forward and shattered, too. Feeling her come around him was like heaven on earth.

When they finally pulled apart, he gave one last gentle lick of her nipple. She stood up on wobbly feet, and he kept his hands on her hips to steady her.

"Damn, that was good." Her husky voice held him as if in a trance. When she slipped out of the gazebo and back into the pond, he followed, the sight of her bare ass in the moonlight a beacon drawing him closer. He saw her shiver as she sank into the deeper water.

"You cold?" He followed her, wanting to wrap her back in his arms.

She waved at him. "No! Stay. I have to pee."

He laughed, laying a hand on the side of the gazebo. His hand gave way, causing him to stumble. A piece of the concrete had shifted, so he grabbed it to move it back. But it ended up falling out instead. He grabbed it as one corner hit the ground. With a sigh of relief, he saw it didn't crack.

He looked into the large black hole that had been created and frowned.

"What's that?" Her voice was low and soft behind him. "Oh! It's a pirate's treasure! Quick, let's get it out before they find us stealing it!"

She reached in quickly and pulled out a plastic grocery bag. He slid the concrete back in and glanced around. Why would there be pirate treasure hidden in the middle of the town square?

"I don't see pirates. Are you sure they're here?"

She nodded furiously as she opened the bag. Gasping, she held up two cans of gold spray paint.

"It's the treasure! It's stuck in the cans! Quick, before they find us."

She handed him a can as she pulled off the lid. She leaned down and sprayed the concrete blocks at the base of the gazebo in wide arcs. He glanced around with a frown and looked at Maryanne.

Smart girl like her, she knew what she was doing. If she said there were pirates, there probably were somewhere.

Popping off the lid, he sprayed and sprayed until they'd gotten all the gold out of the cans. Maybe he needed to make a mess for the greater good. The Pirates had always

The Sheriff Gets His Girl

been Crimson Creek's nemesis, after all. What a funny word. Nemesis. Nem. A. Sisssss.

"There. Now the pirates won't be able to spend it on illegal stuff."

He tossed the can back into the bag. Holding it open, she tossed hers at him, hitting him on the chest. She giggled as it fell to the ground. A gold spot was now on his left nipple. He tried to wipe it off, but it wouldn't budge.

"Maybe the water..." He tossed the bag into the garbage can and stumbled into the pond again. She floated in after him, still giggling as they swam to the opposite shore.

When he got out, he tried using his white shirt to wipe off the spot, but it didn't work. Then he used it as their towel.

They snuck back to her apartment, where they quickly jumped into the shower together to warm up.

The elation of not getting caught, of foiling the cops and the pirates both, led to another round of furious sex, her back pinned to the wall as he held her up.

They came together, but the water and the orgasm had them shifting enough for her foot to accidentally hit the faucet, turning it to ice cold.

She shrieked, then they both dissolved into laughter as they turned off the water, dried off, and finally closed tumbled into bed. When he wrapped his tired arms around her, the bedside clock struck three.

Chapter Eight

First day of November

Gunner woke up to the blinding light from the window. What time was it? He glanced around, looking for his bedside clock. But he wasn't in his bed. This was Maryanne's bed, with her brightly colored comforter, purple side tables, and green curtains. He groaned and sank back into the pillows.

"Good morning, sleepyhead! How are you feeling? I've brought some water and Tylenol, if you need it."

She bounced into the room wearing a tank top that had a picture of two bees wearing ghost sheet costumes and the words *Boo Bees*. Her short shorts were practically panties. The little bees on them were bright yellow in the morning sun.

"What time is it?" he croaked, sitting up and reaching for the offered water. Their fingers met when he grabbed the bottle, sending a bolt of electricity down his arm that made him frustrated. Why did she keep doing this to him? She'd cast a lure to reel him in, and he couldn't get away.

"Only about nine-thirty. Bakery is closed on Sundays, but I grabbed the left-over bear claws. And I made bacon and eggs, in case you wanted something heartier." She shifted on her feet, looking nervous.

"You went out in your pajamas?"

She rolled her eyes, which made him even more frustrated. "I wore my red jacket. And it was early enough, no one saw me cross the street."

He cleared his throat; she wasn't really his, so his opinion didn't matter.

"I'll eat it all, thanks."

He chugged the water, and she turned and rushed into the kitchen to grab the plate, her ass swaying and making his cock even harder than normal morning wood. He swung his legs out of the bed, adjusting the sheet to keep his nakedness covered, and leaned his head into his hand with a groan. It was like a hangover, but he'd only had two or three beers.

"Here you go." She slid a tray onto the bed beside him, so he turned and made a breakfast sandwich with the toast.

She continued chatting nervously. "I had a lot of fun last night. Thanks for bringing me home. You can hang out as long as you want. It's kind of nice to have someone to cook for."

He barely listened while she talked, his brain still foggy and slow. His head ached, and he couldn't see straight. Why was she still talking? All he could think about was shutting her up by shoving his cock in her mouth. He'd fantasized about messing up her red lipstick for years, not that she was wearing any this morning.

When he finished eating, he shuffled to his feet, the

sheet drifting to the floor when he walked naked to the connecting bathroom.

"Oh! Um, I'm going to put the tray up. Be right back." Her voice barely registered while he used the bathroom. Maybe he could find her lipstick in here, have her put some on. She kept up a steady stream of chatter while he took care of business and washed his hands.

He splashed water on his face and wiped it off with the hand towel. When he glanced in the mirror, he saw the spot of gold paint on his chest and froze. Flashes of memories flew through his head—her olive skin glowing in the darkness, the feel of her wrapped around his cock and in his arms... something about running from cops and...

He walked back through the connecting door and stood staring at her, naked and hard. When he had woken up to the cinnamon scent on the pillows, he'd wanted her, craved her, needed her. His mind was at war with his body, and she seemed to sense it, because she now sat silently on the bed, biting her lip.

"Maryanne... why do I have gold paint on my chest?"

"Well, it's a funny story. You ate the brownies, and then one thing led to another and—"

"Wait, why was eating the brownies the start of this story?" He stalked toward her, only stopping when he was within arm's distance, and stood with his legs spread and arms crossed. Her gaze drifted across his biceps and down to his cock, her eyes going glassy when she opened her mouth to talk.

"They were THC brownies." Her voice was almost too low to hear, and she shifted on the edge of the bed, pressing her legs together. She refused to meet his eyes, instead sneaking glances to his cock jutting out in front of her.

Her words slowly penetrated the haze in his brain,

making his body run cold in dread. This could cost him everything, his job, the chance to run for the sheriff's position in a few years. His entire life plan could be derailed because of one fucking night.

"Shit." He raked a hand through his hair. "Keep going."

"We went to the gazebo and had sex a few times; then we found gold spray paint. There was talk of pirates because the gold was hidden. Then we got the gold out, so the pirates wouldn't be able to use it anymore..."

Her voice trailed off when she looked up at him, uncertainty flicking across her face and making her eyes wider than normal.

"So let me get this straight. You got me high. Then we committed indecent exposure. Before we vandalized public property." He clenched his jaw, and she nodded. Would he need to arrest her? Or arrest himself? This was fucking hell.

He always knew what was right and what was wrong, what to do and how to do it. But he didn't know what to do here.

She leaned forward on the bed, her brows drawn to stare at the ground. "To be fair, I didn't get you high. It was an accident. You ate those brownies on your own. I just, I'm sorry I—"

"You're sorry? You're sorry. If you hadn't had pot brownies, this wouldn't be a problem, would it? So yes. *You* fucking got me high." He waved his hands out wide. "Never in my life have I committed a crime. Not even a traffic violation, and in one fucking night, you got me to break three separate laws. Are you fucking kidding me? I can lose my job over this! I'll never make sheriff!"

She jumped up and pressed herself against him. He knew she was trying to pacify him, to calm him. It only partially worked, as her touch settled his nerves but also caused a familiar ache in his cock.

"It's going to be fine. No one knows. No one will find out. They don't have cameras or anything in the park in town. It's not that big a deal—"

"I know they don't have fucking cameras. I would've been the one to install them if they had. But what about fucking fingerprints, M? What about this fucking gold spot on my chest? That's pretty damning evidence." He grabbed her arms, holding her tight, not knowing if he wanted to push her away or pull her closer. The feel of her pressed against him made some of the tension ease from between his shoulders, so he wrapped his hands around, anchoring her to him.

When he breathed in, her cinnamon scent grounded him, made him think maybe it would be fine. She pulled back and looked at him.

"Well, don't get naked with anyone else for a few days." The twinkle in her eye made his breath hitch.

He growled, arching a brow. "And what if they do a random drug test at work, hm? What am I supposed to do then?"

"Um, call in sick for a few days?" She pressed her breasts against his chest, one brow lifted to mirror his own.

His vision went white when she pressed up against him, those perky tits pulling him deeper under her spell. The need for her overwhelmed him, making him run his hands down to grip her ass. Grinding her against him, he saw the glaze of lust settle in her eyes.

"You drive me crazy, Maryanne. You know that?" He stepped back and swiftly yanked her shorts down. He slowly turned her around and pushed the center of her back between her shoulder blades. "Put your arms on the bed, M."

He ran his hands along her spine, and she shivered at his touch. She looked over her shoulder, a smirk on her lips. She settled her arms on the bed, she wiggled her ass in the air, grazing it against his cock teasingly.

"Like this?" Her husky voice raked across his skin, taunting him, making the hair on his arms stand up.

He caught her daring gaze, so he lined up with her from behind and slammed hard inside. She squealed, and the sound went straight to his soul, soothing the worry and frustration. He slid out and slammed into her again, over and over, harder and harder, until she quivered beneath him.

"God, yes, Gunner! Harder!"

Grunting, he felt her clench tighter and tighter. Reaching a hand around, he pressed hard on her clit and hammered in. Her scream was silent now as she came hard, and he held still while he waited for her to stop spasming.

When she finally was just panting into the bedspread, no longer squeezing him for all he was worth, he took his palm and smacked her ass. She clenched around him and jerked in surprise. God, she might have gotten even tighter.

"You like that, don't you?"

"Gunner!" She panted, pushing back onto his cock, squirming closer as he smacked her ass again.

"Answer me. You like it when I spank that ass?"

He pulled his cock out slowly until only the tip was inside. She wiggled, trying to pull closer.

"Well?" He wasn't sure how long he could control himself or even if he could walk away at this point. All he could think was burying deep and filling her up. "If you want me to stop, say so, for fuck's sake."

She pushed back again, but he held himself just barely inside until she hit the bed with a fist. "Yes, alright? Yes."

"Beg for it, M. Tell me what you want."

She took a sharp inhale, her body tensing as she turned to look at him. The sun lit up the golden flecks in her dark brown eyes, and his heart skipped a beat. Her beauty was heart stopping, but the thought of losing her was even more terrifying. He mimicked her deep breath and tried to calm his racing heart as he took in her stunning features once again.

"Fuck me, Gunner. Hard and rough. Spank that ass." Her pupils were dilated, whether from last night or from passion he no longer cared. On some level, he'd known she'd match his darker needs.

He slammed back in, forcing her to break eye contact when she pressed her head into the bed and moaned. Then he spanked her, causing her to clench on his cock and squirm. "God, yes."

"That's for getting me high." He started to move, picking up speed and spanking her again, harder.

"That's for the illegal substance."

Smack. Moan.

"That's for indecent exposure."

God, she was driving him wild. She was moaning incoherently now, spasming around his cock and pushing back to take him deeper. *Smack.*

"That's for the... vandalism." His brain was still foggy, and her pussy was making him forget what he was supposed to be doing. It made him angry, that he was still feeling the effects of it, so he spanked her harder.

She flailed under him with a grunt when she came, choking the life out of his cock and making him pulse inside her. He froze, massaging her ass, soothing the redness.

God, the feel of her wrapped around him, the uncontrollable spasms... Had sex ever been this good? It'd been so long; he couldn't remember any others before her.

That would never do. If just two nights with her had led to breaking the law like that and forgetting all others, he needed to get away from her and stay away. His entire career was on the line otherwise. He needed his job more than he needed sex with her. Probably.

Her panting slowed, and she fell onto her stomach on the bed, causing him to slide out. The light from the window bounced off her perfect ass, shining red. The need to see a tattoo on her ass saying she was his bit through the haze in his brain.

God, what was she doing to him? He stomped to the bathroom, cleaned up, then slipped his jeans on. This was it.

No more messing around with Maryanne. She was too dangerous, too spontaneous, too chaotic. He had to stay away from her, for both of them.

He paused near the bed and couldn't stop his hand from reaching out and brushing the hair off her face. She sighed in contentment, then snored. This was a bittersweet goodbye, and she wasn't even awake for it. He sighed, then found his shirt and shoes.

Once he was outside, he locked the door behind him and scrolled through his phone as he went down the stairs. Frowning, he saw several missed calls from the Sheriff.

"Ray? What's going on? I'm not supposed to come in today." He opened the door to his truck and dug into his go bag for a clean shirt.

"I know, son. But there were some punk ass kids who tore up the gazebo last night. Can you go check it out? Joey and I are still dealing with some crap from last night.

You know how Halloween brings out the worst of everyone."

His stomach bottomed out. Shit.

"Sure thing. I'll go check it out, then swing by the station to file the report."

He hung up the phone and pulled on his extra t-shirt. The white shirt he wore last night was dirty and showed the gold paint. Plus, he didn't want anyone knowing that he hadn't been home yet. He quickly brushed his teeth in the parking lot too, then walked to the park. Maybe he could cover up any evidence that pointed to him or Maryanne...

Dear God, what had happened to him, if he thought obstructing justice was the best course of action? He clenched his jaw and stomped through the trees to the gazebo.

Chapter Nine

November

A week later, Maryanne was exhausted. By that Friday at 6:32am, Maryanne felt sick to her stomach as she accepted the truth.

Gunner hadn't come in at all for his bear claws. Instead, he'd sent another deputy to collect the pastries and coffee for the entire station. God, she'd really fucked up.

And it hadn't even been on purpose. The entire thing was a misunderstanding. The pot brownies hadn't even been pot. The THC had been left over from Colorado. Her anxiety was interfering with a decent night's sleep, so she'd made some brownies to see if it'd help.

Now Gunner thought the worst and was avoiding her. Her heart broke a little as she smiled a brittle smile for her customers, now a steady stream as they tried to stock up on baked goods for the weekend.

She really needed to hire someone so she could be open

on weekends, instead of just three hours on Saturday before soccer.

When she finally closed up shop, the sense of dread in her stomach had turned into a rolling boil. She picked up her nephew from his daycare and took him to the park.

Owen ran to the slides as Maryanne walked to the bench and sat down. She leaned forward and placed her head between her knees, trying to get the knot in her stomach to go away. Something felt off, and she needed to hear her mama's voice. She sat up and pulled out her phone.

"Hey, Mom. How's your trip? Did you make it safely to Houston?"

"Hey, hun! Yeah, it's great. The other Army wives and I are enjoying the spa already. You alright?"

"Yeah, I'm okay. Just a little tired, I guess. Probably had too much sugar because I'm just a ball of nerves today."

A scream pierced the air, and her head jerked up in time to see Owen fall from the playground equipment to the ground.

"Oh my God—Mom, Owen just fell. Hold on."

She ran over in her black heels and scattered wood chips all around as she dropped beside him. "Don't move! It's alright. It's going to be fine. Breathe, Owen. Tell me where it hurts."

She pushed his brown hair back from his eyes, and tears ran down his face. He wailed. "My arm! Ow!"

"Maryanne? Maryanne!" Her phone lay on the ground beside her, and shouting could barely be heard over Owen's screams. Swiping up the phone, she pushed the speaker button as she gently touched Owen's head to make sure it wasn't bleeding.

"Mom? Owen fell off the top of the playground. His arm hurts pretty bad."

"Nanarita? It hurts! It hurts! It hurts!" Owen kicked his feet and held his left arm with his right hand.

"Lay still, Owen. I can hear you moving, but you have to be still. It's going to be okay." Her mom took charge, even over the phone. Maryanne felt tears stream down her cheeks but was too busy checking for open wounds and blood on Owen to wipe them away.

"Maryanne?"

"Yeah, Mom?"

"Call Cindy. If she's at work, call Andy, then call her work number. Once you figure out what's going on, call me back, alright?"

"Okay, Mom. Love you. Bye." She hung up and called her sister, but it wasn't Cindy who answered the phone.

"Andy? Oh my God, is Cindy there?"

"No, she left about ten minutes ago. What's going on?" Maybe he could help.

"It's Owen. I picked him up from school and took him to the park. Somehow, he climbed onto the outside of the playground tube thing and fell off. I think he's hurt and I—I —" Her throat closed up, making her swallow several times to get past it. Tightness in her chest rushed in, threatening to crush her.

"Maryanne? Calm down. It's going to be okay. Stay there. I'm on my way, and we'll figure it out. Is he awake?"

"Yeah, he's awake. That's him screaming. I'm putting you on speaker." She pushed the button on the phone, then sat on her butt next to Owen, who refused to stay still any longer. He crawled into her lap, cradling his left arm as Andy's smooth voice calmed them both.

Ten minutes later, Maryanne had gotten her tears under

control. She was glad her sister had finally taken a chance on love. They were good together, and Cindy had been a single mom for way too long. There hadn't been a male around since their dad had died, but it was nice to have a brother now. Well, she hoped he'd be a brother soon, anyway.

Andy's truck squealed into the parking lot, and he ran over to them, his prosthetic leg shining in the afternoon light. Her chest ached. He'd lost his leg in combat; if he could handle that, maybe he'd know how to handle Owen.

"Okay, let's see what's going on, big guy. What'd you land on?"

"His left side. I don't think he hit his head, though. No lumps or blood."

"Is it your arm?" Andy reached out to touch it gently, but Owen just whimpered and curled further into her arms. She held him, careful not to touch his left side.

"I have an idea. Let me go get something from my truck. Then we're going to put your arm on it to keep it still, okay? That will help it not hurt while we drive to the hospital, okay?"

"The hospital? Is Mama there?" Owen mumbled into her shoulder, making her heart skip a beat. She just wanted to protect him and fix him. Another tear fell as hopelessness swept through her.

"No, your mama is at work but she's on her way to come fix it, alright?" She kissed his head and breathed deeply to stay calm.

Andy jogged to his truck and came back with some cardboard and paracord.

"We're going to make a splint, okay? The cardboard will hold your arm still while we drive. We're going to wrap it with this paracord too, but you'll need to lay flat on the ground while we make it, alright?" Maryanne helped Owen slide off her lap slowly, then lay down on his back. Andy praised him as he tied the cord around the cardboard and helped Owen sit up.

Maryanne jumped up and twisted her hands. She wanted to gather him up and keep him safe, but at least Owen wasn't crying anymore. He really looked up to Andy and was taking the cue from him that it was going to be all right.

"There! Now you're ready to hop in the truck, right? Maryanne, do you have his booster seat? You can ride in the back and make sure he doesn't move or bang it on anything." Andy winked at Owen and ruffled his hair, lightening the mood. Owen gave him a wobbly smile as they started trudging toward the truck.

Maryanne felt the energy balling up inside her stomach. She ran over to her car, her heels sinking into the dirt as she took the straightest route and not the sidewalk. Grabbing her purse and his booster, she hastily wiped her cheeks and slammed the door with her hip.

Andy was carrying Owen in his arms now, the cardboard held on top of his stomach. She opened the back door and placed the booster inside. Andy set him in the seat, buckled him, and shut the door. He seemed to have it all under control, so she went around to the other side and climbed into the backseat through the other rear door.

When they backed out of the parking lot, Owen started crying softly, his sniffles filling the cab and making the knot in Maryanne's stomach twist higher. When they pulled into the hospital parking lot, Andy carried Owen inside as Maryanne checked in with the front desk nurse.

Owen was now clinging to Andy in the waiting room while Maryanne filled out the paperwork. Soon, the nurse called them back to a room where Owen made Andy sit on the hospital bed and hold him.

Maryanne texted her mom to let them know they were in the hospital now. She still felt the nerves crawling over her entire body, the knot in her stomach twisting as she paced in the room. The nurse interrupted to take Owen back for x-rays, and he begged Andy to go with him.

When she was alone in the room, she sat in the chair and bit her nail. She was such a failure. Owen had gotten hurt on her watch. If she had been paying more attention, she would have seen him before he fell. This was the same problem she had in Colorado. If she'd been paying more attention, all that crap wouldn't have happened.

When Andy returned and Kendall came in, they chatted. Kendall must be the doctor on shift today.

"Is he going to be okay?" She shifted on her feet.

"Do I need a shot?" Owen squirmed in Andy's arms at the idea.

Kendall smiled. "You're going to be fine, and no, you don't need a shot. At least, not yet. You've broken your elbow, though. Your bones are tiny, and you'll probably need surgery to fix it. The orthopedic surgeon at Children's Hospital in Dallas will tell you for sure. We can wrap it for now, and he can make an appointment, or he can go now and try to get it all taken care of this weekend."

Maryanne blinked, wide-eyed. "Surgery!"

There was a commotion in the hallway before the door swung open and Cindy rushed in. Her eyes were wide, causing guilt and shame to course through Maryanne's veins. She'd let her sister down again.

"Mama!" Owen almost fell off the hospital bed as he reached for her. She swept him into her arms, careful of his arm now wrapped in a plastic brace.

"I'm going to guess you won't be in to work tonight, Cindy?" Kendall asked.

Cindy ignored the question. "What's the verdict?"

"Surgery at Children's for the broken elbow. Do you want to make an appointment for next week or take the ambulance now?"

Cindy nodded slowly, checking Owen over. "Ambulance. It doesn't seem so swollen that we'll need to wait a few days for the surgery. Let's just get it over with."

Kendall left to put in the transfer. Maryanne couldn't take the guilt anymore. She opened her mouth and talked without taking a breath, telling Cindy every little detail of what had happened. While she talked, Cindy set Owen on the hospital bed and checked him over. When Maryanne finally stopped to take a breath, Cindy pulled her twisted hands apart and hugged her.

Maryanne sank into her sister's hug with a sob. "I'm so sorry, Cin. I'm so sorry. If I had been paying more attention—"

"Shh. It's alright. These things happen."

"I don't know how it happened, though. I'll pick up James and Cody and take care of everything, alright? I'm so, so sorry."

"Boys get hurt all the time. Remember two years ago when Cody got stitches in his leg?"

Cindy pulled back and rubbed her upper arms, a soft smile on her face that reminded Maryanne of their mom. It was comforting but didn't dislodge the guilt that ate up her insides.

"But this one was my fault!" Maryanne's jaw clenched.

"It's no one's fault. These things just happen."

"I—I'm going to go to the bathroom." Maryanne sighed in defeat. It was useless arguing with her sister. She was as stubborn as a mule and experience had taught her that they'd just talk in circles if they kept going.

The knot in her stomach was rising anyway, so the bathroom might be a necessity soon.

"Here, take my keys to the SUV. You can pick us up when we're released from Children's, okay?" Cindy handed over the keys and hugged her quickly as paramedics came to roll Owen to the ambulance. Now that he was hooked up to the IV, the medication was making him talkative and excited to ride in the ambulance for the first time.

Maryanne's hand shook as she grabbed her purse and hurried down the hospital hallway. Her stomach churned as the scent of antiseptic made her gag. When she finally reached the bathroom, she stumbled in and barely made it to a stall before losing her lunch. The sound of retching echoed through the small space, drowning the sound of her pounding heartbeat in her ears.

Eventually, Maryanne sat back against the wall, panting heavily. Her forehead was slick with sweat, and she wiped it off with a shaky hand. After flushing the toilet, she stumbled over to the sink and splashed cold water on her face, trying to calm her racing heart. She wanted to curl up at home in her bed and ignore the world, but she couldn't leave Cindy and the boys.

Touching up her lipstick in the mirror, she grabbed a peppermint from her purse and gave herself a wobbly smile in the mirror. She had to take care of her other two nephews while Cindy handled Owen's surgery. She sighed as her phone buzzed.

"Yeah, Mom... They just left in the ambulance. They're going to Children's in Dallas... No, I don't know how long they'll be there... I'm assuming Andy gave Cindy her phone back, yeah. You should be able to call her, yeah... No, stay there until we get an update. You know that's what Cindy will say, but yeah, call her and see what she thinks... Love you too, Mom. Bye."

She was still shaky, but maybe a nap would help before picking up her nephews from school. Holding her head high, she stepped into the sunshine in front of the hospital and towards Cindy's SUV.

Chapter Ten

The next day, Maryanne pulled up to the soccer game with her nephews, Cody and James, and hopped out of the car. Parker waved from the next parking spot.

"Hey, Maryanne! Thanks for volunteering to help with the Christmas program at church."

"I guess I didn't do too bad last year, huh? If they invited me back." She chuckled while Cody got his bag out of the trunk. She glanced at her phone; the alarm for the bakery was going off.

"Hey, Cody, go join your team, and I'll be back soon. There's something wrong at the bakery."

"Everything alright?" Parker asked.

She nodded and smiled. "Yeah, just an alarm. I'll get it figured out and be back soon. Can you watch Cody?"

Parker nodded and the two walked to the fields as she and James climbed back into her little red car. The anxiety from all the drama from yesterday's hospital trip still left butterflies in her stomach, and the alarm wasn't helping.

When she opened the back door to the bakery, water gushed down the step.

"What the hell?" Her jaw dropped. A large bubble of water covered the ceiling and spread all the way to the storage room. She pushed the door and groaned. Water dripped down the connecting wall to her office.

An overwhelming sense of despair weighed her down, pressing like a brick on her chest. All she wanted to do was sit and cry, but she had to save the bakery, and fast. She didn't have time for a pity-party yet. She sucked in a breath and sloshed through the wet floor, glancing into her office and hurrying to the swinging door that connected the kitchen to the front.

"What happened?" Eight-year-old James set his book down on a dry shelf by the back door.

"I don't know." Maryanne turned around, furiously wiping her cheeks. Hell no, she would not cry. She was fucking tired of these tears. She pointed to the corner. "We have to get the water out. Quick! Grab the brooms and mop!"

Her sister was in Dallas with Owen for surgery today, and her mom was on her way to help at the hospital. Who else could she call?

She wanted to call Gunner, but he was still avoiding her. After she's woken up alone the day after Halloween, she'd texted him, but it'd been nothing but silence. If he were here, his muscular arms would wrap around her and just hold her while she cried over the loss.

But she couldn't cry. It was up to her to fix this. She shook herself out of her misery, she called Andy to see if he could grab Cody from the game. She'd deal with this mess herself.

Then she rolled up her sleeves and helped James sweep

and mop. When Andy arrived, she had a headache from holding in all the emotions.

"What happened?" Cody glanced around wide-eyed at the mess. Maryanne shook her head and a tear rolled down her cheek. She swiped hard at it and frowned.

"I don't know. I had a security alert this morning, so I ran over after I dropped you off at the game. Flooded pipe, I think. Half the inventory is ruined." Her voice sounded flat, even to her own ears. She stomped across the floor to her office.

"Did you shut off the water to the building?" Andy asked, eyeing the still dripping ceiling.

She massaged her temples and groaned no, leaning her head against the door frame. Why hadn't she thought to do such a simple thing? Why hadn't she Googled what to do?

Cody stepped up and hugged her. She loved the kids' hugs. They always made her feel better, with their unconditional love and support.

Andy went back outside as she directed Cody to help with the storeroom. Then she went to make a dent in her office. Later, Andy leaned against the desk as she looked up at him.

"I don't know what to do." She looked around at all the papers on her desk. It was too overwhelming to think about them.

"Do you have insurance?" When she nodded, he continued. "You'll want to call them now. And your landlord so he knows about the upstairs problem. I asked Landry to come help. He'll know what to do on the repairs, alright?"

She nodded again and began to sort the papers on her desk when the phone rang. He stepped out of the office to help the boys clean up as she talked to her mom. She whined about the flood, but Mom didn't put up with a lot of dramatics, even though Maryanne always tried to push that limit.

Sure enough, fifteen minutes later her mom said, "Alright, Maryanne. Enough of the pity-party. Pull up your boots and go call the landlord and the insurance adjuster. Let's get this cleaned up."

When she hung up, she called the others like they'd both suggested. Half an hour later, she heard fresh voices so she stepped out of her office.

When she saw Gunner in the middle of the bakery workroom, she froze. She stared at his boots, worried he was still mad. The butterflies in her stomach seemed to twist and turn inside, making her heart rate speed up. His presence was both comforting and overstimulating.

They'd agreed to the one-night stand—which had turned into two nights—but she hadn't agreed to him avoiding her. After what they'd done on Halloween and their fight the next morning... Well, she didn't blame him for avoiding her now, but damned if she'd take it lying down. Biting her lip, she lifted her chin and met his gaze. She felt her chest constrict at the pain of missing him, only to see him so unexpectedly now.

Landry was already inspecting the ceiling, walking between the storeroom and the main workspace with a frown while writing notes and taking measurements. He asked her questions and made a plan.

A knock on the open back door had Maryanne glancing over. Holly's face was wreathed in a deep frown. "What is going on here?"

"It's a shit show of a weekend. Want to help with the office?" Maryanne asked, hugging Holly as she stepped inside.

"Of course, hun. Anything you need."

Maryanne headed to her office, eager to escape Gunner's piercing stare. She couldn't handle his stoic silence and the bakery at the same time. She waved her arm dejectedly as she stepped into her office. "Boys, you can do... whatever you think will help here."

Holly dodged around the lingering men and slammed the office door behind her.

"What happened?" She pulled Maryanne into another hug.

Maryanne sighed, relaxing into her arms. "The bakery flooded. I might need to shut down for a few days while insurance comes out. And who knows how long repairs will take? I have a ton of orders for Thanksgiving in a few weeks, and I can't afford this to still be under construction then."

Her chest felt tight, thinking of all the things she'd need to do for the next few days. The pressure was building, and she didn't handle the stress well. She'd need to grab the CBD or something tonight, to help manage it all. In fact, her THC was in her purse. She pulled it out and dropped some under her tongue.

"Is that all?" Holly asked, as she sat on the extra chair.

"What do you mean, is that all? Isn't that enough?" Maryanne sniffled, pulling a tissue from the box on her desk.

"Yeah, but it seems like you're more emotional, like you've been crying..."

Maryanne laid her head on the desk. "Just worried about Owen's surgery."

Holly tapped her finger to her chin. "No, I think there's something else going on. Are you sleeping alright? It's either that or a break-up, and it can't be that."

The Sheriff Gets His Girl

Maryanne groaned, making Holly gasp. "Is it? Is it a break up?"

"Not really seeing anyone, no, but…" Maryanne needed a friend. She couldn't seem to hold herself together anymore, but maybe Holly could help. She sighed. "Remember when we did girl's night at your house for the bake sale?" She couldn't look Holly in the eyes when she told her and kept her face on the desk.

"Yeah."

"I—I took Gunner home. And—and we slept together. And then he ghosted me. He's not been in the bakery since."

"What? Why would he ghost you? Was he embarrassed by his performance?"

Maryanne burst out laughing and lifted her head, finally met her friend's curious gaze. "No, the man has nothing to be embarrassed about. Trust me. It was... magical. Three times magical."

They laughed, and she felt some of the pressure on her chest ease. It felt good to finally talk about some of this with someone. Rubbing her forehead, she continued.

"Then on Halloween, we hooked up again. But I made him mad, and he's still ignoring me, refusing to come into the bakery when he was here every day before... I don't know what's going on. I mean, we said it'd just be a one-night stand, but I didn't think he'd ignore me." She grabbed a tissue and spun to her wall mirror to make sure her mascara hadn't made a mess.

Yikes. Her makeup was a nightmare, and there were flour hand prints on her long leopard print peasant skirt. She tried to brush them off as Holly crossed her arms and leaned back in the chair.

"Well, the only way to find out why he's ghosted you is

to ask. We can kick his ass, but I think it'll be better to focus on the bakery first. Then you can manage him later."

Maryanne chuckled as she laid her head back down on her desk. Holly massaged her shoulders for a few minutes. Between the THC and the massage, Maryanne felt the knot in her stomach dissolve. Her heart was still heavy, but things were going to be alright.

"Thanks, Holly. You're a good friend." She lifted her head and patted her friend's hand.

"I know." They both laughed, then started working through the office, moving documents away from the wet, dripping wall. Hours later, when Holly had left, Andy poked his head into the office and frowned.

"I talked to Landry. He doesn't think it's going to keep you shut down for more than a few days. Well, after the insurance adjuster comes out and does his thing."

Maryanne nodded. "Insurance is coming out on Monday."

"That's perfect. Then Landry can start right after. Hell, he can even meet with the insurance adjuster and take more measurements. I talked to the rest of the guys, too. We're all going to pitch in and get you back up and running in no time."

She sighed in relief. "So it's not that bad?"

"Not that bad at all. I think you caught it in time. You okay?"

She groaned and leaned her head back on her desk. With as often as she did that today, you'd think there'd be a permanent forehead spot on it. Her shoulders were stiff from the stress, even if it was less than it'd been earlier. She sat up and popped her neck and back, stretching her arms.

"Yeah, just tired, hungry, and already sore from moving all this crap around."

"You didn't eat the lunch I brought earlier. Let me grab it. It'll help." Andy grabbed the Sonic bag from the main room and sat it on the desk. "Can I take the boys home? I think you've got enough to worry about here. They're going to need dinner soon."

Maryanne practically inhaled her burger. Slurping a melted slushy, she leaned back in her office chair as they made the arrangements. Andy and her sister, Cindy, hadn't been dating very long, but if he took the boys, it would be a big help for her. Silence descended on the office when they left.

She breathed a sigh of relief and leaned her head back down on her desk. Maybe it was just a few rough days. Everything was going to be alright. Between food, friends, and family, she'd make it through.

Chapter Eleven

Gunner put the mop up and walked to her office. He'd never been in this part of the bakery before, but it was all Maryanne. It was controlled chaos.

There were bright colors everywhere. The walls were painted bright pinks, purples, and orange swirls, resembling frosting. The concrete floor was stained a bright blue.

He'd never thought that a bakery could be fun to work in, but he imagined with her as a boss it would be. She made everything fun.

That was partly why she'd always driven him crazy. She'd blow into town for the summer and trouble followed. Every year there was a unique incident. The city pool had been dyed red once; he still didn't know how that had happened. Then there was literally the running of the bulls down Main Street. Lola's dad had been furious about that one, as they'd been his bulls the two girls had let out of the town stock pen.

She'd blown back in town two years and was still causing trouble, but of the adult variety. With her perfectly kissable lips and her tiny waist that he could wrap his hands around, he just wanted to toss her over his shoulder and carry her to the nearest fuckable surface. That big ass that he loved to grab and spank had driven him wild with dreams for years. He'd thought once would be enough. He'd almost convinced himself that twice was a mistake too.

But as he stepped into the doorway of her office and watched her sleep, he realized there was something else between them.

She snored softly, head on the desk, and it was the most adorable thing he'd seen since... Well, since the last time he'd seen her. He'd been too high and drunk to pay attention to how cute she was while sleeping on Halloween night, and now it seemed a missed opportunity.

He brushed the hair away from her face, unable to stay away from her. She moaned softly, snuggling into his palm. The sound went straight to his cock, making it twitch to remember their two nights together.

"Maryanne, come on. Let me take you home," he whispered. Her eyes fluttered open while she leaned back and stretched. When she stumbled to her feet, he wrapped an arm around her waist and held her steady, his heart thumping. How had he made it an entire week without touching or seeing her?

She felt good, snuggled up to him, like home. The knots in his muscles finally loosened and a sense of calm washed over him. It had been too long since he last held her, and the relief he felt was palpable.

He grabbed her purse from beside the back door and flicked off the lights, checking the doorknob and making sure it was locked. Then he wrapped an arm around her waist to walk through the alley. What was it about her that made him relax so easily?

"I can walk, you know." Her alto whisper was like fingernails up his spine. If he was a dog, her voice would scratch behind the ears. The hairs on his neck stood up when she spoke.

He stared at her, his mouth slightly open as if he wanted to respond. But every time she spoke, his mind went blank and his words tangled in his throat. It frustrated him, because he wanted to hear her thoughts on everything and anything. He struggled to overcome this hurdle in their communication so he could finally see if what they had could be more than physical.

Wait, no. He didn't want to overcome it. She was dangerous, and he was supposed to stay away. When they walked up the outside stairs to her second-floor apartment, he sucked in a breath. His gaze narrowed to her ass while she ascended the stairs in front of him. There was no way he could stay away.

As they neared the door, his heart started to race. Would she invite him inside? Or had he blown it by ignoring her the past week?

He cleared his throat when she unlocked the door. Then she threw a glance over her shoulder, one eyebrow arched. "You're coming in, right? Or are you going to continue avoiding me?"

Heat crept up his neck, embarrassed that she'd noticed. "It's easier to shut you out, M."

She tipped her head to the side. "As opposed to what, Gunner? To taking a risk and having some fun? Isn't that all you wanted this to be?"

He felt his shoulders relax; denying her wasn't an option. He was drawn to her like a moth to a flame. Where she went, he wanted to follow. The danger she presented had faded over the past week, until he was left craving her—

a glimpse, a touch. The longer he went without seeing or touching her, the grumpier he became. Even the guys at work were calling him an ass.

She swung the door open and grabbed him by the belt buckle to pull him in. She slid the deadbolt home as she pushed him up against the wall. Her mouth reached his with a groan.

His heart skipped a beat at her aggression. He loved that she was so aware of what she wanted, and it made him want the same for himself. Maybe he could let loose and do what he wanted, be who he wanted.

He tasted the tears, the slushy from earlier. But most of all he tasted the intoxicating spicy taste that had haunted his dreams for ten years. For the first time in weeks, he felt like he could let go of all the stress of his job and just be himself.

He gripped her hips and spun around to pin her to the wall with a fierce kiss that curled his toes. He kicked off his boots as she moaned and arched her back, her long skirt riding up her legs. Pushing it higher, he froze in surprise.

Son of a bitch, she was commando. This woman was everything he'd ever wanted, and it scared the hell out of him. But he was so tired of running from her.

He circled her clit with a thumb, making her moan and buck against his hand. With his other hand, he unzipped his pants and kicked them off. Then he grabbed her by the ass, lifted, and plunged inside as she wrapped her legs around him.

She groaned into his mouth and gripped his hair, their lips locked in a furious kiss. He began to pound her into the wall, fast and hard, just like he liked it. From the sounds of it, she liked it too.

It made his heart soar when she cried, "Yes, Gunner. Harder!"

Her little squeals and gasps drove him wilder, making him push harder just to hear her. And when she clenched around his cock as she came and raked her nails into his back, it caused a chain reaction in him.

He roared and fucked her through their orgasms, finally slowing so he could feel her aftershocks and muscles clenching around him.

Leaning his head into the crook of her neck, he breathed deeply. The scent of cinnamon surrounded him, comforting his erratic heart. He'd never felt like this before.

He didn't want to run from whatever this was anymore, but he wasn't sure how to move forward with her, either. Surely he could have her and his job too?

Even now, he felt his mouth clam up. He couldn't think of anything to say. Damn it, he was still tongue tied around her. Why couldn't he just tell her how he felt, how he wanted to take her out for a proper date?

He lifted her slightly and carried her to her bedroom. Gently, he placed her on the bed. She moaned as he slipped out of her. He didn't want to leave her either. She rolled over onto her side and pulled up the covers.

She was so beautiful. The glow of the streetlight shone through the bedroom curtains. Her hair was spread out on the purple pillows, her caramel complexion smooth against the green blanket.

His hand reached out and smoothed the hair back from her face. It was like he couldn't control it. He couldn't stop touching her, wanting to be with her. The more time he spent with her, the more addicted he became.

He wanted to crawl into bed with her. But he knew that was a slippery slope, because then he'd want to date her and sleep with her every night. He couldn't afford to be distracted right now. Taking her on a proper date would need to wait. The Sheriff had a heart attack this week. Rumor had it he was thinking of retiring early.

He shook his head, walked to the bathroom to clean up, and got dressed. When he stepped out, she was asleep. He shoved his hands into his pockets so he wouldn't be tempted to touch her, sighed, and locked the door behind him.

Chapter Twelve

First week of December

"Gunner. Gunner. Are you even listening?" Sheriff Ray asked in exasperation.

Gunner blinked as his mentor leaned back in his chair and crossed his bulky arms. The sheriff's tan button-down shirt nearly popped its buttons as he sighed and ran his hands through his thick, white hair.

Mayor Charlie chuckled in his wingback seat next to Gunner. Gunner sat straight, feet flat on the ground, hands loosely clasped in his lap, but Charlie had his black, shiny boots propped up on the desk as he picked under his fingernails with a pocketknife.

"I was listening." Gunner frowned. He might've been listening with just one ear, but no one could blame him. The two always droned on about whatever topic of interest when the Mayor came into the Sheriff's office.

Well, former Mayor, as he'd retired a few months ago.

The Sheriff Gets His Girl

Sheriff Ray's recent heart attack and his long-time best friend's pushing was why this meeting had been called.

"Was not," Charlie said with a grin. "I've seen that look before. Man doesn't get to my age without recognizing that look. Who's the lucky lady?"

Gunner's heart tripped a beat and a bead of sweat dripped down the back of his neck. No one could know. There was no way in hell he'd had a 'look.' Even if he had been thinking about her, keeping his face impassive was second nature at this point.

Gunner shook his head, meeting Charlie's pointed gaze. "No woman."

Ray slapped his desk with both hands. "Better not be. This election needs to go smoothly. A woman would be a wild card that we don't need that right now, especially when we know that someone is running against you. We just don't know who yet. So, are you on board with the plan or not?"

"Calm down, Ray. Remember your blood pressure. You're just getting over one heart attack. You don't need another." Charlie folded up his pocketknife and slipped it in his jeans.

Gunner nodded slowly as his heart leapt. This was all he'd worked for. For years.

"I'm on board, Ray. I'll run for sheriff. I didn't realize your heart attack was serious enough to put you to retiring. You were just re-elected last month."

The scowl on Ray's face deepened into his signature frown. In the six years Gunner had been working as a police officer in his little hometown of Crimson Creek, he'd never actually seen the man smile.

"My doctor thinks retiring will help prevent future attacks. I need to de-stress."

"And I don't want to go on that senior's single cruise in

February by myself. He needs to get well. I need my wingman." Charlie slid his feet off the desk and stretched.

"I know it's ahead of schedule. I hadn't planned on retiring for another few years. Are you up for this? Being sheriff ain't easy." Ray scrubbed a hand over his face as he leaned back in his chair.

Gunner had worked his entire life to become sheriff. He'd watched the cops work, especially in high school, and knew how stressful and hard the job would be. But it was his childhood dream. Every step he'd made in his life had been leading up to this. Well, every step except where she was concerned.

"I know, but I can handle it," Gunner said firmly. As long as no one found out what happened on Halloween with Maryanne a few weeks ago, he'd be a shoo-in for sheriff.

He'd been preparing to take over as sheriff for years, ever since he'd moved back home after serving his four years in the Marines. Ray could question all he wanted, but he knew Gunner was ready. Hell, he'd practically been grooming Gunner for it for the past six years.

The police radio in the corner went off. The three listened to dispatch call in a wreck on Route 31 just south of town. One of the younger cops popped his head into the office as the call ended. "Your turn or mine?"

Gunner hopped up, nodded to both Ray and Charlie, and strode out of the office. "My turn. If I need you, I'll call."

The Police Station shared a parking lot with the Court House and the Fire Station, but all the buildings matched the rest of the buildings on Main Street. Floor to ceiling windows with display cases and a glass front door.

There were four deputy desks in the front. Gunner

turned down the narrow hallway to the back kitchen / conference room. The cells were on one side of the hall and the sheriff's office and bathrooms were on the other. He pushed open the back door and hopped into his county-issued SUV.

Maryanne leaned her elbow on the open window of her little red convertible. The top was down, whipping random red highlights and black hair out of her messy bun as she cruised down the highway. She played with her stray hair dyed to match the upcoming Christmas season and yawned.

Why was she so exhausted? She'd been sleeping more the past few weeks. For once in her life, she actually had time to sleep, now that she wasn't so busy helping raise her nephews. She was happy her sister and Andy had gotten engaged on Thanksgiving.

She was even more glad that Gunner had been working and hadn't been there. It would have been difficult acting like nothing had happened between them if he'd shown up for Thanksgiving dinner at Cindy's house.

She still hadn't seen him much. She would watch from inside the bakery as he went into work, then he'd send another deputy to get his bear claws and coffee.

Just the barest glimpses of him walking down the street still made her heart race. What was it about him? Why couldn't she get him out of her head? He obviously wasn't interested. He hadn't texted her and was back to ignoring her.

She pushed the sunglasses back up her nose as she drove home with one hand. She'd been feeling frustrated for a few weeks now, but this afternoon, she'd driven down to help her sister, Cindy, say yes to the wedding dress in downtown Fort Worth.

It had been grueling. Hours had slipped by before she'd found "the one." Maryanne remembered the one-shoulder strap mermaid dress that hugged her sister's curves to perfection. It would need hemmed, of course; both of them were short, petite, busty women with curves that made men drool.

In the dusk, she saw movement out of the corner of her eye. She blinked, just in time to see several deer leap from the trees across the road.

She swerved, spinning in circles. She screamed, her hands firm on the wheel, and she slammed into something. Then everything went dark.

Gunner slowed as he arrived on the scene, the sun setting behind him. Red metal flashed in his siren lights. He sucked in a breath and his heart stuttered in his chest. No, it couldn't be her. Red was a popular color, but surely it was someone else's red car.

He slammed on his brakes, and his SUV slid on the pavement. His chest tightened as he pulled at his seatbelt. It was too tight, trapping him in panic. His pulse slammed against his veins as he threw open the door and stumbled out, not even bothering to shut it behind him.

It was only a few shaky steps before his feet froze in place. An old farmer leaned over the front door of the red sports car, talking to the woman in the driver's seat.

He turned to Gunner, his gaze hovering on his uniform before he spoke. "She's in and out of consciousness, but I don't see any major broken bones or gushing blood." He stepped aside and slipped his hands into the pockets of his jeans as Gunner stumbled forward.

His skin felt like it was on fire. He ached to scratch the itch but when he drew closer, his body went ice cold.

Maryanne's head was leaning against the back of the seat, her black hair matted to her head and streaked with red. It wasn't just this month's highlights, red for the Christmas season. There was more blood smeared across her forehead, neck, and hand, but most of it already appeared to be drying.

Her left hand gripped the seatbelt still buckled across her chest, and her eyelashes fluttered slowly, revealing glimpses of her brown eyes underneath. Her olive skin seemed paler than normal, but she was alive and that was all that mattered.

"Maryanne."

His voice was like gravel, and he swallowed hard, twice, to get past the lump in his throat. The ice was inching its way through his veins, the pressure in his chest threatening to suffocate him if he didn't reach out a hand and touch her.

Her eyes fluttered again, but this time her head rolled toward him. He opened the driver's side door and paused, needing to touch her but hesitating in case he hurt her.

"Maryanne, sweetheart, can you hear me?"

Her eyes opened and her vacant gaze floated to his. He wasn't sure if she could see him, but they stayed open longer between blinks.

"Maryanne, if you can hear me, blink twice." He touched her cheek with the tips of his fingers and trailed them down her neck. Her pulse was steady, and it made part of the knot of worry in his stomach release.

The echo of the ambulance sounded in the distance,

and he blew out a breath as she blinked twice, rapidly, then met his eyes. That time, he saw recognition flicker on her face before she croaked, "Gunner?"

"That's it. I'm here. You're going to be alright. The ambulance is coming."

He soothed his hand over her hair, and it came back sticky with blood. He remembered what it looked like spread out on her pillow, her eyes glowing in the moonlight. Now she looked so lifeless, it made him ache in a completely different way.

"No. Don't want it," she moaned, slipping her hand down to fumble with the buckle.

"No, M. Just stay still." He reached across her and wrapping her hand in his. If the only way to keep her from moving was to hold her hands, he'd hold them all night long, but she was stubborn and tried to move her legs anyway. "No, no. Wait for the paramedics. They're going to check and make sure you can move. Just hold on a minute, sweetheart. We'll get you out of there."

"Wanna go home." Her words slurred, and her eyelashes fluttered closed again. "So sleepy."

"No, Maryanne, don't go to sleep. Not yet. I need you to stay with me. You can't leave me." He stroked her hand gently before releasing it as the EMS team arrived.

Chapter Thirteen

Gunner stepped back and gave the EMTs a quick assessment of her condition before they took his place at the side of the car. Gunner shifted on his feet, watching silently. His body had gone numb, unable to process the fear seeing her like this had caused.

The farmer cleared his throat. "Um, do you want me to give a statement or anything? Pretty sure she tried to avoid that deer over there in the ditch, then hit the tree."

Gunner swung his head, blinked at him several times before he registered what he'd said. How had he forgotten him? "Yes, that'd be great."

He shook his head to clear the worry and pulled his notebook out of his cargo pocket to ask the standard questions. He was on autopilot, copying the man's answers and struggling to listen to the EMS team as they worked on Maryanne.

Would he see her smile again? There was so much blood and head injuries were unpredictable. Her smile always had everyone eating out of her palm. The dimple on one cheek made those full lips stand out and drove him crazy, especially when she always wore that bright red lipstick. He wanted to smear that lipstick from her lips every time he thought of her, which lately was all the time.

She'd been back in town for two years, and she mesmerized him every morning at her bakery. They'd flirt—or rather, she would.

He could flirt with the best of them, but with Maryanne's wide eyes reeling him in and her perfectly arched brows and flawless lipstick begging to be smudged... she left him tongue-tied. He'd never been able to think of a thing to say until a few months ago.

When he'd finished taking the man's statement and information, he turned back to Maryanne. They'd pulled the gurney next to the car and had secured her neck in a brace.

He hovered on the other side of the door as they eased her free. Her cries of pain raked across his skin, and he gripped the top of the door before she passed out. They slid her limp body onto the gurney, and his heart raced.

The EMS team talked with him, but all he heard was broken bones and hospital. Her painful cries still rang in his ears. He then called dispatch to update on the status and call for the tow truck.

His voice felt robotic; his entire body numb. As the ambulance pulled out, he stared at it until the lights faded out of sight. The farmer had gone home too; he was the only one there, but his feet wouldn't let him leave.

It felt like his heart was scattered across the road with the debris. He couldn't go back to the office and just sit. There was too much nervous energy building up, too many questions about her condition. He wanted to chase the ambulance to the hospital. Would she be okay?

She could have died. He felt his knees go weak and a wave of dizziness washed over him.

He tried to cut off his emotions like he'd learned in the Marines. He forced himself to her car and inspected it, routinely looking for alcohol, her phone, or anything else that would have caused the accident.

Even though the dead deer on the side of the road gave him a pretty good clue about what had happened, he had to investigate all possibilities.

He gathered up her phone, purse, and the two shopping bags that were in the front seat, he took them to his SUV and pulled out his phone. He pulled up the number for Andy, Maryanne's almost brother-in-law.

"Hey, Andy, this is Gunner... Yes, we're still on for poker night Tuesday, but that's not why I called. Is Cindy with you? I'm on Route 31. Maryanne's been in a wreck... Yes, she's stable and on her way to the hospital now... Okay, I'll swing by there later with some of her things... Yep, you too. Bye."

A few hours later, he walked through the doors of the hospital and turned left to the ER. He couldn't say what he'd done for the past few hours, his mind solely occupied by Maryanne. The hospital was one big square, single story, with the ER on one side, regular rooms on another, special equipment and tests on a third, and... well, Gunner didn't know what was on the fourth section of the hospital as he'd never been there. Cafeteria was in the middle though.

Spying Andy in the waiting room that served both the ER and regular rooms, he walked over. Andy's head was leaned back against the wall, eyes closed, and feet stretched out in front of him.

Andy'd practically grown up with Gunner and his

brothers. They'd kept in touch, even when they'd both moved away and joined the military.

Andy had moved back to town in October, and had quickly fallen for Maryanne's sister, Cindy. Cindy was a single mom of three, and now a former nurse at the hospital. Andy had found out a few weeks ago that he also had a daughter. They were getting married in two weeks, right before Christmas.

When Gunner sat Maryanne's things on the chair beside him, Andy glanced up and grunted.

"Hey, man. Any news?" Gunner glanced around the empty waiting room.

"Cindy's back there with her now. They'll keep her overnight, since she keeps losing consciousness," Andy said as he rubbed his temples.

"Where are the kids?" Gunner sat in the chair next to him, bouncing his leg. He really hadn't been able to stop moving since he'd seen Maryanne in her car, unconscious and bleeding. If he stopped, he might explode and break down. No one wanted that, and it certainly wouldn't help anything.

"Aunt Suzie has them now. She kept them while Cindy, Margarita, Maryanne, and whoever else went wedding dress shopping in Fort Worth. Cindy had just gotten home when you called." He sighed and leaned back, stretching his long legs out in front of him.

Gunner nodded, crossing his arms. "I wondered what she was doing all the way out on Route 31. She probably took the back roads home."

Andy grimaced. "I don't blame her. I'd want to avoid that traffic too."

"Same. More deer on those back roads, though. She probably swerved to avoid one but still hit it and a tree."

The Sheriff Gets His Girl

The silence stretched, causing his leg to bounce faster. He got up, unable to sit still. Looking down the hall, he turned to pace. Andy's laid-back attitude annoyed him.

"You don't seem worried." Gunner accused as he continued to pace.

Andy crossed his arms even as he shrugged. "I'm not. Cindy is in a tizzy, but if it was that serious, she'd be acting shocked. You okay, man?" His eyebrow arched.

Gunner nodded and took a deep breath, raking his hand through his hair. "Yeah, I'm fine. Just... it wasn't the worst wreck I've seen, but it wasn't good either."

"Shook ya up, huh?"

"Yeah, a bit." Gunner turned to pace towards the hall, avoiding Andy's narrowed eyes. No one knew about his hookup with Maryanne, and it had to stay that way. He had to stay away from her until after the special sheriff's election was over, at a minimum.

He'd already been avoiding her the past few weeks, but seeing her in that car, blood dripping down her cheek... he wanted nothing more than to wrap her in his arms and never let go. How else would he keep her safe? Hopefully, Andy'd just think he was shaken up about the wreck and not these stupid feelings that he couldn't seem to dismiss.

"We'll know more soon. They took her to get all kinds of tests."

It didn't help calm the itch under his skin at all. Lately, that itch was only eased when he was near Maryanne.

The sound of voices floated to them, but it was the cough that caught his attention. Gunner whipped his head around and saw Kendall standing in a doorway down the hall. Andy stood, and Kendall waved at them to come join him. Kendall must be the doctor on shift tonight, which relieved Gunner; he'd only been in town a few years, but everyone knew he was the best doctor in the county.

Gunner slowed his pace to match Andy's, but his heart felt like it was lurching ahead of him, pulling him closer to her. They entered the room to find Cindy hovering, checking the bandages and the work of the nurses they'd passed in the hall.

"I told you. They did a fine job," Kendall said with a sigh.

Cindy gritted her teeth as she tucked the sheet around her sister. Gunner couldn't bring himself to look at Maryanne, too afraid of what he'd see. Instead, he focused on Cindy's hands and gripped his own to keep them from trembling.

"Doesn't matter. I'm still going to check. Just like I'm going to stay the night tonight, so don't even try to stop me." If Cindy's glare were a knife, Kendall would be skewered.

Kendall held up his hands. "I wasn't going to. Technically, you still know all the codes to get in here anyway, so it'd be kind of pointless to stop you."

Cindy had only stopped working at the hospital a few weeks ago. She was preparing for her wedding and a new job as the Home Health and Therapy Director in January.

Andy walked over and put his hands on her shoulders, pulling her slowly away from the bed and wrapping her in a hug. Gunner hung back, glancing away from the couple. His heart stopped as his eyes fell on Maryanne. She looked so fragile and pale on the stark white bed with the IV and things monitoring her. His arms ached to hold her. Her eyes were open but unfocused, as if she wasn't really there with them.

Her black hair had come out of its bun at the scene, but

Cindy must've brushed it out and put it back up. She might have even been the one to wrap the bandage around her forehead. He forced himself to breathe evenly, to steady his erratic heartbeat.

"What's the verdict, Doc?" Andy broke the silence as he rubbed circles on Cindy's back.

"Broken collarbone and wrist and several lacerations from the glass of the windshield. Concussion is the biggest problem and why we're keeping her overnight. Doesn't appear to be any brain swelling, which is good." Kendall flipped through the chart, frowning. "Give me a second. I'll be right back."

They waited in silence as he left, the beeping of the machine the only sound in the room. A nurse came back in with Kendall, then moved Maryanne's IV to attach to the bed.

"What's going on?" Cindy panicked as they began to set up her bed to move.

"I want to take her back for one more test before we let her get some rest for the night." Kendall rechecked the chart. "That alright?"

Gunner took a step back as the nurse unlocked the hospital bed and wheeled past him. His fingers twitched at his sides. He wanted to reach out and touch her, make sure she was still warm and not cold and lifeless.

But that was irrational; the beeping meant her heart rate was steady, and she was still alive.

She was going to be fine. Just a few broken bones and a concussion. It could have been worse. Much, much worse.

He stared at the door as he lost sight of her. Cindy cleared her throat, and he glanced at them. Andy held her in his arms, but she had her face turned towards him, staring at him with eyes so eerily similar to Maryanne's chocolate brown ones.

He shifted on his feet and cleared his throat.

"I gave Andy the stuff from her car. It's been towed to the impound lot. Call me in the morning when they release her, alright?"

Andy said, "Will do. Thanks for stopping by, Gunner. You didn't have to do any of that, but we appreciate it."

"You're a good man," Cindy whispered. "Don't let anyone tell you different."

He felt his cheeks burn as he nodded and left. He used to know exactly what he was doing. His entire life, growing up with five brothers on the horse ranch, he'd been the strait-laced, by-the-book, never-break-the rules kid.

He sighed as he walked to the SUV. After doing his time in the Marines, he planned to become sheriff of his hometown. He was thirty-three, but his goal had been to make sheriff by thirty-five. With this morning's meeting, he was ahead of schedule. Provided everything worked out with the election.

Things had shifted, though.

He wasn't sure he was the same by-the-book guy he used to be. And even though he told Ray there were no complications, there were. Had been for weeks. He'd caught *feelings* for the hot little baker.

Ever since Maryanne and Halloween, he didn't deserve sheriff. Was he even the best candidate for the job anymore? He rubbed his temple as he opened the door and hopped inside his SUV.

Chapter Fourteen

The beeping was annoying. The steadiness of it was soothing, but the sound was too loud. She was barely awake and already she wanted to rip out whatever machine made that noise. Was it her alarm clock? No, her alarm was different.

She breathed deep but paused as a wave of pain washed through her head. The tang of disinfectant flooded her nose, making her want to gag. Instead, she held her breath before releasing it slowly.

Maryanne's eyelids fluttered. The bright lights of the room hit her eyes, making her head spin. She closed them again quickly, thinking. She was in the hospital. She'd wrecked her car. Gunner was there. Where was he?

Peeking through her lashes, she didn't see him. But she also didn't think she was too badly injured, even though her head hurt like nothing she'd experienced before.

"You're awake!" she heard her sister say beside her.

"Bright," she croaked, shifting her head slowly on the

pillow. She heard the light switch flip off, then the curtain of the window slid along its track.

"Here. Have some ice chips." Cindy's whisper helped soothe the frustration of the beeping.

Maryanne cracked one eye open enough to see a piece of ice held up to her lips. She opened her mouth and sucked it in, the cool cube quenching her thirst.

"What happened?" She asked Cindy, who must have been very relieved Maryanne was awake. She was talking a mile a minute, telling her of every detail of the wreck and the hospital stay.

Maryanne was still dizzy and most of what Cindy said just went in one ear and out the other.

Kendall walked in, shutting the door behind him. Holly's brother was the newest town doctor, having moved here less than two years ago. In the dim light, she opened both her eyes as he neared.

"You're awake! That's fantastic. How do you feel?"

She moaned as she blinked away tears. "Hurts. Hurts everywhere."

He nodded with a frown. "I figured. We've given you some painkillers in the IV, but you can't have more yet."

Kendall caught Maryanne's gaze. "You have some broken bones. Collarbone on the left side and your wrist."

Maryanne felt her head and the bandages with her free hand, frowning at the tenderness.

"But the bakery?"

How was she supposed to run a bakery without her wrist? She wouldn't be able to do all she needed to do. And her sister's wedding! She was supposed to make the cake!

"Nothing you can do there for a while, especially since I'm putting you on bedrest for a few days. Want to try drinking water? Let's see if you can keep it down. Are you feeling nauseous?"

"Not really. Just dizzy with a killer headache."

He waved to Cindy, who leaned forward with the cup, straw extended for Maryanne.

She sipped as Kendall continued. "You kept losing consciousness, and I wanted to monitor that, so we kept you overnight."

Cindy's phone rang. Maryanne grabbed the water with her free hand, as Cindy answered, "Hey Mom! Yeah, she just woke up..." She stepped out into the hall, the door closing softly behind her.

Kendall leaned forward, his face earnest as his voice dropped. "Maryanne, before she gets back, I need to make sure you understand the importance of the bedrest. I know you're stubborn like Cindy, but it's to protect the baby too."

Maryanne choked on her water, crying out as it moved her shoulder and clavicle. "The what now?" Surely, he'd been mistaken.

"The... baby? You—you didn't know? I wasn't sure because Cindy didn't mention it. So, I didn't want to say anything with her in the room in case you were keeping it from her. The ultrasound showed you're nine or ten weeks along."

Maryanne felt her stomach roil. A baby? Hell, no! She glanced at Kendall, gasping, "I'm going to—" Kendall pulled the little pink bowl over just as she threw up. She cried as the pain in her shoulder just got worse. It was like a hot poker stabbing where her neck met her shoulder.

When she'd finished, Kendall handed her back the cup of water along with a wet cloth. She drank. Then used a shaky hand to wipe her mouth. Screw it. She was over this already. Pushing the wet cloth onto her face, she laid her head back and tried to ignore the pain as her thoughts whirled.

"Are you sure?" she mumbled behind the warm cloth. The tightness in her chest increased. She couldn't be pregnant.

"Yes, we did a blood test first, then the ultrasound. Both show the pregnancy." When she didn't respond, he continued. "I didn't know you were seeing anyone. Holly hasn't mentioned it."

She winced. Oh, God. What was she going to tell Gunner? She needed to buy herself some time to think about this. And Kendall was friends with him. She couldn't tell Cindy either, because she'd tell Andy who'd tell Gunner. They all played poker together once a week.

She breathed deeply and evenly, trying to get the monitors to beep normally. Her heart still felt like it was speeding down the road, so she just gritted her teeth. What should she tell Kendall?

"I'm not. I—I had a brief fling with the insurance adjuster. The one who came when the bakery flooded. But I don't want anyone to know about the baby until after the wedding, Kendall. I don't want it to take away from Cindy's big day. Are you bound by patient confidentiality?"

She removed the cloth and narrowed her eyes at him. If he didn't tell, it should give her some time to figure out what she was going to do and if... or how she was going to tell Gunner. Good God, a baby!

"I won't say a word. Don't worry."

"Can you hand me my phone? Is it here?"

Kendall looked through her purse sitting on the little couch. "Are you going to call the father?"

Gunner had avoided her after their first night together. That they'd had a second and third night was beyond her understanding, since he was still avoiding her. What would he do when he found out about the baby?

And the bakery. She couldn't close the bakery while she recovered and was on bedrest. She'd just gotten everything sorted out from the flood last month.

She snorted, hoping Kendall didn't do the math on how nine weeks pregnant equaled a fling from last month. Or that he'd find out the insurance adjuster was actually a woman. But she couldn't afford to close for a few more days; she'd have to hire someone now.

Cindy came back into the room as Maryanne said, "Hell, no. I need to find someone to run the bakery. How long will I be on bedrest?"

"You'll need to meet with the orthopedic surgeon next week for your fractures. Bedrest will be two weeks at a minimum, then we'll re-evaluate."

He glanced from Cindy to Maryanne and raised an eyebrow.

"But the wedding is in two weeks!" Cindy screeched. Maryanne winced, the headache getting worse now.

"I'll be at the wedding. Don't worry, sis. It'll all work out."

Cindy shifted from foot to foot. "I talked to Mom. She's going to swing by later."

"While I post the job ad, can you call Mom back? Ask her if she can stay with me while I'm on bedrest? And if she can run the bakery this week while I interview people?"

Cindy stepped out again, and Kendall said quietly, "You'll need to schedule an appointment with an OBGYN within the next two weeks. If they say it's safe for the baby, then you can go off bedrest then. You'll get a cast for your wrist, and it'll be on about six to eight weeks, but the ortho will tell you for sure."

Maryanne turned her phone on as a knock sounded at the door. Sucking in a sharp breath, she saw Gunner walk quickly to the foot of the bed, Cindy following to the little couch by the window.

His face was expressionless, as it'd always been in high school, as it'd always been when he'd stopped by the bakery.

Dear God, they were going to be parents, and she couldn't even read his facial expression! Tears pooled in the corner of her eyes, the light from the partially closed window landing on his face. His eyes darkened as he stared at her. They spoke to her, but she didn't know what he was trying to say.

When a tear rolled down her cheek, his eyes widened. He leaned down and placed a hand on her foot. She felt the sparks shoot up her leg at his touch, but the racing of her heart slowed.

She dragged in a steadying breath. Kendall and Cindy glanced from the monitors to Maryanne to Gunner, but Maryanne ignored them.

"You're awake," Gunner said gruffly. He wore jeans and boots, but instead of his cop's uniform shirt, he wore a dark grey shirt with his black leather jacket.

He looked like he hadn't shaved, his blond scruff calling for her to run her fingers over it. She clenched her hand, gasping as the pain in her wrapped wrist shot up to her elbow.

"Barely," she said shakily. "Broken collarbone and wrist have me out of action for a while."

"You were lucky." He nodded gravely. Another tear leaked out. Well, at least the baby explained why she'd been fighting tears so much these past few weeks.

Cindy stood, taking the shaking cup of water from Maryanne's shaking hand and turning back to something on her phone. Gunner frowned, and Kendall checked the rest of her vitals.

She pursed her lips. "Are you sure there's nothing more you can give me? My shoulder hurts."

"Anything more will make you nauseous." Kendall turned to check something on the counter behind him.

Maryanne didn't break eye contact with Gunner. If he would only hold her, then she'd tell him about the baby now, tell him everything.

She took an unsteady breath, then turned her unbroken wrist so her palm was up. She clenched her hand, opening and closing it in a come here gesture. Gunner's eyes widened. He understood.

And he slid his hand off her foot and stepped back. She felt her chest tighten now that he wasn't touching her. Her heart felt like it was pounding too loud as it cracked into a million pieces.

Another tear fell down her cheek. With a wobbly, tear-filled smile, she nodded and leaned back, putting the now cool washcloth over her face again.

So. That was that. She'd wait to tell him until things settled down a little. Shouldn't be too hard, if he kept ignoring her like he had been. Maryanne felt more tears leak out the edges of her eyes behind the washcloth.

Cindy's voice echoed in the room. "Mom will meet us at your apartment this afternoon. She'll be released today, right?"

Kendall murmured. "I'd prefer tomorrow. We'll monitor her for a full twenty-four hours, since she kept losing consciousness. We're also hoping the swelling in the wrist goes down today. I'm about to head home, but orthopedics will be by later to review everything and make the appointment for your cast. You'll make sure she sticks to bedrest, right?"

"Absolutely."

Maryanne groaned. Her sister was a pushover, but not with medical orders. She was more stubborn than—well, than Gunner following laws and rules.

Gunner cleared his throat. "Well, I'm glad to see you awake. Let me know if there's anything I can do to help."

She snorted. He didn't mean that, since he'd just shot her down.

He turned to go, but she heard him shuffle back. Tears leaked out of her eyes, but she was glad he couldn't see them behind the cloth.

"By the way, I need your statement. What happened last night?"

She sighed, her chest growing tight. Of course, he was only here to get her statement. "Herd of deer crossed the road. I swerved. Not sure if I hit one or a tree or what it was."

"Hm, I thought so. Okay, I'll close out the report when I get to work later. Get well soon, Maryanne."

His tone had been so final. So formal. It made her cry even harder. She held it in as she heard Kendall leave with Gunner. Then she sobbed loudly before snapping her mouth closed.

"Oh! M, it's going to be okay!"

Cindy rubbed a soothing hand over her uninjured arm, then brushed the hair back carefully from her head. Maryanne just shook her head, a deep pit of dread settling in her heart.

Gunner had felt a million miles away. She just wanted him to come in and wrap her up in his arms, hold her, and keep her safe and warm.

She sucked in a breath and wrestled control of her tears. The washcloth on her face couldn't fool her; she knew tears still fell, but at least she wasn't loud about it. Stupid tears. Stupid emotions. Stupid Gunner.

For a second, when he'd come in, she'd imagined him being with her in the delivery, holding her hand as she brought their baby into the world. He'd kiss her as they looked at their little guy.

She pushed that brief dream back, mentally stomping it on it as she cried silently.

Chapter Fifteen

A few days later, Gunner stood in front of the window of the police station, arms crossed, jaw clenched. After weeks of surliness, Joey—another deputy—had stopped trying to have conversations with him.

Normally, they'd be knee-deep in smack talk on their favorite NFL teams this time of year, but Gunner just couldn't handle it right now.

The sheriff's office faced the town square, with the park and that damn gazebo. He avoided staring into the trees at it and instead, he leaned against the window frame and looked down the street.

Diagonally across from him were four shops all in one big brick building: Clip & Curl, Half Baked, Eden's Flowers, and Yoga & You.

Both the bakery and Holly's yoga studio had only been around for less than two years, but the town was growing. Maryanne did a great job with her social media marketing for the bakery. It was popular with the younger crowd, teenagers, hipsters, and people his own age.

The Sheriff Gets His Girl

Even when she'd been in the hospital and on bedrest the past three days, he'd seen the notifications that she'd been posting recipes and mouth-watering pictures of past creations.

Most people probably wouldn't realize that those pictures were ones she'd already posted a long time ago, but he knew. He always followed, paid attention, and remembered anything she did, whether in person or online.

He glanced down at his watch, shifting his feet impatiently. Maryanne sat with her back to the wall in a booth by the window. If she looked his way, she'd see him standing there, but she never did. She was smiling at customers and talking like she hadn't been in a wreck just a few days ago.

What the hell was she even doing over there? Kendall had ordered her to bedrest, but Joey had said she was there this morning when he'd gone for their normal pickup order. And she hadn't left yet.

A steady stream of customers filed in and out of the bakery shortly after seven when Maryanne got up and walked away from the window.

Two customers made Gunner narrow his eyes. They walked up the street, but not together. The dark-haired hipster in front swaggered, hands in pockets acting all nonchalant.

He seemed familiar somehow. The short little old man behind him tripped on the sidewalk, making the younger one turn and glare. Gunner almost would have taken them for a rich boy and his lackey, but the image didn't quite fit.

The man leading the charge walked slowly past the bakery, appearing to glance casually inside before continuing down past the Clip & Curl and to the side of the building. The white-haired man swiped at his nose as he hurried after him, looking furtively around before sliding around the building.

Legs wide, arms crossed, the arrogant jackass glared down his nose at the older man, who waved his arms around nervously, then raked a hand through his already messy hair. Then the hipster unbuttoned his coat and slid a yellow manila folder out.

The white-haired man glanced around nervously before reaching out and snatching it, turning slightly away from the hipster to look inside.

He jerked his head up, eyes wide, jaw gone slack. Whatever was in there surprised the old man. There was a bloom of color on his cheeks, then he glanced inside again, nodded jerkily, and reached out a hand to shake.

The hipster snarled but reached out and grabbed the man's hand. Based on the wince on the old one's face, the hipster was making some kind of threat... and judging from the cruel smile on the hipster's face, he was enjoying it.

The old man then pulled out a piece of paper, shoved the manila folder under his shirt and tucked it in, then turned and practically ran to the bakery, paper flapping in his hand. The hipster leaned against the wall behind him, propped one foot up, and shoved his hands back in his pockets to wait.

The entire thing caused the hairs on the back of Gunner's neck to stand up. Of all the people walking around downtown, why did these two stand out?

"Hey, Joey." Gunner called out behind him, never taking his eyes off the dark-haired man.

"Yeah?" came the shout from down the hall.

Footsteps echoed as they approached and without taking his eyes off the guy across the street, Gunner nodded toward the man. "Ever seen that guy around town before?"

The Sheriff Gets His Girl

Joey ambled up beside him, sipping his Mt. Dew. "Nope, but we're getting new people moving to town all the time. Just in the past two months, there's been three families alone. Not to mention the foot traffic of tourists just sliding through between Decatur and Denton."

"See if we can get a picture of him from the town cameras. I want to run it through the database because something feels off."

Joey walked to his desk and started pulling up the program on the computer. Fifteen minutes later and the old man hadn't come out yet. The entitled prick hadn't left either, but was just standing there, picking at his nails and scrolling on his phone. The printer in the corner startled Gunner, as the white-haired guy walked out of the bakery.

He looked around the street, smiling at those he passed. But he was still too jittery. When he rounded the corner and reported back to the man, he handed over a little purple and pink brochure. That was Maryanne's menu. Was this guy a competitive baker from a neighboring town? Why the subterfuge of sending in someone else?

"Here ya go, Gunner. Guy was in juvie in Cali, then had an arrest in Vegas for domestic violence. Not much on him, though." Joey handed over the printout.

"Did you see what vehicle he came into town with? Did anything pop up on that?"

Gunner glanced down at the printout and sucked in a breath. That face. He had cornered Maryanne on Halloween. Heat blossomed out of his chest as he glanced back up in time to see the two men go separate ways.

"There wasn't anything out of the ordinary. Cameras on 3rd Street show it's parked at the grocery store."

"See that guy with the white hair crossing the street into the park? Follow him. He was given a suspicious package that should be under his shirt. Call in the Aussie to meet you in the park. Make it look casual, like you're just meeting him to go through standard training with Abigail, the drug dog. See if she picks up the scent of anything while that guy is around."

"You sure that's necessary, Gunner? He's just an old man." Joey rubbed his hand down his face with a sigh.

Gunner frowned with a nod. "Better safe than sorry, yes?"

The icy fingers of fear ran down Gunner's spine as he folded the paper and walked toward the back door.

"Where are you going?" Joey called, his voice annoyed.

"Traffic stop. I'm assuming he's walking to the grocery store now to leave town."

"License and registration, please," Gunner said flatly as the man rolled down the window.

"What seems to be the problem, officer?" The man pulled out his wallet and handed over the registration while Gunner inhaled. Yep, same cheap cologne from Halloween.

"There was a stop sign that you didn't quite stop at, Mr... Davis." Well, this was interesting. The license did not match the printout Joey had pulled up for his face. "Give me just a minute to run your details. I'll be right back."

Gunner walked back to his SUV and got in. He typed up the details from the license into the passenger side database computer, his mind whirled. What was this guy's deal? His face was registered; he had his mug shot as Bruce David. The license was a Colorado one registered for Barry Davis.

The computer flashed to the next page. Gunner sucked

in a breath as his eyes widened. Shit. This was some major stuff. Their small town didn't get a lot of this kind of thing. Gunner read the details as the scanner crackled.

"Gunner. You there?"

Joey called from the other end. Gunner picked up the CB radio, pushed the button, and pulled it closer to his mouth.

"Yeah, I'm here. What's up?"

He released the button. Frowning at the computer, he breathed deeply to slow the adrenaline pumping fast in his heart as he processed all the steps he'd need to take next.

"You were right about the old man in the park. He's been picked up on possession of cocaine. We're processing him now."

Shit. Gunner rubbed the back of his neck, then grabbed a drink from his bottle of water.

"Joey, can you send Garrett and Abigail to Hwy 57, just past the Myer's place? Call in the Sheriff too. This is going to get complicated."

"What's going on?"

"Guy gave me a fake license out of Colorado. But even the fake license has warrants out for him for possession and intent to distribute."

"Shit."

"Yep. Exactly."

The silence stretched as Gunner waited for the drug dog and her Aussie handler to arrive. He wasn't about to make this arrest without another set of eyes and hands. He'd prefer the Sheriff be here too, but he might have to settle.

If it was up to him, he might end up punching the guy in the face, just for scaring Maryanne.

He sat up straighter and typed in the name Joey had pulled up from the picture. When he read up on the guy's history in Vegas and Cali, Gunner clenched his jaw. Had the guy done any of that shit around Maryanne? To Maryanne?

If so, that explained a lot of her behavior and words from Halloween. That look in her eyes, the defeat, the fear. It still haunted him.

He hated seeing her scared or crying. Even the thought of it brought such pressure to his chest. What could Barry or Bruce or whoever he was want with Maryanne now?

Another government-issued SUV pulled up behind him. Gunner clenched his jaw as he opened his door and stepped out. It was go time, and this fucker was about to go down.

Chapter Sixteen

"Mom, I'm fine. I can't just sit in bed all the time. This still counts as bedrest," Maryanne cajoled, as she waved to her feet propped up in her office at the bakery. Her mom stood in the doorway, arms crossed over her silk shirt, flour already on her dress pants. Her olive complexion shone in the harsh glare of the overhead lights, the frown marring her perfectly smooth skin.

Maryanne pushed her hair out of her face, re-tucking it into her messy bun with her bound hand.

"This is not what Kendall had in mind, M, and you know it. I'm going to call Cindy," Margarita said as she pulled out her phone. Maryanne rolled her eyes and adjusted her arm on the desk where she'd propped it up.

"Mom, I deliberately scheduled all four interviews for today so it'd be the only long day I'll have. We also need to meet Lola and Holly to complete the wedding details. We don't have time for full bedrest this week. I will do my best to stay still. Hell, I'll keep my feet propped up and only walk from here across the street to my apartment once a day. I'll be fine."

The bell for the front door rang, and Margarita glanced behind her. Pointing a finger, she said, "Don't move." She turned with a flick of her hair and went into the front of the bakery to help the next customer.

Maryanne had done well the past three days. She'd stayed home until she'd felt like she could move less stiffly. She glanced at the save screen on her phone. She'd put the baby's first ultrasound picture on it. She teared up, hoping she was telling her mom the truth and being in the bakery today wouldn't hurt the little peanut.

"Maryanne, this is Chester. He's here for an interview?" her mom said as she poked her head into the office. Maryanne smiled wearily and waved him in as Margarita walked away.

Chester was on the shorter side and very skinny. White hair sticking every which way and sweating profusely, he smiled nervously as he glanced around.

"Please, won't you have a seat?" she waved to the other chair in the room at the edge of her corner desk. She had her back to the wall with her feet propped up on the third chair. She picked up his resume from her desk. "Thank you for coming in today. I see that you've worked in Decatur at the Wal-mart bakery?"

He nodded and babbled about his experience. His eyes kept shifting around, refusing to meet hers. She glanced from him to the resume and back again with a frown. She recognized the tweaking, the profuse sweating. This guy wasn't going to work out. Not with whatever drug problem he had.

Twenty minutes later, she waved him goodbye with an, "I'll call you after the interviews are over and let you know."

The Sheriff Gets His Girl

The next interviewee was a local teenager. Ivy really wanted the job, but she was still in high school, so she could only work until eight in the morning and on weekends. Maryanne smiled as she left, wishing she could hire the peppy girl. She reminded her a lot of herself at that age, so full of hope and big plans of going to culinary arts school. The third interviewee called right before her scheduled interview to cancel.

The last interviewee arrived just before lunch. Maryanne blinked as his dark, bulky frame filled her office doorway. His black hair was cut into some kind of design on the side, the top long and curly like Patrick Mahomes. He was easily six foot five, with tree trunks for arms and legs.

"Good Lord, you're a giant," she said, blinking in surprise. She stiffened, hoping she hadn't offended the man, but he threw his head back and laughed, his flat belly rippling with muscle as his white teeth flashed in the light.

He grinned as he sat down. "That I am. Nice to meet you."

"I'm Maryanne, owner of Half Baked. It's nice to meet you too," she smiled as she picked up his resume.

"I'm Zarrel. Love the name of the bakery, by the way. Used to toke up in college. Great stress reliever, but I'm guessing you don't actually sell edibles here? I checked your online menu before I agreed to the interview, just to make sure. Not wanting to do anything illegal, you know." He crossed his meaty arms, the sleeves of his grey polo shirt nearly ripping as he arched a dark brow.

She laughed. "No, we are definitely legal. I used to own a bakery in Colorado that specialized in edibles, but we don't do that here in Texas. We offer traditional baked goods, and some CBD infused goods, but of course there's no THC in any of our products. If hired, you'll see the local police force in here regularly to 'verify' our goods are legal." She rolled her eyes, which made him laugh.

She felt like her heart was in a vise from missing Gunner coming in to do just that.

He shifted in his seat, glancing away before meeting her eyes again. "I want to be clear that I'm technically a felon. So if you haven't run a background check yet, don't be surprised when that pops up."

She tilted her head to the side and frowned. "What did you do and how long were you in?"

He took a deep breath, but didn't look away. "Marijuana cultivation and two years. Then I was on probation for another two years."

"Why were you cultivating?" she asked, as she narrowed her eyes at him.

He shrugged. "Personal use. I was tired of buying from shady guys in my neighborhood, so I grew my own. I pissed off a neighbor because I wouldn't share. He turned me in. Crazy neighbors is just another reason to get out of Dallas."

She nodded. "How long have you been out? What are your parole or probation terms?"

They talked about what the requirements were, his experience working in downtown Dallas at some local restaurants, and his desire for a more rural and slower lifestyle. She told him about the car accident and the upcoming wedding and bedrest. He was open, warm, and honest, which she valued.

Her mom popped her head into the office and frowned. "Maryanne, I just got off the phone with Andy. Cindy's taking her physical therapy test today. I need to go get Owen and Mandy from daycare. Will you be all right for half an hour?"

Maryanne nodded and waved her off. "Sure. Go. This will give me a chance to test out Zarrel here."

"Make sure she stays off her feet, young man," Margarita frowned.

He grinned as he said, "Yes, ma'am. Don't worry. My sister was on bedrest with her last pregnancy, so I know how it is."

Maryanne froze, her smile in place. Hopefully, her mom didn't connect her bedrest to being pregnant.

Margarita just laughed and checked her phone. "Thank God she's not pregnant. Can you imagine juggling that, the wreck, and Cindy's wedding? Whew. I'll see y'all later."

As her mom left, Maryanne stood, ignoring her blushing cheeks. "Feel like doing a test run? I'd like to see where you're at, skill wise. I need to know how much direction and oversight you'll need."

"So I can have the job?"

She grinned and took him into the bakery to show him around, including where her recipe books were housed. "I'll pay you for today's trial run, if you're up for it?" He insisted she sit down in the bakery and not lift a finger while he made a batch each of donuts, bear claws, and kolaches. He was a perfect gentleman, carrying two chairs into the large room for her to sit down on and prop up her feet. While he worked, she told him about the town's history, the people, and where things were located.

When the bell rang, they both went to the front where she showed him how to run the register. She sat in one booth, her back against the wall and her feet up as she chatted with those who came in for the lunch rush. Everyone asked about her wreck, but many were talking about the commotion across the street at the police station.

State troopers rolled by just after lunch, several even stopping in for coffee.

"Well, hello officers. What brings you fine specimens to our little town today?" She smiled her flirtiest smile, lifting her chin as she tried to figure out what was going on. The other gossip wasn't specific.

"Two arrests, one needing extradition out of state," one said gruffly. He crossed his arms and rattled off a complicated order to Zarrel. Zarrel seemed to take it in stride though, a small smile plastered to his face.

The other state trooper rolled his eyes and slid closer to Maryanne in her booth. "Don't mind him. He's just mad he didn't get to make the arrest."

"Oh?" she smiled, making her dimples pop and sliding a fingertip along the edge of the table. "Who did?"

"Officer Williams. He did some mighty fine detective work, too. Pieced it all together this morning and picked up the out-of-state guy just outside the city limits. Timed it perfectly too. There was nowhere for the guy to run but wide open fields."

She gasped. "Did he run? Was he armed?" A wave of nausea washed over her, making her light-headed and dizzy. The thought of Gunner chasing some bad guy and getting hurt was the thing of nightmares.

The officer shook his head. "Nah, he knew his time was up. Clammed up and hasn't said a word except to make his phone call to a lawyer."

Breathing shakily, she kept a brittle smile on her face as she chatted. Other customers asked the nice officer questions. She noticed the newspaper lady, Isabel, furiously typing on her phone in the back corner; this would be on the local news now.

Maryanne was careful to keep her voice light and peppy until the last customer left around one-thirty. She rubbed her temples and breathed a sigh of relief. When she opened her eyes, Zarrel had placed a cup of peppermint tea in front of her, then sat across from her with a bottle of water.

"So how'd I do?" he asked as he drank.

She smiled tiredly. "Fantastic. When can you start?"

He laughed as he said, "You sure? You haven't even run the background check yet."

She grinned and shrugged, wincing at the pull on her shoulder. "I'm sure, but before we move forward, know that I can be pretty picky about things. Some have called me bitchy in the past. I'm not always the easiest person to work with."

He took a sip of his water. "I doubt you're worse than any of the guys from prison. Or my sister while she was pregnant with all her babies."

She laughed, nervously picking up her tea and taking a sip.

"It's rude for a guy to ask a woman if she's pregnant, but you're on bedrest and that peppermint tea is already making you look less green about the gills." Zarrel's left brow rose as he leaned back in his seat.

Maryanne sighed as she sat down her cup with a shaky hand. She cleared her throat and glanced away before taking a deep breath and meeting his chocolate brown eyes. "Ok, yeah. I'm pregnant. I found out while I was in the hospital from the wreck, but you and the doctor are the only ones who know so far, and it needs to stay that way until after my sister's wedding this weekend, okay?"

He nodded as he rubbed a hand over his jaw. "Yeah, that makes sense. I can do that."

"Good. If you can keep that a secret and help me survive through the wedding, then you're definitely hired. Might even need to give you a bonus."

They laughed as the door opened, the bell ringing as someone stepped inside.

Chapter Seventeen

Maryanne glanced over and her chest seized. Gunner stood just inside the doorway, his cop's uniform stretching over his chest and visible beneath his leather jacket. His jeans were pressed and his boots shone like always. He held his cop's cowboy hat in one hand, spinning it as he slowly glanced between her and Zarrel. She pasted on a brittle smile.

"Hey, Gunner, this is Zarrel. I've just hired him to run the bakery while I'm on bedrest and dealing with the wedding this weekend. I hear you're a hero! Congratulations on the arrest." Her chest hurt just looking at him. She wanted him to hold her, but this was the first time she'd seen him since the hospital. Rejection still stung, making her shoulders stiff.

His face was unreadable, as always. Only his eyes shone, piercing into her soul as he blinked slowly.

Zarrel stood up and offered a hand. "You're the local police? It's nice to meet you. Heard a lot about you today. I need to come by the police station later to file an intent to move form."

Gunner frowned as he shook Zarrel's hand. Gunner's height had always amazed Maryanne when they were teenagers, but next to Zarrel, he looked like a normal sized man. Now that they were grown, he'd added bulk to it. She blushed as she remembered running her hands across his wide chest. The pool of longing in her heart made her a quivering mess.

This wouldn't do. This was the first time he'd been into the bakery since the beginning of October, since their first hookup. She blinked rapidly, thinking… that would have been when they'd made the baby.

"I'll be working late. Stop by after you're done here, and we'll get it worked out," Gunner said gruffly.

A ding sounded in the back. Zarrel turned and said, "Just a minute. Let me unload the oven."

Gunner stood, shifting slightly as Zarrel walked down the short hall, past the bathrooms, and into the kitchen. As the kitchen door swung behind him, Gunner walked toward her and sat down, pushing his hat onto the table in between them.

His five o'clock shadow was prominent, making her want to reach out and rub against it, but there were bags under his eyes. Was he not sleeping well, either? He frowned as his hazel gaze shone in the light from the windows beside them. "You're hiring a felon? Is that the best you could do?"

She narrowed her eyes and glared. "At least he's honest about it. I need to work with someone who's an open book, Gunner."

She hoped he got the message. Gunner was anything but an open book. If he were a book, he'd be a diary with a lock that no one had the key for. Then the diary would be in a welded shut metal box.

His jaw clenched, distracting her from her thoughts. "What was he in for?"

Oh boy, he was gonna love this. "Marijuana cultivation," she smirked.

His eyes widened. "Is it wise to have him around you, then?"

She shifted in her seat, sitting up straighter. "What do you mean by that?"

He crossed his arms and leaned back. "I mean, do you still have pot somewhere? From Halloween?"

She rolled her eyes. "I told you then and I'll tell you now. I don't have pot."

He snorted. "Yeah? Then what the hell was in them?"

She held up her cast bound hand. "Hold up, G. Are you asking me as a cop? Because civilian to cop, I don't know what you're talking about. I deny having any pot, now or in the past."

He huffed in frustration and leaned forward, his gaze intense and stern. "So it's all gone? That was the last of it? I don't need to search your apartment?"

She rolled her eyes, even though her heart beat fast in her chest as he came closer. "Well, if you want an excuse to come to my apartment..." she wiggled her eyebrows with a grin.

He sat back and crossed his arms, making her roll her eyes in response. "Yes, Gunner. It's all gone. It was leftover liquid THC from 'Buela's Hospice days. It wasn't pot. I don't have contacts with the town pot dealers or run an underground drug ring. Just chill out, ok?"

The flash in his eyes said he was still mad. As an awkward silence descended, she glanced away from him and out the front door. How could she help them get past this? If she didn't fix it, he wouldn't come back in and would continue ignoring her. That would make the news of the baby even more awkward.

"So... what happened with the arrest today?" she asked softly. Maybe he'd be able to talk about work.

But... maybe now was the time to tell him about the baby. She glanced back at him as she bit her nail, her heart in her throat. She *should* tell him now. Her heart raced, and her palms were sweaty. The cast on her wrist itched.

"The arrest was... interesting. I actually need to ask you some questions, if you don't mind?" His expression gave nothing away, but he was using his cop voice, and it made her nervous. She nodded slowly as he pulled out his phone, swiped, then set it in front of her.

She gasped, her eyes widening. "That's Barry!"

"Yes, it is. He was the one I arrested today, and I have some questions about your connection. He was here Halloween, correct?"

She nodded, swallowing the knot that had formed in her throat.

"What did he want?"

She shook her head, whispering, "I—I don't know. He—he was into some shady stuff in Colorado. He mentioned drugs over in Dallas, but I don't know why he was *here* or how he tracked me down or—or why he was in town and you arrested him. Gunner—" She was hyperventilating now. Clutching her chest, she slid out of the booth and put her head between her legs.

She felt a warm hand rub circles on her back slowly and the tension seeped out.

"It's ok, M. He's locked up now. Were you afraid he was going to hurt you?"

She nodded her head, still trying to regulate her breathing and heart rate.

"Have you seen him since Halloween?"

She shook her head no and sat up slowly. Gunner stood next to her as she sat on the edge of the booth seat. He slid his phone over to her with another picture on it. She gasped, "That's Chester. He interviewed for the open position earlier this morning."

"Have you met him before today?"

She shook her head no with a sigh, the headache growing. "No, but he was acting shifty in the interview. He was sweating a lot and wouldn't make eye contact. I got the feeling he was on drugs."

Gunner nodded, then picked up his phone and slipped it into his pocket. He started to slide away, but she reached out a hand and grabbed his. Standing up, she looked up into his eyes as they darkened, light swirling around them.

"Gunner, I have nothing to do with whatever they're mixed up in. Believe me." Good God, what if he didn't believe her? Would he arrest her too, for what happened on Halloween? Would he arrest himself, too?

"I know you're not. Chester is singing like a canary, and Barry is being extradited to Colorado. You won't see either of them again." His confidence made her knees buckle. He caught her around the waist and pulled her in for a hug. The smell of cedar and pine mixed with the scents of the bakery to comfort her. His arms wrapped her up safely, and it was everything she'd been craving since waking up in the hospital.

She took a deep breath, leaning back to meet his eyes. She would tell him about the baby now. She needed to. Opening her mouth, Gunner broke eye contact and looked toward the kitchen before stepping away. A moment later Zarrel pushed through the kitchen door and walked towards them.

She smiled as he neared. "Got it all taken care of?"

He nodded, "Yes, ma'am. It's almost two. Do you want me to flip the sign on the door and show me how to lock up?"

She nodded as Gunner moved away from her. "Can I take some bear claws to go?"

"Of course," she said as Zarrel went behind the counter to bag them up. Gunner walked to the checkout counter. She couldn't take her eyes off his ass. She remembered how soft his skin was there, the dimple on the bottom of his back. Her fingers tingled.

When he finished paying, he walked toward her. His eyes had darkened like they did before he kissed her. Her heart sped up, thinking maybe he would kiss her goodbye.

But he just reached for his cowboy hat on the table. Setting it on his head, tipping it at her as their eyes met. Then he slipped out the front door. Before she could catch her breath, Zarrel flipped the sign and locked it behind him.

"So… that's your baby daddy, huh?"

Maryanne sank down onto the seat with a shaky laugh. "Was it that obvious?"

Zarrel shrugged as he picked up her empty teacup. "It was to me. You sure no one else knows? Because if anyone saw you together… it's in the eyes. It gives you both away." Her heart leaped. Did Gunner look at her differently than he did others? She doubted it.

"We aren't often in the same room together, so no one else knows. Well, except my friend, Holly. She knows I slept with him but not about the baby." Maryanne glanced out the window just in time to see Gunner go into the police station.

"So what's next for the bakery?" he said. She shook off her thoughts of Gunner and walked Zarrel through how to

The Sheriff Gets His Girl

close up the bakery and the end of day checklist. They planned for him to arrive the next morning.

"My mom, Margarita—you met her earlier—will be here in the morning to show you how to open up. I'm going to hire a teenager, Ivy, to help in the mornings too, at least this week and through the Christmas rush. But she will only work until eight when school starts. We'll need both of you, and my mom, in order to do the baking for the wedding alone."

An hour later, she walked across the street and down the alley to the rear of the Pharmacy. She yawned. She'd check the arrest stories later on the Crimson Creek Facebook page, or the Newspaper's website.

When she made it to her apartment, she removed the sling from her left shoulder and collapsed slowly on the bed. She needed a long nap. It had been good to get to the bakery, but she was definitely tired.

As she slept, her dreams turned fitful. Gunner chased her through a field, rain pouring all around them, waving his gun and shouting at her.

When she awoke with a start, her heart pounding, she groggily wondered... was he going to hurt her? Or protect her from something else?

Chapter Eighteen

Second week of December

"All the Bachelorette dinner stuff is in the bag in the pantry. I was going to make it earlier, but Mom wouldn't let me." Maryanne said from the couch Cindy had forced her onto. She sat with her feet propped up on the chaise lounge, a pillow under her arm.

Cindy's glared at Maryanne. "Exactly why we came over early. Kendall said bedrest, M. You're lucky you're on the couch and not in bed right now."

Holly plopped onto the couch, her silver hair pulled back in a ponytail. Still in her twenties, she'd dyed it to match her grief before moving to Crimson Creek.

She tucked her feet under her on the floor, her black yoga pants stretching, the movement causing her dark grey oversized shirt to fall off one shoulder. She twisted her ponytail with a finger as she talked with Maryanne.

"Don't worry. We'll make sure it's all put back where everything belongs."

"And exactly in the right order, too," Lola said with a firm nod, bringing a throw blanket to Maryanne. "Don't worry, M. I got you. I won't let them destroy your kitchen."

Maryanne chuckled softly and laid her head back, closing her eyes briefly.

"So, how have you been feeling?" Holly asked softly, while Lola and Cindy bustled around in the kitchen. Maryanne opened one eye and saw Holly's frowning at the floor. She watched her shift in her seat, pick at the hem of her sweater.

"Fine. It's been a long week, but I'm glad I hired Zarrel and Ivy to help this week and with the wedding. How've you been doing?"

Holly arched an eyebrow and glanced back at Cindy and Lola in the kitchen before lowering her voice and staring at Maryanne. "Girl, you're on bedrest. That can't just be for your shoulder and wrist."

Maryanne sucked in a breath and glanced away, adjusting the throw blanket tucked around her. "I don't know what you mean," she mumbled.

"Maryanne, it's me. I might've been pregnant for just a short time, but I know the signs. You were sick before Thanksgiving when the bakery flooded, remember? You've been more emotional. And you slept with Gunner. Are you gonna make me say it?"

Maryanne bit her nail, blinking rapidly. Holly may be the only one she could talk to about this right now. She glanced furtively over at her sister and leaned closer to Holly. "Okay, fine, but you can't tell Cindy. You can't tell anyone, not until after her wedding."

Holly snorted. "You'd be surprised. She probably suspects the truth by now."

"Are you kidding? She's too focused on the wedding, her

new job, getting settled over at Andy's house. It has been ridiculously easy to keep it all quiet." Maryanne frowned, the pressure on her chest growing at the thought of lying to her sister. They'd always been close. At least, until she'd gone to Colorado. Her sister knew nothing of Barry and that mess.

"Gunner is the father?"

Maryanne finally met her friend's gaze, her own filling with tears as she nodded, blinking furiously to keep them from falling. Sucking in a breath, she glanced around wildly. "Yes, but he can't know yet, either. I just need to get through the wedding first. Then I can tell him and everyone else."

They sat in silence, the soft murmurs of Lola and Cindy in the kitchen floating through the air. Tears spilled onto her cheeks, and Maryanne brushed them quickly aside.

Remembering why Holly had moved here with her brother Kendall just made Maryanne so sad. She couldn't imagine losing this baby, even if it was unexpected.

"Will you be able to still hang out with me? Or will it be too much to see me with a baby over the next few months or years?" She was afraid this would drive a wedge between them, and she desperately needed her friend right now. "You don't have to talk about it if you don't want to, Holly. I understand. I just... I don't want to lose you over this."

Holly shook her head, her eyes sad. "This won't drive us apart, don't worry. My therapist says it'll be good for me to face this. It's been two years. I—I have to ask, have to talk about it. It's the only way to move past it."

"You'll never move past it, Holly. It'll always be with you." More tears crested Maryanne's eyelashes. "*They'll* always be with you."

Even though her own dad had been strict, she still missed him now that he was gone. Losing a spouse and baby wasn't the same, but sometimes grief transcended the details.

Holly gave a wobbly smile. "I know. I miss Eric, but I missed out on raising our little girl too. You being pregnant... it's bittersweet, but I'm happy for you. Are you're happy for you?"

Maryanne closed her eyes again and leaned back on the couch. "I guess so. I mean, I've only known a few days, but so far I've just been overwhelmed by it. I don't think I've entered the happy stage yet. All I seem to do is cry."

"That makes sense. I mean, Eric and I had been trying for ages. We were both ecstatic when we found out."

"Yeah, but you were in it together. I'm—It's just me, you know?" Her voice choked.

"Hey, none of that. It's going to be alright." Holly scooted closer on the couch, wrapping her in a side-armed hug, Maryanne sighed as she continued. "You're not alone. You have all of us. And your mom."

After a few minutes, Maryanne got her emotions under control, and Holly leaned back, letting her go. "How do you think Gunner will take it?"

Maryanne winced and shook her head. "Probably not well. We'd agreed it was just a one-time thing, and he's still ignoring me."

"He has a right to know, though. And he'll probably help with child support, which you're going to need to pay for a sitter if you're going to continue running the bakery."

"I know he does, and I know he'll do the right thing. I mean, come on, it's Gunner. I just... I need to wrap my head around it first, you know? After the wedding. I don't want this to take away from Cindy's big day." That would give her one more week to figure out how to even get Gunner to talk to her. Should she go to the police station while he was working? It was the most logical way to pin him down.

Holly reached over and squeezed her knee. "Text him now and ask him for a date after the wedding. Wedding's on Saturday. What about Sunday?"

"Sunday is the big Christmas pageant, and I'm singing a special. My nephews are in it, then there's a big potluck after."

"Sunday evening? Monday evening?"

Maryanne sighed, but nodded with a smile. When Maryanne glanced at Lola and Cindy finishing in the kitchen, Holly nudged her knee again. "Seriously. Get out your phone and text him. Invite him over for dinner."

Maryanne frowned, but pulled her phone out of her shirt pocket. Her stomach was in knots, but he hadn't responded to any of her text messages in over a month. He might have even blocked her.

Hey, G. The wedding has me crazy, but I need to talk to you. Can we have dinner Sunday evening, after all the church pageant potluck hoopla? Say, seven o'clock?

She turned the phone around and showed Holly it had sent while Lola came to sit on the lone, wide chair in the living room.

"What are we looking at?" She lowered her six-foot frame into it. Her strawberry blond hair was piled into a messy bun like Maryanne's own dark hair. But while Maryanne looked tired and drained, Lola looked fresh as a spring day with her green plaid shirt and freckles dotting her nose and cheekbones.

Cindy walked to the bathroom, saying over her shoulder, "Dinner will be ready in seven minutes."

When the door shut behind her, Holly leaned toward Lola to whisper. "I was right. Maryanne's pregnant but no one can know until after the wedding. She's promised to tell the father next Sunday evening."

"Holly! It's gotta stay quiet! Stop telling people!" Maryanne sat up quickly as she hissed, slipping her phone back in her pocket.

"The bastard better pay child support." Lola smirked. She didn't look surprised at all; instead, she looked like the cat who ate the canary.

Maryanne frowned. "He's not a bastard. Quite the opposite, actually. He's a very honorable man. Straight laced and by the book."

Cindy came out of the bathroom and sat on the end of the couch. "What are we talking about?"

"Your wedding, of course," Lola said smoothly, arching an eyebrow. Cindy's face lit up, making Maryanne smile.

"I was telling them about the new hires. I think they'll do a great job on the cakes and pastries, and I'll be there the entire time they'll be making them on Friday." Maryanne shifted on the couch.

Lola pulled out her phone. "We also need to confirm the details of the rehearsal... I have the lists. Are we ready to get down to business?"

Cindy clapped, her brown eyes shining with joy in the light. Maryanne was so happy for her sister, but her chest ached at how alone she felt now. The feeling had been rising since October when Cindy and Andy had first started dating.

Then she stopped watching her nephews every day and on weekends. Now she only got them one night a week. Cindy was getting married so fast too. She never would've thought her cautious sister would have jumped into a relationship like this.

The timer dinged, and they moved to the kitchen table to eat. Lola worked down the to-do lists, confirming who was doing what. It'd take place at Holly's yoga studio and be a dinner wedding. Lola and Holly would get the tables and chairs from the church and decorate on Friday. Then they'd have the rehearsal dinner there Friday night, catered by the Diner. Then the wedding would be Saturday at four with the reception right after at the yoga studio.

Maryanne would make the deserts for Friday night and the cakes for Saturday. Or rather, have Zarrel and Ivy make them.

"I still think Mom can make the cakes." Cindy wiped her mouth with her napkin.

Maryanne rolled her eyes. "I know, Mom makes a great cake. But you deserve the best and that's me."

They all laughed, making Maryanne grin.

"You better not do any of the actual baking, though." Lola lifted a brow.

"At least keep your feet up the entire time." Cindy frowned, pointing her fork at Maryanne.

Maryanne rolled her eyes and leaned back in her chair. Her feet were already propped up on a stool Holly had found from some corner of the apartment. "I ordered a couch from IKEA today. It'll be delivered tomorrow, and Zarrel is going to put it together in my office so I can stay laying down as much as possible."

"Ohhh! Tell me about Zarrel! I saw him walking around town yesterday." Holly leaned forward to get all the details. Maryanne filled them in on his background and move to town.

"I can't believe Mr. Pike got the apartment above the

bakery fixed already. He's normally not that quick to get stuff paid for." Lola got up to grab the pitcher of sweet tea and refilled their drinks.

Holly snorted. "You know it was Landry and Andy who pushed for it, right? Landry got it all fixed in about a month. It was a priority project."

"I told him not to make it a priority. I just wanted the bakery to not flood anymore and to fulfill all the Thanksgiving orders." Maryanne wrinkled a brow as she thought about the work Landry must have put in it.

"Well, it wasn't just Landry and Andy. All the Williams' boys chipped in too. That's how they could get it done so quickly and how Landry didn't have to put any other projects on the back burner." Holly reached for the last piece of bread.

"Oh, I see. That explains why they were always coming into the bakery there for a while." Maryanne rubbed her forehead. She'd seen all of Gunner's brothers over that week... but not Gunner. He'd been conspicuously absent.

Lola narrowed her eyes, making Maryanne's heart trip. That evil smile never led to anything good. "I thought you were going to hook up with Gunner there for a while. Didn't you leave with him from Holly's house the night of the bake sale fiasco?"

Maryanne's breath caught in her chest. She held it as her heart skipped a beat before exhaling slowly. She slid on her fake smile and shook her head. "Yeah, but I just dropped him off at home. The man is totally closed off. Trust me. I've tried for two years and not had success barking up that tree."

Holly exchanged a look with Lola, but Cindy just giggled. Maryanne glared at Lola as Cindy got up to refill her water. Now was not the time to talk to Cindy about Gunner.

Lola rolled her eyes, but changed the topic. "Did you hear about the special election?"

Maryanne shook her head while Cindy sat back down. Frowning, Maryanne asked, "What special election? Didn't we just have an election in November?"

Lola nodded her head. "Yep, but then the old Mayor decided he wants to go on the senior cruise in February, so he's convinced the Sheriff to retire and go with them."

"Wow, good for them! I can't imagine the town without them, though. They've been running it since we were babies." Cindy stood up again and started grabbing the dirty plates from the table.

"Who do you think will run?" Holly asked, as she picked up the cups and took them to the sink.

Lola hopped up to help Cindy. "Gunner's running for sheriff, of course."

Maryanne's heart seized again as she sucked in a deep breath. Was this going to happen every single time someone said his name? Her reaction to thinking of him was getting ridiculous.

"He'll make the perfect sheriff!" Cindy cried from the sink as she washed the dishes. "He's never done a thing wrong in his life." Maryanne felt her lips twitch, then she couldn't hold back the grin as she thought of the night of Halloween. She caught Holly's gaze, who lifted her brow.

Maryanne mouthed, "Later."

If only they knew! She got up and walked to the couch. Laying back down, she thought back to one of the hottest nights of her life.

Outdoor sex had always been fun before, but everything with Gunner was on a different level. He was overwhelming in his intensity. Her heart grew heavy. He was such a good man, but so stern and strict.

She sniffed as she realized he was exactly like her father. She always felt like she was going to get in trouble, and it just made her want to act out so she could get it over with. The waiting for the hammer to drop was the worst feeling.

She swiped a tear off her cheek. Falling for a man like that was not part of her life plan, but hopefully they'd be able to work out some kind of arrangement with the baby and be cordial to one another. If she kept her distance, then it'd all be okay... He'd become sheriff like he wanted, and she'd become a mom.

Shit. Would the baby impact his election? The town was growing with new families and people, but the older crowd wasn't going to be happy about the new sheriff having a baby out of wedlock, much less having one with her. They weren't a fan of her CBD, alternative choices.

She bit her bottom lip as she tried to think of how to tell Gunner. Maybe she'd bake some of those little, tiny plastic babies into a cupcake or something.

"Does it work? Can you hear me?" Maryanne asked into the tablet. She tapped on the screen, flipping from camera angle to camera angle.

"I can hear you. Can you hear me? See me?" Andy asked, as he waved from one of the six boxes on her screen. She clicked on his image and the camera zoomed in to full screen.

"This is so cool! Wow. This is exactly what I wanted, Andy. Thank you so much." She smiled, even though the cameras were just one way, and they couldn't see her.

"No problem. This is what I love to do." He shrugged, his long sleeve blue shirt pushed up to the elbows. He'd installed six cameras in the bakery, so she'd be able to see every angle. Not only that, but he'd made it so that she could tap a button and call in to any of them and talk to Zarrel.

"Seems like overkill when you're only on bedrest for another week, but it's your bakery." Andy's cocky grin made her laugh while he packed up extra wires into his milk crate box.

Zarrel kneaded dough on the pastry table. "Yes, but it's good pre-planning on her part. She can take more time off and still keep her head in the game."

"You're not spooked by the thought of eyes constantly watching you?" Andy asked as he leaned against the counter. Maryanne snuggled deeper into her bed and smiled as she watched them on her screen.

"Not in the slightest. You get used to that in prison. And since I don't break the law anymore, there's nothing to be spooked about." Zarrel grinned and winked.

Andy laughed. "Fair enough. You know, next Tuesday we're having our last poker night of the year. You should come. You'll get to meet some guys, make friends, and all that shit."

"That'd be great! What's the stakes? Because the move has cut into my savings pretty bad."

Andy waved a hand. "Pennies, dimes, and nickels, man."

She listened to them talk about their moves into town and how it felt to be the new guys as she flipped between screens.

The box with her new couch had been delivered, but Zarrel wouldn't put it together until after the bakery closed this afternoon. She felt the itch to go bake something and turned over in the bed.

She probably needed to budget for the baby and figure this out, though. She flipped over to a different app and started searching for lists of everything a baby would need.

She downloaded several so she could print them off when she went over to the bakery tomorrow. Then she downloaded the *What to Expect* book so she could figure out exactly what she'd gotten herself into.

Chapter Nineteen

Gunner stepped into his brother's closet and grabbed a t-shirt. He and Hunter still lived at the bunkhouse on their parent's ranch, but on Tuesdays he couldn't run home, change, and get back to town for poker night. So most of the time, he just grabbed something from Landry and Parker's closets or from his go-bag. He pulled off his uniform shirt as he walked into the en suite bathroom and tossed it to the floor.

Some days as a cop were more difficult than others. The domestic call today had been hard. He splashed water on his face, trying to wash out the image of the woman crying, her face bruised.

Had Maryanne gone through stuff like that with the Barry Bruce bastard? His stomach knotted up at the thought. There'd been more information passed along this week on the case. He'd even been asked to speak at the trial in February, although he wasn't sure how it was going to work to go to Colorado for a few days if he was elected sheriff.

The Sheriff Gets His Girl

Pulling on Landry's shirt, he reached down and grabbed his uniform. He shoved it into his go bag from his truck, emptied his pockets, and set off down the hall. Already, voices were ringing through the air.

Just as he reached the open concept living and dining room, the front door opened. Andy and the new bakery assistant walked in.

"Hey, everyone! Zarrel is new in town and working with Maryanne at the bakery. Zarrel, this is everyone." Andy swept his arm around the group.

Gunner reached out a hand to shake. "Hey, Zarrel. Good to see you again." He'd run a background check on the man after Joey had come back to the station talking about the new hire. When he'd confirmed that Maryanne wasn't at the bakery, he'd gone by to introduce himself and size the man up.

So far, Zarrel had no red flags, but with the Barry Bruce arrest and the cocaine, Gunner was keeping his eyes and ears open.

"You too, man. Thanks for letting me join in tonight." Zarrel's smile spread wider on his face as he turned to shake hands with the rest of the guys. The dark man dwarfed over most of them, a cross between a gentle giant and a linebacker, but his calm smile and quick laugh set them at ease.

Landry came out of the kitchen with Mardi Gras style beads around his neck and a tray of drinks. They were all beers that had been opened, with koozies that said *Groom's Last Day Out*.

"Zarrel! You made it! Did you bring the package from the bakery?" Landry's eyes were bright and his lips tipped mischievously. Uh oh. What was he up to?

"This doesn't appear to be a normal poker night." Andy glanced around at the dining table.

"Nope, it's a bachelor party!" Landry grabbed a handful of something from the tray and tossed it on Andy. Confetti rained down, covering Andy like snow as he blinked rapidly, shook his head, and caught some in his hand.

He looked at it and burst out laughing. "Boobs?"

Landry smirked, handing out the beers. "You betcha!"

"You like those? Just wait until you see what we whipped up at the bakery today." Zarrel set a pastry box down in the center of the now confetti covered table. The guys all crowded around as he opened it with a flourish. When they saw the sugary treats, laughter echoed out as hands reached in to grab for the cookies and cupcakes. The cookies were hearts, but decorated to look like a girl's ass in a thong or boobs in a bra.

"Did Maryanne do these?" Gunner kept his face neutral, but he felt his blood pressure rise. She was still on bedrest but if she wanted to do all the wedding things for Cindy this weekend, she needed to take it easy. She'd never be well enough if she was making cookies like this all day with just one arm.

"We both did. I baked them, and she iced them."

"Nice teamwork." Andy took a bite out of a cookie.

"Look at these cupcakes!" Landry held up two of them in front of his chest. They looked like boobs, complete with nipples. He picked one up and licked the icing off it as he stared deadpan at Andy. The guys snickered as Andy rolled his eyes.

"So, what's the plan for the bachelor party?" Andy swiped a beer and washed down the cookie.

"You're not going to fight me on it?" Landry lifted an eyebrow and sat down the cupcakes.

"Nah, no point. As long as it doesn't involve a strip club or driving in the dark or staying out all night, let's do this."

Landry grinned. "We're going to play games but not poker. On the agenda tonight, we have food, beer, and games, like this bead necklace game. Anyone who says bride, Cindy, or wedding will get his necklace taken away by whoever calls him out on it. Whoever gets the most necklaces by the end of the night wins a prize."

"This sounds dumb." Andy snorted, then took a drink of his beer.

"Wait, what's the prize?" Zarrel scratched his chin and eyed Landry.

Landry grinned. "Two tomahawk steaks worth about $100 and a box of .22 ammo." Silence reigned for about three seconds before the guys started talking over each other.

"Damn. How'd you find .22 rounds?"

"I've always wanted a tomahawk steak. Are they as massive as they say?"

"As massive as my cock," Landry said with a wink. They busted up laughing again, several talking smack over each other about how they were going to win the most necklaces.

Gunner rolled his eyes as he took the necklace Landry handed him. "Who put you in charge of this? Only a woman would come up with a game involving necklaces."

Parker, his other brother who lived with Landry, laughed. "Trust me. It was way worse, but I toned him down some."

"Oh shut up, both of you. We're going to play Cards Against Humanity, the drinking version. Then we'll go outside and play Drunk Jenga and Drunk Cornhole before chilling around the firepit."

"And food?" Andy asked, just as Kendall came through the door carrying bags.

"I got the food. Fried chicken from the Diner for everyone, specifically breasts. We also have russet potatoes, the blue ones for blue balls, and baby carrots for micro penises." Kendall lifted the bags to put them on the table.

"Who has a micro penis?" Gunner snorted. All the guys tripped over themselves to deny it, causing the entire group to burst out laughing.

"All right, everyone have a seat and let's eat first." Landry waved to the chairs. Place settings were already laid out, so they passed the large containers of food around the table.

A few hours later, Gunner was lounging on the back patio, a mild buzz making him sleepy. It was the middle of December, but no one told Texas that. With the fire pit and a throw blanket for everyone, it was quite nice out. The inaudible murmur of voices hummed around the fire. The party had been a riot of fun, and he'd maintained his buzz since the card game had started.

Zarrel passed him another beer as he sat down in the empty chair next to him.

"So... how are you liking Crimson Creek so far?" Gunner hated small talk, but he knew it was the right thing to do. Besides, he wanted to get to know this man who was going to be working so closely with Maryanne.

"Loving it. The people are pretty friendly out here, except for the older crowd. It's nothing like downtown Dallas, though. Way less judgment here."

"Yeah. There's good people here. How are you liking the bakery?"

Zarrel gave him the side eye before glancing back at the fire and taking a sip of his beer. What did that look mean? It seemed like he was hiding something. Gunner's intuition about that kind of thing was never wrong, even if he was buzzed. He shifted in his chair and waited for Zarrel to answer.

"Job's good. Maryanne is fantastic. She knows her recipes like the back of her hand and runs a tight ship."

Gunner breathed a sigh of relief. Respect echoed in the man's voice.

"Then again... it doesn't hurt that she's fucking hot. I'm damn lucky to have her as a boss, that's for sure."

Gunner jerked in his chair, a low growl seeping out before he could control it. Reigning it back, he sucked in a breath and released it slowly. When he was sure his voice would be even, he said woodenly, "Yeah, she's pretty hot. It's never a good idea to get involved with someone from work, though."

Zarrel glanced at him. Meeting his gaze, Gunner saw him lift a brow in the firelight as he nodded slightly. "True. Besides, I get the feeling she's pretty hung up on some other guy anyway."

Gunner's chin jerked slightly before he forced himself to hold still. Did Zarrel mean him or was she seeing someone else?

Before he could think to question it, Zarrel continued. "I doubt she'd go for me, even if she is mighty lonely and depressed. Poor girl."

Gunner blinked, then took a sip of his beer. Maryanne was lonely? "But she's always so vivacious and happy-go-lucky."

"Yeah, but that's her mask, not the real her. Why do you think she uses so much CBD?"

Zarrel's question made him jerk in his seat again. "Because she was smoking pot in Colorado and only CBD is legal here. I'm sure she told you of her experience, considering your background."

Zarrel nodded but looked into Gunner's eyes in the dying firelight. Gunner could well imagine how this behemoth survived prison, because he was intimidating even sitting down and relaxing in the chair.

"She's lonely and under a lot of pressure running that bakery and helping raise her nephews. CBD helps, but it's not a cure, especially not for the busy body old ladies in town who snub her over it."

He'd known Maryanne for at least twenty years. How had this man who'd known her less than a week already figure she was lonely? And why the hell did he not know that the older folks... "Do they avoid the bakery?" He needed to stop interrogating the man, or Zarrel would figure out why he was so interested.

Zarrel nodded and leaned his head back to look at the stars. That damn itch began under Gunner's skin as he thought about this man knowing her better than he did.

What would another month reveal to him? He couldn't stand the idea of them becoming more than coworkers. But the election was at the end of January. He had to stay away from her until then, especially now that he knew the older crowd didn't like her. Maybe he should ask Ray about it.

But no, Ray had already said he couldn't afford a distraction with a woman. In February, though, he'd be able to ask her out on a proper date. Hell, he'd even like to take her out on Valentine's Day, publicly declare to all that she was his.

Maybe it wouldn't be too late by then.

Maryanne laid on the couch in her apartment and huffed a

breath as she watched Zarrel work in the bakery from her tablet.

This fucking morning sickness had to hit this week of all weeks. Two days ago, she'd woken up nauseous. Today was Friday, the dress rehearsal was tonight, and she had to get the desserts done and the wedding cakes baked today.

But instead of being at the bakery, she was holed up here. Crackers and ginger ale sat on the coffee table. Holly had made sure she'd been running the diffuser and using her essential oils to help, but she still didn't feel like she could make it across the street yet.

"What time will Ivy be here today?" Zarrel asked through the speaker. He was kneading the dough for the rolls tonight. That, at least, was something that didn't need decorating. He was in complete charge of that task.

"She gets out at three, and the rehearsal is at the yoga studio at seven. We need to have the food there by six-thirty."

Ivy was going to help Zarrel with last-minute baking while Maryanne went down to decorate around four. She still had hours to go, though. Hours to get over this stupid morning sickness. Wasn't it supposed to go away by afternoon? She moaned.

"Still not feeling well?" Zarrel asked.

"Nope. I feel like death warmed over."

"My sister's morning sickness lasted about three months, but you're almost out of the first trimester. Maybe you'll only have a few days of it and then be right as rain!"

"That would be the best-case scenario. All the books have different answers on what to expect." Maryanne snuggled down into her blanket further and closed her eyes. Zarrel hummed a familiar tune, but she couldn't quite place it.

Zarrel's voice crackled through the tablet. "Maryanne? Darlin, wake up. I've hit a wall. You there?"

Maryanne groaned as she stretched. She'd fallen asleep again. How long this time?

She glanced at the clock. "Four-thirty! What the hell, Zarrel! Why'd you let me sleep so long?"

"Your snore was pretty adorable. Besides, I held down the fort, and Ivy's here. We're almost done for tonight and are getting started on some of it for tomorrow. But is this the recipe you want me to use for the wedding cakes?" He held up a paper to the camera lens.

"Give me half an hour. I'll be right there. Hold it up closer."

She looked through the tablet and nodded, but he couldn't see her. "Yes, that's the one. Start with the one on the back, the groom's cake for Andy. It's a whiskey chocolate cake with chocolate raspberry ganache filling and a touch of citrus essential oil. That's kept in my office desk. I'm going to go take a shower, do my hair and make-up. I'll hopefully be down within an hour to decorate the scones and cream puffs."

"No worries. We got this, Maryanne."

She tossed down the tablet and raced to the shower. Thankfully, the nap seemed to do the trick and kicked the nausea.

Now she just had to fight the nerves at potentially seeing Gunner tonight. He would probably be at the dress rehearsal dinner, but if not, he'd definitely be there tomorrow for the wedding.

She bit a nail as she waited for the water to heat. She glanced at them, then quickly grabbed the file and filed them down. The red polish looked fine, but it wasn't like she had time to re-do them anyway.

Shit. She'd have to wash her hair with one hand. Her mom had been doing that for her the past week.

Maybe Ivy could fix her hair at the bakery. She quickly undressed, careful not to jar her shoulder as she removed the sling and slid a bag over her cast. There was so much to do and not enough time to do it in.

Chapter Twenty

Maryanne sucked in a breath as her mom zipped up her bridesmaid dress.

"It's a little tight, hun. Suck in a bit more," her mom said. "Why's it so much tighter? We just got the dresses two weeks ago."

Maryanne felt her chest tighten. Was she already gaining weight from the baby? If she was ten or eleven weeks, then according to the books, she would start to get a belly soon.

"I don't know, Mom. Maybe because I've had to sit on my ass all week on bedrest with nothing to do but eat?" Maryanne's snark caused her mom to jerk on the dress. Her mom glared at her reflection in the mirror, and Maryanne smoothed out the wince on her face and held still.

"Don't start with me, Maryanne. I can't handle it today. We have to take care of Cindy." Her mom finally got the zipper up on her pale green dress. She adjusted the one shoulder that barely kept her boobs contained and stepped into her heels.

The Sheriff Gets His Girl

Maryanne let out a huff of frustration. "I know, Mom. I just needed to get that out. I'll be good the rest of the day. Promise." Maryanne held up three fingers in scout's honor promise, causing her mom to roll her eyes.

"You were never a Girl Scout. That means nothing."

Maryanne laughed, then hugged her mom. The scent of vanilla and coconut surrounded her, making her nerves settle even as she squeezed her tighter. Mom shifted, drawing her closer.

"You okay?" Her mom's voice was soft in Maryanne's neck. Maryanne nodded, the knot in her throat too large to talk around. The tears welled up, and she pulled back quickly. She grabbed a tissue from the counter, leaned forward, and made sure her mascara hadn't gotten wet. With a deep breath, she glanced at her mom in the mirror.

Her pale green dress sparkled in the bathroom's light. They were still at Maryanne's apartment, getting ready. Cindy had slept over the night before and was in the kitchen talking to someone on the phone about the wedding.

Mom shifted, crossing her arms and narrowing her eyes. Did she suspect about the baby? Surely not.

The past few days, her mom had become more stressed about the wedding than the bride. She'd been gone practically from sun up to sun down, which Maryanne was thankful for. It meant that she hadn't been around for any of the morning sickness. Thank God this morning she'd awoken with no symptoms at all.

But just in case, Maryanne needed a distraction. She arched a brow at her mom in the mirror. "What? It's nothing. Just missing Dad today. That's all."

Her mom's shoulders sank, her own brown eyes misting up as she unfolded her arms. Sure enough, that worked like a charm and distracted Margarita.

"I know, I do too. That's why we have to take such care of Cindy today."

"And we will. Let's go fix whatever's going on out there. I'm ready, I think."

Maryanne followed her mom through her bedroom to the kitchen. Cindy was pacing, still in her pajamas, but her hair and makeup were done. Kate from the Clip & Curl had come to the apartment and done all their hair this morning. It was now just after lunch.

"Who was on the phone, dear?" Mom asked, as she sank onto the couch carefully so as not to wrinkle her dress.

Cindy sighed as she picked at the finger foods that littered the table. "That was Eden. There was a mix-up with the flowers. I wanted snowberries, but they didn't get the shipment in."

"Want me to run down there and see what we can do with what's on hand?" Maryanne asked. Cindy's face lit up as she clasped her hands.

"Would you mind? Then Mom can help me into my dress. The kids will be here within half an hour for pictures."

She walked to her sister and gave her a quick hug. "No problem. This is what the maid-of-honor and best sister in the world's job is, after all. I'll handle it and be back in a bit!"

Maryanne grabbed her red short trench coat from the coat rack and swept out of the door, careful not to catch her dress as she closed it. She breathed a sigh of relief, inhaling the scent of the crisp December air. Even in the middle of town, it still smelled like the country, like dirt, hay, and grass and instantly calmed.

The Sheriff Gets His Girl

A few hours later, Maryanne peeked down the stairs into the yoga studio below. Circular tables had been spread out and people talked quietly among their table mates. The floor to ceiling mirrors along the side wall were now covered by white fabric. A white floor runner led from the bottom of the stairs to the white archway decorated with greenery and white twinkle lights.

"Maryanne, are they ready?" Cindy's voice wavered behind her. Maryanne ducked down even more to see the guys standing under the archway. Then she stepped back up the stairs and nodded.

"Yep, they're all standing where they're supposed to. Are we ready?" Everyone nodded as Cindy took a deep breath, her grin wide as she bounced on her feet. She prompted the kids to walk down the stairs. Her nephew, Owen, and Cindy's soon to be daughter, Mandy, stomped down the stairs together, throwing red rose petals every which way.

They could hear the small crowd below laughing and awwing at the same time. Next went her nephews, James and Cody, each bearing a ring box on a pillow. Their matching suits brought a tear to Maryanne's eye; they were looking entirely too grown up.

Next was her turn but her stomach twisted in knots. She stared at the boys as they descended. Then turned back to wrap Cindy into a fierce one armed hug. "I'm so thrilled for you, sis. I love you so much." Her voice cracked when she caught Cindy's surprised gaze. But Maryanne just smiled a watery smile, spun on her heel, and sauntered down the stairs.

She'd refused to wear her sling with her dress. She'd tried to get white satin gloves to go over her cast, but it hadn't worked. The flower bouquet hopefully would cover up most of the cast in pictures.

When she reached the bottom of the stairs, she stopped and glanced at the archway. Andy stood next to the minister and Landry, Mandy's arm wrapped around his leg. She began walking along the floor runner, but immediately spied Gunner sitting at a table to her right. Her gaze flicked to him as she started to walk closer. He looked delicious in his navy blue suit.

She tried to tear her gaze away, but her heart melted when his eyes captured hers. His hazel eyes were darker, and it wasn't just the lighting. That look said he wanted her... it was the one that made not just her heart melt, but her pussy too.

She looked damn good in this figure-hugging dress. His face may be cast in stone and unreadable, but his eyes said he wanted to fuck her.

It made her knees weak and her hands tremble. Gripping the flowers in her hand harder, she sucked in a breath and winked at him. Would he get the message, that she wanted him too?

As she strolled down the aisle, she finally broke eye contact with him and held her head up high. She might want him. Her heart might ache for him. But with a baby coming, that wasn't enough. She was tired of being his secret fuck buddy.

Her palms began to sweat as she realized this wedding was probably going to be the closest she'd get to having a wedding of her own. Soon she'd be a single mom and even though Cindy was getting her happily ever after, she was probably the exception to the rule.

Single mom and business owner were jobs that wouldn't leave any time for dating or falling in love. She turned at the end of the archway and took her place next to her nephews, her heart racing in her chest. She glanced furtively at

Gunner as everyone stood and the bridal march began. His biceps seemed to barely fit his suit, and it made her drool a little... maybe she'd get one last hurrah before she told him about the baby. After, he probably wouldn't want anything to do with her other than pay child support.

A tear slipped down her cheek as Cindy stepped off the stairs. At least this time, no one could fault her for crying.

Chapter Twenty-One

"Maryanne, oh my God, this groom's cake is to die for!" Holly gushed as she licked the chocolate icing off her finger. Lola nodded her approval as she stabbed another forkful and shoved it in her mouth. Maryanne grinned. If Lola was too busy eating it, it must be pretty damn good.

Maryanne ate one bite and moaned. "Isn't it the best? The raspberries and that citrus essential oil really bring out the flavor of the whiskey and chocolate."

"Can I get drunk on this? I mean, I've had two slices." Lola scraped the last icing off her plate.

"Maybe a slight buzz, but not drunk. Still, we have signs posted on the groom's table that it's whiskey and not for children."

"And that's why you only ate the one bite, right?" Holly's eyebrows raised pointedly.

Maryanne nodded, looking around to see who was listening. "Right."

"The Diner did a great job on catering, didn't they? The

chicken and roasted veggies were so flavorful." Lola leaned back with a sigh.

"I loved the potato soup the best. And the bread! Did you do the bread, Maryanne?"

She shook her head. "No, Zarrel did those. He's a bread genius, right?"

"Oh, yeah."

"I'm so glad I hired him. He and Ivy both have been life savers this week."

"How's the arm and shoulder holding up?" Lola took a drink of her wine.

Maryanne winced, scrunching up her nose as she shifted in her chair. "They're okay. Sore, but not too bad unless I twist my shoulder the wrong way. Getting tired though."

"Getting tired just from going without the sling, huh?" Lola arched a brow and winked.

Maryanne frowned and glanced around. The back of the studio had an impromptu dance floor with Landry playing guitar and singing. Most people their age were gathered around dancing. Some kids ran through the tables, and her mom sat with some of the church ladies near the front door, whispering about the older gentlemen who sat around a table across the room.

"Sh. Not here. Yes, I'm tired, but I'm okay."

Holly twisted her napkin in her lap and glanced around nervously. "Yeah, but technically the wedding's over. So you could tell the—"

"Hello, ladies. Would you care to dance?" Kendall asked as he came up behind them. Gunner stood just behind him, shifting from foot to foot. His brother, Parker, stood beside him.

Kendall reached for his sister, Holly's, outstretched hand

but Parker slid it into his own as she stood, tucking her hand into his arm.

Kendall's face turned pink as the two laughed at him and joined in the dancing. Lola smirked as she caught Maryanne's eye, then threw down her napkin on the table and stood. She grabbed Kendall's hand and hauled him toward the dance floor as he spluttered in surprise.

Maryanne chuckled, the sound causing Gunner to freeze his movement in time to the music. His eyes bored into hers, making her breath hitch in her throat and her stomach twist. He held out his hand as the song changed. She glanced at it. This might be her last chance with him, before all hell broke loose.

It wasn't even a conscious thought to reach out and take his hand. Sparks shot up her arm, but amazingly enough the butterflies in her stomach stopped and the tension drained out of her shoulders as he swung her into his arms. Cedar and pine swirled into her nose as she sucked in a sharp breath, instantly sweeping a deep calm through her body.

He pressed her close, causing her nipples to harden. His hand on her back and his other holding her hand by their shoulders made her feel safe. She tucked her head into his shoulder with a sigh as Landry began singing *At Last* by Etta James.

Gunner bent his head toward her ear and sung along with Landry.

His deep voice, smooth as syrup as he sang just to her caused a shiver to run up her spine. Did he mean it? Were their lonely days over? She was so tired of being alone in the world. When the lyric about the smile came, he leaned back and tipped up her chin as he smiled. She smiled, tears in her eyes as everything around them became hazy.

The Sheriff Gets His Girl

He'd backed them off the dance floor and floated them down the little hallway that led to the back door. The bathrooms were on their left but behind that was Holly's office. He glanced over her shoulder at the crowd, then opened the office door and slipped them inside.

The light from under the door gave just enough light to see the desk and chair in the corner. She slid around Gunner and leaned against the clean desk.

"Hey." He shifted closer and ran a finger down her cheek. She sighed as she leaned into his palm.

"Hey yourself." She didn't think she could say anything else right now. Her heart was racing, her brain was foggy, her stomach was hungry or nauseous—she didn't know which. "Are you talking to me now?"

He hunched his shoulders and put his hands in his pockets. "I—never know what to say, so I just don't say anything."

"Even to my texts?"

He shrugged. "Dinner tomorrow is fine."

She smiled slowly. "See, that wasn't so hard, was it?"

He growled, "I'll show you hard."

He dipped his head closer and kissed her. It was a sweet kiss, but it still sent a shiver through her body and a beam of electricity straight to her pussy. When she gasped, he swept his tongue inside, and the fire quickly spread. He was pulling up the hem of her dress, and she was unzipping his pants.

When she wrapped a hand around his cock, he groaned and nipped her bottom lip. She twitched in his arms and rocked against him. His hand found her thong. Brushing it aside, he slowly teased up and down her soaking slit. She slid back onto the desk and wrapped her legs around his hips, pulling his cock towards her entrance as he held her thong to the side.

He slid in slowly, causing her to gasp and lean back. That was a mistake, with her shoulder, so she sat back up and wrapped her good arm around his back. He held still when he buried to the hilt.

She groaned. "Holy fuck, Gunner. You feel so good."

"You're so wet, Maryanne."

"Always wet for you."

"Only me, M. Only wet for me." His gaze was fierce as he slid out and slammed into her. He started a furious pace that barely left her time to breathe. With the song and now his words, she didn't know what to think about their future.

But all other thoughts fled as he hiked her leg and slid his fingers to her clit, flicking and making her gasp. Squirming on the desk, she clawed at his back. God, it was too much. It had been too long. She came hard, clenching down on his cock just as he groaned. She stilled to savor the moment and felt him spasming with her.

Then he pulled her closer so her head was on his shoulder as he held her shaking legs around him. Laughter rang out from the party as Landry continued to sing, his words now slurring.

Gunner leaned down and kissed her softly. Their tongues dueled slowly, and her body returned to earth from the soul shattering high. She felt like she was floating. As he pulled away and tucked himself back into his pants, she stood, wiping herself off with a tissue from the box on the bookshelf.

When she threw it in the trashcan, Gunner traced her cheek again and kissed her chastely on the other cheek. What did all this mean? He was so sweet tonight.

The Sheriff Gets His Girl

He opened the door and glanced down the hall with a frown. She had to tell him now, or she'd lose her nerve.

"Gunner, we need to talk. I—"

"Hold on, M. Something's not right up there."

Her heart tripped a beat. Had something happened to Cindy? The party sounded like it had livened up. She followed him down the hall, patting her hair with one hand to make sure it was still in the elaborate up do.

When they stopped at the end of the hall, her jaw dropped. The kids were watching tablets in the corner. They weren't the issue. Oh, no. It was everyone else who had gone nuts.

The older ladies from the church were giggling and patting each other's hair. A few had taken off their blazers, and it looked like one was trying to take off her bra under her silk shirt. Her mom's smile was crooked as she licked the icing off her plate. In public! Her mom, the picture of decorum and Southern gentility, was licking the fucking plate!

Some older guys were asleep sitting at the tables, their faces in their plates. The minister had taken his tie off and was just staring at it like it held the answers to the universe. Two ladies were standing over the food tables, giggling and eating the rolls. Ivy looked confused, her brow wrinkled as she kept handing them bread and pastries.

The dance floor was the worst, though. Cindy and Andy were practically dry humping. Landry was singing forlornly, clearly drunk, and staring at Parker and Holly who were whispering in each other's ears as they swayed side to side. It couldn't even be called dancing, really. A few others were dancing like they were at the club. One guy's hand was even inside the dress of the woman he was dancing with. And Lola and Kendall were kissing.

"Fucking hell. They're finally kissing!" Maryanne's jaw dropped.

Gunner raked a hand down his jaw. "What the fuck is going on here?"

Zarrel saw them and circled the food tables. Twisting his apron in his hands, he squared up to Gunner and sucked in a breath. "Gunner, man, I'm not sure what's happened, but everyone's stoned."

"What?" Maryanne gasped, her hand flying to her mouth.

Gunner glared at her as he ran his hand along the back of his neck. "You sure?"

"Oh yeah. I know this feeling. I'm definitely stoned." Zarrel looked at the ground and scuffed his toe along the floor. "I don't know how it happened, man. That's the thing. I haven't had pot since I got out of prison. I swear, it wasn't me, Gunner."

Zarrel's expression was so dejected and panicked, Maryanne reached out a hand to comfort him. She patted his hand. "No one thinks that, Zarrel. What motive would you have? None at all."

Gunner bounced on his feet, shifting side to side as he watched the crowd. Finally, he sighed and slapped Zarrel on the shoulder. "I don't think it's you, but protocol has you as a prime suspect. You and Maryanne, that is."

"Me?" Maryanne squeaked, her stomach twisting.

"Yeah, you." Gunner glanced around the room before eying her pointedly. "Halloween, M. Remember?"

"I told you, I haven't had pot around in a long time, not since Colorado. That was THC, and it's all gone."

"Are you sure? Think, M. What could have got the entire guest list high?"

"I had two bottles left, and just finished one bottle back

before Thanksgiving. Remember, in my office the day the bakery flooded? That's why I was so sleepy, because I'd just taken the last of that bottle, and you walked me home."

"Umm, you had THC in the office?" Zarrel looked like a deer caught in the headlights. Frozen in place, eyes wide, mouth ajar.

She nodded slowly. "Yes, I kept one in my desk, and another bottle in my purse. But one was empty."

"Well... the citrus essential oil I put in that whiskey, raspberry, chocolate cake sure didn't smell like citrus..."

Gunner and Maryanne stared at Zarrel, who had paled and was now hyperventilating.

"I—I didn't think it smelled like pot, but it sure didn't smell like citrus or orange or anything either. If—if it was the THC..." His jaw clenched and his shoulders slumped as he sank into a nearby chair. He held his head in his hands and groaned. "This is going to send me back to prison, isn't it?"

"What? No, Zarrel, absolutely not. We don't even know if that's what's causing all this." Maryanne slid over and rubbed circles along his back with her good hand. Gunner growled, his body stiffening as she touched Zarrel. She glared at Gunner, nodding her head to Zarrel and mouthed, "Say something."

"Maryanne is right. We don't know for sure that's what did it. But if it is, someone will have to be arrested." Gunner spoke hesitantly, softly, as he scanned the crowd.

Maryanne's head shot up, and her hand stopped on Zarrel's back. A knot settled in the pit of her stomach.

"Why? No one needs to know about the THC. Maybe we just tell everyone the whiskey cake was just stronger than expected. It's not a crime to get drunk, right?"

Gunner arched a brow at her. "I'm running for sheriff. I

can't just turn a blind eye to something like this. What if one of these fine citizens takes a home drug test? Or someone gets tested at work tomorrow? The truth will come out, in a town this small. It's better to tell the truth from the start than get caught later on."

She snapped her mouth closed and nodded, narrowing her eyes at Gunner. She wanted to argue more, but if it came out that he'd covered something like this up, it would cost him the election. She wouldn't fight him but it was much better for her to go down for this than Zarrel.

She stood in front of Zarrel and squared up with Gunner. She poked him in the chest and his eyes flashed, sending a shiver up her spine. "If you have to arrest someone because of your fucking morals, then it'll be me. Not Zarrel. Got it?"

Gunner met her stare and nodded. "Yeah. Got it. This isn't your fault, Zarrel. Maryanne is right. This wouldn't have happened without her THC. I'll arrest her tonight but release her immediately, because we'll have to send the cake off for testing to see if that's even what happened."

Zarrel rubbed a hand over his face. "This is fucking hell. I'm never attending a wedding again."

Maryanne snorted and crossed her arms, relieving some of the pressure on her broken arm. "That sounds like a great idea."

Gunner ran a hand down her back and squeezed her free hand.

"You won't hear an argument from me on that one, but we need to take care of all these people now. Maryanne, see if all the kids' parents are alright first. Let's get the kids home or with sitters, then we'll take care of the church ladies and the older crowd. By then, hopefully, our friends will have come off their high."

Maryanne turned to go find Andy's aunt and uncle, to see if they were taking her nephews home or if they were stoned too. She got two steps away when Gunner growled.

"And someone better fucking remove that cake and stop serving it!"

She swung by the table and talked with Ivy about the cake, then went to round up the kids. After getting everyone home safe, she'd talk Gunner into delaying her arrest until the cake's test results came back.

Maybe she could tell him about the baby instead of waiting for their dinner date tomorrow night. Although, he wasn't going to be thrilled to find out the woman who had gotten half the town high was also having his baby.

Chapter Twenty-Two

Gunner sighed after he dropped the last of the wedding guests off at home. It had been a long night already, and now it was almost one in the morning.

But he couldn't go to bed yet; instead, he had to do the actual paperwork for the entire fucking incident because he was the deputy on call.

He glanced over to the passenger seat where Maryanne was curled up asleep. She'd helped Zarrel, Ivy, and the Diner ladies clean up the yoga studio while he took people home, but he'd asked her to accompany him on the last trip.

It was time for her to pay the piper. He pulled up to the police station and parked the SUV in the parking lot behind it. Turning off the engine, he faced her.

Clenching his jaw, he fought the urge to reach out and touch her. He wanted to tell her earlier to wait for him, just a few more months until the election settled down. He wanted to tell her how he felt. Hell, he'd even sung to her.

He couldn't do it now, though. She was going to be in so much trouble over this. If he got involved with her and the town found out about the pot cake, the election was all but over. Anyone could beat him then.

The thought of arresting her made his whole body hurt. He'd love nothing better than to carry her up the stairs to her apartment, lay her down, and remove that glorious dress. Sometimes, he really didn't enjoy being a cop. His heart argued with his head, pulling him apart from the inside out.

Sighing, he opened his door and hopped out, rounded the front, and slowly opened hers. Her eyes blinked open, and he was reminded of how she'd looked at the wreck.

Was that less than two weeks ago? It seemed like just yesterday he'd seen blood dripping down her forehead. It haunted him more nights than he cared to admit.

Reaching up, he brushed the hair out of her face. It was coming out of her fancy up-do and made him want to pull the rest of it down, loose and wild just like he wanted her.

"Come on, Maryanne. Let's get this over with."

"Aww, Gunner. Can't we do this in the morning? It's not like I'm going to skip town or anything."

She yawned, unbuckled, and slid out. Her calves in those fuck-me heels made his mind travel down a dirty road.

He groaned. It would be so easy to walk her back to her apartment and forget the whole getting the entire town high situation. But he couldn't. This was his job, and ignoring her crimes would be a one-way ticket to unemployment or worse.

"I know you won't, but I've thought about it all night, and I think there's a solution. I'm going to book you tonight, but I won't process it until we get the results back from the test on the cake. I won't be able to send the cake for testing until Monday anyway."

"Then why book me at all? Can't we just go back to my apartment and maybe have sex in an actual bed?"

She grabbed his arm with her free hand and rubbed his bicep, making shock waves sweep through his body and straight to his cock.

"I'd love nothing more, but I'm on call tonight. I have to sleep here. Let's just get this done now, then you can go home to sleep. The Christmas pageant is tomorrow morning at church, remember?"

She snorted, and they walked to the back door of the police station.

"You know good and well I haven't missed a Sunday morning service in the two years I've been here. Neither have you, Mr. Choir Director."

"And that will bode well for you with the judge, if the cake tests positive for THC. So come on. Let's get this over with."

He led her through the conference and kitchenette room to the front. Pulling out the required equipment, he grabbed her hand to take her fingerprints.

His heart ached at the idea of dirtying her hands with the darkness the ink represented. Pausing before he pressed them into the ink, he lifted her hand and kissed her palm.

His eyes pleaded with her to understand; he didn't have a choice here. She kept asking him to forget it, but he couldn't.

Her whole body seemed to melt at the contact of his mouth on her skin, and she smiled, her lips trembling. Those lips made him dream wicked dreams at night. And some not so wicked and much more domesticated dreams of her by his side forever.

No, not yet. He couldn't let himself think about that yet. They had to jump this hurdle first.

Quickly, he took her fingerprints, only stopping when he switched to her other hand and kissed the palm of it too. Then he led her to the wall and had her stand against it for the mugshot.

He stepped back with the camera but paused before he snapped her picture. She was so annoyed, her arms crossed, her eyes glaring at him, one brow raised. He winced, but walked back toward her and brushed the stray hair out of her face. He tucked it behind her ear and felt her shiver in the cool night air as he kissed her on the cheek.

Stepping back again, the soft sound of the Polaroid echoed through the empty building. Their small town didn't have the resources to do much electronically, the exception being the computers and tablets in their SUVs. He set the picture down on his desk next to her fingerprints, grabbed her hand and walked down the short hall to the jail cell, reading her the Miranda rights while he walked.

He stopped next to the cell and waved to it. Her lipstick had long worn off her frowning lips. "So I can go home now?"

He shrugged. "Sure, I can walk you home, or you could stay here with me?"

She glanced through the bars and sucked in a breath, then glanced back at him. Her eyes shone in the soft light, and his heart pounded while he waited for her answer.

"Do you... *want* me to stay here with you?" Her voice was soft and shaky. The only other time he'd heard her talk like that had been Halloween when Barry Bruce had left.

He shoved his hands in his pockets and nodded slowly. "I do. There's a bed here. It's clean, comfy, if small for two people."

She glanced around, then her eyes searched his face like it held the answers. Only, he didn't know what the question was. Then she cocked one hip out, placed her free hand on her hip, and smiled that mischievous grin of hers that made his heart jump.

"Do you want to play big, bad officer has his way with the prisoner?"

He couldn't help the answering grin that spread his lips wide. "I'd love to but there are cameras." He shook his head.

She tipped her head to the side. "So why ask me to stay then?"

He wasn't sure how to answer. How did he tell her he just wanted to hold her all night? He felt his throat closing up, and he choked on the emotions.

He cleared his throat, crossed his arms and scowled. "Do you want to stay or not?"

She looked at him for a few tense minutes. "Are we still on for our date tomorrow night at seven?"

He nodded.

"Then sure, I'll stay. I'm getting the wall, though. I don't want you to push me off this tiny bed and break another arm." She flounced over to the bed against the wall and sat on it, bouncing a few times. Then she kicked off her heels and slid under the blankets.

The pressure in his chest eased, and he walked over to join her. It didn't matter where they were as long as she was in his arms.

The sound of retching woke him. He rubbed his eyes and blinked slowly. Realization slammed into him, and he sat up with a start.

The cell door was open, along with the bathroom door

across the hall. He slid off the bed quickly and pushed open the bathroom door more.

Maryanne was on her knees in front of the toilet, her green dress wrinkled. God knows how long she'd been there, but panic raced up his spine. He ran to the kitchenette and grabbed a dish towel and ran it in the sink before laying it on the back of her neck. She dry heaved and reached back to pull it off. Then she wiped her face and sank back onto her butt to lean against the wall.

With a shaky hand, she folded the rag and placed it on her forehead and breathed deeply.

"Maryanne? Are you okay? Was it the food? Did you eat the cake? Hangover?" He knelt in front of her and caressed her cheek. She didn't feel warm, so it wasn't a fever, but his own stomach was in knots from seeing her so weak. He hated being helpless.

She shook her head slowly, pulled the rag off her face and met his gaze. Her brow wrinkled, and she sighed, her eyes shining in the light from the hall.

She was tired and disheveled, nowhere near the perfectly put together Maryanne he knew. But his heart still tripped a beat when her eyes met his. He could get lost in those eyes.

She opened her mouth to answer, but the front door dinged as someone came in. He stood and leaned out of the bathroom door, frowning.

"Justine? What are you doing here?"

Her red velvet dress was way too short for December, but she'd paired it with black thigh-high boots and a white fuzzy jacket. Her blond hair billowed around her shoulders under her black and red beanie hat that matched her red lipstick.

She was bright eyed this morning and way too chipper

for—he glanced at the clock on the wall—eight in the morning.

"I brought you breakfast, silly. Figured we could ride to church together this morning."

His brows rose, and his head jerked back. What the fuck? He had seen her occasionally at the bar, church, and around town. But he hadn't talked to her in months, since the night they'd... well, not broken up, but talked it out at the Electric Cowboy. He crossed his arms, frowning while he stood in the doorway to the bathroom.

The toilet flushed behind him, and he glanced over his shoulder to see Maryanne washing her hands and face at the sink.

"Who's that? Oh, Maryanne, right? I didn't know you were back. It's good to see you again."

Justine smiled, her face friendly and open. But Gunner knew her enough to see that glint in her eye. She'd been snarky and mean in high school, and that look always preceded something.

"Gunner, why are you in the bathroom with her? Give the woman some privacy."

Justine swatted him on the arm, ran her hand on his bicep, and pulled him down the hall to the conference table where she set down a bag. She pulled out a Tupperware of homemade breakfast and released his arm. "Poor Maryanne. She had too much to drink at the wedding to make it home, eh?"

He shrugged, wanting to shake off her touch, and not knowing what to say that wouldn't have Justine mouthing off all over town about Maryanne. Turning back, he saw Maryanne had followed them to the end of the hall, shifting on her bare feet.

She gave a half-hearted shrug and swallowed hard. She licked her lips and took a deep breath.

"Gunner, can I talk to you?"

Before he could answer, the back door beside him opened, and the Sheriff walked in.

"Wow, the station is a lot prettier this morning! Hello, ladies." Ray's permanent frown smoothed out into a sort of smile. The man looked like he hadn't smiled in so long his face didn't know how. "What are y'all doing here?"

Justine smiled her megawatt smile and flicked her hair. "I brought Gunner breakfast before taking him to church."

"I—um..." Maryanne glanced at him, the wrinkle between her brow deepening when she glanced at Justine.

"Maryanne wanted to talk to you, Ray, about a problem we're having. Got time to give her some advice? I'll join you in a minute," Gunner interrupted.

Ray nodded. "Yes, ma'am. Won't you step into my office?" He waved for Maryanne to lead them down the hall. When they disappeared into the office, he swung his head to Justine and narrowed his eyes.

"What do you really want, Justine?"

"I miss you, that's all."

Gunner snorted and reached for a sausage biscuit on the table. "Yeah, right. Maybe six or seven years ago, but not now. Whatever you're trying to do, forget it. Thanks for breakfast, but I'll find my way to church." He waved the biscuit and turned to go down the hall to join Maryanne.

"Wait! Gunner, think about us, will you? It makes sense. I've taken over my parents' pizza place. You're going to be sheriff. We fit. We can run this town. You know I'd make the perfect sheriff's wife."

Ah, there it was! Her ulterior motive. She'd heard about

the election and wanted to capitalize on it. He arched a brow at her and chuckled. "Yeah, not gonna happen. Never again. You're outta luck, Justine. Go find someone else to string along. In fact, didn't you move back with a boyfriend?"

She shrugged. "Yeah, but he couldn't handle small town life. Come on, Gunner. Go cleanup for church, and I'll drive us over."

He grabbed the rest of the sausage biscuits and glared. "No. Not now, not ever."

Then he stomped towards the office, slamming the door behind him. He set down the breakfast container on the desk and saw the evidence bag of cake, fingerprints, and mugshot spread on the Sheriff's desk. Maryanne was sitting in a chair, biting her nail and bouncing her leg with her broken arm wrapped around her stomach.

When he slammed the door behind him, she looked up. Fire flashed in her eyes when she straightened her spine.

Ray tapped his fingers against his desk. "There you are. Now, Maryanne here has caught me up to speed, and I agree with her. There's no need to process her arrest because the evidence is circumstantial. Could've been some punk kids brought in pot to the wedding. Too many variables to know for sure."

"If we send the cake for testing—" Gunner began.

"Is this all the cake that's left?" Ray held up the evidence bag, and Maryanne nodded. He shook his head. "I'm letting her go. You and I both know half the state isn't prosecuting, or hell, even arresting, anyone for less than two ounces possession. And the medical marijuana laws surrounding THC are even more of a grey area."

It didn't matter that it was legal where she bought it, since it was illegal in Texas. Gunner crossed his arms.

"But she shouldn't have brought any from Colorado at

all—" Gunner tried to point out but Ray cut him off with a sigh.

"Yes, that's true, but do we really want to spend tax dollars on sending this cake for testing, processing the arrest, taking witness statements, and holding her for a few days... all so the judge can order her to do community service? No, we do not. The only thing I need to know, Maryanne, is where the THC bottles are."

Their department already didn't have enough resources, so Ray was right, but it wasn't their job to decide who had to follow the law and who didn't.

"One was in my purse and the other was in my desk." She sat up straight, her posture stiff, eyes staring at Ray and avoiding Gunner's.

Ray nodded. "Fine. We'll confiscate those bottles so no misunderstandings like this happen again. Gunner, go with her to get those bottles."

"But, sir—" Gunner growled. She'd broken the law and needed to go through the proper procedures to pay for it.

"No, Gunner. If you're going to be sheriff, you have to learn what fights are worth fighting. Are you prepared to die on this hill today? Pick your battles, son. Save our resources for actual crimes and not misunderstandings."

Gunner's face heated and his jaw clenched. His body was tense, but his heart was relieved. She wasn't going to get in trouble with the town after all. That was good news, so why did he feel so frustrated?

"Take care of that baby, Maryanne. It was good seeing you, but it's time to stay out of trouble, all right?" Ray smiled, and she hopped up and reached out her good hand to shake Ray's.

"Thank you, Sheriff. I'm glad someone around here can

see sense. If you'll excuse me, I have to get ready for church. Gunner, did you want to get those bottles now?"

She didn't even wait for him before she slid around him, opened the door, and walked down the hall to the front door.

"It's difficult being an unwed mother in this town, especially when so many are already against her with the CBD in the shop. She didn't need the arrest after getting knocked up. Damn that insurance adjuster for leaving her all alone with that baby." Gunner glanced at Ray, his mind whirling because Ray made no sense.

He stepped out of the office and breathed a sigh of relief to see that Justine was gone. He barely missed the front door banging shut in his face when Maryanne let it close behind her and stomped outside.

The early morning sun hadn't burned off the mist yet, and it was chilly outside. He was glad Maryanne had her jacket.

"Shit, Maryanne, you're barefoot. Hold on, let's get your shoes."

She whirled on him in the parking lot and pointed a finger under his chin. "I don't fucking care about the shoes. How long have you and Justine been back together? And even talking marriage? Fucking hell, Gunner."

He caught up to her on the sidewalk. "Forget about Justine. What the fuck was Ray talking about in there?"

"You know what? I was going to wait until dinner, but this is fine. It's better than fine, actually. I'm pregnant, Gunner. Now go back to Justine and enjoy your life together."

He stumbled to a stop in the middle of the street. Fuck. He hadn't even realized he was jaywalking. How did she make him break so many fucking laws without even realizing it?

His face went slack, and he blinked slowly, Ray's comments about the father on repeat in his mind. He tried to speak, to ask any of the million questions running through his head. But the knot in his throat was too big. His jaw clenched, and his feet shifted back and forth to an unknown rhythm on the road.

"Pregnant?" His voice was soft in the still morning. Not even the birds seemed to be awake while the entire world tilted around him, freezing in time even as his heart rate sped up.

Maryanne stomped across the street, hiking her dirty green dress and out pacing him. He shook his head, and his mind went into overdrive with the new information.

His chest felt like it was being torn apart from the inside out. She'd been sleeping with someone else? Shit, she flirted with everyone.

Gunner felt like a fool. He'd begun to think it was just the two of them, that maybe he could ask her out and turn this fuck buddy thing into something more after the election was over.

Robotically, he shuffled forward to the sidewalk. She had the front door of the bakery unlocked before he'd even finished crossing the street.

He pushed the door open, hearing that door bell match the ringing in his ears. The front was empty, but he shuffled to the beverage fridge and grabbed a bottle of water.

He chugged it, trying to swallow the news and push past the knot of disbelief that had lodged in his throat. When she stomped back into the room from the back, she slammed the two bottles against his chest, making him grunt.

"Here's the THC. The labels must have been smudged in the flood, which is coincidentally when you were ignoring me and getting back together with Justine."

The tone of her voice was hurt and angry, but what the hell was she talking about? He wasn't back with Justine. He opened his mouth to correct her, but she spun away and waltzed to the front door, wrenching it open with her free hand.

"She's right, though; she's a much better fit for you as sheriff. As opposed to me, who gets half the town high at a wedding." Her jaw was set, her body stiff when she lifted her chin in defiance.

He shuffled to the front door and stopped beside her. "She's not right for me, though." His voice sounded hollow to his own ears, and Maryanne snorted.

"Not sure anyone is, G. Don't worry about coming to dinner tonight. I wanted to talk about the pregnancy then, but now it's all out in the open."

She locked the bakery door and strode across the street, not even looking either direction or walking on the crosswalk. Her head was held high while she walked away, leaving him reeling, dizzy, and mind spinning. His heart was being torn to shreds with every step that took her farther away from him, and he had no fucking clue how to fix it.

Chapter Twenty-Three

Maryanne sat in the shower and let the water wash over her, her broken wrist hanging out of the tub in a bag. Thank God, Gunner helped her mom to her own house last night. She needed to sing at the top of her lungs and let out this frustration, which is why she had her favorite playlist going and the volume on full max.

It was so stupid. The whole thing was stupid. She should have just told him last night while they'd been alone in the cell.

But no, she'd wanted him to come over for a date, eat a home cooked meal to butter him up, then have him bite into desert and find the stupid plastic baby. But apparently he'd been seeing Justine again. It was high school all over again. He'd kissed her and left, running back to his ex. Well, good riddance. She could be a mom on her own. Lots of people did it. Hell, Cindy had done it for years.

Zombie by the Cranberries came on her phone's playlist, and she started to sing, tears of anger and frustration mixing with the water. Gunner was going to marry Justine and never know about his baby.

It broke her heart; she wanted to tell him. She wanted to start a life with him, even if as just parents and not as a relationship. But he was so hung up on winning that damn election and Justine could help him with that.

Maryanne was too alternative for the little old church crowd. Yeah, some of them loved her baked goods, but many of them boycotted her bakery because of the CBD. Her mom liked to pretend they didn't, but Maryanne knew her demographic for the shop, and teens, twenty, and thirty-year-olds were it.

The song ended, and she sighed. Her family was expecting her at church. There was the Christmas pageant, and she had to be there to support her nephews and do her song. She stepped out of the tub and clicked her phone to the one she was going to sing this morning at church.

When she out of the shower, she dried off, lathered up the lotion, brushed her teeth, and dropped some CBD under her tongue.

The books said it was fine while pregnant, and hopefully, it'd help release some of the tension from her... what did she even call it? It wasn't a breakup because they'd not even been dating.

Maybe just call it an incident. That was much better than admitting heartbreak. Much better than admitting that it felt like her entire body had been run over by a dump truck, and her heart was shredding into a million pieces.

With a shaky hand, she brushed out her hair. It'd have to hang loose today, since she was only working with one hand. Last night it'd been a bad idea to go without her sling. She threw on her makeup and Christmas dress for church before searching for her heels.

Crap. She'd left them at the police station. There was no way in hell she was going back down there. She pulled out her black heels. They'd have to do.

She walked back to the kitchen and whipped together some scones, adding the little plastic babies she'd ordered into two slices. While they were baking, she tidied the apartment with one hand. She supposed it was going to be harder to be a clean freak with a baby.

When everything was done, she locked her apartment and headed to church. Without a car still, she juggled the scones in the shoulder bag on her good arm as she walked across the street to the church, her jaw set as she strode through the park, past the pond and gazebo.

Gunner was—was... She sighed. She'd tried being fun Maryanne, side piece Maryanne, and it'd been nothing but trouble. She was tired of being who she thought he wanted her to be.

The thought broke her heart, and she quickly swiped a tear away as she neared the end of the park to cross the street. She'd brought this on herself; now she had to make the best of a bad situation.

She pasted on her fake smile at the crowd walking toward the main entrance.

"Auntie M!" Owen called, racing down the steps to meet her. He slammed into her knees, and she wrapped him in a half-hug, careful not to bump her arm.

"Well, aren't you the handsomest angel I've ever seen!"

His toothless grin soothed her broken heart. Cindy smiled from the top of the stairs as Owen led her by the hand the rest of the way to the door.

Maryanne grinned at her sister. "Well hello, Mrs. Reynolds. How was your wedding night?"

Cindy blushed and glanced behind them. Andy was

shaking hands with the guys just inside the vestibule. He must have felt Cindy's gaze, because he looked up and grinned at her. She could practically feel the love bursting between them in just that one look.

It made her nauseous because she'd never have that. She sucked in a breath, straightened her spine and nodded at some of the other churchgoers while she took her regular seat, carefully setting her bag on the floor in front of her.

Owen squeezed her hand. "I gotta go find my teacher. Take pictures of me? You know, like you do for Cody at his games?"

Maryanne leaned forward and kissed him on the cheek. "Of course, little man. You're going to rock this. I can't wait to see you up there." He beamed at her, then skipped up the aisle and to the side door. She could see a flurry of activity through the open doorway.

Her mom swept into the seat beside her as the band started playing. Maryanne gulped, blinking furiously as she spied Gunner.

He had showered and was dressed in his Sunday best. Justine was flapping her arms and talking to him animatedly, but he wasn't even looking at her. His gaze bore into Maryanne's.

He crossed his arms as he stood near the front, waiting for his brothers to finish tuning up their instruments. He glanced down at Justine, said something, then turned on his heel and went up the two steps to the stage.

He pasted on a fake smile and grabbed the microphone.

"Merry Christmas, everyone! Today is a special day indeed. Let's start it off with *Oh Come All Ye Faithful.*"

His eyebrow arched when he said the last word. She gulped, sucking in a breath as the congregation stood and started singing along. The sheriff had probably told him about the insurance adjustor.

The entire time they were singing was an act of pure torture. The songs either talked about babies or love. Halfway through, she went to the bathroom, then snuck outside to just stand on the front porch. She couldn't stand the look in his eyes. It made her entire body hurt. The bitter December wind bit at her cheeks, whipping her hair into a mess around her face.

With a shaky hand, she shifted to face the wind, letting her hair blow behind her. She couldn't let this go on. It was time to cut off the heartstrings and go numb. She'd tell Gunner eventually, but for now—if anyone asked, she'd avoid saying anything.

She couldn't deal with Gunner anymore right now. Her head was already hurting, and when she stretched her neck carefully, she winced. By the time her wrist and collarbone healed, hopefully her heart would be healed enough that she could tell him.

She went back inside just as the announcements started and slid into her seat, grabbed her phone, and took pictures of Owen, Cody, and James. The play was about a little lost boy who searched for a place to belong.

When it was almost over, she slipped back out to walk around the back through the hallways. She found Dot, the newlywed waitress from the Diner, who looked frazzled but smiled when she saw Maryanne.

"There you are! Are you ready?"

"Yep, now or never."

Dot laughed. "Good, this is the big finale. We literally can't do this without you."

"That's what I like to hear," Maryanne grinned, making

Dot laugh as she handed over the microphone. When the kids on the stage said their last lines, Maryanne slid through the door and flipped on the mic. She stood behind the curtains, out of sight as the music started for *You Say* by Lauren Daigle.

Maryanne shifted on her feet and caught sight of Gunner sitting in the back. She was only visible to a handful of people behind the curtain. She turned away from him, sucked in a deep breath, and began to sing as the lost little boy in the play acted out the lyrics. She sang for all she was worth, about not feeling good enough or measuring up to people's exact standards. She glanced back at Gunner.

Her heart broke a little more as his face didn't change expression. Not that she'd expected him to. He was made of granite. If only she could see his eyes, maybe she'd be able to tell what he was thinking or feeling.

So she sang to him, pouring her heart out, tears streaming down her face. She closed her eyes and let the song overtake her. Gunner may have tossed her aside, or maybe she pushed him away, but she had her family and her bakery. It was going to be alright.

When the song ended, she felt drained, but in a good way, like a cleansing rain had washed over her, giving her strength and peace.

When she opened her eyes, she refused to look at Gunner, glancing to the door to look for Dot, who bustled out to the front of the congregation. Maryanne slipped through the side door and set the mic on the chair before walking back down the hallway.

Soon, they were all eating in the fellowship hall, and she had put all but the two special scones on the buffet table for everyone. Owen and Cody hadn't stopped talking about the play long enough to eat. When everyone was eating dessert,

The Sheriff Gets His Girl

Maryanne pulled the two special scones out of her bag and placed them on her mom and sister's plates. Cindy said goodbye to one of the church ladies and turned back to their table.

"Oh, you made scones? Thank God, I need some breakfasts this week. Did you make extras? I'm going to save mine for tomorrow."

Maryanne blinked, sucking in a breath as she glanced between her mom and Cindy, frowning and biting a nail. She couldn't save it for tomorrow; she had to eat it now.

She watched her mom bite into the scone and moan. "Maryanne, this is delicious, as always. I don't know why, but I've been so hungry since the wedding last night."

Maryanne felt her cheeks heat and rolled her eyes. "It was the whiskey cake, Mom. You had too much of it."

"Seems like we all did." Andy reached over and swiped the scone off of Cindy's plate and popped half of it in his mouth. Cindy swatted him on the arm with a smile. Maryanne's heart rate sped up as she grinned, nervously shifting on her chair.

Her mom took another bite as Andy started to frown, chewing slowly. He reached up and pulled something from his mouth. Holding it up, he swallowed.

"Uh, Maryanne, did you bake something into the scones?" Andy dipped it into his water and cleaned it off with a napkin, as her mom reached up and took out an identical one from her own mouth.

Maryanne chewed her lip and shifted back and forth in her chair.

"What is this, Maryanne? It's not Three King's Day until January." Her mom looked at her with her head tilted to the side.

"It's a baby, Mom." Maryanne's leg started bouncing

under the table. She hoped they would be supportive. They had been when Cindy had gotten pregnant as a teenager, but she honestly didn't know how her mom would react.

"For baby Jesus?" Cindy glanced at the piece of plastic in Andy's hand.

"For my baby." Maryanne took a deep breath. "Surprise!" Maryanne glanced at each of them, then pulled out her phone and showed them her save screen, her heart beating fast as she waited for them to process.

Her mom's jaw dropped as the plastic baby fell from her hand onto the table.

"You're pregnant?" She screeched so loud, several tables around them stopped what they were doing and turned to face them.

Maryanne felt the heat climb up her neck to her face, but she kept her smile as she nodded. She probably should have waited until she was alone with her family to do this. But with all the drama with Gunner finding out, she needed to just get it all over with.

"I wanted to wait until after the wedding to tell you guys." Maryanne twisted her hands in her lap.

"I knew it! Oh thank God, you finally admitted it!" Cindy jumped up and rushed around the table, pulling her out of her chair for a hug.

Maryanne's shoulders sagged in relief. "You knew? You're okay with it?"

"Okay with it? This is fantastic! I'm so excited for you. You're going to make such a great mom." Cindy bounced on her feet.

Maryanne's heart dropped again, guilt over Owen's injury gnawing at her. "I don't know about that."

Her mom stood and walked calmly around the table.

The Sheriff Gets His Girl

She grabbed Maryanne by the shoulders, leaned in close and caught her gaze. No words were spoken, but her mom's eyes widened as she smiled. "Cindy's right. This is fantastic, and you're going to make an exceptional mother. First a wedding and now a new baby in the family?"

Those around them started calling out their congratulations. The sounds of laughter and chatter rang out, getting louder and louder around her. Her stomach flipped, and she looked around as her mom and Cindy discussed whether it'd be a girl or boy.

Cindy turned to face her. "Who's the father?"

Margarita asked, "How far along are you? When's your due date?"

Maryanne's heart pounded in her chest, beating in tempo to the beat in her head. Maybe she couldn't get it over with. She didn't want to lie to them. She glanced around, her eyes wild as she took in everyone around her.

"Um, Mom? I—I'll talk to y'all about it later. I'm going to head home and take a nap, okay? I was fine last night at home by myself, and I'll be fine tonight too, if you want to stay home and sleep in your own bed."

"What? No way, I'll be over there later. I'll bring dinner, alright? What have you been craving? I'll make whatever you want."

Maryanne smiled a watery smile as she wiped the sweat from her forehead. Her head was pounding now. "That's okay, Mom. I just need to lie down."

"Okay, honey. I'll see you later." They kissed and hugged, then Maryanne grabbed her purse and walked out the door. When the icy December air hit her sweat-covered face, she sucked in a grateful breath. On wobbly legs, she slowly made her way back to her apartment.

Gunner flipped through the digital file the clerk had shared with him. A lot of it he already knew, but if he was going to win this campaign, he needed to know all the issues that had been presented to the City Council in the past year.

He shook his head at some of them. Did people seriously think the city was going to pay to put up a possum sanctuary on the outskirts of town?

He loved his hometown, but sometimes the people here were just nuts. He glanced over as the front door of the Police Station opened up. Joey brought Gunner's lunch from the Diner and plopped it on his desk, a woman trailing behind him.

"Hey, Gunner, this is Marigold Adams with Allstate. She needs in the impound lot. Do you want me to escort her while you eat your lunch?"

Gunner stretched and eyed the woman. She was around his age and wore khaki slacks, a blazer, and was chewing bubble gum loudly as she looked up from her phone. Her brown eyes met his, and her eyes widened. She patted her hair.

"It's nice to meet you. I need to inspect a vehicle that was recently towed there, and I'd like to get that done today, if possible. I'm trying to wrap up all the things in this area at once."

"I can take her, Joey. I need to get out of the office for a while." He grabbed the bag and waved her back out the front door and to the parking lot. "Just follow me, ma'am."

"Oh, would you mind if I rode with you?" She slid her hand on his forearm.

He blinked and nodded, turned and walked to the SUV, opening the passenger door for her. She smiled and batted her eyelashes. He strolled around the back to get in the driver's side.

Her touch had done nothing, but she was flirting like she was interested. He most definitely was not. Maryanne had messed him up even worse than Justine had.

His mind shied away from thinking of Maryanne, and he started the SUV and buckled up.

"I appreciate the help. I have to come out here about once a month for something or other it seems." Her sigh was louder than the faint song on the radio.

"Where are you coming from?" He turned down the street and took a left.

"My office is in Denton. Allstate tries to keep the same person assigned to the same region. I drew the short straw six months ago when I got started there so here I am."

"Short straw being coming to the small towns like Crimson Creek?"

"Oh, I didn't mean to imply—" she said as they pulled up to the impound lot.

"It's fine." He cut her off and lowered his window to punch in the access code on the panel. The chain-link gate slid open on the rails, and he drove inside. "What are you here to inspect?"

"An '07 Ford Mustang convertible," she said.

He felt the hair on the back of his nape stand up. "Red?"

"Yep." He drove around to the back of the parking lot where they'd towed Maryanne's car. She gasped as she saw it.

"Oh gosh. That poor woman. I heard she survived the crash?"

He nodded, his throat too closed off to speak while he parked and they got out of the vehicle.

She continued to chat as she took pictures of the car. "That's good. I really like her. She's so easy to work with." The more she talked, the more he felt like throwing up.

"Do you only do auto insurance claims?"

She laughed and waved her hand. "Oh, no, I'm everything. Most people who insure with us insure several things: auto, house, life... in this case, business."

"You—You insure her bakery?" He cleared his throat and crossed his arms to lean against his SUV. He felt like his legs were going to give out on him.

"Oh yes. Maryanne was devastated when it flooded, but we got her fixed up pretty quickly, I think. She's reopened, right?"

He cleared his throat again and nodded. He realized she might not see him as she was taking her pictures, so he cleared his throat. "Yes, her bear claws are the best in town. Same with the coffee."

He saw her nod. "That's good. I'd hate for her to be still dealing with the flood and then this wreck. Goodness, she's lucky to have made it out alive! You sure she's okay?"

He nodded. "Yes. Few broken bones, but alright. Are you the only insurance agent that came out when her bakery flooded?"

"Yep, I manage Mr. Pike's insurance too—all his buildings and real estate—as well as your previous mayor's. So I had to process the claim for Mr. Pike and the second-floor apartment too."

She flipped through her phone pictures, then pulled out the clipboard from her shoulder bag. She started reading quietly out loud, scratching and making notes on the form.

Soon, they were back in the SUV, and he turned the heater up. She continued to talk as they closed up the lot and drove back to the station. He sat in the SUV and waved goodbye to her as she got out.

There was no insurance adjuster other than her. He had to talk to Maryanne. He glanced over at the Diner bag, then called Joey on the radio to let him know where he'd be if anyone needed him. Then he turned off the SUV and grabbed the food before walking to her apartment.

Chapter Twenty-Four

Maryanne woke up to knocking on her door. She stumbled out of her bedroom, placed the tablet on the kitchen table, and opened the door. She blinked, wiping away the sleep from her eyes.

"Gunner? What are you doing here?" She rubbed her eyes while he huffed a breath and pushed into her apartment. She shut the door behind him and saw a note from her mom telling her she'd left lunch in the fridge. Gunner set a bag from the Diner on the kitchen table.

He opened his mouth to say something, but the smell of the food hit her. She froze, held up a hand, and sprinted to her bathroom. She barely made it to the toilet before she threw up. This was great. Gunner was in the next room, and she had morning sickness.

She flushed and washed her face with a shaky hand. She brushed her teeth, then brushed her hair and put it back up in a clip. The mirror showed she was a mess, in her red long sleeve shirt that read *Dear Santa, it's actually a funny story* and matched her red and green flannel pajama pants. Her left arm was still in the sling from earlier, when she'd come home from the bakery and fallen asleep.

Whatever, she wasn't going to change or dress up for him. He could take her as is or get out. Her heart ached at the thought of him leaving. She squared her shoulders and walked back out to face him.

He was standing at the window, looking out over Main Street. He'd taken off his jacket, and his light brown hair looked darker in this light. With his jeans dirty and dirt scuffing his black boots, she wasn't used to seeing him so disheveled.

He turned and caught her gaze, standing at attention with hands clasped behind his back, feet slightly spread as he faced her. His body was eerily still, his expression like stone.

But his eyes blazed in the light when he stalked towards her on silent feet. She shifted, feeling cornered but refusing to back up.

She felt her heart skip a beat and her chest tighten as he neared. He was hunting her, upset about something, and her stomach flipped as she tried to think what it was.

When he was within arm's reach, he stopped, and frowned. "The insurance adjuster is a woman."

She felt her body go cold. Oh, no. Not that. "Wh—what?"

He crossed his arms, drawing her eyes to his biceps, and glared. "The insurance adjuster. Is. A. *Woman*."

"My insurance adjuster?" She fought the panic, trying to slow her breathing and stall him. How had he found out?

"Yes. Your insurance adjuster for both the bakery and your car." His nostrils flared.

"Oh," she said, turning to the fridge and grabbing a bottle of water. Maybe she could play this off, and he didn't actually know. "I suppose she is. Nice woman, but too chatty."

He slammed a hand down on the kitchen table, making her jump. "Maryanne, you told Ray the father of your baby was the insurance adjuster. If she's a woman, then who the *hell* is the father?"

She bit her lip and jutted out her chin. Her brain panicked and her heart raced. "It's—it's not what you think."

He paced between the window and the kitchen table, running his fingers through his hair, before spinning to face her. "What I *think* is that I'm the father. Am I?"

Fuck. This wasn't how it was supposed to work. He wasn't supposed to be angry. If only she'd been able to do this the way she'd planned.

The nausea was back and a headache was forming behind her eyes. It was all piling up and making her frustrated. She flicked her hair over her shoulder and walked to the couch, slid her free hand to her hip, jutting it out. "Does it matter?"

He reared back like he'd been punched in the gut. "The fuck it does. If that baby is mine, you better straighten up and tell me right the hell now."

His tone sent a thrill through her, reminding her of how good they were together and making her core clench in anticipation.

She searched his eyes, standing stoic in the kitchen, hands on hips now, and that thunderous expression on his face. She rubbed her temple and closed her eyes, unable to look at him while she came clean. "Yeah, you are."

She sighed and sank onto the chaise sectional. Her hands were shaky, matching the turmoil in her stomach. When she opened her eyes, he was pacing in front of the coffee table, running a hand through his hair, glancing at her and scowling.

She watched him, her heart hurting and scared of the unknown. She was afraid to hope for their future, especially with the sort of lies and all the trouble she'd caused for him the past few months.

After a few minutes, he stalked over to her and took a deep breath, and she finally met his eyes. They were a dark green today, like rain pouring through the trees, shining and vibrant. He sank onto the coffee table with a sigh, his shoulders sinking in defeat.

"Why lie about it? Why didn't you tell me sooner?"

She leaned her head back on the couch, closing her eyes. "I wanted to, but I didn't want it to come out until after Cindy's wedding. She deserved to have all the attention."

"Yeah, but you could have told *me*."

The silence stretched accusingly, breaking her heart for what she didn't think she'd ever have. She'd always wanted this man, and now he seemed further away than ever before.

It made her angry, and she snapped her eyes open to glare at him. "I would have, if you—" She wiped a hand down her face and ground her teeth. "Ugh, Gunner. I said in October I wasn't looking for a relationship, and you didn't want to get involved, so I figured there was time to wait until after the wedding."

Her chest felt tight, and she adjusted her sling, hoping to dislodge the knot in her heart. "Plus, you were ignoring me and had been for weeks, which didn't make it any easier to find time to actually talk to you."

He reached out a hand and stroked her face with his fingers, wiping an angry tear off her cheek and causing something to shift in her chest. He was so close, but so far away. His green hazel eyes peered into her soul, frowning and making her afraid to hope.

"I was going to tell you on the dinner date we were supposed to have Sunday night." Her voice was soft, her lip trembling.

"Tell me now then." He traced her face with his fingers. She wasn't even sure if he realized he was doing it.

She sucked in a deep breath as another tear leaked out of the corner of her eye and his fingers played with her face. "Gunner, I'm pregnant."

"With my baby?" His voice raked across her skin like sandpaper. She nodded sharply.

"Was there ever anyone else?"

She shook her head, hating that she couldn't read his expression.

He blinked, then gave a small smile as he palmed her face, running a thumb over her lip. That smile made her stomach flip; maybe it would work out. He leaned forward slowly, a question in his eyes. She felt her breath hitch in her chest, but she leaned back and frowned.

"What about Justine?"

He growled, the sound seeping under her bones and making her want to purr in response. "I haven't talked to her since you came to the Electric Cowboy."

"In October?" Her heart hurt to think of him with anyone else, much less the girl he went back to dating two weeks after their first kiss in high school.

"Yeah. She's delusional and doesn't hold a candle to you, Maryanne. Nothing can compare to what you and I have." His words were a balm to her soul, easing her troubled heart. His eyes burned into hers before he slid onto the couch beside her, wrapping an arm around her shoulders.

The Sheriff Gets His Girl

She glanced at his lips and licked her own. He knew she was pregnant, wasn't with Justine, and still wanted her. It was like she'd won the lottery. She felt him take a deep breath before his lips met hers softly.

She felt the pressure ease in her chest as she gasped. He swept his tongue inside, his hand cupping her face as he leaned over her. It was the sweetest kiss she'd ever had. She felt him groan as her tongue met his. Sucking in a breath, she smelled his cologne. Her core tightened, her stomach growled, and she shifted and lifted her hand up to his chest. It shook until he slowly broke the kiss and grabbed her hand in both of his.

She smiled softly and palmed his cheek, his five o'clock shadow raking deliciously along her hand. "You're not mad?"

He frowned. "Yeah, I am. I feel cheated. You not only broke the law with the THC but lied to me."

"I didn't lie. I just omitted the truth."

"The insurance adjuster—"

"I told Kendall and the Sheriff that to buy me time to tell you privately. I never told *you* that."

He rubbed his forehead. "A lie of omission is still a lie, and you need to be punished."

She grinned and winked. "You could always spank me again. Would that help?"

His laughter echoed through her apartment, vibrating through her heart. She could count on one hand how many times he'd laughed the past few years. She was determined to see him laugh more.

"It might, yeah. But first, we need to talk. Have you eaten?"

He reached for the couch pillows while she shook her head. He propped one under her sling, and another behind her back before grabbing the bag from the diner and bringing it over. The smell was more than appetizing now and her mouth watered. He pulled out a burger and cold fries, then grabbed her now empty bottle of water.

"What do you want to drink?" He threw it away and walked to the fridge, pulling out her mom's casserole. She reached for the burger, amazed that he was waiting on her and taking care of her. Perhaps this was more than physical for him too. Hope bloomed within her soul.

"Would you rather have—oh, I guess not." He chuckled as he looked over at her to see that she'd already half finished his burger. She grinned, her mouth full as she chewed and watched him.

He made himself a plate and brought her a sparkling lemon lime water and a cup of sweet tea. She grabbed the water and popped the top, guzzling it down. When the microwave dinged, he sat on the other end of the couch and waved his fork at her.

"Talk. Kendall knew?" His command made her stomach flip in excitement.

She cleared her throat as she took another drink. Eating seemed to have settled her shaking. She turned slightly to see his face and took a deep breath.

"When you came to the hospital that morning after the wreck, I'd just woken up. Kendall told me about the baby, but I didn't want to tell you with him in there or take away from Cindy's wedding—plus you turned me down when I tried to hold your hand. I knew I wanted to talk to you about it first, before telling people, but it never seemed like the right time."

She glanced down and picked at the hem of her shirt.

He nodded slowly as he chewed. She felt the silence pressing on her while she smoothed the hem of her shirt.

"At the bakery, I was going to tell you, when you arrested Barry. But we ran out of time after arguing about Zarrel. Then I was going to tell you at the jail but we had the date already set for Sunday, and I wanted to tell you with the little babies baked into bear claws. It was going to be cute."

"Like you did with your mom at the potluck at church."

"Yeah, but that was before all the mess Sunday morning with getting sick and Justine and the Sheriff showing up. Ray asked about the smell from the bathroom, so I had to tell him about the pregnancy, but I didn't want him to know you were the father before I told you so—so... sorry I didn't tell you sooner."

She sighed and tossed her trash back into the Diner bag while he drank the sweet tea, guzzling until it was empty. Then he sat both plate, drink, and bag on the coffee table and pulled one knee onto the couch to face her. He shrugged.

"I can't say I'm happy about how it all came out, but at least it's out now, and we can both plan and prepare."

"Are you... happy at all? About the baby, I mean? What do you want to do?" She hadn't thought this part of the conversation out.

"I'm not sure yet. I know I want to be a part of everything, though. I know my parents are going to want to be involved. It'll be their first grandchild. When do we find out the gender?"

His sudden question made her heart flip in surprise. His green hazel eyes shone on his tanned face. Even in winter, he was still the golden boy from her high school days. She was happy that, if even for a few months, she'd have his attention.

They were going to have a baby together. She frowned as nerves clawed at her stomach.

"Grab my tablet from the kitchen table. I was reading the *What to Expect* book, and it'll tell us. Oh, and grab my phone; I think it's in my bedroom."

She watched his ass as he walked away, wondering if he'd—no, he wouldn't want to have sex. She was pregnant, and they had to figure out what they were going to do. When he returned, he handed over the tablet as he sank down onto the couch and stared at the save screen on her phone.

"Is this—is this the baby? What am I looking at exactly?" He frowned, sliding closer to her and propping his feet up on the chaise lounge next to hers. He slid an arm behind her head, so she turned to lean back against him and pointed to the dot.

"See this peanut-shaped bean looking thing? That's it."

He lazily traced his fingers up and down her shoulder as he stared at her phone in his other hand.

"Wow," he whispered. He glanced down at her, their faces close, leaned down, and kissed her softly.

It was like electricity raced straight from her lips to her heart to her clit. Her whole body ached for him. Too soon, he pulled back and glanced down at her stomach. He set her phone in his lap, then reached over and slid his hand along her abdomen. She gasped and squirmed in her seat.

He chuckled in her ear, nuzzling her neck. "Calm down, M. I'm just saying hello to the baby."

She moaned as he rubbed slow circles, bunching up her shirt. He dragged it up, revealing her still flat tummy. He rubbed slow circles on her skin this time, and she sucked in a breath.

"Breathe, M," he demanded softly. She exhaled as his hand settled low, but not nearly as low as she wanted. "We should probably talk about some basics." He nipped her ear, making her shiver.

"Let's start with non-negotiable things. First, you're keeping the baby, right?"

She gasped and twisted away from him. "Of course I am!"

"Calm down." He threw his hands up and pulled back, the relieved smile on his face making him look younger and more carefree. "I'm just checking. Second, I guess, should be..." He paused, frowning.

She sighed and snuggled in close to him again, casting her eyes down as she laid her head on his shoulder.

"Second should be us. I know we've been casual the past few months and said we'd only do one-night stands—which then led to two and three—but what do you see happening now? I mean, are you going to date Justine? What about me? Should I date someone else?"

She kept her face down, hoping he wouldn't see on her face that she wanted the opposite of that. The idea of him with Justine curdled her stomach, and she felt her face heat just from asking the question. This baby was changing her; she'd never been embarrassed about these kinds of questions before. Or maybe it was Gunner?

He reached out and tilted her head up with his fingers. Her eyes met his. His fierce expression took her breath away as he said harshly, "You won't be dating around, M. That baby is mine, and by proxy so are you."

Her heart thrilled at his tone, so forceful and with that don't argue with me attitude she loved. But she didn't want to be his by proxy. She just wanted to be his. "Then neither will you, G. What's fair is fair."

He nodded, then crushed his lips to hers. She moaned as he slid his tongue around hers, then slid his hand down her stomach and under the elastic of her pants. She gasped and lifted her hips to encourage him. He slid a finger down one side of her leg in the crease, then back up the other, making her groan.

No, this wouldn't work. If they were going to raise a baby, she didn't want to just be his by proxy. She pushed his hand away.

"Gunner, being yours by proxy doesn't mean you get an all-access pass."

He growled and slid his hand back up her leg. "Fuck proxy. You're mine, M."

He stroked her clit, making her gasp and throw her head back. He circled it once, twice, then dipped a single finger inside. When she clenched on it, he moaned before sliding it in slow and deep.

She gasped. "Promise?"

"Body and soul, M."

His voice vibrated through her body, making her clench on his finger. Her heart wept that he'd left out heart; she didn't hold his heart, but maybe someday.

"Then take me already."

She raked her nails down his arm, trying to pull his hand closer, deeper. The ache was burning for him and wouldn't go away with the little he was giving her. She wanted the whole Gunner package.

He plunged deep and moved his thumb to circle her nub as he shook his head. He increased the pressure, but before she could even gasp and demand he go harder, she broke apart with a cry. She arched her back and clamped down on him as he groaned. "God, I can't wait to take you again." He nuzzled her neck.

"Well, what's stopping you?"

He pulled his hand back and laid it gently on her stomach. He bowed his forehead to hers as he breathed deeply.

"When do you go to the doctor next? I want the all clear first. I don't want to hurt you, your shoulder, or the baby. I don't even know if I did damage at the wedding in Holly's office."

Maryanne grinned and kissed his cheek. "Gunner, that's adorable, but absolutely ridiculous. The books say—"

The front door handle jiggled. He leaned back to glance over his shoulder as it opened. Her mom walked in and shut the door, making it into the kitchen before she saw them frozen in horror.

She glanced from Gunner to Maryanne and back again. Gunner lifted his hand from her stomach and pulled her shirt down.

Then he stood up and faced her mom, who was frowning now. He stood still, eyes locked with her mom's, arms behind his back with legs spread slightly apart in that parade rest stance she loved.

Maryanne sighed. "Mom, Gunner's the dad."

She moved to slide off the couch. Gunner grabbed her elbow gently and helped her up. Her mom took in the gesture with narrowed eyes, then blinked rapidly.

"Oh my." Her mom seemed to wilt into a kitchen chair with a deep sigh. She rubbed her eyes as Maryanne walked toward her.

"Mom, are you alright?" Maryanne sat on the chair beside her and rubbed her back. Her eyes went wide as she felt her mom's shoulders shaking in silent sobs.

"Well, this is a good surprise. Oh, this is so much better." Margarita rubbed her temples.

Maryanne frowned, noticing the dark and deep bags under

her mom's eyes. Gunner was shifting nervously on his feet on the other side of the table, so she waved at him. "Gunner, can you grab Mom a drink? Mom, talk to me. What's going on?"

"It's just the stress, M. The wreck, then the wedding, and now the baby. It's just, well, I haven't been sleeping very well either, you know. Not that your couch isn't comfortable because it is. It's just—oh!"

Margarita's shoulders shook as a shudder wracked her small frame. Maryanne moved her chair closer and wrapped an arm around her mom. Gunner washed his hands and made her mom a glass of sweet tea. He sat it in front of her, but her mom reached out and grabbed his hand before he could move away.

She met Gunner's eyes over her head. His brows arched in surprise. She mouthed 'just wait.' He slowly sank into a chair, her mom's hand still locked on his in a vice grip.

"Mom, stay at home and sleep in your own bed. You need a good night's rest, and I'm fine by myself. You don't have to stay here."

"But you'll forget to eat if I don't tell you, and you can't clean anything. You can't even wash your hair. I've been so worried, Maryanne." Her mom sat up and threw her hands in the air, freeing Gunner.

He sat back quickly, but she kept her eyes locked on her mom's smooth olive toned face. She smiled reassuringly.

"Mom, I'll hire Holly to clean the apartment. And I'll go to the Clip & Curl and have them wash my hair. I can do this, Mom."

"You can't do this alone, but you're not alone. You have Gunner. Oh, I'm so relieved." Margarita looked up, tears on her eyelashes but a wavering faint smile on her lips.

Maryanne narrowed her eyes and leaned back. "Cindy

did this alone for years, Mom. And this is just one baby, not three kids like she had."

"But she wasn't running the bakery. And how are you going to get to your doctor's appointments? You don't have a car anymore."

Her mom huffed a breath, jutting her chin out and making Maryanne smile faintly. Her mom's stubborn streak was where she got it.

"When I get off bed rest, I'll go get one."

Gunner cleared his throat. "I can help with that. I know a good dealership in Denton that's honest and fair."

Her mom turned to face him, her eyes shining with tears as she grabbed both his hands in hers.

"Oh, would you? That would be so helpful. And her first doctor's appointment is going to be Tuesday. Can you take her to it? We're hoping she gets off bed rest then so she can be more active for Christmas."

Maryanne rolled her eyes at her mom's dramatic damsel in distress pose. She was clearly trying to rope Gunner in for baby stuff.

She tapped the table with her nails. "Of course I'll be off bed rest. Kendall said it was just precautionary. Either way, I'm not missing Christmas. The boys would be so disappointed."

Gunner narrowed his eyes. "You'll do what the doctor says. What time is the appointment? I'll need to take time off work."

Her mom rattled off the details, then even made him put it in his phone calendar. Maryanne grabbed her mom's tea and drank as they talked.

"How are you feeling, dear? Any morning sickness today?"

Her mom's eyes were now clear, hope shining bright as she leaned forward and rested her elbows on the table.

Maryanne winced, nodding. "Yeah. Just been nauseous the past few days."

"Oh! Your mom!" Margarita sat up sharply and pointed to Gunner, who blinked at the sudden change in topic.

"Uh, what about her?" Maryanne asked with a frown.

"She's going to be so excited. Let's go tell her right now. Wait, you're on bed rest. Let me call her."

Margarita hopped up and walked to the front of the apartment to look out over Main Street while dialing on her phone.

Maryanne glanced at her, then back to Gunner. "You know it's going to be all over town by nightfall, right?"

He nodded with pinched lips. She sighed and rubbed her forehead.

"You said you didn't need the distraction of a girlfriend with the election. How is this going to impact that?"

He shrugged. "It can't be helped. I'll try to keep the election stuff away from you and the baby, but I've already had random people coming up to ask me all kinds of questions about what I'm going to do as sheriff."

"Is there anything I can do to help?" She frowned at her mom, dreading what she was planning with Mrs. Williams.

He shook his head. "Nope, I'm going to go meet with the Sheriff and Mayor to let them know. Don't want them to find out from someone else." He pulled out his phone and texted them. He paused, then looked around before spying her phone on the couch and grabbing it. He opened it, clicked something, then looked at his phone.

"What're you doing?"

His grin lit up the room and made her heart soar as he glanced at her. A matching smile tugged at the corners of her own lips as he flipped his screen around and showed her.

"New save screen. Sent the baby photo to myself. Also, you need to add a pass code to this; it's a safety concern without one. What are you calling it?"

"Uh, I call it my phone." Maryanne smirked while he handed the phone to her.

He laughed, making her heart jump to see him so happy. "No, the baby. I don't want to call a baby an it."

Happy tears filled her eyes again. "Peanut. It looks like a peanut."

He nodded, glancing at his phone once more as he laid hers on the table. Margarita walked back with a grin, her tears forgotten. "Okay, your mom and dad will come into town tonight. We're going to have dinner here at six to celebrate."

"I don't get off shift until seven." Gunner frowned and slipped on his jacket.

"Fine, we'll push it to seven." Her mom looked back down at her phone and typed.

Gunner turned to Maryanne and smiled ruefully. "Looks like I'll see you tonight? Do you need me to bring anything?"

Maryanne shook her head no, her throat closing up as he leaned down and kissed her swiftly on the lips. She sucked in a breath, smelling his cologne as he waved to her mom and left.

Her mom plopped down into the chair as the door clicked shut behind him. "This is *quite* the turn of events. Now, start talking, but don't give me details." Her eyes shone brightly, excitement pouring out as she chatted about the menu for tonight's impromptu announcement party.

Maryanne laughed, feeling her body relax for the first time in days. The truth was out, and it felt good.

Chapter Twenty-Five

"What the hell, Gunner?" Sheriff Ray said from his office later that afternoon. "I thought we talked about this. You said there were no complications, no women, much less a baby out of wedlock!"

"What would you have me do, Ray? Deny it? Refuse to accept my responsibility? This isn't the fifties; women can have babies out of wedlock."

Gunner crossed his arms as he sat in the chair across from the sheriff's desk. Mayor Charlie had his black jeans pressed and a blue pearl snap shirt, his hair slicked back with gel.

Charlie snorted. "Can't have that. It'd cost him the entire election."

Ray rubbed his temples and placed his hands on his knees. "What are we going to do?"

Gunner shrugged. "We can't do anything about it right now. We'll have to see how it plays out."

He wouldn't tell them he planned on moving in with her and being there every step of the pregnancy. Shit, and the birth. A year from now, there'd be a baby. Would they need a house?

"How it plays out?" Ray shouted, bringing Gunner's mind back to the matter at hand. "The town is going to go nuts over this. The future sheriff can't knock a girl up right when an election starts. It shows a lack of morality."

"Relax, Ray. It's not like the end of the world. It's not like it was thirty years ago." Charlie propped his elbow on the chair and rested his head in his hand.

Ray slammed his hands onto the desk and glared at them both. "That's not our only problem. I found out who's running against you. It's Mr. Willowby."

Gunner blinked. "My old Government teacher? The man despises the government! Why's he running for Sheriff?"

Charlie glanced at his phone. "The man's our age and has been retired for years. Makes no sense."

"Gunner!" A woman's voice rang out from the front office. Gunner felt his eyes bulge as his spine snapped straight in his chair. He jumped up and strode through the open door.

"Ma? What's wrong? Are you alright?"

He froze in the hallway, staring at her. She stomped in, her scuffed cowboy boots announcing her arrival. Her faded jeans clung to her legs, and a red plaid shirt peeked out from under her worn brown jacket. She pushed back the hood, revealing frizzy brown hair and a deep furrow between her brows.

She pointed her finger at him. "I thought it'd be Parker! He's the ladies' man around town. But you?"

She marched to him, her boots stomping, and threw her arms around him. She was a big woman, tall and muscular, built tough to run the ranch with his dad. Her hug nearly crushed him, but he clung to her like a child, confused about life and finding comfort so easily in her arms.

When she pulled away, he captured her stormy green eyes in his, tears shining bright. He only remembered her crying once in his entire life, and that was the day his little brother Chase went to prison.

She hastily wiped her eyes, stepping back and frowning at him. "Now, what's your plan here? I want to know before we go into this family dinner."

Just then, his dad and brothers walked in behind her. Gunner blinked as they stomped their boots on the mat and crowded into the front of the office.

"See, Dad? She didn't kill him." Parker raked a hand through his hair with a lopsided smirk. He was the only one wearing dress slacks, his cowboy boots peeking out from under the hem.

Hunter slapped a hand on his back with a grin. "She's too smart to kill him in the sheriff's office."

"And look. The Sheriff and the Mayor both are right there. Too many witnesses." Landry laughed, pushing the hood back on his jacket, a streak of mud on his forehead.

"Gunner! Congratulations, my boy." His dad's grin was identical to all his sons. The same green hazel eyes sparkled with mirth in the fluorescent lights above.

A song started playing from the group. Parker waved his phone in the air while Shaggy's *It Wasn't Me* played through the speakers. His brothers doubled over in laughter, and Gunner lunged for the phone.

"Enough." His mom's lips twitched as she tried to keep her frown in place. "We need a game plan, not just for tonight but for everything."

"That's what we were trying to do before y'all came in." Ray leaned against the doorjamb of his office.

Charlie peered over his shoulder, a grin on his face at Gunner's obvious embarrassment.

They all murmured their agreement and started talking at once. Gunner lifted his hand and whistled into his fingers. When silence descended, he jerked a thumb behind him.

"Let's go to the conference table, and we can sit down and have a rational discussion. Joey, can you handle the front?"

Joey gave him a thumbs up from his desk, a shit-eating grin on his face too. Gunner scowled at the group, their faces all lit up with dopey grins. He let out a frustrated sigh and rubbed his temples as he led them down the hall to the table.

"What do you mean, that's what you were doing?" his mom asked.

"We were trying to figure out how this was going to work with the election, now that Willowby is running." Ray gave Gunner the stink eye.

Gunner sighed. "There's nothing we can do right now. Maryanne and I have barely talked about it. Give us a few days to talk it over."

"You don't have a few days. The election is next month. Get it settled sooner rather than later, son." Ava took off her jacket before sitting at the table.

Gunner frowned. "Don't ask her a ton of questions about it tonight at dinner, Mom. Let us work it out."

Ava waved her weathered hand and narrowed her eyes. "I won't pry, but you should move in with her."

"What? Why would I do that?" His brows rose and his heart leapt at the idea of being with her in all his spare time, sleeping with her, taking care of her. Maybe his mom could help convince Maryanne, but it was a big step. They needed to talk it out.

Parker rolled his eyes. "Duh, you knocked her up and are campaigning for public office. The people will want to see that you're in a committed relationship."

Landry snorted. "It's not just about the election. Andy said that Mrs. Martin has been staying there since the accident. You should be the one taking care of Maryanne, not her mom."

Hunter and his dad nodded, frowning, as Ray tapped his chin. Landry had a point. Mrs. Martin had been relieved when she'd seen him earlier. He knew she'd be thrilled to turn over Maryanne to him. His fingers tingled to think of Maryanne as his, his to take care of, his to protect. He'd take such good care of her, she'd never want him to leave.

Ray sat forward. "If you immediately jump in to take care of her, that could help us with the election. The people need to see you as dependable."

Gunner rubbed a hand over his face. "I've been nothing but dependable in this community for six years. And I never caused problems in high school either."

His mom shrugged, leaning back in her chair. "Doesn't matter. You know how everyone loves gossip around here. They'll be talking about this for a long time, even more so than Dot and John's surprise wedding or Andy and Cindy's whirlwind courtship and wedding."

"You'll be in the spotlight, even after the election." Landry smirked.

Gunner glared at him. "So? I'm used to it, singing with you fools on stage."

"That's different. This is going to be a lot of scrutiny, Gunner. Are you willing to do what it takes?" Charlie stared hard at him.

Gunner swallowed as he narrowed his eyes. "What do

you mean?" Silence echoed, his brothers looking at each other and avoiding his eyes.

"I'm going to guess marrying her," his dad said into the silent room.

Gunner frowned, even as his heart leapt at the idea. "It won't come to that. The election will go according to plan. Besides, none of y'all have asked her about any of this, have you? It takes two to get married."

He didn't even know if marriage was something she'd want. Sure, most women around here wanted to get married, but Maryanne wasn't most women. She was different, special.

"She can't deny that it makes sense for you to move in for a while though." Ava crossed her arms and narrowed her eyes. "That's our plan going into this family dinner tonight to celebrate, okay? Don't be pushy, but we're going to convince her this is the best course of action for now."

"Then we'll see where it goes from there." He rubbed his jaw. He was getting a headache from information overload. They heard dispatch through the speakers for a domestic call just out of town. Ray pushed back and stood at the same time as Gunner.

He waved at him, saying, "I'll go with Joey. You stay here and plan more. When Billy gets here, you go take care of that girl."

Gunner sat back down and listened to his family talk over one another. It frustrated him that they were planning out his life, but experience taught him to wait and see what happened. Most of the time their half baked plans fell flat. Deep down, he hoped they were right, and he could move in with her.

Chapter Twenty-Six

That night, Gunner led his family up the stairs to Maryanne's apartment. He knocked, but it was almost immediately opened by Andy who grinned wide.

"Gunner, I hear congratulations are in order." Andy stepped aside and shook his hand. Gunner smiled tightly and nodded as he walked into the apartment. He'd thought it would just be their parents, but his three brothers, and her sister and Andy made the small space very crowded.

"Good thing you brought in the extra table, Andy, because there's no way we'd all fit in here otherwise." Landry laughed and helped Andy set up the folding chairs.

Andy shrugged. "Margarita arranged for the loan from the church. All I did was pick it all up."

Cindy bounced over, also smiling ear to ear. "Here, let me take the jackets into the bedroom. Food's almost ready."

He passed his worn leather jacket to Cindy, but his gaze naturally found Maryanne sitting on the chaise lounge, surrounded by soft pillows and nestled under a colorful throw rug. The piercing intensity of her eyes sent a mix of excitement and nerves down his spine.

They shone in the light, and she looked equal parts terrified and excited. That was the same look he'd seen on her face countless times in the past, right before she'd done something truly outrageous. It made his skin itch and his stomach clench with worry, but at the same time, he also wanted to see what crazy thing she did next.

He took a seat beside her on the couch, leaving a small space between them, and offered a gentle smile. Her brown eyes met his, and she inhaled deeply before releasing it slowly. The warmth of their shared silence filled the air around them.

"Hello," he said quietly as everyone chattered around them.

"Hello. So much for a small, parents only dinner. Cindy demanded to be here too, once Mom called her." Her bright red lips curled in a soft smile. Like always, he wanted to smudge that perfect lipstick with his mouth. Or his cock, he wasn't picky.

She looked so beautiful, so put together. Her hair was pinned up on one side in a few tiny braids, revealing that beautiful, flawless makeup that Gunner loved.

He wanted to run a hand over her long hair, which fell in waves down her grey plaid over shirt. His fingers twitched as he glanced down at her ample cleavage busting out of a red tank top, itching to trace that soft skin.

He wanted to throw her off-balance like she did him. He wanted to see her lose control like she had in bed. He wanted—

"Gunner? Are you ready to eat?" Mrs. Martin asked across from him. Her head was cocked to the side, one brow arched as if she'd caught him being a peeping tom. He cleared his throat and nodded before he stood up.

Maryanne threw off her blanket to reveal black yoga pants and thick, fluffy red socks. He gently helped her up by the elbow, careful not to jar her.

When she smiled up at him through her thick lashes, he felt a pressure build in his chest. He rubbed the back of his neck where his skin itched and walked to the kitchen.

His dad cleared his throat. "Bow your heads as we bless this food. Thank you, God, for bringing us together tonight. Thank you for merging our two families at last and for the blessing of this little baby. Bless this food to the nourishment of our bodies. Amen."

Everyone said amen then got in line to fill their plates from the buffet laid out on the stove and counters.

"Where are the kids tonight?" Parker asked, looking around for Cindy and Andy's kids.

Cindy's eyes lit up with a laugh. "Oh, they're at Suzie and Mike's. This apartment is barely big enough for all of us, but to add four screaming kids to the mix?"

Gunner glanced around as he waited to fill his plate. She was right. This apartment wasn't the best for kids. What was Maryanne going to do once the baby came? Haul up a carrier and groceries up those stairs? What about getting a stroller in and out? She didn't just need a house, she needed a vehicle that could haul those things too.

A soft hand touched his forearm, and he blinked to focus on Maryanne's upturned face. She leaned in, biting her lip with a crease on her forehead.

"Are you alright?"

He nodded, then moved forward to fill his plate, and she kept talking.

"It's a little overwhelming, isn't it? But don't worry. We

have time to figure it out. At least six months. We'll figure it out by then. Right?"

She shifted on her feet nervously. Turning to face her, he set his plate on the counter as she looked at their family, talking among themselves, and then back at him.

As her worried gaze caught his, he smiled and brushed her hair behind her ear. "We'll figure it out. For now though, what do you want to eat?"

He grabbed another plate and fixed it according to what she wanted. Then he carried both plates to the kitchen table where his parents and her mom sat. His brothers, Cindy, and Andy sat at the extra table that had been set up behind the couch.

When they'd both taken their first bite, his mom asked, "So when did you two take things to the next level?"

He choked on his rice, which made Maryanne giggle. He glared at her, but the humor sparkling in her eyes made him want to smile back.

He grabbed his drink as Maryanne winked at him and responded. "Right before Halloween. Not sure what changed. I've been hitting on him for years with no success."

They all laughed, but Gunner's brain spun. She'd been serious in her flirting? He'd always thought it was who she was. She flirted with every guy he'd ever seen her around.

"Then on Halloween, one thing led to another. When the bakery flooded, he helped me clean up. He was my hero."

The smirk on her face sent a flash of heat through his body as their moms sighed in unison.

"Hey, I was there too!" Parker said from the other table, waving his fork at them. "Don't I count?"

"We all were," Andy chuckled.

"I feel like that makes me a hero too, since I'm the one that fixed the place. Y'all mostly stood around," Landry said.

Maryanne rolled her eyes as she replied. "You all helped fix it. You also ate my extra inventory for weeks."

Landry shrugged as Parker laughed. "It's the best inventory I've ever eaten."

Gunner clenched his fist on his lap as his brothers continued to flirt with Maryanne from across the room. She smiled and sassed them back like it wasn't a big deal.

See? She always flirted. It was in her nature. She was the life of every party. He watched as she pulled her phone out and passed around the baby's sonogram photo. His mom teared up again as he finished his food, making it difficult to swallow.

Ava sighed. "I'm so happy. He's going to be the most loved baby in Texas!"

"Or she." Margarita flipped her hair over her shoulder.

Ava frowned. "He's a Williams. We have boys. I had five of them."

Maryanne's mom shrugged. "I had two girls, and my mom and both aunts had all girls. I guess it's up to the Good Lord now."

"We're just calling it Peanut for now." Maryanne cut in as she pushed the food around on her plate.

"When will you find out the sex? Will you have a gender reveal party?" Cindy asked. Really, they should've shoved the tables together, the way everyone was joining in on the conversation from over there. Gunner took another drink as Maryanne shrugged with a wince.

"We haven't talked about anything yet. I don't want to plan anything for a while, though. With the wreck and the wedding, I need things to calm down. Did I tell y'all about the wedding fiasco?"

Maryanne's arched brows and mischievous glint in her eyes did things to his insides. He wanted to smooth a finger over them. They were so delicate but strong, just like her. Good God, what was wrong with him? Was he seriously mooning over her eyebrows?

"You mean when everyone went home drunk?" Cindy asked.

A shiver of alarm went through him as Maryanne grinned and winked. "Yeah. Drunk. Because that whiskey cake was too strong. *Right...*"

Margarita frowned. "What aren't you saying, dear?"

Maryanne's grin widened. "Well, after getting everyone home safely, Gunner arrested me for being responsible for all the public intoxication."

Her mischievous eyes turned on him, and he froze in place. It wasn't the truth but a half-truth. She was practically daring him to tell the full truth, but that would expose Zarrel. His head and his heart warred with each other as the tables talked one over the other and Maryanne finished the story.

His brothers razzed him about it, but his mom was the worst. "I'm so disappointed in you, Gunner. How could you arrest her when you'd been sleeping with her?"

He crossed his arms and leaned back in his seat. "Someone had to be held responsible."

"You're going to make such a great sheriff." His dad nodded approvingly.

Gunner shifted in his seat as the conversation moved to the upcoming debates. Maryanne laughed when she heard Mr. Willowby was going to run for the sheriff's office.

"But he hates the government. Why would he run for

sheriff?" The knot in his stomach eased to see her face bright with laughter.

Gunner frowned. "You didn't go to school here. How do you know that?"

"They live in my old apartment complex," Cindy said.

Maryanne nodded. "He also comes into the bakery and complains a few times a week. He's a sucker for bear claws too. Must be a sheriff thing."

He arched a brow, which made Maryanne's grin deepen, the cute dimple popping out to tease him. He felt his own mouth tilt in response. Smiling softly, he slipped an arm around the back of her chair. "Who knows why he decided to run. I'm sure it'll be all over town soon. Otherwise, we'll find out at the Town Hall meeting when they have the debates."

"When will those start?" Hunter asked from the other table.

Gunner shook his head. "Not until after New Year's. It'll be every Monday night in January. Then the special election will be held in February."

The conversation turned to the new mayor. Gunner looked at Maryanne's plate. She'd barely eaten anything, but her drink was empty. He got up and refilled it from the pitcher of sweet tea. When his mom raised her glass, he filled it too before checking the rest and refilling as necessary.

He felt Maryanne's eyes on him the entire time he moved around the tables. It made the hair on the back of his neck stand up.

"Gunner, slice up the apple pie and pass it around too," his mom ordered. He obeyed because no one messed with his mama.

When he sat back down, he had two slices on the same

plate for him and Maryanne to share. She gave a secretive little smile that made his stomach flip as she took a bite.

His mom patted Margarita's arm softly. "Are you okay, Margarita? You're holding your shoulders a little stiff there."

Her mom sighed wearily. "Yeah, I'm fine. I'm just not used to sleeping on a couch, you know?"

"Maryanne wouldn't let you sleep in the bed with her?" Ava asked incredulously.

Maryanne chuckled and shook her head. "Oh no, don't go blaming me for that. She refuses to sleep in the bed."

Margarita shrugged. "I'm still helping open up the bakery in the mornings. I didn't want to wake you."

Maryanne rolled her eyes as she replied. "Mom, I've gotten up at three in the morning six days a week since moving here, and before that almost as regularly for years. My internal alarm is set for it now. I hear you every morning."

Gunner waited. He knew where his mom was going with this. Sure enough, she smiled and raised a finger like she'd just had a new idea. "Why doesn't Gunner move in? He could help just as much as you, Margarita. Then you could sleep in your own bed."

Cindy agreed from the other table. "I could use your help, Mom. With Maryanne on bedrest, there were some errands that she was going to take care of before Christmas and our honeymoon."

Apparently, they were all in on his mom's plan. He glanced at Maryanne to see her blinking rapidly, a smile frozen on her lips, her eyes wide.

"Oh, that's a great idea, Ava. This will give them time to talk about the baby and how they want the future to go." Margarita clapped her hands.

"That settles it." His mom's satisfied smile showed just how happy she was to have gotten her way.

Maryanne opened and closed her mouth, but said nothing before the conversation turned to another topic. Within half an hour, the ladies had cleaned up the dishes, and the men carried the table and chairs down the stairs.

Maryanne and Gunner waved at them from the top of the landing as they pulled away. Shivering in the cold, she turned to go back inside, and he shut and locked the door behind him.

Landry had brought up his go bag from his SUV, so he carried it through her bedroom to the bathroom where he put it on the floor next to the counter.

When he walked back to the living room, Maryanne was reclining on the couch with her head resting against the back cushion, eyes closed. He sat down gently beside her and propped his head in his hand, elbow bent on the back of the couch as he faced her.

He traced the lines of her face with his gaze. He saw her throat swallow and her nostrils flare as she breathed deep and slow.

"You okay with this?" His voice was gruff, his body excited to have her all to himself again.

"Hm." The sound went straight to his cock, reminding him of the sounds she'd made when he was buried in her wet pussy.

"I would've fought it, but I was too surprised to think of a way out. Sorry. You don't have to stay if you don't want to. They'll never know. I promise to sleep the whole time, if it makes you feel better."

He snorted. "I'm not going to just leave. I gave my word."

"No, you didn't. You just sat there and let them plan it

all. You never agreed to it. Although it's curious that you had an overnight bag. Did you expect this?" She cracked one eye open to glance at him.

He shook his head. "Mom swung by the station earlier and told me it was going to happen, but the go bag is always in my SUV, in case I need to change at work. Things get messy sometimes."

Truth was, he wanted to tell her he'd already been thinking of asking to move in when his mom mentioned it. But his damn throat kept closing up when he tried to think of the words to say.

He paused, switched tactics, then reached a finger out and brushed her hair off her shoulder. "They think it'll help with the election if I'm taking care of you after getting you pregnant."

It was her turn to snort. "It takes two for that to happen." After a few moments, she rolled her head and looked at him. "Do you really think it'll help with the election if you stay here?"

"Probably. You know Crimson Creek. The people are all pretty old-fashioned. Gossip can make or break a man in this town."

She sighed as she rubbed her forehead with her right hand. "Very well. You can stay as long as you need to. I feel bad enough already about distracting you from the election when I clearly said months ago that I wouldn't do that. I really am sorry, Gunner."

He shrugged. "I am too but like you said, it takes two to make a baby. We're not going to play the blame game, alright? Let's just face forward and not back."

Maryanne's twinkling eyes found his as she slyly said, "Well, I guess this makes us even then, huh? I've messed up your election, and you've arrested me."

Gunner grimaced. "Quite a pair we make, huh? And now we're going to have a baby. Think little Peanut will be a rule follower or a rule breaker?"

She smiled and palmed his cheek. "I hope he's a strong, upstanding man like you."

He kissed her palm and grinned. "Or a hellion that turns my world upside down like you." She snuggled into his arm, leaning back on his chest. It felt good, like he was exactly where he was supposed to be.

After a few minutes, he continued softly. "By chance do you know how it happened? I thought you were on birth control. Just curious. No blame or anything."

"Hm, not sure. I was on the shot, but Kendall said it's not one hundred percent effective. I was supposed to get a new shot in December, so it wasn't expired in October. Really, if we were to play the blame game, it'd totally be on me for not having a more effective method. Again, I'm sorry."

She'd turned her head and opened her eyes while she'd been talking. Her brown eyes shone in the light, tears sparkling at the corners. He reached out a hand and traced a thumb over her cheek, wiping one away.

"No blame here, M. There's a baby for a reason, even if we don't know why yet. We'll figure it out." She sighed into his palm, closing her eyes slowly. "Come on, let's get you to bed. Mama needs her sleep as much as Peanut does." He leaned forward to help her up, and she reared back with a gasp.

Alarm raced through him, and he reached for her. "What? Are you okay?"

She looked back at him, her eyes wide, her breathing shallow. "You... you said Mama. I'm—that's me." She scrambled up and started pacing in front of the couch.

"Is that a good thing or a bad thing?" He stood, crossing his arms.

"It's good, I guess. But Owen got hurt on the playground, and I couldn't protect him. How am I going to take care of Peanut?" She huffed a breath, pulling on the ends of her hair as she spun around.

He stepped in front of her path and placed his hands on her shoulders. "You're going to be a great mom. You've been taking care of your nephews for years and nothing like that has happened before, right?"

She nodded, so he pushed her chin up with a finger, making her meet his eyes. "Well, there you go. One accident in years among three kids is pretty good math. You've been doing something right in taking care of them. When I was a kid, between my brothers and I, one of us would get hurt at least once a month. Accidents happen, and it doesn't mean you're a bad aunt to those boys. I have no doubt that you're going to be a great mom, Maryanne."

Her eyes grew glassy and a tear eased out. He swiped it away with his thumb, leaned forward, and kissed her. It quickly took over his soul, and he devoured her like a starving man eats cake.

When he finally broke the kiss, she had the well-loved relaxed expression that made him happy, proud that he'd put that look there. He leaned his forehead on hers and tried to calm his breathing. "Well, after that, I need a cold shower."

She laughed, and he pulled back to see the beauty of it lighting up her face. "Do you want company in there?" She wiggled her eyebrows.

He growled, turned her around and spanked her lightly on the ass, making her jump and laugh. "That won't accomplish what I want to, no. I was serious earlier. We'll get the all clear from the doc on Tuesday."

She glanced over her shoulder and rolled her eyes. "Fine. I'll just watch a show while you get ready for bed then."

He swiftly walked away from her, his hand still aching to spank her properly, pull her flush against him. His shower was cold, but not nearly cold enough to keep him from needing to rub one out.

When he came back into the living room, he smiled. She was curled up asleep on the couch. Slowly, he eased his arm under her legs and stood, carrying her into the bedroom and easing her down on the bed and under the blankets.

He hesitated, then walked into the living room and to the couch. They hadn't exactly talked about sleeping arrangements, and he wanted explicit permission before invading her bed. Plus, he wasn't sure he could keep his hands to himself if he was next to her.

The brightly colored pillows and throw blanket smelled like her, so he snuggled deeply. But his brain wouldn't turn off. All the questions about how to be a dad, how to provide for Maryanne, and how to make this work swirled in his head.

An hour later, he got up and grabbed a bottle of water. The couch was more comfortable than his bed in the bunkhouse, but he wanted to sleep with Maryanne. His arms ached to hold her, and he found himself in the bedroom. He looked at her, tossing and turning in the bed. Maybe she couldn't sleep either. Setting the water on the bedside table, he reached down and stroked the hair out of her face. At his touch, she stilled, sighing in her sleep.

When he grabbed the water for another drink, she

fidgeted again, rolling over and twisting the blankets. He leaned down and straightened the blankets, covering her up. He ran his hand down her arm, and she shivered then stilled. When he sat back up, she turned over and reached out, latching onto a pillow.

Realization dawned. She needed him to touch her, hold her; otherwise, she wouldn't get a good night's rest. He sighed, her body calling to him. There was really no better option, if he wanted her to get a good quality sleep for the baby. He would control himself and be what she needed.

He slowly tugged the blankets and straightened them again. Then he slid into bed beside her, settled the blankets, and slid closer to the middle of the bed where she faced away from him. As soon as he slid his arm around her waist, she stilled.

He was pleasantly warm both inside and out. Why hadn't he slept with her like this before? He'd been missing out. His bed in the bunkhouse wasn't nearly this comfortable, but somehow he knew that if she were in it, it would be. Her cinnamon scent cocooned him as her hair tickled his nose. His limbs grew heavy as he slipped into a deep sleep, at peace for the first time in a long time.

Chapter Twenty-Seven

Maryanne blinked awake, stretching her limbs out underneath the soft sheets. A weight pressed down on her legs, creating a cozy cocoon that made it hard to want to leave the bed. She turned her head to check the clock, not surprised to see three-thirty in the morning.

A soft snore had her turn further. Gunner's legs tangled with hers, and his arm wrapped loosely around her stomach. She'd never spooned with a guy before.

It was... magical, maybe because it was Gunner and not some random guy. Was he the reason she woke so refreshed and ready for the day? Was he why she'd slept so good? Perhaps it was just because she wasn't nauseous.

Maybe it wouldn't be so bad to live with him for a while. She grinned as she slipped out of the bed, adjusted her sling that she must have slept in, and went to the bathroom. After getting ready for work, she walked through her bedroom and paused at the bed. His blond tousled hair made her want to grip it. Without realizing it, she found herself reaching for him.

When she brushed the hair back, he turned from his side to his back, nuzzling into her hand with a sigh. Her heart melted, and she wanted to snuggle up to him. Instead, she forced herself down to the bakery, the brisk air helping wake her.

"Morning, Zarrel!" Maryanne called. He stood at the counter reviewing the to-do list for the day as he drank his coffee. The smell hit her, and her stomach rolled. Perhaps she wasn't quite over her morning sickness after all.

"Good morning, Maryanne. How are you this morning? Wait, something's different." He tapped his chin with a frown.

She grinned as she bounced to the coffee machine and made her own cup. "Well, I slept great, if that's what you mean."

"Hm, maybe. You seem happier."

"Could be because Gunner found out about the baby, Mom's moved out, and he's moved in."

"Whoa. That's a big deal, but I'm glad it's all out in the open now. He's a good man and an even better cop. I still can't believe he didn't arrest me for that THC at the wedding, Maryanne. I—I was so certain it was back to jail with me." Zarrel's voice wobbled as he sucked in a shaky breath.

She laid a hand on his large forearm. "It was an accident. He may love his rules, but I wasn't about to let him get away with pinning it on you."

He smiled and breathed a sigh of relief. "I still can't believe he arrested you, his baby mama."

She shrugged. "Like you said. He's a good man and his sense of duty, right and wrong... I'm not sure he'll ever be able to just let things slide, but I think he's getting better. Did I ever tell you what happened with that arrest? God, not even Holly knows about this, but you'll get a kick out of it."

She told him the story as they worked. There was more laughter that morning than she'd had in quite a few weeks. She returned home around noon, leaving Zarrel to finish the lunch rush and close for the day. A note on the kitchen counter simply said *Gone to work. Be back at seven.* —G

She grabbed lunch with Holly, took a nap, and wrapped Christmas presents for her nephews. When seven arrived, she re-heated leftovers, then wrapped Christmas presents for her nephews while watching a re-run of *Lucifer*.

A knock on the apartment door surprised her. A peak through the peep hole made her frown and throw open the door. Gunner lowered the flowers, a grin on his face that reminded her of when they'd been carefree kids.

She laughed and took the offered flowers. "Well, hello, handsome. What are you doing?"

He stepped in and shrugged off his jacket. "I don't have a key, but if we're going to live together, I wanted to start us off on the right foot. You're a woman, so I got flowers. Do you like them?"

Laughing but with tears at the corners of her eyes, she gazed at the bouquet in her hands. "I can't believe you got me flowers. No one's ever gotten me flowers before."

The mix of vibrant orange, deep purple, and bright yellow wildflowers flooded her with the earthy, floral scent and calmed her nerves at having him back in her space. They brought a sense of warmth and joy, like sunshine after a storm, filling her with hope and dreams for the future.

He walked past her, draping his jacket on the back of a kitchen chair. "What's this? Dinner?"

She smelled the flowers deeply as she searched for a vase. "Yeah, leftovers from yesterday. I'll heat it up again."

He walked to the bedroom, unbuttoning his uniform shirt. Her voice trailed off as she set the flowers on the counter and followed him. God, even his back was sexy. With a white undershirt, she could see his muscles rippling, so she walked closer and ran her hand down his spine.

He stiffened, then looked over his shoulder and peeled off the undershirt. He stood there shirtless in his jeans and boots, making her swoon as the scent of pine and cedar and that manly musk that was all him. He pulled her slowly into his arms, that feral gleam in his eye, and dipped his head lower.

He brushed his lips over hers softly, the kiss light. She longed to take it deeper, to take his cock deep inside her. She moaned when he pulled back and smirked. "When is that doctor's appointment again?"

"Tuesday."

"Just a few days. When we get the all clear... I'm going to fuck you so hard you'll forget your name." His growl sent a shiver up her spine. The anticipation might kill her, she wanted him so bad. He threw on a shirt and walked into the kitchen before they sat down to eat and watch tv.

It was all so domesticated and normal, and a natural rhythm developed between them. The next few days repeated much the same. Maryanne got up around three am to battle her morning sickness, which was back. She grew bolder as she left for work and now kissed Gunner goodbye on the cheek without fear of waking him.

They were too busy at the bakery getting ready for the Christmas rush to think about the baby or their future. In the afternoons, she anxiously awaited last minute presents to be delivered, hung out with Holly, or napped.

When they sat to eat at night, they developed the routine of watching tv to break the silence. Well, she tried to watch it, but she ended up just watching his reflection, falling asleep on the couch in his arms, or they made out like teenagers.

She'd expected the passion, but his sweet side surprised her. She'd fall asleep on the couch, but find herself tucked into bed later, Gunner's arm around her and legs entwined with her own. It was adorable and easy to be with him, but he was still so far away. They weren't talking much, and she had so many questions.

Primary among them was how long he planned to stay with her. Until her arm healed or would he want to stay until after the baby was born? The questions swirled around her head, making her more exhausted. Maybe that was why she was sleeping so well now.

Tuesday, she'd done the same as every day. She'd been decorating cookies one handed at the table she'd commandeered in front when the door rang and someone stepped inside. She did a double take to see Gunner standing there, twirling his black cowboy hat. Thank God for small towns that set their own police uniforms because that black leather jacket over his uniform shirt and pressed jeans fit him to perfection.

Quickly, she wiped her mouth with a spare napkin, discreetly getting rid cookie crumbs. His hazel eyes locked on hers, and he smiled softly. Her heart raced as he walked closer and slid into the booth across from her as Zarrel came out from the back.

"Oh, Gunner. How's it going? Congratulations about the baby, man."

Gunner grunted, nodding his head as Zarrel stopped by the table. "Thanks, Zarrel. It's been a crazy week, but it's going. Got any leftover bear claws to go? We have to get to the first baby appointment."

Maryanne blinked. "Oh, it's Tuesday, isn't it? Dang it. Okay, I'll finish these when I get back. Zarrel, can you cover them and set them on a tray? You'll probably be closed by the time we make it back from Denton."

Zarrel grinned as he boxed up some pastries. "Sure thing, boss. I'll hold down the fort." Gunner got up and went to the register while she ran to the bathroom.

When she came out, she heard Zarrel say, "I'm serious, Gunner. Any other cop wouldn't have thought twice about locking me up for that cake. Doesn't matter that it was an accident. I'm indebted to you for life, man. Whatever you need, just call. I'll be there anytime. Day or night, I'm your man."

Zarrel was standing on the edge of the counter with the box of bear claws, his brows drawn in a straight line. Gunner's easy-going smile made her heart flip as he slapped Zarrel on the back and reached for the box with the other hand. "It's all right, man. It was the right thing to do."

They walked to Gunner's truck, and he held the door for her. The feel of his hand on the small of her back shot awareness through her limbs, making them tingle. How long would she feel like this at his touch? A few months, she guessed. Then the newness would wear off.

The thought made her sad as they drove. When they reached the edge of town and continued toward Denton, he cleared his throat. "Will you put in the GPS where we're going exactly?"

She jumped at the sound of his voice, then plugged it in. Fiddling with the radio, she turned a sly grin on him. "Gunner, what's this?" She had popped out his favorite mixed CD labeled 'Gunner's shit, not Landry's.'

He grinned. "I like to sing at the top of my lungs on the way home from work. These are my favorite."

She pushed it back in and The Black Eyed Peas started singing *I Gotta Feeling*. It immediately picked her spirits up, so she started humming along, but by the end she was practically dancing on her seat.

When the song switched to Kelly Clarkson's *Since You Been Gone*, she noticed Gunner thumb drumming on the steering wheel and singing along. She pretended to hold a microphone and sang into her fist, then held it out to him. He grinned before belting out the song at the top of his lungs. The rest of the drive, she alternated giggling and staring at him as they sang together.

Her heart was light and in that moment, nothing else mattered except the road, the song, and Gunner. Her mom called as they were entering Denton, so she turned the radio down and answered.

"Hey, Mom... yeah, we're almost there... do you need anything from town... Okay, love you too. Bye."

He navigated lunch traffic to the hospital with ease. Music continued in the background, and she started to bounce her leg as she picked at the hem of her sweater.

"That was Mom. She's invited you to Christmas, by the way. When does your family do Christmas?"

"Christmas Day, usually around lunch."

"That works for us because Mom does hers Christmas Eve. Oh no! I forgot your family. Can we go shopping after the appointment? I didn't get them anything."

Gunner glanced at her with his brows drawn. "Sure, but you don't have to get presents." He parked and opened her door. They walked to the door, she twisted her hands in front of her. This was going to make it more real, and she wasn't sure if it was nerves or dread fluttering in the pit of her stomach.

Chapter Twenty-Eight

They walked into the office, and she checked in before sitting in the corner next to Gunner. She scrolled through her phone and bit her nail as her leg bounced. When her name was called, Gunner stood up with her.

"You're going in too?" her voice squeaked, and she cleared her throat.

He nodded, putting his hand on her back and leading her down the hall after the nurse. When they arrived in the room, the nurse took her vitals and some blood, then asked her to undress for the initial ultrasound. The door closed behind her, leaving them in silence under the glaring lights.

She sucked in a breath as Gunner sat in the corner with his legs crossed at the ankles, phone in hand as he scrolled. Well, if this was the way it was going to be, then fine. She set down her purse on the extra chair, took her red jacket off, then slowly eased her sling and sweater off over her wrist. She pulled it gingerly over her head, took another deep breath, and turned slightly away from him as she folded it.

She kicked off her heels under the chair. Then she reached for the button on her blue jeans to drag them over her hips. Her ass wasn't quite right in front of Gunner when she bent to pick them up, but she made sure he had a nice view. She glanced at him through her lashes as she stood up and folded her pants.

She smiled in victory. He was watching, his phone long forgotten. Next she reached behind her and unsnapped her pale pink lace bra before sliding it slowly down her arms and wedging it between her shirt and pants. She slid her fingers along the waistband of the matching panties before hooking a thumb on each side and sliding them down her legs slowly. She stepped out, added them to the pile, and reached for the hospital gown on the exam table.

Gunner's hands shot out and grabbed her by the waist. She tumbled softly onto his lap with a gasp, both her legs to one side.

His arms wrapped her in a cocoon of warmth in the cold sterile room. His touch that made her shiver, and her head tipped back when she met his eyes. The green flecks popped under the bright lights and that predatory look was back, like he wanted to gobble her up.

"You're going to pay for that little strip tease. You know I can't do anything about it right now, but later…"

His deep, gravelly voice made her even more wet than she already was just by being in the same room with him. His lips hovered before slightly kissing hers. Then another, so light as to be barely felt. It made her lips tingle because she just wanted him to sweep in already.

Instead, he leaned back and set her on her feet, nodding to the exam table. She slipped on the hospital gown and sat on the table with shaky legs, her heart racing. Before it had time to calm down to an even pattern, a knock sounded on the door.

"Ready?"

"Yes," Maryanne called out. Dr. Patel was a short, little Indian woman with a British accent. After introductions, she explained how the appointment and ultrasound would work.

"But first, we need to just chat and ask some questions, alright?" She asked about health history and clarified some things Maryanne had written on her paperwork.

"We're going to do the pelvic exam now." The doctor set up the stirrups, and Maryanne leaned back. She heard Gunner shift in his chair beside her as the doctor did her thing.

"Does that hurt the baby?" His gruff voice caused the hairs on her arm to stand up.

The doctor chuckled. "Not at all. As first-time parents, you're probably wondering about sex while pregnant, huh?"

Gunner grunted, which made Maryanne roll her eyes. "I've told him the books all say it's fine, but he'd rather have your opinion."

"Yeah, because you were in an accident three weeks ago. It has to be safe for both of you, Maryanne."

The doctor held up her hands with a smile. "Sex is perfectly fine for both mom and baby. It all feels healthy down here, so we'll do the ultrasound now to verify. Let me grab the ultrasound tech, alright?"

She disposed of her gloves, covered Maryanne's lower half, then leaned her head out the door before closing it behind her again.

"While we wait for her, do either of you have any further questions?"

Maryanne sat up and looked at the doctor. "Can I continue dying my hair? What about yoga?"

The doctor nodded. "Dye should be fine, but if you can, consider switching to a vegan one, as they typically have fewer chemicals. Yoga is a definite yes. Exercise is recommended but don't start a new exercise regimen. If you've already been doing yoga, keep it up, but don't start to train for a marathon now if you haven't already been. Does that make sense?"

"Yeah. That works for me. I like yoga with my girlfriends, so that's good."

"Keep it low impact and non-strenuous, and you'll be okay."

Gunner interrupted. "What about diet and nutrition? Vitamins or minerals?"

The doctor nodded as the door opened and the tech came in.

"Avoid caffeine as much as possible. Everything in moderation. The more fruits and vegetables, the better. Scale back on carbs and sugars. You run a bakery, right?"

At Maryanne's nod, she continued. "Do you sample a lot of your own goods?"

Maryanne nodded again, laying down as they set up the equipment. "Yeah, but mostly because I forget to eat, and it's there. The books said one cup of coffee was fine, right?"

"Right, one a day is fine. Dad, if you want to help, preplan meals so when she gets hungry, there's healthy food available. As for vitamins, take a prenatal, but the blood work will tell us if there's anything else you need. Ready for the ultrasound now?"

When the tech lubed up the wand and the doctor pulled out the stirrups, Maryanne glanced at Gunner and reached out to beckon him closer.

He stood and locked their fingers together. With his other hand, he tucked a stray hair out of her face. His touch steadied her heart rate a little, and she leaned into his hand as the tech rolled the wand inside.

The machine lit up as she started to take pictures. Silence reigned for several minutes until the tech reached over and hit a button on the keyboard. *Womp--womp--womp--womp* echoed.

"That's a steady heartbeat for a healthy little tyke." The tech's cheery voice echoed in the sterile room, and the doctor started pointing to the machine, explaining what they were seeing. Tears pooled in Maryanne's eyes as she stared and listened.

"When do we find out the sex of the baby?" Gunner asked, and Maryanne's heart skipped a beat.

"Looks like you're measuring about twelve weeks now, so your due date is going to be July 10. Normally, we'd be able to see the sex, but the angles are wrong today. Are you alright waiting until your next appointment? Maybe the baby will cooperate more then."

The doctor had the tech print out about a dozen images as they discussed more details. When they both left, Gunner helped her sit up before wrapping her in his arms.

It felt nice to have him holding her, keeping her safe with his scent wrapping around her. Having his hips between her legs wasn't too shabby, either, but it wasn't about the sexual tension.

What she felt with him was much deeper than she'd ever felt before. She kept her face buried in his shirt and breathed deeply of his pine and cedar aftershave, the tension leaving her shoulders. She didn't want him to ghost her or go back to ignoring her. This felt too good, too right to give up.

The Sheriff Gets His Girl

She swallowed hard. "Are you really in this, Gunner? And if so, for how long?"

He leaned back and palmed her cheek, tilting her head up until their eyes clashed under the bright lights.

"I'm here, Maryanne, and I'm not going anywhere. I'll be at every appointment, and anytime you need anything, just ask. It's going to be alright. Didn't I already tell you this?"

She swallowed her emotions. "I'm just afraid you're going to leave, that you'll move out, and I'll have to do all this alone."

Her lips trembled and a tear escaped. He wiped it with his thumb before he gently met her lips with his own. He tasted like coffee and sugar, and it made her crave him even more. She moaned into his mouth, opening wider as his tongue dueled with hers. Her fingers clutched at his waist, pulling him closer between her legs.

He broke the kiss with a gasp and looked into her eyes. "You're strong, Maryanne. If you had to do this alone, you could. But the only thing that would keep me from being here for you is death. Come hell or high water, I'm still gonna be here."

Her heart ached, and she breathed deeply of that comforting scent of his. He was right, because she *could* do this. She'd been alone a long time, but she figured out how to run a bakery, and she could figure this out too.

He stepped back until he hit the wall, where he nodded to her clothes on the chair. "Get dressed." The deep command sent shivers down her spine, but it was that predatory look in his eyes that made her legs wobbly as she stood up and obeyed.

Chapter Twenty-Nine

When they were walking out the door of the doctor's office, he took her hand in his, lacing their fingers together. "So, what would you like to do first? Shop and then food or food and then shop?"

She beamed at him as he opened the door for her and helped her up into his truck. "Walmart first. I want to make some photo gifts from these pictures for your parents and my mom. Then we'll eat, and if we need to shop more while we wait for the photo gifts, we can hit the mall."

He nodded as he shut the door. Walmart was packed, being the week of Christmas, and it took way too long to get in and out. When they arrived at Outback and sat in their booth, Maryanne tried to make conversation.

"I haven't been here in forever. Is this your favorite restaurant?" They talked about their favorite restaurants and foods before the waitress came to take their orders. He preferred meat, while she loved spicy foods. Neither of them cared for vegetables, but if they had to pick a favorite green vegetable, hers was lemon Brussel sprouts with bacon while his was French style green beans.

"Breads are my weakness. I love bread." She tore into the loaf that had been set in front of them. When she moaned, he chuckled and sliced half for himself.

"I'm partial to your bear claws, myself." He winked, making her grin. It probably wasn't a pretty sight, with her mouth still full of food. She took a hefty sip of her water.

"What about favorite drinks? Alcoholic and non. Like, what do you drink every single day?" She raised her glass of water in salute.

"I like a good Bud Lite Platinum. I drink coffee in the morning from your shop. Sweet tea at lunch. And water all afternoon. What about you?"

"I like wine coolers. Getting drunk isn't my thing anymore, so only in social situations. I enjoy sparkling waters but will occasionally have a sweet tea or lemonade at Cindy's or Mom's. Maybe a soda every once in a while. Holly's really into health stuff, so she sort of influenced me to be more healthy."

Their food arrived as they were talking about their friends and all the people who had moved to town in the past few years.

There wasn't a break in conversation. For once, he didn't clam up or just speak a few words. They talked about their families, his brothers and the band, and why she had wanted to become a baker. Then they moved on to bucket lists, where they wanted to travel and things they wanted to do, before talking about trivial things like favorite movies and tv shows.

When he paid for lunch, her cheeks hurt from laughing and smiling so much. It might have been the most engaging and fun date she'd had... well, ever. She fought down a rush of anxiety at the thought. He was the best date, best kisser, best sex. What if he decided he wanted out? What if she got used to having him around, to having the best, and then he left?

Her heart skipped a beat as they walked to his truck. It was so easy to be with him like this, and she could feel the foundation of their relationship strengthening. She just hoped it was the start of something permanent.

When they reached the passenger side, he spun her around and pressed her up against the door. His eyes locked on hers, his brows drawn down in a frown as he seemed to search her wide-eyed gaze.

Then he dipped his mouth to hers, and everything stilled. Her racing heart. The swirling thoughts in her head. The air around them even seemed to pause as his tongue swept into her mouth.

All the jagged pieces of her heart clicked into place. It was too late. She already loved him, perhaps had since that first kiss in high school, perhaps even before that when he'd rescued her from the pool when she was ten. She might not survive if he broke her heart, but she was going to enjoy every moment they tried to make this work.

She wrapped her arms around him and gave up thinking.

Gunner dumped the last of their purchases into the living room by the couch. How did women shop like that? They'd gone from Outback to the mall where they'd spent two more fucking hours walking around before circling back to Walmart for their photo gifts.

The only good thing about it all had been watching Maryanne's facial expressions change whenever she would find the "perfect" gift for someone. And every time she'd ask if he could carry the bag, she gave him a kiss and that saucy little smirk. She'd reapplied her lipstick in the truck after lunch, and it took twelve little kisses in the mall before he could smudge them to his satisfaction.

Maryanne came out of the bathroom, her face scrunched in a frown while she bit her lip.

"Um, Gunner? Can you, um, help with the laundry?" She waved at her arm still in the sling.

He smiled, liking that she was leaning on him now and accepting him in her home. The date had definitely helped. She seemed more comfortable than she'd been earlier in the week, and the awkwardness that had been between them was gone.

She directed him to the laundry closet off her bedroom, where he bent to put the clean clothes into the empty hamper. Such a simple chore, but it reminded him of the non-permanence of their situation.

"We need to talk about the baby and living arrangements, M." She froze like a deer in the headlights, then turned, frowned, and sat on her bed. He stepped back, piled the clean laundry beside her, and started to fold the towels.

She slumped over the hamper, her fingers digging into the fabric. "I appreciate you taking me around today, but I can do this on my own," she gritted out, her voice trembling. "You don't have to take care of me." She looked up at him, her eyes defiant.

"I know you're cleared from bedrest," he said, gently placing a hand on her shoulder. "But I just want to make sure you're okay."

She cast her eyes down then jerked her clothes out of

the hamper. "I told you to go home, Gunner. You can go anytime you want, and I don't need you to stay here."

Gunner's heart tightened at Maryanne's words, the vulnerability hitting him in the gut. He knew she was strong, independent and had always been fiercely determined to take care of herself. But seeing her vulnerable and in need of help tugged at his heartstrings.

He crouched down beside her, ignoring the laundry scattered around them. "I know you can do this on your own," he said softly. "But that doesn't mean you have to. I want to take care of you." The truth of his words scared him, but he didn't try to take them back.

Maryanne shook her head, tears threatening to spill from her beautiful eyes. "Why?" she whispered, her voice full of pain and confusion.

"Because...because I care about you," Gunner replied, his hand reaching out to brush a strand of hair behind her ear. "And because I want to." He knew it was true, but he didn't know why it was so. It was simply the way it was.

Maryanne looked away, unable to meet his gaze as the weight of his words settled around them. He knew she'd always faced everything on her own and rarely asked for help, but the need to wrap her up in a protective bubble and hold her was becoming stronger and stronger.

"For how long, Gunner? You're being sweet helping me out this week, even with the laundry, the dishes, the trash. This time next year, we'll have a baby though. And it's been my experience that no one ever sticks around when I need it. I don't want to be a burden," she said softly, still refusing to look at him.

"You're not a burden," Gunner insisted firmly. "You never could be. I know you don't need me, but I—I need to take care of you and the baby. I want to give us a real shot at a relationship. For the baby's sake, we should try, right?"

He gently lifted her chin with his finger until their eyes met again. "But if...if you don't want me here, I'll leave. If you don't want to have a relationship, I'll back off and move back to the ranch," he added reluctantly. With the way their parents had pushed them together, the decision had to be hers. His chest tightened at the thought of leaving again, but he waited, crouching in front of her as she bit her lip.

"No," she said softly, placing her hand on his cheek. "Don't leave."

Gunner let out a relieved sigh and pulled Maryanne into a hug, wrapping his arms tightly around her small frame as he kneeled on the floor in front of her.

They stayed like that for a few moments, taking comfort in each other's embrace. He sighed and reached for the stack of towels. He walked to the bathroom and put them up, came back to the bedroom, and continued folding the laundry.

She bit her nail, her leg bouncing. "What does a relationship mean though? You want to date?"

He raked his hand through his hair as he paced away. He didn't want to date her. It was so much more than that. He spun around, knelt at her feet and took her hands into his. He kissed her knuckles, somehow enjoying kneeling at her feet. He needed to lay the plan out and see if she liked it.

"I don't want to just date you, Maryanne. I want us to live together, permanently, but not here. A second floor apartment is going to be a nightmare with a baby carrier, stroller, all that stuff, so we need to buy a house."

She sucked in a deep breath as her brow wrinkled in a frown.

"Gunner... I'm doing alright, financially, but I'm not ready to buy a house."

"I'll buy the house. I've been saving for a long time. There are perks to living in my parent's bunkhouse for so long."

She stood up and stepped away from him, holding her elbow in the sling. She paused at the window and stared out at the street.

"And what happens if we move into a house and then break up? I'll need to move again—and with a baby? Come on, Gunner, that's too much pressure."

He stepped behind her and ran his hands up and down her biceps. He leaned forward, breathing in the cinnamon scent of her shampoo and kissing the back of her neck.

"I'll purchase the house and sign it over to you. If we happen to go our separate ways, then I'll be the one to leave. It would give me peace of mind knowing that I can still take care of you and the baby. Please, Maryanne."

He stroked her hair with one hand, the other holding her about the waist. She turned into his chest, her head settling over his heart. The itch that threatened just under the surface of his skin whenever they were far apart was completely gone when she was in his arms. It was soothing, peaceful, and made him horny as hell.

Maybe she wouldn't notice the raging boner being pressed up against her.

She sighed, shifting her head slightly on his chest. He kissed the top of her head and held her tight.

"Fine, let's buy a house. I'll pay the down payment though, and you pay the rest, okay?"

He tipped her head back and stared into her beautiful face. He wanted her to see all of him, the good, the bad, the mundane, even the things he kept hidden from himself.

The Sheriff Gets His Girl

Her eyes relaxed, and she smiled with a sigh as he leaned in and kissed her. Electricity shot down his lips to his fingertips and his cock. Pulling up the other hand, he cupped her face in his as their kiss deepened. Would he ever get enough of her? He didn't think so. Thank God, she'd agreed to the house plan.

Chapter Thirty

"Maryanne, this photo magnet is perfect. And the ornament! Thank you so much, hun." His mom grinned, showing the magnet to his dad.

Gunner shifted on the couch, making Maryanne glance at him with a smile. When her hand settled on his knee, he relaxed. This was going to be fine. Christmas lunch had gone well, even if it was loud and chaotic.

Maryanne's flirting with Landry and Parker hadn't bothered him as much, since she'd taken her sling off for lunch and kept her broken hand on his leg under the table the entire time they'd eaten. He'd noticed her wince a few times, but she didn't seem too bothered by it. She was strong, his Maryanne, although he'd made her put the sling back on right after she'd finished eating.

His Maryanne? God, that was so lame. She wasn't his yet, but he wanted her to be. For now, she was just his baby mama. Right?

"Did Gunner already give you his Christmas present,

The Sheriff Gets His Girl

Maryanne?" His mom raised her eyebrow, making him shift in his seat again, his stomach clenching in knots.

Maryanne just laughed, the deep throaty sound sending shock waves straight to his cock. "Not yet. We're saving that for later, right, G?"

He shrugged and grinned, his stomach flipping in anticipation. "No need to wait. It's fine." He pulled out the small box from his pocket and handed it over. Maryanne's eyes widened, and she sucked in a breath when the room went eerily quiet. What were they all staring at? Yeah, everyone else had already opened their presents, but they didn't need to all stare.

She glanced down, her hands shaking as she opened the box. The pause seemed to last minutes before she exhaled, glanced at him with a big grin, and held up the keys. "What are these for?"

"The black key is to the red Fusion waiting back at your apartment. The gold key is to our house."

Her jaw dropped and her eyes widened. She started to shake as her mouth opened and closed. His heart lurched, and he swiftly pulled her onto his lap, her legs dangling to the side when he wrapped his arms around her and laid her head on his chest, careful of her arm.

"Is it alright?" He nuzzled her hair quietly as his mom beamed at his dad and his brothers started talking to each other again. Maryanne gave a small nod, and he slid his hand up her good arm. "Are you tired? Do you want to go take a nap?"

She sucked in a shaky breath and nodded again, so he slid an arm under her legs and stood.

"Mom, Maryanne needs a nap. We'll be back soon." He juggled her into a better position to carry as he strode down the hall and to the stairs.

Parker's voice echoed behind him. "Is that what we're calling it these days?"

When he reached the room at the top of the stairs on the right, kicked the door shut with his boot and strode to the full bed under the window. He laid her down gently, then sat beside her and brushed the hair out of her face. Maybe the house and car had been too much for their first Christmas.

"I'm okay." She cleared her throat and turned onto her side, careful of her sling and avoiding his eyes. He kicked off his boots, walked around the bed, and laid down behind her. He pulled her into his arms to spoon and breathed deeply behind her, some of his worry releasing at the feel of her.

"You sure? You freaked out a little."

She chuckled and turned onto her back, causing him to sit up on one elbow. "I know. It was just so overwhelming. You got me a car and a fucking house? Gunner, I got you a couple's coupon book and a mixed CD."

His lips twitched, making her grin before they both burst into laughter.

"God, that's such a middle school gift, M."

"I know! I thought it'd be funny, but I didn't know it'd be this funny. The look on your face..." They laughed as he slid a hand to her stomach, his head falling into the crook of her neck. When he kissed the exposed skin of her shoulder, she laughed again.

"Stop. That tickles." His heart leapt at the sound of her laughter, and he needed more of it, more of her. He snuffled into her neck, making her gasp and squirm. "Gunner," she laughed, then twisted the wrong way.

"Oh! Ow. Gunner—" She hadn't even finished saying

his name when he pulled back with a frown, his stomach dropping.

"Shit, I'm so sorry. Your shoulder. Are you okay?"

She raised her one good hand to his cheek, so he turned his head and kissed her palm. Smiling, she sighed. "Yeah, just twisted the wrong way." He worried about her shoulder, but her eyes were clear of pain and happy. "Now about these gifts…"

Nerves jumping, he tried to force his mouth to talk, to say anything. He needed to push past this mutism where she was concerned. "I promised I'd take care of you and the baby, M. For now, that means the house and car because you need them."

Her eyes searched his. "And a year from now? Two years?"

The thought of not being with her in two years made his body run cold and his heart stutter. But he didn't want to get together with her just because of the baby, either. They needed to make the relationship work, outside of having a baby.

He leaned down and kissed her nose, laying his forehead on hers. "We'll see how it goes, won't we? Come on, I told Mom you needed a nap, so let's get some shut eye." He pulled her ass back against his crotch, and she squirmed against him, making his semi harden immediately.

"You sure it's a nap you're wanting?" Her husky voice was like a scratch behind the ears, making him growl.

"I'm not having sex in my old bedroom with my family downstairs, Maryanne. They could walk in."

"Exactly. That's the thrill, Gunner." She pressed her butt against his cock again, and he leaned forward and nipped her ear before licking it.

"Not now, M. Save it for later. Sleep for peanut, okay?"

She sighed. "Why is this your old bedroom? Why do you live in the bunkhouse and not here?"

He shrugged and wrapped her closer. "Mom smothered me when I moved home after the Marines, so I moved out there with the other ranch hands. She doesn't set foot in the bunkhouse."

Maryanne chuckled, and the sound shot Cupid's arrow straight to his heart, making him hot and cold at the same time.

"Sleep, M." He growled into her hair and threw a leg over both of hers, holding them down. With an arm wrapped around her, he felt at peace, knowing she was safe and protected in his arms.

After they woke and said their goodbyes, Gunner bundled her into her favorite red jacket and ushered her to his truck. When she was settled inside, the anxiety climbed higher in her gut, and she bit her nails. A freaking car and a house. How could she ever balance that out? She didn't want him making all these life altering decisions for her. She'd had enough of that to last a lifetime already.

Maybe this was just a step on the road to controlling her. It wouldn't be the first time, and it hadn't worked out with her dad or with Barry. Her dad had kept grounding her, taking away the car and all the things, even things she'd bought with her own money. Barry's had been less obvious, but by the end he was in complete control of everything, even the finances.

She wasn't sure how to talk to Gunner about this either. Maybe she needed to start therapy like Holly, to work out how to talk to him about her fears.

The Sheriff Gets His Girl

They went the long way back to town before turning onto Old Mill Road. Trees lined the street and kids were riding shiny new Christmas bikes on the sidewalk. Houses were spread along on big lots—Craftsman, Victorian, and everything in between—and he turned down a side street, stopping at the last one on the street. It was a two-story Craftsman with a porch along the front. Grey brick with blue shutters and a blue door stood stark on the dreary December day.

"What are we doing here?"

"This is your new house. If you like it, that is." His gruff voice sent shivers up her spine and made her heart pound. He hopped out, opened her door, and slid his fingers into hers as they walked from the driveway around to the front porch. His touch warmed her up and kept the cold at bay.

"Oh, a porch swing! I've always wanted one just like this." She let go of his hand and sat on the swing as he unlocked the front door. The wind bit through her beanie hat, whipping her hair around her face. Gunner leaned on the front doorjamb, arms crossed, a half-smile on his face.

That smile... was he smiling more this past week? Did she make him happy? If she could make him happy, maybe he would stay with her. She shivered, chilled to think of life without him.

"Come on, before you get too chilled."

She hopped up and followed him inside. The scent of pine and lemon filled her nose, reminding her of her 'Buela. She always used that cleaner. The smell, the warmth, the shiny cleanliness of it all felt like home, and a sense of peace settled over her.

The foyer was two stories and led to a wide, well-lit hallway with a staircase on one side. On either side of the foyer were open rooms, but the living room on the left caught her immediate attention.

With a brick fireplace painted white, wide windows facing the front porch and street, and tall ten-foot ceilings with crown moldings, she fell in love. She put her cold hands to her overheated face as she took it in.

"The floors are in decent. I had Landry come by and inspect it yesterday. He said we might need a new air conditioner come summer, but that's alright. Everything else is in good shape for being a few decades old."

"It's more traditional than I expected, but it feels good. It feels... like it could be home."

She spun in a slow circle, noticing the room across from the foyer for the first time. She walked toward it, a dining room with white wainscoting below a sea foam green wall and matching windows from the living room.

She caught sight of the open doorway in the dining room and walked through it. With a gasp, she came to an abrupt halt. Tears filled her eyes. She had been afraid of having an old, non-functional kitchen, but this...

"Do you like it? It's what made me pick this one." His voice was soft behind her as she walked into the room. The kitchen took up the entire back quarter of the house.

Cabinets were on three sides, with a giant island in the middle, big enough for a few bar stools. The back wall was all counter space with several windows above them looking out onto the backyard. She peered into the double wall-mounted ovens.

"Do you know when this was renovated? It's newer than I expected."

"Actually, Landry remodeled it five or six years ago, so everything is up to code."

She walked to the sink and looked out. "What a cute backyard! And bigger than I thought it'd be."

"That row of trees along the back fence over there? They're fruit trees. Peaches, I believe. Might come in handy for fresh produce for the bakery."

He really had picked the perfect house. She turned and leaned against the counter, staring at him across the kitchen with a smile.

"Do you like it? If you don't, that's fine. We can look at other houses."

She shook her head, nervous to talk to him about this but knowing it needed to be said. "No, I like it. I'm... conflicted though. I don't like having decisions made for me. My dad was like that, and Barry was even more controlling. That's why I was so afraid earlier, when you gave me the keys. I want to be part of the decision-making process."

"They decided for you, were controlling, or both?"

She picked at the hem of her sweater and glanced down.

"Both. With Dad, nothing was ever good enough, and I was always getting things taken away when I disappointed him. He controlled what I could and couldn't have, and it was just part of growing up. Barry... was more subtle. But by the end, he was in complete control of all the finances, what I wore, who I hung out with, when I worked, everything."

Gunner's face was expressionless again. He wore that mask well, but her heart rate sped up as he stalked across the room toward her. He slid his hands to the counter on either side of her, boxing her in.

"Are you afraid I'm going to take the house and car away?" His voice was soft, and she couldn't bring herself to look up into his face. She focused on a button on his green plaid button-down shirt and nodded.

He tipped her chin up with a finger.

"I gave my word about the house being in your name. The realtor hasn't drawn up the contract yet though, because I wasn't sure if this was the one you would want or not. I absolutely am not taking away your right to make this decision. We have an appointment to return the key on Monday, and if you don't want this one, we can set up appointments to look at others then."

He kissed the corner of her mouth softly, making her tremble.

"But we do need to get a few things straight. You're the driving force in my mind. When making decisions that impact us both, you'll be there for everything. I might narrow down options for you, but if you don't like them by all means—find something else, and we'll talk about it. You and the baby will always come first. With this house. With your car. With everything."

She leaned back, meeting his hazel eyes, the light from the windows behind her illuminating his rugged face. "About the car... Why a Ford Fusion? I loved my little Mustang."

He smiled and kissed the other corner of her mouth.

"The Fusion has a back seat, darlin'. And the safety ratings were excellent. I knew you wouldn't take well to a truck or SUV; you've been driving that car for a long time. And I figured you'd want to stick with red since that's your favorite color."

She tilted her head to the side. "How do you know that's my favorite color?"

He arched a brow. "You wear your red heels more than any others, prefer red lipstick, have a red purse, and mostly red accessories, plus the red car. That your apartment is a lot of purples and greens actually surprised me."

She grinned. "Yeah, red makes me feel confident and powerful and sexy. I didn't know you paid attention to little things like that."

"With you, M, I pay attention to every detail, no matter how small."

Her heart raced, and she placed a hand on his bicep and ran it up his arm. His words gave her hope, made her think they could turn this into something permanent.

"You put a lot of thought into the house and car though, didn't you." That must've been what he was doing all week and why she'd barely seen him.

"Yeah, no shit." He snorted, making her giggle.

She placed her hands on his chest, his eyes gleaming in the light and changing colors, either from the sound or her touch. She didn't care which, as long as he kept that happy look on his face.

"This is where you say—Thank you, Gunner. It's the best Christmas I've ever had. Please bend me over that island and fuck me."

When he talked like that, it sent her heart racing, and she chuckled. "An intriguing proposition."

She pressed into him, rubbing her breasts against his chest. They both sucked in a breath, and he backed them up toward the island. She grinned, then sashayed through the kitchen door and into the hallway.

"But I haven't seen the rest of the house yet, Gunner. Maybe later." She glanced over her shoulder. He growled, he clenched his fists and jaw and stomped toward her.

She squealed and ran around to the stairs, sprinting up them as her heart pounded with excitement and desire. She looked over her shoulder to see he was grinning like a lion toying with its prey. He stomped up the stairs slowly, allowing her the head start.

Chapter Thirty-One

She ran up the stairs and slowed to throw open doors, finding four bedrooms and a big bathroom at the end of the hall. She spun on her heels and grinned as she spied him prowling closer, trapping her.

"You done yet?" He growled, the sound sending shivers up her spine, making her pussy ache for him. She shifted on her feet as he stalked closer and backed up into the corner by the bathroom door.

He leaned in close enough for her to feel his breath on her cheek. But he didn't press her up against the wall like she wanted.

Instead, he slid his hand under her sweater and grazed the flat of her stomach just above her jeans. She sucked in a breath at his touch. When he hooked a finger into the top of her jeans, she tilted her hips up to him, trying to get his finger to go lower.

He chuckled, the smile on his face looking feral as he slowly started pulling her back towards the stairs by that one damn finger in her pants. She could have stood her ground.

She could have easily grabbed his hand and removed it, but she didn't want to. This was too much of a turn on.

"Where are we going?" Her hands trembled with excitement.

He walked backwards a few steps before glancing over his shoulder. "You forgot the room behind the living room, little girl. Can't leave any area unexplored, now can we?"

His voice was deep, the sound echoing around her head and bouncing in her body down to her pussy. She ached for him and going down the stairs was torture, as she felt the jeans put pressure onto her clit in just the right way. He glanced back at her with a smirk.

"Is it the master bedroom? I just saw regular bedrooms up here."

Her heart raced when they rounded the stairs into the hallway. Across from the kitchen were two doors. One was open; a half-bath. Gunner pushed open the other to reveal the master.

The walls were a tranquil shade of pale blue, creating an atmosphere of calm and peace. The ship-lapped wall added a touch of rustic charm to the room. Through the open doors, Maryanne was drawn to the master closet. Her eyes widened. "It's the size of a bedroom."

"Big enough for your wardrobe?"

"Psh, I'll say," she said, going on to the luxurious bathroom.

The air in the room was crisp and clean, with a hint of lavender from scented candles that sat on the countertop. More shiplap covered the recessed area of the toilet, but the rest of the room was calming pale greens and blues. The jacuzzi tub, with its glistening white surface, took up most of the back wall, surrounded by pale blue tiles. Above it, a wide window was set high into the wall.

The oversized shower had a clear glass door and was also tiled in pale blue and green, with multiple shower heads and a built-in bench. The shower seemed to be a cathedral of cleanliness and relaxation, promising to wash away all her worries and stress. The bathroom—no, the whole house—created a safe oasis to escape from the outside world.

"Oh, wow. I could probably lay down in that thing."

Gunner stopped beside it, his brow raised as he turned to face her. "Probably, but not today. Right now, I need you to get on your knees."

Her jaw dropped as she spun to face him, brows rising. "What?"

"You heard me. On your knees. I've been wanting to see those cherry red lips wrapped around my cock for years, Maryanne. We'll consider it part of my Christmas present. I bet one of those coupons could make that happen?"

She grinned slyly and nodded as he reached for the fly on his jeans. She got such a thrill from him talking like that, knowing that he'd been dreaming of her like she'd been dreaming of him... Her heart melted and she stepped closer.

Unbuttoning them, he slid them down around his hips and pulled out his thick cock. Her mouth watered when he fisted it and spread his legs slightly. She reached out to touch it, but he slapped her hand away, sending a thrill through her body.

"Uh-huh. I could've fucked you real good in the kitchen, but you didn't listen. So now... get on your knees and suck my cock, Maryanne."

The command sent ripples of awareness up her spine as her eyes snapped up to his. Holy shit, he was serious.

"Oh, so bossy. I like it."

He caressed her cheek, swiping his thumb over her

The Sheriff Gets His Girl

lower lip and leaning on his other hand against the wall, caging her in. His hand was the only thing touching her, but she ached for so much more. She wanted all of him. The doctor had given the all clear earlier in the week, but he'd not touched her at all. Her eyes flicked down, his hard dick jutting out between them, before sucking in a breath and licking her lips.

"I know you like it, what you want and what you don't. Do you trust me, M? Do I need to beg and ask again?"

She tipped her head to the side as she raised a brow. "What happens if you have to ask again?"

"You're about five seconds from finding out, little girl."

She grinned, reaching her hand out to stroke him, triumph lighting up her heart that he didn't smack her hand away this time.

"Oh yeah? What are you gonna do, spank me? That would involve me letting go of your cock, and you wouldn't want that, now would you?"

He groaned, slapping his other hand against the wall and holding himself rigidly still. She could hear the grinding of his teeth, his ragged breath. His eyes went feral.

"Damn it, Maryanne. Suck my dick, and I'll make it worth your while. For the love of God, woman."

The thrill flipped her stomach, nerves dancing in excitement. With a soft laugh, she slowly sank to her knees and reached for him, more than ready to rock his world.

But damn, he was so big her hand didn't even make it all the way around. She looked up at him through her lashes and licked the tip. His breath shuddered. There was power in obeying him, in reducing him from demanding to begging. Power in having him literally in the palm of her hand.

She tucked her chin and slid her tongue along the

underside, from the base to the tip. He growled, his hand stealing around to cup the back of her head. When she slid the tip in her mouth, he stilled.

"Fuck. Maryanne—" he gasped, his voice raspy, raw. She adjusted her angle and then slid him as far into her mouth as she could. He was too wide, but when she got as deep as she could, she held still.

He wrapped her hair around his fist and pulled her back. He set the pace, slow and methodical, his hands soft but firm on her head, sliding in and out. He didn't go too deep or pushed her boundaries, and it made her chest ache that even in this, he was so sweet and considerate.

She glanced up at him, catching that glazed, feral look in his eye. She refused to break eye contact, and he sped up, making her heart thump in excitement to watch his face. Even the ache between her legs paled compared to her need to see him come.

Before she knew it, he was there. He growled and pulled her deeper than before, spilling down the back of her throat. She swallowed, and the look on his face was priceless. No walls, barriers, or hiding between them, nothing but raw emotion. Just the two of them. Damn, she loved him so much. His gasp, his fluttering lashes, the grip on her hair, she soaked up his response along with his cock.

A few minutes later, she rocked back onto her haunches and stood up. Still panting with one hand still on the wall, he wrapped the other on her hip. She placed a hand on his chest and raised her brows.

"Thank you, Gunner, for letting me suck your cock and the best Christmas I've ever had. Now will you make it worth my while?"

He barked out a laugh. "God, I don't know why that sass surprised me."

The grin that slid onto his face was worth every word out of her mouth. She'd do just about anything to keep him smiling and grinning like that. He pulled her into his arms, not caring that his pants were still around the top of his thighs. She snuggled into his chest and breathed in his pine and cedar musk. She felt so cherished and appreciated.

He cleared his throat. "Was that okay? You didn't mind the bossiness?"

She grinned into his shirt. "Nope, it was pretty hot."

He leaned back and tipped up her chin with a finger. Their eyes met, and he wore the biggest grin she'd ever seen. His eyes were relaxed, playful, and happy. It was a new look, one she wanted to see every day.

"You loved it, didn't you?"

She winked, slowly grinning too. "You bet your hot ass I did."

He leaned forward and kissed under her ear, nipping and causing goose bumps to race along her spine. "In that case, you're gonna love what I have planned for New Year's."

"Aw. Why ya gotta wait for New Year's? Is it another present? A surprise? I've never been—well, I haven't..." She glanced away, then pulled out of his arms. He situated himself in his pants as she faced the mirror. Her hair was mussed, her lipstick smudged. She looked so wicked... but happy too. She sighed.

"You haven't what, Maryanne?"

She met her own eyes in the mirror. She loved this man. Surely she had to be honest with him if she wanted him to stay with her.

Hadn't he pined for Justine because they hadn't been clear and straightforward with each other? That was a bunch of miscommunications. It was a win for Maryanne, but she didn't want to make the same mistake.

She turned to face him, leaned against the counter, and crossed her arms. "No one has ever given me stuff like this before."

He snorted. "I hope no one has ever given you a house or car before. It's kinda extra."

She laughed, finally meeting his eyes. His brow was arched as he just stood, waiting for her to talk.

"Not just big stuff. Little stuff too. I've only had a handful of boyfriends—"

He snorted again, making her frown.

"What? It's true. I've only had four boyfriends in my whole life."

"You're kidding me. You're a babe, Maryanne. You're *the* babe every guy in town wants to be with."

She shrugged. "Flirting's just to get people to like me. It means nothing. My first boyfriend was in high school, and specifically against my dad's rules."

He frowned. "I'm not going to place a ton of rules on us, but I do want exclusive."

She waved a hand. "Yeah, I do too. It's not about that. Listen, my high school boyfriend took my virginity on prom night and broke up with me. I had two boyfriends when I went to community college in Houston, one right after the other. We partied a lot, but they were more of a friend with benefits situation. We always went dutch and bought our own stuff, didn't celebrate any major holidays together."

She scuffed her foot on the wood grain tile, her mind whirling through the memories.

"And the fourth?" he prompted.

"That was Barry. He bought me flowers once, the week after we met, but somehow I always ended up paying for everything. Dinners, rent, the bakery I started after graduating. It was all me, although it was supposed to be a joint business. Only thing he did for the bakery was take over the finances. It took months to figure out how I could shut it down and leave without him knowing what I was doing. Thank God nothing was in his name."

"Why did you leave? What happened?"

She rubbed her temples and sighed. "I had seen some suspicious activity on the accounts for the bakery. When I tried to confront him, he wanted to talk it out over dinner. Then I'd forget what we were talking about, or I'd wake up the next day, and he'd say that we already talked about it and solved the problem."

"You're forgetful but not about stuff like that."

It warmed her heart that he knew small details about her.

"Right, it's why I have everything in my phone calendar. I hate forgetting things."

The silence stretched, comfortable and easy, before he asked, "So what exactly was happening there?"

"Same scenario every few weeks for about six months. I dug into our finances and our shared computer server at the bakery and found some nasty stuff. That's when I decided to audio record another confrontation on my phone."

She rubbed her arms, holding her broken one to take the pressure off. She didn't want to admit the next part, but he needed to know her past if they were going to make this work. She took a deep breath and stared at the tile.

"We'd gone to a restaurant, he slipped something into my drink, and I passed out. Some pretty nasty things were said between him and two other guys about me, my shop, and then some crazy shit involving drugs. After that, it took about a month to find a secret buyer for the bakery without him finding out. The same day I signed over the bakery, I packed up my car and headed home to Texas."

"What kind of crazy shit?"

She rubbed her forehead, relieved to finally have someone to talk to about this. "He was using the bakery as a money laundering front. We were legally selling edibles, but he was also funneling other drugs out of the store."

"Do you have proof? Is it in the accounts? The audio recording?"

She nodded, finally meeting his eyes. "Yeah, it's in my closet at the apartment."

"That's a big deal, M. Why didn't you go to the cops, if you had all that?"

She glared at the accusatory tone in his voice. "One of our regulars was a cop. He came in like clockwork, much like yourself. But unlike you, I'm pretty sure he was on someone's payroll, someone higher up than Barry. I didn't want to get further into it, didn't know who I could trust up there. All I wanted was to come home and forget any of it ever happened. Not even Mom or Cindy know about this stuff, Gunner."

He held up his hands, palms towards her and nodded. "Hey, it's alright. I'm on your side here."

"Are you sure? Because the tone of your voice makes me feel like I've done something wrong. You've already arrested me once. You could book me and extradite me to Colorado like Barry for being an accessory."

Gunner didn't look away from her. The silence stretched as he stood stoically, his granite expression never changing. She couldn't read his eyes, either. Finally, he walked to her and ran his hands up her arms.

"Maryanne, I'll always be on your side. No matter what, no matter how crazy the situation might be. Yes, I'm mad about your complete disregard of the law. I hate breaking the law, but that's my own internal mess to deal with. It'll never keep me from being on your side, alright?"

Her heart soared at his words. Maybe he was falling for her too? She placed a palm on his chest, over his heart. "Gunner, I've never broken a law that would hurt someone. I like order. Have you seen my apartment? There's control everywhere; otherwise, I'd find nothing."

"It's cute how you rearrange all the couch pillows to be exactly where they're supposed to be." He grinned, and she rolled her eyes.

"But all the stuff with Barry... that's why you need to understand that I never meant for the wedding to go the way it did. Drugged against your will... I've been there. You have to know how sorry I am that all that happened."

He arched a brow. "Hm, no mention of the brownies though?" His lips toyed with a grin, drawing her in and making her love this teasing side of him.

She settled her hands on his hips and smiled. "Hey, those brownies were on you. Those were in the safety of my own home, and you stole them."

He mock gasped. "How dare you. I would never steal."

But my heart. Her head unhelpfully supplied the thought that caused her stomach to roll and her heart to skip a beat.

She smiled shakily, his soft teasing smile making her want to draw out a real grin. "My own personal hero."

He kissed her softly on the lips. "Always yours, M. I'll always be on your side, but I can't ignore the law either. I can't risk my job or the election."

"I know. And I'm going to help. I'm going to meet with Ray and Charlie to talk campaign strategies next week."

Now he grinned. "That's sweet, babe, but you don't have to do that. It's going to be all good."

"I know, but it wouldn't hurt to have another pair of hands. Let me help, Gunner."

He nodded, then bent to kiss her. It was sweet, slow, and reminded her of how wet her panties still were. She deepened the kiss, and it quickly escalated. He grabbed her ass before reaching around to slide her zipper down. She kicked off her heels, and he pushed her pants and underwear all the way down. He knelt on the floor as she raised each leg, and he took them off.

He trailed his fingers up her legs softly, making her core pulse with need. He spread her legs slightly and blew on her overheated pussy, making her gasp. He glanced up, his eyes shining greener in the light, and smirked. When he slowly pressed her legs wider, she leaned back against the counter.

He saw her wince in pain, his eyes narrowing. "Shoulder?"

"It's fine. Keep going."

He frowned, then stood, which made her whimper until he grabbed her by the ass and sat her on the counter. He stepped between her legs and gave her a swift, hungry kiss. She was light-headed when he broke it off and knelt again. He spread her legs and slid a knee over each of his shoulders.

"There. Now lean back against the mirror. Gotta take care of my girl, now don't I?"

His words made her heart melt but when he glanced up and winked before licking her sopping pussy, she forgot what he'd said. God, those five o'clock whiskers raking across her sensitive skin and made her legs quake.

"Gunner," she gasped. He repeated the motion, slowly licking from pussy to clit. Only this time, he circled the nub once before applying with extra pressure. Her hips bucked, and she gasped, leaning back against the wall. Then he repeated the motion, circle and press, circle and press. Every time he repeated, he circled her clit an extra time.

She lost count after three. Her mind went numb as it tried to process all the sensations shooting through her. Of all the times they'd had sex, they'd never—he'd never...

Oh, God. He started sucking on her clit now, and that finger was teasing her entrance, making her quake and quiver and holding her on the edge.

"Gunner!"

At his name, he plunged two fingers inside as he sucked. Her hips bucked as he set up a fast rhythm. She moaned, reached forward, and grabbed the back of his head, pulling him harder onto her.

Those whiskers—she wanted more of that abrasive scratch on the itch that always started up when she thought of him. He slipped his fingers out, crossed them, then went back in.

She groaned as she came. He flattened his tongue and soothed her sensitive skin, lapping as her spasms slowed. He slid his fingers out, then slowly licked all the way up again, making her legs jump and her hips buck. He did it again, making her jerk.

When he did it a third time, she groaned. "Gunner, stop. I can't—"

He did it again, making her moan as he pressed his tongue against her clit and then rolled it. Only then did he ease back and stand, slipping between her legs and holding her close in his arms.

Chapter Thirty-Two

New Year's Eve was cold and wet. Maryanne had been sleeping better the past few weeks, and she couldn't be certain if it was the baby hormones or the fact that Gunner was beside her. Or maybe it was the mind-blowing sex they'd been having every day.

They settled into a sweet, domestic routine, even though he still had all his stuff at the bunkhouse. They'd returned the key to the realtor the Monday after Christmas, and she'd started the paperwork for purchase. They'd close on the new house in three weeks, and there was no need for him to move twice.

Tonight, Gunner would sing with his brothers at the Electric Cowboy to celebrate the New Year. All their friends were going, but this was going to be the boys' last hurrah. After this, Gunner and his brothers were only going to play once a month.

Gunner had told her they'd be getting a karaoke machine for the house soon, so they'd be able to sing together.

The Sheriff Gets His Girl

She liked the idea of them hanging out and having fun, but she hoped he wasn't giving up singing with his brothers just to have more time for her and the baby. She didn't want him to resent her.

When she asked, he said it was to prepare for being the sheriff, to give him more time to do that job more effectively. In her heart, she hoped it was because he wanted to be with her, though.

Maybe if she could be his First Lady and help him win the election, standing in the wings supporting him, he'd see she could be a good sheriff's wife. If he loved her, that is. Lord knows she didn't want to get trapped in a loveless marriage just because they were having a baby together.

Not that he'd given any kind of hint to his feelings or to marriage. Damn her female heart that was conditioned to get excited when the man she loved dropped to one knee or handed her a ring-shaped box.

Marriage hadn't crossed her mind at all until he'd done those. Then her heart had started to yearn for something more permanent with him.

Maryanne was in the bathroom putting the final touches on her makeup when he came home from work.

"Maryanne? You about ready? I got off work late, and we're going to miss opening if we don't hurry."

He stomped through the apartment, then rustled in the closet as she called out, "Yeah, I'm ready. Just one more thing."

She fiddled with her mascara while she waited for him to make his way to the bathroom. He stepped into the doorway and pulled his long sleeve shirt down over those abs she enjoyed so much.

Snap out of it, M! Remember the plan. Flirt, drive him crazy with want, and he'll fall in love and stay forever.

Blinking, she leaned against the counter to get closer to the mirror. Raising her ass in the air, her skin tight blue mini-skirt shining in the light, she grabbed her bright red lipstick and slowly put it on.

She finally met his gaze in the mirror. Her heart was already beating wildly as she capped the lipstick. "Hey, handsome. How was work?"

He grunted, then stepped behind her and placed his hands on either side of her on the counter. Never breaking eye contact, he smelled her hair, then slid his nose down the side of her neck before kissing the soft spot there. Goosebumps broke out over her skin, making her squirm and graze his crotch with her ass.

He pushed into her, slipping a hand into her v-cut orange top and cupping her breast.

"We can't be late, M, but I'm not sure I can survive the night with you looking like this and not do something about it. I've dreamed of you in this shirt since October when you came to the Cowboy wearing it."

She gasped when he rolled her nipple. "You saw me that night?"

He nodded, his jaw clenching. "It took everything I had to not punch every single guy who looked at you."

Her eyes widened, and she grinned. "You were jealous? Even then?"

He snorted. "Even always, Maryanne." He arched a brow, but she couldn't say anything over the knot in her throat. Had he always wanted her like she'd always wanted him?

Gunner growled, flicking her nipple as he stared at her in the mirror. "This is gonna make us late, but fuck, Maryanne."

Her eyes flared, and he moved both hands to her hips, grinding his cock on her ass in that mini-skirt. He ran his hand up the outside of her leg, making her sigh.

Those were the black thigh-high heels she'd worn on Halloween. His hand smoothed over her ass, and he groaned. She was going commando again. Damn it.

"Lean forward, elbows on the counter." Thank God her arm was healed, and she wasn't using the sling anymore.

The mirror in front of them made the little room feel bigger and gave the perfect view down her orange top. The vee that went to her navel showed her braless tits hanging down. She must not have realized because when she leaned forward, she gasped.

She tipped her leg forward a little, giving him access to dip a finger down her ass to her pussy. God, she was so soft and smooth. As he stroked gently back and forth, he smiled. It was like warm butter, creamy, rich, and wet. He just wanted to stick his corn on the cob inside and never take it out.

He slipped a finger in, and she moaned while he rubbed circles around her clit and then stroked in and out. She was ready and waiting for him.

He unzipped himself, pulling painfully free, and teased her opening with his cock. He slid in just the tip and breathed.

"See those tits? How they look when you bend over? When you wore this shirt and went to play pool, all those guys were hanging around. That's why. Because your tits are fucking magnificent."

He slid in and out slowly, amazed that his mouth was working at all as her tight snatch clamped down on him.

"All I thought about for months after that night in the bar was bending you over the pool table and fucking you until you screamed. You ready to scream for me, little girl?"

"Hell, yeah."

Her mouth was open, and he ached to feel her mouth wrapped around him again. The flare of excitement in her eyes caused an answering flare in his veins.

Adrenaline rushed in as he slowly withdrew and slid back home. He picked up the speed and grabbed her hips to slam in harder. Her tits bounced, and he reached a hand forward and pulled them free of the shirt.

Grabbing her hips again, she moaned. "Yes, Gunner. Yes, harder."

"Have you been a bad girl, Maryanne?"

She gasped and her eyes widened. Then she nodded quickly, moaning, "God, yes."

He set up a steady pace and kneaded her ass with his palms. "Is this what you need, M?"

She groaned in response. He reared back and spanked her ass the way she liked it. Just hard enough to make a satisfying smack.

She gasped, "Oh!"

"You like that, babe?" He reared back and spanked her harder.

She clenched around him as she said, "God yes, spank me, G." He slammed in and out, trying to distract himself from the rising need to fill her pussy.

He spanked her again. "Is that what you want? Say it."

"Yes, Gunner. Spank my ass."

He looked up from her pinkening ass and met her eyes

in the mirror. Raising a brow, she moaned as he slammed into her again, hard and fast now. Her eyes were wild, drawing him deeper under her spell.

God, this woman. He spanked her a little harder. Her moans escalated to gasps and then to tiny incoherent screams of "Yes—" and "Fu—" before she shattered inside. She screamed, "Ahh" as she spasmed around his cock.

It sent off a chain reaction in him, and he slammed her hips into the counter as he came with her. He slowed his pumping until he finally held still.

He wrapped an arm around her waist and leaned his head on her back, the other hand holding a breast as their breathing slowly returned to normal. When he slipped out, she grabbed some toilet paper, and they cleaned up in silence, their breath still ragged.

He bent forward and rested his forehead on hers. Sucking in a breath, he sighed slowly and leaned back, smiling softly as he kissed each corner of her mouth.

"Just wait until tonight. I've arranged with Katie to close up for her, and I intend to lay you on that pool table and feast on your decadent pussy before bending you over and watching those tits move as I fuck you."

She moaned, leaning in to follow him as he stepped away and strode through the apartment to the front door.

She slipped her makeup into the drawer, and followed him, her mind still trying to catch up from having her brains screwed out. When she reached the front door, he held open her jacket and she shrugged it on.

She'd stopped wearing the sling and was only feeling a

slight twinge in her shoulder now. The doctor's appointment was next week to get the cast off. They walked down the stairs to his truck.

"You already started it?" She held her hands up to the heater, the cab warm.

He shifted into gear. "Yeah, when I left work and walked over, before coming upstairs to change. I didn't want it to be cold for you or peanut."

Her body melted, and it wasn't from the seat warmers. "Gunner... that's so sweet. No one's ever—well, taken care of me like that." He was constantly taking her by surprise.

"I told you, M. I know what you need, what you want, and will take care of you."

"Yeah, but saying and doing are two totally different things."

Music played softly as they left town and drove to the bar. The darkness was stark, the mist not heavy enough for the windshield wipers.

When they arrived, Gunner kept his hand on the small of her back as they wove through the crowd. He waved at his brothers already tuning up on stage, but turned her toward the back room.

When they stepped through the saloon doors, she saw that all their friends had already taken up nearly every booth in the room. Cindy and Andy were still gone on their honeymoon, but Holly and Lola were here, along with some of their other friends from yoga and girl's night.

"Hey, guys! Are we ready for some dancing?" Maryanne grinned as she stood next to their booth.

"Let's do it!" Holly practically bounced in her seat.

Gunner leaned over and kissed her on the cheek, growling into her ear, "I'm going to go join the boys. Be safe. Don't flirt too much, or I might punch someone, alright?"

Maryanne leaned back to look at him in surprise. His arched brow told her he was dead serious, and it made her blush. A grin spread across her lips as she nodded. "Sure thing, G."

"Lola, look out for my girl tonight." Lola grinned and gave him a thumb's up before he walked out the door.

Maryanne's stomach twisted. He'd just publicly called her his girl. That was a first, and it felt good, right, loved.

When she slid into the booth, they both looked at her expectantly. "What?"

"You're his girl." Holly squealed.

"That was so fucking adorable. And I've never found Gunner to be adorable before, not even when we were kids." Lola crossed her arms as she leaned back in the seat. Kendall walked up and slid into the booth with Lola. She pushed against the far wall, trying to keep space between them.

"Hey, what are we talking about?" He was probably the only guy in the place dressed in slacks and a button-down shirt. He might have acclimated to living in Crimson Creek, but he hadn't changed that much.

"Gunner called Maryanne his girl." Holly grinned, elbowing Maryanne.

Maryanne blushed as Kendall swung his eyes to hers. He frowned. "Yeah, about that. Don't lie to your doctor. Just say you don't want to discuss it if a question makes you uncomfortable, okay?"

"Fine, I won't lie to the doctors, but you gotta admit, that question wasn't necessary."

"What are y'all talking about?" Holly frowned.

Maryanne raised a brow and crossed her arms. "Kendall asked me in the hospital who the father was."

Lola smacked Kendall on the arm. "Ken doll, that's so unprofessional of you. You're practically asking for gossip."

A waitress came over with a pitcher of water and a pitcher of something fruity while Lola and Kendall started bickering.

"Oh, we haven't ordered anything yet," Holly said to the woman.

She just smiled. "It's alright. Gunner's sent it over. He's also ordered appetizers for the table and told me to ask Maryanne if she wanted anything specific." The woman looked at each of the three friends at the table. Holly and Lola stared at her as she blushed and raised her hand.

"That'd be me. Um, whatever he ordered is fine. What's in the pitcher?"

"This is a mocktail Caribbean sunrise. So orange and lemon juice, grenadine—completely alcohol free."

Holly sighed with a grin. "Aw, he's so sweet."

Maryanne grinned. "Thank you," she told the waitress. When the woman walked away, she leaned forward and said, "He takes *such* good care of me. It's unreal."

"Did I hear something about a house?" Kendall asked.

Maryanne beamed. "Yes, we move in a few weeks. You'll have to help. We'll make a weekend out of it and order pizza and beer for everyone."

"And he bought her a fucking car for Christmas!" Lola raised a brow at Kendall, who just rolled his eyes at her.

"I'm going to miss you not being right across the street," Holly said softly. Maryanne met her eyes across the table and smiled sadly.

"Me too. Maybe someday we'll live across the street from each other again." Holly seemed to perk up at that thought. Just then the waitress returned with their appetizer sampler platter as the band started to play in the main room.

"Oh, jalapeno poppers are my favorite!" Holly clapped her hands, but Maryanne pushed them away. Her stomach was not going to handle those tonight. Those little mini burgers though... she swiped all three onto the tiny plate that had been passed to her.

Chapter Thirty-Three

"About time you showed up." Parker mouthed off like the annoying little brother he was.

Gunner shrugged and hopped onto the stage. "Y'all get the song list I sent earlier this week? The group text has been weirdly quiet."

Hunter grunted, ignoring them as always.

Landry slugged him in the arm with a sly grin. "You just want to dance with Maryanne, don't you? That's why there are no slow songs until after midnight."

He tried to play it cool, but Parker egged him on. "It's more like he doesn't want to see Maryanne dancing any slow songs with anyone else, I bet."

Hunter even joined in with this brotherly smack talk. "It's probably both, but he can't come right out and tell her not to dance with anyone else. He's probably not ready to send that kind of message yet."

"What kind of message?" Gunner growled, crossing his arms as they tuned up their instruments.

Landry rolled his eyes. "The one that says you're completely in love with her, moron."

"I am not in love with her."

"She's definitely more than just a baby mama." Hunter piped up from the drum set.

Gunner wiped a hand down his face. "Maybe she is, maybe she isn't. It's too early to tell. I'm trying to look at this objectively."

Parker snorted, then choked on a cough. Landry slapped him on the back until he gasped.

"That's fucking hilarious. You're in so much denial."

He raked his hand through his hair and turned away from his dick head brothers. No, she wasn't just his baby mama, but he didn't want to have a relationship just because of the baby. People who got together because of a baby or people who had a baby to save a relationship—well, it'd never worked out for any of his Marine buddies. He didn't want to jump in too fast with Maryanne; he wanted to develop something real and lasting beyond sharing a kid together.

He bounced on his feet and frowned as he grabbed the microphone. "Whatever. Are you assholes ready yet?" At their murmurs of assent, he flipped on the microphone and welcomed the crowd. They started the party with *Uptown Funk* by Mark Ronson and Bruno Mars, and the dance floor overflowed.

Soon, Maryanne shimmied onto the dance floor, drawing his eyes like a moth to flame. He watched with a smile as she danced with abandon. It didn't matter what song they played, she sang with them and danced like she hadn't a care in the world. He ached to dance with her, to hold her in his arms as they swayed to a slow song.

Maryanne stayed mostly in sight until almost midnight.

She'd gone to the bar for some water and sat with one of his poker buddies, Nick, for a while.

Gunner had seen him and Kendall taking turns hovering. Both former military, he was glad he'd asked them to watch out for her tonight. Not that she couldn't handle herself, but because he needed to know she was safe and had help if she needed it.

Landry caught his eye as they finished the song and tapped his watch. Gunner checked his.

"All right, all you cool cats and kittens. We have time for one more song before the ball drops at midnight. We're going old school on it too." Etta James' *At Last* started up and Maryanne froze on the dance floor. Everyone else paired off, but she stepped closer until she was right before him.

His eyes locked with Maryanne's, his entire body hummed with awareness of hers, and he sang to her. Why was it so much easier to communicate with her like this? Her eyes were tearing up as she swayed in place. When the last notes faded, he jumped down in front of her.

He grabbed her hands as Landry turned into the mic. "All right, we've got less than a minute 'til midnight. Pair up if you're gonna. Otherwise, grab your drink, and we'll raise a glass as we ring in the New Year."

She smiled a watery smirk at him, and he wanted to wrap her up in his arms and never let go. How did she do this to him? How did she twist him to pieces and toss him around? His chest felt like it was going to explode, and he didn't even know how to make it better. Did he need space from her? Or did he need to be closer?

His cock voted for closer. And there was that midnight kiss...

She didn't speak, not that they could hear each other

over the din of the wordless music or the chatter of those around them.

Landry spoke into the mic. "Here we go, folks! Ten—nine—eight—"

He watched her lips count, her ruby red lipstick drawing him in closer. The faint smell of cinnamon teased his nostrils, a clean haven in a sea of salty sweat around them. The lights flicked off at each number, pitching them in semi-darkness, the stage lights on his brothers illuminating her beautiful face.

His hands squeezed hers, then slid around her waist as hers wrapped around his neck. She was so small compared to him. It made him feel like a bull in a china shop anytime he was around her, afraid she was too fragile and would break everywhere. His lips tingled as he heard the crowd chant.

"Two—one—Happy New Year!"

He crushed her lips. Sweeping his tongue inside, he groaned, picking her up and tilting her head back with his as he took the kiss deeper. She pulled at his hair, clawed at his back, and made his dick leap in his jeans.

Setting her on her feet, he placed little kisses along her jaw to her ear. He felt her gasp when he nipped it, then licked and sucked the soft spot beneath. The band played *Auld Lang Syne*, then seamlessly transitioned into Pink's *Raise Your Glass*.

When the second started, Maryanne pulled back. Eyes wide, grin wider, she started jumping and singing along. It was infectious. Besides, it'd be weird for him to just stand there. He started jumping and pumping his arm in the air with her, the other hand finding and holding hers the entire time.

Her smile was as bright as those stage lights. Her

smudged lipstick made him happy too. It was the best New Year he'd ever had, and he hoped they could do this every New Year, actually.

Holy shit. Did he really want that? The song ended and another up-tempo one started. He got her attention and made the drinking motion with his hand, nodding to the bar. She nodded, then turned back to the stage to keep dancing.

Well, he'd wanted her to come with him, but no matter. He'd grab their drinks, then take a break in the back room with her. Just a little longer, and then she'd be all his.

For the night. She'd be all his for the night. It'd take time to make her his forever. He ordered a beer and her mocktail. While he waited, he turned to watch her, and Kendall joined him, nodding at Maryanne.

"How's it going?"

Gunner shrugged. "Fine, I guess."

"Congrats on the house. That's a big place for you, her, and a baby. Y'all gonna make a relationship work and fill that house up with more babies?"

Gunner's heart seized. Was that what he wanted? He was just focusing on the relationship now; he hadn't even thought of more kids. The vision of her in the kitchen danced in his head again. There were kids and dogs running around, causing chaos as she laughed in the midst of it. It was loud and messy and joyful.

His palms were sweaty, so he raked them down his jeans and shrugged again. He took a sip of his beer to ease the knot in his throat.

"What about marriage? Holly said there was a proposal vibe going on between you two."

He frowned, glancing at Kendall. "What do you mean?"

"Well, Holly said that you got down on one knee but

then asked her to buy a house instead of proposing. Then for Christmas, you gave her a ring box, but it had keys in it. So, are you just teasing her or what?"

Gunner's blood ran cold as he blinked at Kendall. Kendall's eyes widened, and he laughed. "Holy shit. You didn't realize you did that, did you?"

Gunner just blinked again.

How could he have been so stupid? Of course, a girl he'd knocked up would read that kind of thing into those gestures. Fuck. He raked his hand through his hair and turned back to the bar.

This was going so fast. He wanted to date her, get to know her, and see if they could work long term, but she was already expecting a marriage proposal? He felt his blood run cold and his hands shake.

Kendall slapped him on the back, making him jump.

"Hey, man. It's okay. She's obviously fine without it, so don't think about it. I mean, you're moving in together, right?"

"Yeah, but if she's expecting a proposal—"

"Hey, just take it day by day, okay? No need to put a label on anything. Although..."

"Although what?" What kind of bomb was he going to drop next?

"Well, with the election this month, there's probably going to be questions about your relationship status. How are you going to answer that? You know how these old ladies in town get. So—while you don't need to label anything or define how long you'll live there or whatever—you may want to talk with Maryanne about at least acknowledging publicly that she's a girlfriend."

Gunner snorted. "I called her my girl earlier, but then told my brothers she's just my baby mama."

"But—" Kendall stuttered to a stop as a hand slid between them to the mocktail on the counter. Gunner turned his head to meet the blazing eyes of Maryanne.

"Don't let me interrupt. Please, continue. I'm just gonna stand here and listen as I drink." She wrapped those luscious red lips around the straw. She swirled her tongue around it, then she bit the straw with her teeth before sucking a drink. His cock twitched even as his head registered the deep shit he was in with her.

Kendall cleared his throat and waved at someone across the dance floor. "Oh look. Holly's dancing with two guys now. I'm going to go break that up. See y'all later."

Gunner glared at him for leaving but as Kendall stepped behind Maryanne to walk away, he just shook his head and mouthed, "Nope."

Maryanne slid onto the barstool beside him and spun to face the dance floor. "What time are we heading home?"

"Why? Are you tired? We can go now." He didn't want to go now. He had plans for her, but if she needed rest…

She shook her head before he could finish the thought. "Nope, I'm having a blast and wide awake. Zarrel's working in the morning, so I'm good."

"Last call is at one. I promised Katie that I'd help get everyone out the door. Then I need to do some drive-bys and make sure everything's quiet before going home."

"A cop's job is never done, huh?"

"Yeah, something like that."

The silence stretched between them, filled only with two songs from the band. She spun to put her now empty drink back on the bar and hopped off the stool. Her breasts jiggled in that orange sequined top. He both feared and hoped to catch sight of a nipple, but it didn't happen.

"About earlier. If you want to tell the town we're girlfriend and boyfriend because it'll help with the campaign, that's fine. If you wanna tell them I'm just your baby mama, that's fine too. Just give me a heads up on what you decide, m'kay? And I'll act accordingly."

She flipped her hair behind her shoulder and wove her way through the crowd toward the bathroom.

She'd taken that better than he'd expected. Maybe she hadn't been that mad after all. He set down his beer and went to finish the set with his brothers.

Maryanne came back onto the dance floor, mesmerizing him with her hips as she moved with the music. She spun into some guy's arms, and Gunner felt his jaw about crack.

He might have missed a line in the song, but his mind was on the way she was touching first one guy's bicep, then slow dancing with another, only for a fourth guy to cut in and finish the slow dance. His knuckles were white on the microphone as he watched the guy's hands dip dangerously low on her lower back.

It was the flirty smile on her face that kept him from marching across the dance floor and socking the guy in the mouth. He didn't want to break the law, but he also wanted to see that smile on her face, even if it wasn't directed at him.

After an hour of that torture, people started trickling out the door. Maryanne disappeared when they started to pack up their instruments.

"That was fun. I'm going to miss playing with y'all every weekend." Landry wiped a fake tear off his eyelash, making Parker laugh.

Hunter yawned. "I'm not. I'm getting too old for this shit. Best thing that happened was Gunner getting Maryanne knocked up so we could start backing off here."

Landry laughed, but Gunner didn't register it because

he saw orange sequins sparkling through the faint lights, heading toward the back room. Had she heard that too? Was she mad? She'd not come back from the bathroom to dance the rest of the night. Instead, she'd gone to the back room. He'd missed seeing her while he sang.

When the rest of the patrons filed out the door, Katie locked the door and turned to him.

"Door's locked, so when you leave, just make sure it's shut all the way behind you, okay? I'm going to make sure the kitchen's cleaned, then I'll be heading out the back. Don't stay the night and don't make a mess."

"When have I ever made a mess? I'm the guy who cleans them up, remember?"

She snorted as she wove through the tables. "Yeah, I remember that huge mess you made in Chemistry junior year."

"Hey, that doesn't count."

She laughed, waving over her shoulder as she swung through the kitchen door. Gunner stepped into the back room but couldn't find Maryanne anywhere. He searched the rest of the bar, every step feeling like a lead weight slammed into his stomach.

Finally, he pulled out his phone. No texts or missed calls or anything, so he called her.

"Hello?" Her voice was sleepy on the other end.

"Maryanne? Where are you? Are you okay?"

"Yeah, I'm fine. I'm home and asleep. What's wrong, Gunner?"

He pinched the bridge of his nose and breathed deeply.

"Fine, I'm going back to sleep. See you later, G."

He stared at the phone, not believing she'd actually hung up on him. He finished closing up the bar, locked up, and then did his rounds for work. When he got home at three-thirty, he found her awake and in the shower.

He took off his clothes and tossed them in the hamper before walking naked to the shower. He stepped in behind her, spun her around, and quickly wrapped his arms around her in a hug. His heart seemed to thaw in the hot water, the knot in his stomach dissolving at having her in his arms safe and sound.

He ducked to kiss her, but she ducked to the side, making him kiss her cheek instead. When he pulled back with a frown, her eyes were wide awake and flashing in the bathroom lights.

"Morning, G. How was work?"

He growled. "Maryanne, you didn't tell me you were going home. I was worried about you."

She shrugged, then pulled the curtain back and stepped out, leaving him alone in the shower.

"That's weird. Not sure why you'd be so worried about your baby mama. I mean, if we were in a relationship or something, then yeah, I'd keep you informed. But a baby mama? Nah."

He tapped his head against the tile, before sighing and washing his hair and body. When he finished and dried off, only five minutes had passed, but Maryanne was already dressed and braiding her hair.

"Where are you going? You don't have to work today."

He slipped on his shorts and followed her to the kitchen where she slipped on her cowboy boots.

"Does it matter? Don't need to tell my baby daddy my schedule, even if he did buy me a house and a car. Not sure *baby mama* fits what's going on here, as it seems like I'm more of a kept woman than anything."

She glanced at him under her lashes and looked away,

but not before he saw that hurt look in her eye. She grabbed her jacket, purse, and keys.

"See you later, G. Sleep well." She slammed the front door behind her, the icy air just enough to chill him to the bones as he stood wondering what the hell had just happened.

He strode the windows in the living room and watched, hoping and then sighing in relief as she walked across the street and unlocked the bakery door.

He watched her lock it closed, then saw lights flip on as she went deeper into the back of the shop. Her tablet! He grabbed her tablet and accessed the camera app, flipping cameras until he saw her sink onto the chaise lounge in her office.

She curled up on her side. No sound came through the speakers, but he didn't need them. Her shoulders were shaking, and he wanted to throw up to think of her hurting and alone, to think that he was the one who'd caused the tears and couldn't fix it. He was well and truly fucked.

Chapter Thirty-Four

Second week of January

She pushed open the door to the bakery and pasted on a grin for Zarrel. The past few weeks of strictly maintaining her distance from Gunner were making her even more short-tempered than normal, and she didn't want to take it out on him.

"Morning, boss. How's it going today?"

She took a deep breath of the fresh bread he was taking out of the oven. Her stomach rumbled, and she smiled.

"I'm doing alright. Morning sickness is still going strong, but other than that it's fine Dude, this is the best biscuit I've ever tasted!"

He grinned. "It was my mama's recipe. I put some peppermint tea on your desk. You still sick all day?"

She winced. "Yeah."

"Are you going to talk to the doctor about it?"

She nodded. "The books say it should be over by the second trimester, but I'm going strong."

Zarrel put some scones into the oven and frowned at her. "You're already in the second trimester? Are you even gaining weight?"

She swiped a warm roll and avoided his eyes as she walked to the office. "Nope, I'm going to get caught up on some paperwork for half an hour before we open. Holler if you need me."

He didn't respond or press her for more details. She tried to shrug off her anxiety about doing all she could for the baby. She was taking the stupid vitamins, drinking water. Hell, she was even going to bed at a reasonable hour at night.

Of course, she was falling asleep much easier when Gunner spooned her and held her legs down with one of his. Even though she separated them in the bed with a pillow, he still somehow spooned her for a good portion of the night.

As angry as she was at him for sending so many mixed signals, she savored those sweet moments in the early morning when he was deep asleep, just before her alarm went off.

She was almost done with the paperwork when the doctor called.

"Hello?" Why was the doctor calling? Her stomach roiled.

"Yes, is this Maryanne?"

"Yep." Was something wrong? Her palms started to sweat.

"Awesome. We got your blood tests back from your January appointment. Have you been feeling more tired lately?"

"Well, yeah, but isn't that part of being pregnant?"

"Normally, yes. But your blood work says you're anemic, which can cause extreme fatigue. I'd like you to come in tomorrow to get some iron infusions to see if that helps."

"And that's safe for the baby? Will it help with morning sickness too?"

"Yes, it's safe. Are you still experiencing morning sickness?"

"Yes, I thought it was getting better when we had the appointment last week, but it's not really. I'm nauseous when I wake up. Then the rest of the day I'm hungry, but every time I eat, I throw up within about half an hour. Doesn't matter the time of day."

"Hm. Yes, the infusions should help with that too. What's your availability?"

She scheduled the appointment, added it to her phone's calendar and the calendar on the wall, and hung up as she walked to the front of the shop.

Stopping at the restroom, she threw up the honey biscuit she'd eaten earlier, pulled the toothbrush out from under the cabinet, and cleaned up before opening the door. It was like clockwork, her morning sickness.

The hours flew by with customers coming in. Zarrel's breads were a great addition to the pastries, donuts, and such that were already served. She was yawning by two when they closed the doors for the day.

Zarrel shooed her with a dish towel. "Go on. Get to bed with you. I'll clean up here."

"Thanks. I'll only get a small nap before I need to go pick up Owen and Mandy from preschool." She waved as she left.

Her phone alarm went off an hour later. She rolled off the couch and washed up, then grabbed the kids from school. They went to the playground, did some grocery shopping for Cindy, picked up James and Cody, and headed to Andy and Cindy's house.

She'd just finished making chicken and rice around seven when her phone rang.

"Hello?"

"Where the hell are you?" Gunner grumbled on the other line.

"It's Tuesday. You have poker night, and it's my day for babysitting my nephews and niece."

"It's not on the calendar in the apartment."

"Sorry. It's a standing thing. I'll add it to every Tuesday when I get home."

"When will that be?"

"I should be there before you get back from poker night. I have been doing this every Tuesday since before you moved in. Don't you remember last week?"

Her voice was pointedly digging at him. Seriously, he'd moved in almost a month ago, and he didn't know what she did every Tuesday? Just like a man to not pay attention to the details if it didn't apply to him.

"All right. I'll see you later then."

"M'kay. Bye." She hung up on him. If she didn't hang up first, she'd say something stupid like "I love you" or "Fuck off, Gunner. You don't own me." She sighed, unsure of how to resolve the distance between them.

Thursday was girl's night yoga at Holly's studio. Maryanne was in the middle of tree pose, her mind finally clearing from all the emotional upheaval, when her phone rang.

"Hello?"

"Where are you?" Gunner asked. She sighed. This was Tuesday night all over again.

"Thursday night is girls' night, so I'm at Holly's for yoga."

He growled from the other end and the silence stretched. She felt the stares of the rest of the women in the room.

"Are you home? There's a casserole in the oven, if you're hungry." She was trying to bridge the gap between them but it was quickly turning into a canyon.

He sighed. "Yeah, have fun and tell everyone I said hi."

"Will do, bye." She hung up first again. She tossed her phone onto her workout towel and turned back to the group. Their circle had grown in the past few months to nearly a dozen women ranging from twenties to forties. And now all eyes were on her. She gulped, pasted on a smile, and followed along as Holly led them into warrior one pose.

"What was that all about?" Lola whispered beside her. Cindy was on the other side of her and the three of them were at the front of the class right in front of Holly.

She whispered back, "Gunner was just worried. He's called twice this week because I wasn't home when he got home."

"Doesn't he know your schedule by now? It's been over a month since he moved in." Her sister had a point.

"Apparently not. I've even written it on the wall calendar in both my apartment and in the bakery—you know how I forget things—but he still calls and checks." She wasn't sure if she felt loved because he was worried about her or if she felt suffocated because he had to know everywhere she went. The lack of sex was frustrating too.

"It's kind of sweet. I miss having someone care about where I am." Holly sighed, then led them into warrior two.

"How upset was he about the first debate?" Lola asked.

"He was so disappointed. But instead of talking about it, he closed himself off. The man talks as much as a tree—not at all." It would be one thing if she could read his face or knew his emotions. But every time they were in a room together the past week, he projected such a wall of... well, it wasn't frustration or anger that she felt rolling off him. Just —emptiness. Coldness.

It made her want to do something crazy to shake him out of it. She wanted the passion, the fire, the real him that he kept hidden from the world. She missed him.

Holly snorted. "Maybe because you're still punishing him for the New Year's thing."

Cindy added, "Freezing him out isn't going to work, Maryanne. You need to talk to him."

"The silent treatment is a bitch," a woman from behind her said. Maryanne glanced over her shoulder and nodded with a smile. It was the new mayor's sister, the lawyer. They smiled, commiserating together, before Holly led them into the next pose.

The rest of the yoga session ended without incident, but as they were all getting ready to leave, Maryanne walked over to the mayor's sister.

"Hey, Jade. How's it going? Haven't seen you in the bakery in a while." Maryanne remembered swimming with the sisters at the town pool when they were kids.

"It's going well, but I went gluten-free, so I've been staying away from the bakery. Sorry about that!" The blond woman pushed her long bangs out of her blue eyes as she packed up her gym bag.

"That's alright. We do have gluten-free options though, if that helps."

"Oh, I didn't realize. I might stop by next week then." Her blue eyes were so big and the bangs just made them pop even more.

"That'd be great. I was actually wondering if I can stop by your office next week? I have a few questions." Maryanne juggled her gym bag and fidgeted with her water bottle.

"Oh sure. Let me pull up my calendar on my phone. Just a sec."

They made an appointment, and Maryanne put it in her own phone calendar with reminders. A wave of exhaustion hit her as she told the girls bye and walked across the street to her building.

She really wanted to talk with Gunner and get their relationship back on track, but it wasn't going to happen tonight. She yawned as she walked up the stairs.

Swinging by the attorney's office after work, she walked through the door and smiled at Jade.

"Hey, I brought you some of our gluten-free treats. Thanks for meeting with me today."

Maryanne sat the box on the desk and settled into the chair. The office was small with just one big room and two desks in it. The door to the bathroom was visible down a short hallway that led to a private area in the back.

It was in the older part of town by the Old Mill, but it was well kept. The tile floor sparkled in the January sunlight and the cream-colored walls had large forest landscapes that made the whole place feel homey and not like a lawyer's office at all.

Jade tucked her blond hair back into her bun and pushed up her glasses with a smile. "Oh thank you. I didn't stop for lunch today. These are going to be perfect. Would you mind if I ate one while you explain what's going on?"

Maryanne nodded, then started from years ago. She explained all that had happened with Barry in Colorado, the incident at Halloween, the arrest in November, and her thoughts on him trying to plant Chester in her shop.

She explained what had happened on Halloween with Gunner and the THC, what happened with the whiskey cake in December at Cindy's wedding.

Halfway through, Jade passed her a bottle of water. But it wasn't until the story was over and Maryanne realized an hour had already passed that she twisted it open and drank.

"So now I've been called to testify in Colorado later this month, and I'm not sure what all to expect. I spoke with the prosecutor on the phone, and I received this letter in the mail with some details. But can you maybe tell me what's going to happen? Or coach me on some things they might ask? Will they try to pin me as an accessory for what was happening at my shop because I didn't report it?"

Jade read the letter Maryanne placed on the desk, then they talked. After two more hours, a review of one of her old thumb drives from Colorado on the computer, and a phone call to the prosecutor's office, Maryanne left with confidence and peace. She felt prepared and knew what she needed to say.

She also felt better about the fact that Jade had arranged for her testimony to be with the judge and the two lawyers in his chambers. She was adamant that she did not want to see or be in the same room as Barry. Thankfully, Jade had agreed and made it happen.

She drove home and parked, wondering how she was going to tell Gunner about the trip to Colorado next month.

With as overprotective as he'd been this month on needing to know her whereabouts, he might demand to go with her. Her head hurt as she tromped up the stairs to her apartment.

Chapter Thirty-Five

Third week of January

"What a fucking nightmare. Do I have to go through this again?"

Gunner paced at the police station. All the guys had dropped by on their way to the debate next door to give him a pep talk because the last few weeks had been hard. Not just because Maryanne had been giving him the cold shoulder, but because the first debate had left him a tongue-tied fool.

Landry handed him a water, and Gunner wanted to wipe the smirk off his face. Instead, he spun on his heel and paced the other direction, taking a sip to cool down.

"This is the last debate, G. You can do it." Maryanne arched a brow and spun slowly in his office chair.

"Hey, I tried to warn you those old biddies would go for the throat." Kendall didn't look up from him phone.

Parker snorted. "And you just stood there, staring at

them as they asked questions. Why didn't you answer, man?"

"I couldn't fucking think with them all yammering away like that!" Gunner growled.

The courthouse's meeting hall had been crowded last week. It took up the entire bottom floor of the building, as the offices were upstairs. Roughly two hundred residents had crammed into the building, most of them older folks. It had looked like a fucking wedding with Willowby's people on one side of the aisle and Gunner's on the other.

It had started off alright. The new mayor, Ruby, was young and bright-eyed. Up 'til now, she'd run a law practice partnership with her sister, but she was taking to the new role well.

She'd organized the entire shindig. There was an open forum where townspeople came up and said what they wanted out of a mayor. Then Willowby and he had taken turns answering questions that Mayor Ruby had asked.

Except the townspeople still interrupted. And Willowby kept turning to the audience and inciting them to speak up, like he was a preacher encouraging them to go well beyond an acceptable "amen."

The next and thankfully last debate was tonight, and he felt like he was going to throw up. How could he get the whole thing to fall into order and be how it was supposed to be?

"You're going to be fine, Gunner. We've prepped for this, remember?" Maryanne crossed her arms and leaned back in his office chair. He was nervous, not that it showed on his face. He just raked his hand through his hair and turned to pace some more.

Maryanne's voice soothed him.

"I've talked to the girls. We're going to be your backup bitches tonight and keep it all going smooth." Gunner turned to see Holly nod behind Maryanne's shoulder, and Lola crack her knuckles.

Landry and Parker laughed, making Gunner smile, his eyes narrowing in on Maryanne. The past few weeks had been stressful, mostly because they weren't back to that easy camaraderie they had developed over the Christmas break. She kept pillows between them at night, they'd not cuddled on the couch while watching tv, and of course, there was no sex.

Three fucking weeks of being near her but not being able to hold her was pure torture. Speaking of, he sighed, already tired and dreading the debate tonight.

"Come on. Let's get this torture over with." He strode out the building, and his friends followed.

Maryanne watched Gunner walk to the front of the town hall meeting room in the Court House, and she took her seat behind his mom.

Holly leaned over. "You still haven't made up with him? How long are you going to freeze him out?"

Maryanne shushed her, waving at Ava's back in the seat in front of them. "As long as necessary."

Lola sat on her other side. "Y'all didn't touch at all tonight, not even to hold hands as we walked from one building to the next."

"Hey, I'm not happy about it either, but this will make him realize I'm more than his baby mama. Or he'll realize that it's all I am. If he hasn't figured it out by the election, we'll talk about it." Maryanne had tried so many times to talk to him, but one of them was always tired, out of the apartment, or asleep.

Mayor Ruby stood on the stage and tapped the microphone, making Holly and Lola sit back in their chairs. Kendall and some others were spread throughout the room, and Andy and Cindy sat on the back row, kissing and giggling.

"Good evening, Crimson Creek! Hope y'all are ready for tonight's sheriff debate. We're going to keep it more civilized tonight and jump right into it. Mr. Willowby, you're first. Will you please tell the people what your focus will be as sheriff?"

The old man tapped his microphone until it screeched. He reared back and raked a hand through this thick bushy white hair. "Yes, as we all know, the general population of Crimson Creek is split into three groups. My age, the young upstart here, and then the kids. The kids have great programs, and I'd like to expand on that. As sheriff, I'd like to see more patrolling on the ball fields and games to keep the riff raff out. I believe this is the only way the town vandalism will stop."

Maryanne froze on her chair, her eyes riveted to Chase. Would he give them away? Her palms began to sweat as Willowby continued.

"The parents in this town are doing great and taking care of business. But for those my age, I'm going to provide security for the senior citizens single cruise in February and future events like that. We need a monthly town dance where people can get off the streets and mingle. Not just for those my age, but for all three groups. That's my plan as sheriff."

The crowd applauded, murmuring to themselves. Mayor Ruby smiled and then turned to Gunner, who cleared his throat. Maryanne's stomach danced with nervous energy, and she prayed it went well.

"Your turn, Deputy. What do you plan on doing as sheriff?"

He shifted on his feet, then took a deep breath. "Crimson Creek is growing. The past few years have seen dozens of families and people move to town. With the increase in population comes certain security and safety needs. We need to expand the police department and hire at least one more full-time deputy, or possibly two or three part-time deputies."

He looked over the crowd, but when he caught her gaze, his stiff shoulders slackened and he smiled. His voice grew firmer, more confident as he continued.

"We need to be out and about in town and on the roads, helping wherever we're needed. If a cow gets out and crosses the road, the sheriff's department is the one that gets called. If anything happens in this town, anything from a lost kid—both of the human and goat variety—to domestic issues, we come running, but we need more deputies to handle the load."

He looked away, and she felt bereft and cold.

"As sheriff, my first action would be to hire and train new recruits. My second action would be to improve communication by updating our equipment. We have mobile equipment that is relatively modern, but the police station itself needs new Wi-Fi, computers, and processing equipment. This will go a long way in making sure our town is secure if anything major happens."

"Major like the big arrest you made last month?" Some old codger yelled out from behind her. She sucked in a breath, not just because of the mention of Barry but to see if Gunner would let it throw him off his speech that they'd practiced for hours.

"Yes, exactly. When the out of town and state people came in, it was hard to verify that all procedures had been followed correctly because we were missing a lot of standard equipment compared to other precincts of similar sizes. Therefore, my third action as sheriff is to give back to the community. I have been keeping a list of issues that you good townspeople need help with, problems you've brought to the department but we haven't had the resources to solve yet. I plan to go down that list and help however I can. Not just me, but developing that as part of our department's culture to give back to the community."

Gunner opened his mouth, closed it, nodded, then stepped back. His feet were spread, arms behind his back. Maryanne recognized military parade rest. She smiled at him, gave him a thumb's up as his eyes flicked over hers, and the crowd clapped and murmured.

Mayor Ruby smiled. "Thank you, Deputy. Mr. Willowby, you mentioned the town's vandalism problem. Over the past six or seven months, there have been three separate instances of spray paint vandalism on downtown walls. How do you plan on solving this problem?"

Gunner's eyes met hers again as Willowby began to rant.

"Those young kids don't know what's good for them. We'll catch them red-handed, set a trap just like we would for any ole animal we hunt. Then we'll make 'em clean up the whole town with community service. They need the law to be tough on them, or they'll grow up into felons and murderers, and we don't want any of that here in Crimson Creek."

Maryanne's lips twisted. She had some pretty strong

opinions about that, considering Zarrel was a felon and Gunner's own brother was currently incarcerated. Gunner did too, as he barely waited a beat before replying. His face turned red and his lips pursed.

"Some of y'all remember my brother, Chase. He's still in prison for the mistakes he made, and he intends to come home once he's out. What happened in the past is in the past, and if a felon is a productive, upright citizen of the community, then I will welcome him or her to the community. In fact, that's exactly what I've done in the past few years when other felons have moved to the area. I know several people who are meaner and deserve jail time but are not felons because they haven't been caught."

"So you're anti-felon?" someone yelled in the crowd. Gunner shook his head slowly and took a breath before responding, just like they'd practiced.

"I'm not against felons, but I am against breaking the law. I have a track record of treating everyone who comes into town with equal courtesy, regardless of their background, prior convictions, race, ethnicity, gender, or any other factor. That being said, I will respond to anyone who violates the law in the same manner, by following every procedure to the full letter of the law."

Zarrel stood up, catching Gunner's eye. "I can attest to that. When I moved to town, Gunner didn't treat me any different because of the mistakes I'd made in my past. He's been nothing but fair. I know I'm not allowed to vote as a felon, but if I could, Gunner would be the only one I'd trust to be fair no matter the situation."

Zarrel sat back down as the crowd murmured, most not realizing Zarrel had been to prison. Gunner cleared his throat and continued.

"I agree that the vandalism needs to stop. The kids need

to be punished, but they also need to be heard. If I had listened to Chase... If I had listened to him that night, I might have been able to stop it and prevent the tragedy that happened. That's the entire reason I became a cop, so that I could make up for my mistake of not listening, not helping, not taking action when I had the chance."

A murmur went through the crowd, and Gunner's eyes found hers again. She nodded gently, and he swallowed hard before continuing.

"A sheriff needs to be firm but fair. These kids might just be blowing off steam or they could be true delinquents. We won't know until they're caught. Until then, we can take proactive measures to give them outlets to blow off steam safely. The addition of the town gym and the yoga studio opening up to the teenagers has made a big impact. Since school started in August and those places opened up, there has been no vandalism at all. That's telling. We need to give these kids something to do, something productive. Then they won't be interested in or bored enough to go around vandalizing."

Mayor Ruby looked at her notes, then glanced back up as the crowd clapped.

"Deputy, correction. There's only been one instance of vandalism since August, on the night of Halloween. But other than that, you are correct."

Gunner's eyes met Maryanne's as he cleared his throat. "Ah yes, I remember doing the report and cleaning that up." She couldn't control her lips or the grin that stretched ear to ear. He was much better at controlling his; barely a twitch of the lips crossed his face.

Mr. Willowby turned his stink eye teacher glare on Gunner, making him shift on his feet. "That's right. Your brother *is* in prison, isn't he? He probably influenced you a lot. What have you gotten up to that people don't know about, Gunner? You sure that Halloween report of vandalism was handled correctly?"

Parker shouted from behind her. "Hey, my brother may be in prison, but he's a lot better man than many walking around free."

Ava stood up in front of her, fists ready. "You watch your tongue, Walter. That's my son you're talking about." Maryanne stood and grabbed her arm while Gunner's dad grabbed her other and pulled her back to her chair.

An older woman stood up and waved a manila envelope. "He's got a right to question it. Gunner was the one who vandalized the gazebo, and I've got proof!" She stepped into the aisle as the crowd murmured softly then died to nothing. Her cane clicked in the silence, and Maryanne could've heard a pin drop as she held her breath.

Her grey-haired bun was coming loose, and she had a camera strapped around her neck that bounced as she walked. The woman was one she'd seen around town a lot, but she didn't know who she was.

"Ethel, what are you going on about?" One of the church ladies from the other side of the room asked into the stillness. Mr. Willowby looked like he was about to dance a jig. The son of a bitch knew about this and had waited for his moment.

"Who's that?" Maryanne leaned forward to ask Ava. Holly wouldn't know, as they both moved to town around the same time. Ava twisted in her chair as the rest of the crowd started to murmur. Mayor Ruby took the envelope and pulled out the contents, spreading them across the table that was set up on stage.

"That's Ethel. She lived here until her husband left her about twenty years ago. She just moved back a few years ago, and she's a bitter old hag if I've ever seen one. They say she was so hard to live with, her kids kicked her out. She lives in the assisted living side of the nursing home, so she's always running around town and poking her nose into people's business. Remember that fight between Carl and Eddie about the stud pigs they raised? She started it."

Maryanne sat back and bounced her leg. What pictures did this woman have?

Mayor Ruby frowned while she looked at the contents of the envelope. "Five-minute recess while we figure this out folks. Gentlemen, turn off the mics."

"No way," Willowby said. "He needs to admit what he's done. Look right there. He's shirtless and gold paint is all over his chest. And look at the date in the corner. November 1."

The crowd gasped as Gunner looked at the pictures and then at the crowd. His face never changed, even when he met her eyes. He'd clammed up; she recognized that face. He wasn't going to say anything now, and her heart sunk, much like his chances of winning sheriff.

Mayor Ruby held up her hands to calm the crowd. "Now, now. He just said he cleaned up the mess. Don't you think he'd get gold paint on his chest through cleaning?"

Ethel rifled through the pictures, and shoved two more at Ruby, who looked at them, frowned, and then looked at Gunner. Reluctantly, she set them back onto the table.

"What's those pictures show?" someone in the crowd called out.

Ruby sighed. "Gunner is cleaning the gazebo in a clean shirt, not the one he changed out of."

Maryanne's heart sunk when Gunner straightened his spine and stood silent. She'd done what she'd promised not to do and ruined the election for him. Not by distracting him as a girlfriend, but by leading him to break the law.

"What does that mean?" someone shouted.

Willowby raised a fist, his voice triumphant as he said, "It means *Gunner* was the one responsible for the vandalized gazebo."

Her jaw firmed. She was on her feet and marching up to the stage before she'd thought it through.

"No, you can't do this to him." She stopped in front of it and raised a finger to point at Willowby. "You don't get to come in here and cast the first stone, Mr. Holier Than Thou. No one is without sin here."

"That's right. You've done plenty wrong too, Walter!" someone shouted from the crowd behind her, and others murmured their agreement.

"There's no way Gunner would do that," someone in the crowd said.

Walter crossed his arms. "Yeah, but my mistakes were in my youth. What have I done wrong in the past few months, or hell in the past few years? I haven't broken the law repeatedly, now have I? Nope. That's just him." It was Willowby's turn to point his finger at Gunner.

"What do you mean, repeatedly?" Mayor Ruby asked, frowning. Willowby moved some pictures around and pulled out two to hold up.

"See these? These are from that wedding at the yoga studio before Christmas. Look at this. The preacher is face down in his cake, and this entire table of decent, respectable ladies have pulled off their bras. Look at them, waving their braziers around like flags."

He held up the picture as the crowd gasped, but Mayor Ruby ripped it out of his hand and looked at it. Her jaw dropped. "This is my mom! What's going on here?"

"It was the whiskey cake," someone shouted.

"It was the strongest I've ever had," someone else shouted.

Mayor Ruby turned the picture face down on the table. "And just how is that Gunner's fault? He didn't break any laws there."

"He didn't arrest anyone for public intoxication, which makes him an accessory. He was aiding and abetting someone. Oh, I don't know. Maybe a little baker he had a hot and heavy relationship with?" Willowby crossed his arms and smirked at her, but Maryanne saw red.

She jumped up on stage and stood between him and Gunner, jamming her hands on her hips. "No, absolutely not. You don't get to turn this around on Gunner. I take full responsibility for that whiskey cake.

I used a pint instead of a cup, but you know what? Gunner arrested me for it. So even though we're having a baby, he still followed the law, got to the bottom of the problem, and took action. I mean, how many of *you* would arrest your significant other in a similar situation? Your *pregnant* significant other?"

"I haven't heard about any arrest. It wasn't in the county report," someone called from the crowd.

Ray piped up from the front row, arms folded and frown ever at the ready. "That's because I made him toss out the arrest. It was a waste of city resources."

Maryanne held up a finger, waving it at Willowby. "Speaking of resources, without the needed equipment and resources that Gunner was talking about, it wasn't even possible to arrest that many people for public intoxication. Don't you want a sheriff who has compassion? Who helps?"

"But not one that breaks the law himself! He spray painted the gazebo, didn't he." Willowby held up the picture of Gunner shirtless next to his truck outside her apartment. The gold paint was bright as day. Gunner slid a hand to her back, but Maryanne didn't take the time to think what that touch meant.

"He only did that because I told him to!" Her shout echoed in the loud room. She felt the color drain from her face, and Gunner's hand slid from her back, leaving her cold, bereft in front of this angry mob. What had she done?

Chapter Thirty-Six

Maryanne sucked in a breath to calm her nerves. She turned to half face the crowd and half face Willowby.

"Look, you know my shop has some pretty powerful CBD. I experimented with a new brand to see if it'd help me sleep. Before I could try the brownies, Gunner had gotten into them—"

"Uh huh." "Sure." "CBD brownies? Yeah, right." The voices in the crowd talked over each other.

She cleared her throat and kept going. "We'd already been drinking, and the combination wasn't good. We got shit faced and walked to the gazebo for a swim. When we found the spray paint, well—it was a stupid misunderstanding because we were so out of it. An honest mistake, really. Gunner went the next morning and cleaned it all up before noon. I intended to go down there and clean it up after work, but he'd already gotten it done."

She put both hands on her hips and glared at Willowby.

"So when he said there's been no vandalism by teenagers since August, he was telling the truth. The man is a fucking saint, and he's never broken a law before. Even when we were teenagers and running around, sneaking out—he was the one that was looking out for everyone and making sure everyone was safe and not being too stupid."

"That's true, he was always keeping me out of trouble." "Me too." "Remember that one time—" "No, shut up and listen." The crowd's voices continued, but Maryanne ignored them.

"It's only in the past few months that I pursued him so much and goaded him into having fun. It got out of hand and led to breaking a few laws. So maybe you're right, and he was being lenient because—because—well, because we were busy making a baby. But he's the most upright, honest, law-abiding man for the job. He respects everyone and would never willingly or knowingly break any laws, not even the dumb ones like jaywalking. He's the best man in this entire damn town, and if you don't elect him, you're a fool for letting him go."

She crossed her arms, cocked her hip, and stared Willowby down. The crowd's murmuring reached a crescendo as people talked about this newest piece of gossip. Mayor Ruby tapped her microphone to get the crowd to quiet down.

Gunner hooked a finger into Maryanne's jeans and pulled her back against him then shifted to stand beside her. He slid his arm around her waist, so she slid hers around his.

They stood together, facing the crowd as everyone settled, her hands still shaking from the adrenaline and from her first touch of him in weeks.

"This is an interesting turn of events. We're going to open the floor to both sides to speak now, and we're going to take turns to hear a balanced audience. Form two lines please." Mayor Ruby organized the people.

Several people jumped up to the center aisle and formed their lines. It was half an hour of the same thing. Willowby's side argued that they didn't want a sheriff who was going to turn a blind eye to some girl. Gunner's side said they appreciated a cop who would let mistakes go if a person learned from them and no harm was done.

When the floor was closed at exactly nine-thirty, people mingled. Many came up to shake Gunner's hand. He didn't say much, to her or to anyone really.

His mom gave him a piece of her mind, but when she hugged him, she whispered more into his ear. Maryanne only caught the words proud, love, and fools.

She wasn't sure if her nerves could handle much more. She couldn't tell if he was mad, and her stomach churned at the thought of what he'd say when they got home.

They walked back to her apartment, his steps jerky. The debates were just across the street from her building, and as they walked, she reached out to hold his hand. But he just pulled his hand back and slid it into his pocket.

Her heart squeezed at his rejection.

She was taking two steps to his one, but couldn't stand the waves of emotions rolling off him. "It's going to be okay, Gunner. We'll figure out how to—"

"It's over, Maryanne. Willowby will win, and I'm fucked."

"But the people will only put up with him for so long, and then you can run for sheriff again."

He stopped on the corner under the streetlight, shadows falling across his face as he swung to face her.

"I told you this would all come back and bite me in the ass. I told you it was better to tell the truth on the whiskey cake. But no, you wouldn't listen, and now we're stuck together and—"

He cut off sharply and reared back, and she raised a hand to her mouth.

"You're... stuck with me?"

Her heart felt like it was being chiseled slowly, each pound of her heart the hammer driving a deeper crack into her soul.

He raked a hand over his face and clenched his jaw. "That's not what I meant, Maryanne."

She held up a hand, fighting back angry tears.

"No, I get it. I promised you wouldn't be distracted with a relationship, which is why I'm just your baby mama. But we're going to fucking raise this kid, Gunner. I'd like us to at least be friends through this whole mess, so we're going to go upstairs and drink some hot chocolate to warm up, and talk like friends. Got it?"

She glared at him, then spun on her heel and strode down the alley to the back of the building. Her breath was visible in the cold air as they started up the stairs.

They unlocked the door and went inside, discarding jackets and shoes. He paced in front of the couch while she made their drinks.

"You can't give up, Gunner. We'll let it settle down for a few days, then start a new campaign strategy. We can talk to Ray and your mom and whoever else we can think of to help fix this."

"It'll be fine, M. I'll just go back to my original timeline." He gave a resigned shrug, stopping his pacing when she handed over a steaming mug. He sank slowly to the couch.

"What was your original timeline?" She sat criss-cross

on the chaise lounge, facing him, the need to hear his voice and draw him out rising in her heart.

"Make sheriff by the time I'm thirty-five. I can still do that since I'm only thirty-three."

She sipped her drink as the silence stretched, thinking of ways to become friends and get their relationship back on track. "When's your birthday? I don't even know."

They talked about their birthdays and their favorite birthdays from childhood before silence reigned again. It was an easier silence than what they'd had the past few weeks, though.

Gunner looked so forlorn when he looked into his almost empty mug. She shook off her guilt and turned to him.

"You're not the only one with life goals, you know. Sometimes you gotta get back on the horse, even if it's still bucking."

He cracked a smile. "A horse reference? Really?"

She smirked. "Figured you'd get it, growing up on that horse ranch."

She sipped her drink and glanced away from him, staring at the marshmallows bobbing in the dark chocolaty goodness.

"Were you ever bucked off your dreams?" His voice was soft and sent shivers up her spine, making her crave his touch.

She sipped her drink and settled back on the couch.

"I've always wanted to be a baker, but I'd like to specialize in cookies and cakes, like wedding cakes, birthday cakes, things like that. I was making a name for myself with that crowd in Colorado, but then there was the mess with Barry. I thought for a while that my dreams were over, when I first came back to Texas."

She shifted on the couch, his eyes burning into her as he stared, making her stomach flip.

"What made you get back on the horse and open the shop here?"

"My grandmother was sick, but when I wanted to mope and whine, she set me to baking and taking treats around to all her neighbors or to the nursing home. I loved that, spending time with her, baking, visiting and talking to others, seeing the faces of people who get a treat when they're not expecting it... It was like my childhood all over again. It reminded me of how much I love to bake and bring joy to others."

"That's when you opened the shop?"

"She pushed me to open it actually, helped me get the confidence back to step out and try again. Now, it's self-sustaining and turning a tidy profit, especially with the addition of Zarrel and his breads. I think I'll be able to dedicate more time to decorating cakes now, with Zarrel around."

"I'm grateful you have him to help. He's a good man."

She smiled, because it was Gunner who was a good man. He didn't look at Zarrel and see a felon or race or even a man to be jealous of. Gunner could be rather possessive sometimes, but he'd been fine with Zarrel, which had surprised her.

"The point is, Gunner, that if I hadn't tried again, I wouldn't have my shop, or have hired Zarrel, or be on my way to creating these masterful cakes. The debates were a setback, not a permanent roadblock."

He chuckled. "You're mixing metaphors, M. First horses, now roadblocks?"

She grinned. "What can I say? I like variety."

"Is that so? Well, do you have a variety of life goals then? Any other dreams?"

His voice was soft, making the hairs on the back of her arms stand up as she finished her drink.

"The past few years, I've been using all my free time to help Cindy with her boys. I wasn't really expecting to love them so much, or to already miss them this past month. The transition to all of them living with Andy has been smoother on them than it has been on me."

"How so?"

She leaned her head back on the chaise and closed her eyes. "The boys kept me busy. I actually loved going to all the soccer games, taking Owen to the park every day after preschool while Cindy was working."

"And now you only get one day a week with them."

"Yeah, I fully intend to keep going to all the soccer games, science fairs, and whatever else with my nephews and niece. I'm scared I'll be a terrible mom and let peanut get hurt. But I'm so fucking excited too because I get to do all that with *my* kid now. Yeah, we'll have the diaper stage and the late nights. But I... I want to recreate those memories with my grandma with Peanut, taking treats to people and bringing a smile to people's faces."

Her eyes get heavy as she pictured their future in her mind's eye.

"Did you ever picture yourself as a mom before?" His voice was soft, like a dream lulling her to sleep.

"Not really. I just assumed I'd always be the fun-loving aunt. But now that it's happening, I'm getting pretty excited. What about you? Did you ever picture yourself as a dad?"

He chuckled softly. "Yeah, when I was younger, I wanted an entire football team of my own. I loved growing up with all my brothers, running around everywhere and having fun."

"Causing mischief, you mean." Her lips tipped up in a soft smile, thinking back to their childhood.

"Hey, that was mostly you, Landry, and Parker, not me." He chuckled, the sound soothing her.

He slid the empty cup out of her hand and set it on the coffee table.

She dragged her eyes open as he bent to scoop her up into his arms, making her heart race at his touch. Standing, he walked them into the bedroom.

"Gunner?"

"Sh, you're tired. Let's just go to bed, M."

When he laid her down and tucked her in, she grabbed his wrist and peered up into his eyes. "I really am sorry about today, Gunner. Will you let me make it up to you?"

He frowned and stepped away to kick off his boots and shirt. "Taking care of my erection won't win the election, M."

She burst into laughter and leaned on her good elbow on the bed. "Who knew you were so funny?"

"I have my moments."

She turned back the covers as he shucked his jeans, the light from the window flirting on his abs and making her mouth water.

"It's been too long, Gunner. I'm tired of arguing and bickering."

He slid into bed, and his hand roamed her already overheated body. "What man can resist you, M?"

She didn't want him to resist her; she wanted him to love her. Her heart raced, rejoicing at the feel of his hands again.

He kissed the side of her neck. "I thought we were just going to be friends? Friends don't do this, M."

She threw a leg over him, then lifted to slide her body

against him. His groan sent a shock of electricity up her spine.

Her mouth watered when she unzipped his jeans and got on her knees beside him. "We'll be friends with benefits for now. You good with that?" He paused as she tugged his jeans down and they tossed them aside.

She gripped his dick, and he hissed, "Hell, yeah."

She smiled like a Cheshire cat and slowly took him into her mouth. It wouldn't solve the problem with the election, but if she could distract him for just a little while and make him relaxed and happy, it would be worth the lost sleep.

Besides, he tasted so damn good when he exploded in her mouth. She swallowed every drop, then snuggled into his arms with a sigh. Maybe she'd wake up with her own happy ending in the morning.

Chapter Thirty-Seven

The next few days, she couldn't bring herself to wake him up when she went to the bakery at four in the morning. And at night, he was too busy with work and campaigning to even talk to her.

She snorted as she walked down the stairs of her apartment and across the street to the bakery early one morning.

Campaigning—that was rich. He was doing damage control, plain and simple. Ray and Charlie had him hosting daily lunches at the Diner to talk about various problems the townsfolk wanted solved.

Then in the afternoons, he ran around town doing different things for work. He helped Helen, the head of the Ladies Auxiliary Club at church, change her flat tire north of town. And he helped Mrs. Henderson get her cat out of a tree. She knew about those because both of them had come into the bakery this week to tell her how sweet her boyfriend was.

And both times, it felt like her heart was breaking because he wasn't her boyfriend.

She'd thought he was proposing twice, but then she was just his baby mama. Yeah, she was still pissed over it, and it made her hesitate to talk to him and trust him.

Her heart ached to think about him leaving, but at least they were sleeping together again. It was almost like they were starting over, since being friends with benefits had led to them getting knocked up.

The debate had brought them physically back together, but it hadn't brought them closer emotionally. She'd thought she'd done enough damage control of her own with their hot chocolate talk of dreams and life goals, but no.

They sat in silence over dinner, when he was home, that is. This week, he'd only come home around nine, taken a shower, and fallen into bed without saying a word to her.

She was thankful he was cuddling her, but damn it, she was getting stressed over every little thing. They needed to move beyond the friends with benefits zone and into a genuine relationship, and she didn't know how the fuck to do that.

She arrived at the Diner and the bell dinged when she walked through the door for their standard Wednesday family lunch date.

"Hey, Mom! How are you doing this week?"

Maryanne leaned in and kissed Margarita on the cheek before sliding into the booth across from her. Her stomach growled. Maybe she'd get lucky and be able to hold down the food.

"I'm doing good, dear. How are you feeling?"

"So-so. The iron infusions are once a week, and I'm good for a few days, but then it's back to being sick."

"They might need to increase to twice a week until it all gets sorted out."

Cindy walked in, her navy-blue scrubs complimenting

her dark black hair pulled back into a long braid. Strands had come loose and framed her pretty little face, making Maryanne jealous. Her own hair was straight and lacked that whimsical look her sister wore effortlessly.

She smiled as her sister kissed her cheek, then slid in to sit next to Margarita. "Hey, what'd I miss?"

Maryanne shrugged. "Not much. Just talking morning sickness and doctor's appointments."

"You shrugged your shoulder without wincing. Does that mean it's all healed?" Cindy's face lit up. She was such a good physical therapist.

Maryanne grinned. "Yeah, pretty sure. I follow up with my primary doc next week to confirm and get the cast off my wrist."

They talked about the local doctors—there were three in town—Cindy's new job managing the entire Home Health and Therapy Center, and their mom's upcoming cruise in February.

Dot took their orders and brought their drinks, and she chatted with Cindy about newly married life.

Dot turned to her and smiled. "You just missed Gunner, Maryanne. He left about ten minutes before you came in."

Maryanne smiled, and they talked about unexpectedly moving in with a guy because Dot had done that in the fall. Maryanne wistfully watched her walk away. Maybe she'd end up getting married to Gunner like Dot had to John after he moved in.

She sighed, turning to tease her mom. "You going to shack up with some random guy while on that cruise?"

Margarita blushed but waved her hand in the air to brush it off. "Please, I'm a lady. I would never."

"We can't all be like you, M." Cindy wrinkled her nose.

The Sheriff Gets His Girl

Geez, that dig hurt. Her sister sure knew how to push her buttons.

Maryanne scoffed and leaned back in her seat. "When have I ever hooked up with a random guy?"

Cindy frowned, scratching her chin. "I guess that's fair. You're a big flirt, but I guess you haven't slept around much, have you?"

Maryanne shook her head. "Nope, certainly not."

She'd always told her sister everything until nine years ago or so when Cindy got married to the boys' dad. Then they'd kind of drifted apart for a while. It made her sad, and rather nervous that her new husband would cause a similar divide between them.

If she was honest with herself, she'd admit that they were already starting to drift. Not because of Andy but because Maryanne had kept the baby news from her for so long in December.

"Speaking of hook-ups, how are you and Gunner getting along?"

Maryanne unloaded on them about the past week of Gunner scrambling to repair the damage from the debate.

When their food was delivered, she finished her story. "And then at the debates, I went and ruined everything. I don't know what to do now. How do I fix it and help him win the election?"

"It should be less about the election and more about starting your family together, hun," her mom said softly, her brown eyes shining in the light from the window.

Her shoulders slumped as she picked at her food. "I know, but it's what will make him happy, and I want to make him happy. He's been so distant this week, so I *have* to help."

Cindy frowned, then leaned forward while looking around furtively. "M, do you love him?"

Maryanne felt her heart stop at the question. She made the mistake of lying about the baby's father so she could tell Gunner first, and it caused a shit ton of problems.

She was done with lying. Nodding, her eyes filled with tears as her stomach roiled. Shifting uncomfortably in her seat, she saw her mom and Cindy glance at each other before looking back at her.

"Well, for starters the town needs to see that you're both happy together, and it's a permanent thing. Even if it's not, they need to see it as if it is."

Maryanne had trouble following Cindy's logic on this one. She rubbed her temple as Margarita clarified.

"Moving into the house will help, I think. When do you close?"

Maryanne perked up. She really was excited about the house. "Next week. Think we can have a moving in party next weekend to get all our stuff over there and unpacked?"

Cindy grinned. "Oh yeah. Especially if you offer the poker guys food and beer. We'll make it an all day event on Saturday. Say, about nine? Then order some pizza for lunch and grill something for dinner?"

Maryanne frowned. "I'm not sure we'll have a grill. I don't even know if Gunner grills."

Cindy laughed, making Maryanne chuckle. Her laugh was infectious. "He's a man in north Texas. Of course he grills."

"I guess I can ask him. Or his mom. I can ask his mom if he has a grill."

Margarita wiped her mouth and folded the napkin neatly. "Maryanne, darling, you can't avoid talking to him. If you want to get this whole election thing—and even more importantly, the relationship—sorted out, then you need to talk to him. About everything, nothing, and all that's in between."

Cindy nodded. "Communication is key. I think that's the only reason I moved forward with Andy so fast. He was an open book, and we talked about deep stuff right away. We still do. No secrets and no holding back. Honesty always."

Maryanne felt tears fill her eyes again. That wasn't her and Gunner at all. Did that mean that she and Gunner would never make it like Cindy and Andy did? Her stomach revolted at the thought.

She sucked in a shaky breath. "Excuse me. I need to go throw up."

She hustled to the bathroom and made it just in time to lose her lunch. It was not as delicious the second time around. She sat on the floor of the biggest stall and leaned against the wall, breathing deeply as her stomach settled. The door opened and a few women came inside.

"I know, but it's shameful is what it is," one woman said. She sounded like one of the older church ladies, all prim and proper.

A second woman chimed in. "I don't blame her one bit, but she better put a ring on it if she hopes to hold on to a man like that. I mean, sometimes I call him to come rescue my cat just so I can watch those biceps bulge."

There were murmurs of approval. Maryanne felt her stomach twist again, as there were only a handful of guys around town who were called to rescue cats.

"You think he'll beat out Willowby?" a third woman asked.

Maryanne swallowed hard as she realized who they were talking about.

"I sure hope so. I know Willowby is our age, and we

need to vote for him in a show of solidarity. But Gunner's the best person for the job. I just don't like the idea of him being reckless, running around town, and breaking the law. Is that really the message we want to send our kids in this town?" The second lady was obviously the most level-headed of the group.

"See, I see it differently." She heard a toilet flush and a door squeak open as another lady stepped into the stall.

The first lady asked, "He's not the best person for the job?"

The third lady replied. "Oh no, he definitely is. But I think that if he and Maryanne get married, he'll settle down. He's never been the reckless sort before, but if he's in love, once they're married and preparing for that baby, he'll be back to his normal, reliable self."

"She'll settle down with a baby or two, too. They won't both be getting into trouble together if they're starting a family."

"Do you believe that nonsense about the vandalism? Have you ever tried her CBD stuff? It's amazing."

Another flush sounded, then the sink turned on as they began talking about scones and cookies. At least they were customers who liked her products. That made her feel marginally better.

But maybe they were right. If they got married, it could sway the town to vote for him. But could she go through with it, knowing she loved him but he didn't love her?

Chapter Thirty-Eight

First week of February

Gunner swung by the bunkhouse at lunch to grab some more clothes. He was tired and frustrated, mostly because he was trying to wrap his head around losing the dream of becoming sheriff.

There was no doubt in his mind that it wasn't happening right now. Maybe Willowby would be ousted at the next election.

He sighed and hopped out of the truck. That was assuming he could survive working for Willowby as sheriff. The man was a pain in the ass, a crotchety old bastard who had made high school a living hell.

"Gunner! What are you doing out here?" Hunter asked.

His older brother rounded the corner of the bunkhouse and grinned. "Did Maryanne get tired of your bullshit and send you back?"

Gunner snorted. "What bullshit? She's the one who opened her mouth at the debate and cost me everything."

"Dude, no she didn't. Don't be an ass just because she told the truth. The town will come around and see that before the election. Don't worry."

They stepped into the bunkhouse, making Gunner wrinkle his nose at the stench of body odor and leather. How had he lived here for the past six years and not noticed the smell?

He made his way to the back bedroom that he shared with Hunter. "Doubtful. And it wasn't all the truth."

"What's the whole truth, then? What'd she twist?"

Gunner sat on his twin bed, set his elbows on his knees, and put his head in his hands. "She had a bottle of THC from Colorado and made pot brownies. I ate a few on Halloween and—"

Hunter busted up laughing. "You? No way!"

Gunner sat up straighter and slapped his knees. "Yes, yes. I didn't know they were special brownies, okay? It was an accident."

"But the vandalism on the gazebo? That was because you were higher than a kite! Oh, this is rich. No wonder you're so pissed!"

Gunner stood up and started pacing the space between their beds as Hunter leaned against the door jamb.

"I'm not pissed. Just... disappointed, I guess. I've worked so hard to do things the right way, but in one night she got me to break multiple laws—"

"Wait, how many? Just the edibles and the vandalism, right? That's not that bad, Gunner. Lots of us did worse when we were younger."

Gunner spun to face him and waved his arms. "Exactly! When you were younger. But I'm thirty-three. I'm not going to be elected sheriff now because everyone thinks I'm someone I'm not, going around and breaking laws."

Hunter sighed and rubbed his forehead.

"Gunner, this same old argument is so annoying. You're human. We all make mistakes. And if you'd pull your head out of your ass and focus on Maryanne and the future with her and the baby, then you'd see that being sheriff is just a job. It's not the end all be all you've made it out to be. Have you been stomping around and shutting her out the past week since the debate?"

Gunner's shoulders tensed, and he turned away from his brother's piercing hazel eyes.

Hunter snorted. "I knew it. You've always done this, Gunner. You did this when we were kids, and you thought I'd stolen your fishing pole, when you broke Mom's favorite vase and couldn't fix it, when Chase got in trouble—"

"Don't bring him into this," Gunner growled.

Silence rang out, echoing in his head and making his chest feel like it was going to explode.

"I heard what you said at the debate, Gunner. It wasn't your fault." Hunter's soft whisper was hoarse, making Gunner glad he was turned away and staring out the window.

He'd always looked up to his only older brother. Hunter had been the one he'd always hung around with, since there was only a year between them.

Chase had been the loner middle brother, then Landry and Parker had come along with barely ten months between them.

Gunner turned and pulled out his shirt drawer, grabbing a few more button downs. He grabbed his suit jacket from the shared closet and went to step out the door.

As he brushed past his brother, Hunter reached out and grabbed Gunner's arm. He stopped and met eyes eerily similar to his own. It was like staring into his conscience.

"You said you wanted to listen, to help, to take action. That's how you work, but is that how you live? Do you do that with Maryanne? Think about it, bro. Don't shut her out. Or me."

Gunner nodded once and unclenched his jaw. "I'll try to get better about it."

They walked down the hall and out the door, and he tossed his duffel into the truck.

Hunter slapped the front of his truck. "Are you coming up to the house for lunch?"

"Yeah, want a ride? Hop in." He needed to see his mom. Maybe it'd help him get some normalcy.

They chatted about the ranch and the changes Hunter was making, about Gunner's upcoming trip to Colorado, and their parents.

When he stepped into his mom and dad's ranch house, he grinned as the tension seeped out of his shoulders.

Normalcy was overrated, but in this case it was chaotic, loud, and—he did a double take when he glanced over the crowd around the dining table.

"Maryanne? What are you doing here?" He slowly made his way to her, drawn like a moth to flame.

Her hair was pulled back in a ponytail, the silver streak in her hair for winter the only sign she hoped for snow. Her shy smile drew him in and made him want to touch that dimple on her cheek, graze his fingers down her jaw, tracing down to her cleavage in that v-neck green sweater.

"I wanted to see if you could grill Saturday night after everyone helps us move into the house, but I didn't know if you had a grill so I came to ask your mom."

Gunner winced as the conversations around them began to die down. Everyone in this town wanted to know everyone else's business. "Yeah, the closing has been delayed a few weeks. I talked the owners into replacing the air conditioner now, so we won't have to worry about that in the summer when the baby comes. But that means we won't be able to move in this weekend after all. I was going to tell you tonight."

"Oh." Her face fell as she took a deep breath, then pasted on her fake smile. He was happy he could identify it now, but he craved her genuine smile. "That's all right, then. It'll give me more time to pack the boxes."

"How's the packing going?" his mom asked as she sat down a casserole in the middle of the table.

They had two tables, one in the kitchen and one in the dining room. Both were overrun by big, burly cowboys, with Maryanne and his mom being the only females. Gunner washed his hands quickly at the kitchen sink, then kicked the chair leg next to Maryanne.

"Mind if I sit here?" he asked the ranch hand.

The other man lifted a brow but grabbed his plate and shuffled off to the other table. Gunner knew he'd be razzed about that later with the guys, but he didn't care.

He slid into the seat and grabbed a fresh plate, loading it up as Maryanne turned back to his mom. Ava sat in her usual seat at the head of the table, with Maryanne to her immediate left.

They began comparing pregnancies, and he tried to close his ears to the details his mom was describing. He forced himself to listen, though, because he wanted to be part of every step with Maryanne.

Happy to see her eating, he scarfed down his own food. The rest of the table began talking about the upcoming Super Bowl game, so he joined in the smack talk with the rest of them.

When he was finished eating, he slid his arm along the back of Maryanne's chair and leaned back with a smile.

The ranch hands got up, rinsed off their plates, and slid them into the dishwasher before grabbing their jackets, thanking Ava, and waltzing out the door.

When it was just his parents, Maryanne, and himself, the tension started to creep back up his spine.

Maryanne slid her hand on her stomach, then turned to his mom. "Excuse me, but where's your bathroom?"

"I'll show you." He stood with her, then led her down the hallway to the downstairs bathroom.

He'd barely pushed the door open when she slid past him, dropped to her knees, and retched into the toilet. His own stomach curdled at both the sight and smell.

Shutting the door behind him, he grabbed a washcloth and wet it.

Laying it on her neck, he pulled her ponytail to hang down her back and out of the way. Everything she'd just eaten came back up. A knock on the door sounded, and he opened it to see his mom holding a bottle of water.

He thanked her, then turned back to Maryanne. She was already flushing and wiping her face with the washcloth. Leaning back against the tub, she took the water bottle with a shaky hand and took a drink.

"I didn't know you were still sick. Wasn't the morning sickness supposed to be gone by now?" Gunner crossed his arms and leaned against the sink.

"That's because you're never home, Gunner. But yeah, it's supposed to be gone by now, so I've been going to Denton for iron infusions once a week. They keep wearing off after a few days, so the doctor is starting me on twice a week infusions on Friday." She wiped her face one more time and then started to stand up. He helped her up and frowned, his mind churning as he processed.

"You've been going to the doctor without me?" His heart dropped and his skin felt cold and clammy. "We're in this together, Maryanne, and I told you I want to be at every appointment. Why didn't you tell me?"

She shrugged. "You've not seemed very invested the past few weeks since the debates. And it wasn't a regular appointment, just the anemia shots."

How could he have missed that? He'd paid attention to all the details of her life until last month. He crossed his arms and stepped back, staring at the floor and fighting the rising disappointment in himself.

"You have anemia? How does that impact the baby?" His head was spinning and his heart dropped to his stomach. "Why didn't you tell me?"

She glared and set the water bottle down.

"Damn it, it's your own fault, Gunner. You've kept your distance for weeks, pushing me away just like you did after the Halloween brownie incident. Why the hell would I try to talk to you when you're only a roommate at this point?"

His eyebrows pulled together, and he raked his hand through his hair. He'd just thought distancing himself from her would help the townspeople realize he wasn't going to let Maryanne—or himself—break any more laws.

Fine, that wasn't fair. He'd kept his distance because he'd realized she was more important than the election, and it scared him. He'd worked to become sheriff for over a decade, and she'd completely changed his life plan and goals in just a few months?

He hadn't just been trying to wrap his head around losing the election, but also the idea of a new future, a permanent future, with her as the main attraction. He'd been trying to think, but obviously, it hadn't helped.

He jammed his hands into his pockets and moved away from the sink, murmuring, "Keep your enemies closer."

"What?"

He cleared his throat. "I said, maybe I need to do the opposite and keep you closer instead of pushing you away."

She waved her pointer finger under his nose. "I'm not your fucking enemy, Gunner. I'm having *your* baby, or have you forgotten?"

Her sarcastic tone of voice sent a shock wave of pain through his chest. By keeping himself away, he'd been hurting her when really all he wanted to do was hold and protect her.

She flipped her hair and spun away from him to wash her hands.

She took several deep breaths before saying calmly, "Yeah. I'm okay, baby's okay, we're all okay. Or rather, we will be, with these shots and once this fucking election is over."

He glanced at her hands as the water ran over them. Something was different.

"Where's your cast?" He grabbed her hand and pushed up her sleeve. His stomach boiled to see it was gone.

"I got it taken off yesterday. You didn't even notice when you came home last night, ate the dinner I'd left out, and fell into bed. Hell, Gunner, you said two fucking words to me all day yesterday."

She pulled her hand back and dried them on the towel.

She spun to face him, scowling. "My doctor said the wrist and clavicle are all healed, but he said Cindy could work with me for therapy on my shoulder movement if I wanted." She rotated her arm slowly, showing him her range of motion. "There's a twinge now and then, but Cindy will help me get my strength built back."

"Shit, Maryanne. Why didn't I know about that doctor's appointment either?" He raked a hand through his hair, catching sight of himself in the mirror above the sink. Bewildered, lost, angry, he scowled and turned away, disgusted with himself for ignoring the one person who meant everything to him.

His body froze in place, ice spreading through his veins. She *was* everything. When did she become so important that it felt like he couldn't live without her?

She crossed her arms and glared at him.

"Seriously, Gunner? You've barely been home the past few weeks, too busy doing damage control to pay attention. It's not like we've talked about anything. When was I supposed to tell you? How am I supposed to talk to you when I feel like I'm still in trouble and the reason your dream has gone to shit?"

He ran his hands up her arms slowly, unable to keep himself away from her any longer, and saw the awareness flash through her eyes as she shivered.

He pulled her into his arms and gently rested his chin on her head, thinking furiously, feeling the tension in his shoulders release when her soft curves molded against the hard ridges of his body.

His world was spinning too fast on its axis, and at its center was this woman. She was infuriating, but he just kept spinning around her, unable to get away... and not really wanting to anymore.

He felt his inner walls crumbling the longer he held her, realizing that in order to take care of her, he needed to talk to her and keep her close. Not as an enemy, but because maintaining his distance the past few weeks had felt like he was slowly suffocating.

Now she was in his arms, and he could breathe deeply again. He sighed, taking in her sweet cinnamon scent.

"I never meant for you to feel you couldn't talk to me. I push people away when I'm mad at myself, when I feel like I should have done something differently, when I feel like I failed."

"What did you fail at, Gunner? I don't understand." She slid her hands around his waist, but he didn't pull them closer.

"I choked at the debate. I didn't defend myself or anything. It was the same damn thing that happens around you. My tongue was tied, and I couldn't talk through it."

Her hands froze on his back, and her voice was vulnerable. "So you're not mad about what I said? About everyone knowing about us breaking the law?"

He leaned his forehead against hers and breathed deeply. How did she still smell so good when she'd just thrown up? He couldn't even smell that, just her. Just that scent that drove him crazy and made him want to protect her and hold her and love her.

His mind shied away at the big L word. What had she asked? "I was mad, yes, but I'm glad it's all out in the open. And I'm glad you didn't tell them the *whole* truth with the cake and the brownies."

She leaned back, her eyes twinkling in the bathroom light. "So you're glad I told a half-truth? Why Gunner, I'm surprised at you. This is enormous progress from the stickler you've always been."

He grinned and winked. "I'm going to be better and loosen the reins a little. Think you can help with that?"

She nodded eagerly, that mischievous dimple in her

cheek driving him wild. Slowly, she pulled his uniform shirt from his pants, making his breath catch.

They froze when someone knocked on the door.

"Gunner? Your dad and I are going to head to the barn and get back to work. Maryanne, stop by anytime, sweetie!"

"Yes, ma'am."

"All right. Bye." His mom's footsteps echoed down the hall and the screen door banged shut.

Then she raked her fingers along his stomach. The hair on his arms stood up as she arched one of those perfect eyebrows of hers. He grabbed her hands and held them in his. She frowned, and it made him want to smooth the wrinkle on her forehead and make her laugh.

Her voice haunted him and made his cock twitch. "Thought you were going to let go a little? Doesn't that mean having a little fun?"

It'd been too long since he'd had her. Why had he kept away? Why had he only allowed himself to hold her at night?

He growled. "It sure does, but I've wanted to do something since that Christmas Day nap."

He leaned forward and kissed under her ear. The catch in her breathing drew a smile from him, and he nipped her ear lobe.

"Now that there's no one else in the house... run to my old bedroom and take off your clothes." He leaned back and opened the bathroom door. She looked at him wild-eyed, giggled, then literally took off running.

He grinned as he stalked after her.

Chapter Thirty-Nine

Second week of February

Maryanne looked up from the batch of scones she was working on as someone came through the back door of the bakery. Her heart flipped over when she saw Gunner twirling his cowboy hat and stomping his boots on the rug. She smiled as he caught her eyes and grinned back.

God, she loved that smile. They'd been talking more the past few days, and she'd been feeling much better too. The increased iron infusions had her energy levels up and her morning sickness nearly gone.

He was still campaigning for sheriff, but he'd stopped working crazy long hours and was coming home in time for dinner. They'd stopped watching tv and were having conversations at the kitchen table now too, and it made her heart thrill at the domestic bliss. The only shadow was his worry over the election and her worry that he'd leave. She'd catch him staring out the window or just sitting up in bed in the middle of the night, rubbing his forehead and thinking.

Neither of them mentioned the election. Instead, she kept their conversations fun, flirty, and light-hearted, and it seemed to help him balance the stress over the election. His grin now spoke volumes, considering just a month ago, he'd been all scowls and growls.

"Hey, handsome. What are you up to today?" He came over and peered into the large bowl. Wrapping an arm around her waist, he twirled her into a half circle and kissed her square on the lips.

She sank against him, deepening the kiss and dueling with his tongue. Sparks shot through her body, making her tingle all over. When he pulled back, his eyes crinkled from his smile.

"Hey, M. Not much. I had some free time at work, so I thought I'd come see how you were doing."

Her chest tightened at his sweet words and smile. "Well, I'm making some scones for a tea party birthday for a little girl this weekend. Want to help?"

He blinked and let go of her waist, backing away slowly with brows raised.

"Don't look so scared. I just need your big muscles."

"Where's Zarrel? Isn't he the muscle around here?"

She shrugged. "Since I got the cast off, I've started sending him home at one. In a few weeks when Mom goes on the cruise, it'll just be me on his off days."

She ran her hand along his bicep and waved to the bowl with the other. He groaned, then nodded. She jumped up and down and his eyes dropped to her too tight white t-shirt with white lettering that said *Roses are red, violets are blue, I want queso, and tacos too.*

She glanced at her watch and started to walk to the front through the swinging door. If she closed up a few minutes early, maybe she'd be able to convince him to—

"Maryanne, what do I do?" He stared into the bowl like it contained the answers to the universe, and it made her smile.

"First, wash your hands while I lock up. Then you're just going to stir while I add ingredients." She hummed while she went to the front and locked the door.

When she returned, they worked around each other, music playing softly in the background. She danced as she fetched ingredients and when she came close, he'd snatch a kiss before letting her put an ingredient in. They ended up singing almost every song together, their voices blending in beautiful harmony.

An hour later, Gunner groaned as she finished washing the dishes and set the now clean bowl on the counter in front of him. "Another batch? Don't you have a mixer for this?"

Maryanne laughed, then ran her hands up his arms. "I do have a mixer, yes. Several of them actually, but I wanted to see how long I could put you to work." His lips twisted as his jaw firmed, and he glared at her. She grinned, kissed him on the chin, and turned to pull out the last tray from the oven.

"Don't worry, G, this is the last. I was just going to have you keep mixing things so I could keep staring at those muscles of yours, but it's nap time."

Gunner crossed his arms and leaned on the counter. "It would've been faster to use the mixer."

She grinned and turned off the oven. It was time to implement her sex in the bakery plan.

"Yeah, but not nearly as fun. And you're working on that fun factor, remember?" She winked, then sashayed into her office, her heart racing in anticipation. "Speaking of, can you come here for a second?"

The Sheriff Gets His Girl

When he joined her, she pushed him onto the chaise lounge and straddled him.

"Oh, what's this?" His voice sent a shiver up her spine, and she Leaned in as he wrapped his hands around her waist.

"Was wondering if you're up for some bakery sex." She kissed him softly, his groan vibrating through her body. She ground against him, her whole body thrumming with need. She hadn't ever dry humped anyone but damn, this was so good.

The radio on his hip fell to the floor and beeped.

"Yeah, Gunner?"

She broke their kiss with a laugh, and he cursed as he sat up, leaned to the side, and picked it up. He pressed a button while she sat up, drawing his eyes to her breasts. "Nothing, Joey. Just dropped the radio."

He traced her nipple through her shirt and bra, and she barely bit back a moan.

"Ah, um, okay. Well, think you can head back over? We just got a call, and I might want some backup."

Gunner glanced at her, his eyes were smoldering as he raked his thumb across her pouting bottom lip. "Yeah, give me five. I'll be right there."

He tossed the radio behind him on the cushions and wrapped his arms around her waist again. She sat there, listening to his heartbeat as he held her. Her heart rate slowed, but she soaked up the feel of him, the safety, peace, and love. Surely he loved her; she could feel it with how he acted sometimes.

She sighed. "Thanks for your help this afternoon. It was fun."

His arms squeezed her before he released. "It was, wasn't it? Maybe I'll see if I can come over and help you out for an hour on Zarrel's off days. Make sure it's on the calendar, okay?"

"Oh, speaking of. I talked to Andy, and he said there was a way to sync my phone calendar with yours. Maybe we can figure that out tonight?"

She slid off his lap and stood next to her desk, fidgeting with her nails.

He stood and grabbed the radio. "Yeah, I'd like that."

"Why do you need to know everything on the calendar anyway? My dad was like that, and I remember he and my mom arguing about missed events all the time."

He shrugged, and she was afraid he was just going to brush her off and leave. But he tipped his head, making his dark blond hair fall to the side. It was just long enough to run her hands through, and she loved to grip it while his face was between her legs.

She subtly rocked back and forth on her heels, trying to ease the dull ache between her legs. He entwined their fingers together and pulled her closer. The rugged scent of cedar and pine clung to his body, his touch electric as he traced his fingers along her jawline, sending shivers down her spine.

"When I saw you in that wrecked car in December... it scared me, Maryanne. I never want to see you hurt again. To keep that from happening, I want to know where you are all the time. If I find there's some down time at work, I want to pop into the bakery or swing by the apartment and see you. I need to know where you are so I know you're safe."

He searched her eyes, but she wasn't sure what he was looking for. If he was worried, it meant he truly cared for her, right? As more than just his baby mama? Hope blossomed in her chest as she smiled and wrapped her arms around his waist.

"I worry about you going on calls. I try not to think about it, but I do like to know your schedule and when you'll be home. When you were coming home late—there for a few days, I worried myself sick wondering what was keeping you. Then I realized it was just your schedule. Maybe syncing our phone calendars will help us both."

It wasn't fiery or intense, but it was filled with tenderness and promise. In that moment, she felt a surge of hope for their future together. Maybe this was the beginning of something real, something lasting. They were taking small steps towards each other, like sharing a calendar and making tentative plans. They were moving in the right direction, towards a love that could withstand anything.

He pulled back and rubbed his hand up and down her back. "Valentine's Day is in a few days, but I need to go out of town for training tomorrow. Want to go to the Old Mill with me tonight?" Her heart raced in surprise. That was the fanciest place in town. She'd only eaten there three times in her entire life.

"I'd love to!"

"Great, I'll make the reservations. I'll be home around seven to pick you up?" He kissed her cheek and then walked out the office and the bakery. She kept her lips shut before she said she loved him. It was getting harder to keep from saying those words.

Chapter Forty

Maryanne stretched in bed, feeling sore in all the right places thanks to Gunner last night. Valentine's dinner had been spectacular. She'd dressed up fancy in a short dress and her thigh-high heeled boots. Gunner hadn't taken his eyes off her the entire night, not even to stare at their cute waitress or the hostess who had seated them. They'd talked about their friends and family for most of the night, then had played a twenty questions game to get to know each other.

She now knew his favorites, as well as things he absolutely couldn't stand. She'd laughed when he'd admitted to not being able to eat bananas or banana pudding. He'd let her snuggle up to him in the booth and had even played with the hem of her dress for a while. His hand on her bare thighs had her melting in her seat.

When they'd gotten in the truck to leave, he'd taken a back road and pulled down an old dirt driveway. They'd made out like two teenagers before she'd straddled him and ridden him to heaven and back. When they'd gotten home, he'd spent another hour making her come time after time.

Maryanne yawned and glanced at the clock. It was almost seven in the morning, but it was Zarrel's day to open the bakery, and she'd fallen back to sleep after turning her alarm off at three-thirty. Gunner opened the dresser drawer he'd been storing his clothes in and tossed some shirts and jeans onto the bed next to his duffel bag.

"You're going to be okay by yourself? Did you call your mom to come stay with you?" Gunner asked as he packed his bag for his week-long annual deputy training camp.

"I haven't called yet, but I'll be fine, Gunner. It's just a few days, and I don't have any appointments or anything going on. I'll just be going from here to the bakery, the Diner, and Cindy's house."

She felt guilty about lying to him, but he would worry needlessly if she told him she was flying to Colorado tomorrow. There's no telling if he'd even let her go, and she wanted to close that chapter of her life and move on, never to look back.

"Will you call me every night? Maybe we can keep playing twenty questions." She picked at the bed spread, not wanting to admit how much she'd miss him. He'd been living with her for two months now, and it still amazed her how much better she was sleeping with him beside her.

He fell on the bed and pulled her into his arms, the sheet pooling around her naked waist. "I would love that," he growled in her ear.

He nuzzled her neck, making her giggle. She pulled back and wrestled her way on top of him. Running her hands up his chest, pressed her breasts together and made him growl. Then she pulled his hair and leaned forward to kiss him.

He groaned, grinding his hips up and gripping her waist in his large hands. "Maryanne, I have to hit the road if I'm going to get there on time."

"Just a quickie? Come on, take one for the road or you'll miss me too much." She kissed her way down his jaw, running her hands down his abs to his jeans. He refused to break their kiss, but helped his jeans slide down his hips.

When he slid inside, she sighed into his mouth. It was like coming home, and she hoped it was always like this. He tugged her hair to pull her back. "Sit up and ride me, M. I wanna see those tits bounce."

His rough, deep voice did something when he commanded her like that. She was already wet and ready but with his words, she moaned, leaning back and placing her hands on his thighs to ride slowly.

She never broke eye contact, but soon he was gripping her hips and controlling the rhythm. Damn, it was glorious, exactly what her soul craved, exactly what she needed to survive the next week without him.

He gasped and slid a hand down to her clit. He flicked it three times before she felt him filling her up, which triggered her own spasms of ecstasy. She slumped to his chest, and he wrapped his arms around her naked body. Only then did she realize his jeans and shirt were still half on.

Turning her head slightly as her breathing slowed, she chuckled. "You lost a boot."

He grinned and glanced down. "You've fucked me outta my shoes, woman."

They laughed, which made him slip out. She scrambled to the tissue box beside her bed and cleaned up. When she turned back to him, he was put back together and picking up his duffel. He went to the bathroom and grabbed his toiletries while she started the shower.

"If you get bored on the road, call me. I'm going to Holly's for a massage, and then I'm seeing Mom and Cindy for our weekly lunch." She tested the water's temperature.

He slid his arms around her from behind and met her eyes in the bathroom mirror. "I know, I checked the calendar yesterday. But I'll definitely call you. I like that you're naked when I'm leaving. Plan on being naked when I return, alright?" He kissed the side of her neck again, making her shiver.

When Maryanne turned in his arms, she kissed him, hoping he would miss her on this work trip as much as she would missed him. Maybe the time apart would help him realize he loved her. Maybe he'd want to spend forever with her. She was half afraid to hope, but they said absence made the heart grow fonder for a reason.

Their kiss broke apart, and he palmed her cheek, smiled, then walked out of the bathroom. She heard the front door close behind him before she stepped into the shower.

Gunner called three times that morning while she was at Holly's and had even started texting. It was progress because their conversations were all flirty and happy, not angry and accusatory like he'd been in January. Her heart thrilled every time her phone dinged or the *Country Fried* ring tone went off; she'd programmed that last night when she'd found out his favorite song.

She needed to pack her own bag before she went to pick up her nephew and niece from school. She'd switched her regular babysitting day so she'd still see them this week, since her flight was first thing tomorrow. A stab of guilt shot through her because she'd lied to Gunner again. But it was for the best. She picked up her phone and texted her friends from culinary arts school in a group chat to let them know she'd be in town.

Maryanne bounced up and down, waving like a mad woman with a dopey grin on her face. Wendy cut through traffic and pulled her little blue hybrid car into the loading only zone at the Denver airport. She hopped out, her wild curly auburn hair blowing haphazardly in the chilly wind, and rounded the hood to throw her arms around Maryanne.

"Maryanne, oh my God! I can't believe you're back. Girl, it's been too long. Your timing couldn't be more perfect because I have so much to tell you."

Wendy was as petite as Maryanne but wasn't as curvy. It was her wild hair that made her stand out in a crowd, not her lush curves like Maryanne.

"Wendy, I can't believe we made it almost a year without seeing each other. When are you going to come visit Crimson Creek?"

Wendy laughed while they loaded Maryanne's checked bag and her carry-on, her freckles standing out as the cold sucked the color from her pale skin.

"Soon, I hope. Are you hungry? I brought you a welcome back cupcake."

When they were loaded into the car and pulling away, Maryanne devoured the cupcake while chatting recipes.

They'd gone to high school together in Fort Hood, then Wendy's dad had been stationed to Colorado. When Maryanne moved here for culinary school, they'd fallen right back into their high school friendship like no time had passed at all.

Wendy waved her hand to the vehicle behind her. "Alright, I need to concentrate on traffic. So you spill it while I drive and tell me all you've been up to and why you're here. Also, how long do I get to keep you?"

Maryanne laughed. Wendy was so fun, somehow even more vivacious than even Maryanne.

Maryanne looked at her watch. "Fine, I'll tell you but take me to the courthouse before heading to your place, will ya? I need to check in with the lawyer."

"Lawyer? What's happened? Do I need to find bail money?" Wendy's concerned green eyes flashed to meet Maryanne's own.

Rubbing her temples, Maryanne sighed. "It's a long story, but do you remember my ex-boyfriend, Barry?"

While Maryanne caught her up, Wendy drove. When they arrived, Maryanne looked up at the intimidating building. Her stomach was queasy again, and she couldn't wait to get this over with. A part of her wished Gunner was here to back her up.

Wendy glanced over and lifted a brow. "What's with that face? You're mooning over some guy again, because I recognize that face."

Maryanne sighed. "Might as well tell you the rest of it now. Do you remember when I told you about my first kiss, the summer we were sixteen?"

"The kiss that rocked your world so good you passed out and had you turning down all the guys at our school because no one measured up?"

Maryanne met her friend's wide eyes with a frown. Had she really done that? She just hadn't been attracted to any of them. Surely it wasn't because of Gunner.

She rubbed her forehead. Of course, it was because of him. She'd been in love with him forever, it seemed.

"Yeah, that kiss was with Gunner. He was the cop who pulled me over when I first moved back to Texas, and last October things *happened*."

"Oo la la, what things? Do tell." Wendy wiggled her eyebrows, making Maryanne laugh as they pulled up to the courthouse.

"Well, long story short, we got pregnant, and now we're living together."

Wendy slammed on the break in the middle of the parking lot. She hit the steering wheel with her hand and turned wide-eyed to Maryanne.

"You're pregnant? Holy hell, Maryanne, why didn't you lead with that? Congratulations! I'm so excited for you."

Wendy threw it into park and reached over for an awkward seatbelted hug that made Maryanne laugh.

"Thanks. I'm due in July, but it's so complicated. Not sure if we're in a relationship or if he's just my baby daddy or what."

"Well, you have a few months to figure it out before the baby comes." She finished parking, then waved to the building. "Do you know how long you'll be in there?"

"No, the lawyer said today was just a preliminary meeting. The key questions and testimony won't be until later this week."

"Well, I need to be home in two hours to cook dinner for the guests." It was Wendy's turn to look at her watch.

Maryanne reached for the door handle. "Oh, don't wait for me then, hun. If you send me the address, I'll take an Uber and meet you there when I'm done. Save me a plate for dinner though because I'm already starving."

Wendy laughed, which somehow settled the nerves in Maryanne's stomach. Or maybe it was the CBD kicking in. She stepped out of the car with her big purse.

Wendy leaned over before Maryanne shut the door. "And after dinner, we'll go out for karaoke!"

"God, yes, I need karaoke so bad. You don't even know. I've only gone through half the story. Girl, you're going to flip out over the rest of it."

Maryanne's grin widened as Wendy's eyebrows rose in disbelief. Without saying another word, she shut the door and waved.

Chapter Forty-One

Gunner sat in the hallway, arms and boots crossed. He was tired, hungry, and ready to get this whole week over with and back to Maryanne.

"Officer Williams? The judge will see you now." With a creak, the clerk swung open the chamber door, revealing a spacious office. The walls were lined with towering bookshelves, and a large wooden desk sat at the back of the room. Behind it, a heavy leather chair stood tall and imposing.

But his eye was drawn to the large oak conference table in the center of the room. Three men sat around the table, which could seat eight, two on each side. The prosecutor and the defending attorneys were on opposing sides with an empty chair beside each of them.

A tired looking older man was on the far end, leaning back in his chair. The scent of coffee filled the air, making Gunner's nerves settle. The man and the coffee instantly reminded him of his grandfather, who was long gone.

Gunner walked to the fourth empty side and took a seat

across from the coffee drinker. He assumed that was the judge, as that's who addressed Gunner.

"Officer Williams, I hope your trip was satisfactory. Thank you for joining us today."

Gunner nodded as they exchanged pleasantries and introduced themselves. His skin itched, but he refused to give in to the nerves. This differed from normal testimonies as part of the job because it involved Maryanne and Barry Bruce.

"Mr. Williams, will you please explain the circumstances that led to the arrest of the defendant, Bruce David." The judge reached forward and pressed a button on a recorder. "We'll record this, if that's okay with you?"

Gunner nodded, then shifted straighter in his seat. "Yes, sir. I first met Mr. David on Halloween." Gunner continued to explain the discussion he'd overheard with Maryanne.

The lawyers asked questions to clarify. Then they showed pictures he'd already sent them from the town's traffic cameras, and he explained what happened the day of the arrest.

After more questions, the judge rifled through some paperwork and then stared at him, his eagle eyes peering at Gunner. "We just have one more thing before you'll be free to go, Mr. Williams."

He lifted a hand for the clerk, who jumped up and walked swiftly to the door behind him.

Gunner frowned, not looking back as he heard the door open. "Are you bringing in Mr. David? I'd prefer not to be in the same room, if possible."

The defense attorney smiled slowly, sending chills up Gunner's spine. "No, actually. We need to deal with the second issue."

"Right this way, ma'am." The clerk waved someone inside but Gunner's heart raced before he even saw her.

The scent of cinnamon filled the room, and he breathed deeply. Jerking his head to see her, she paused with one hand on the back of the chair next to him.

He met her surprised gaze with his own, and she swiftly looked to each of the others in the room before looking back at Gunner. His head spun with the implications, laws and procedures flying through his head to taunt him. This was terrible, and he wasn't sure how else to handle it except tell the truth.

He sucked in a breath and jumped to his feet to pull the chair out for her. She bit her nail, wisps of her pink highlights framing her heart-shaped face. Her bun bobbed when he leaned forward and kissed her cheek before she slid onto the chair.

He sat back down, running his hand along the back of her green sweater. "Hey, M. Fancy seeing you here."

She smiled wryly before placing her hands in her lap, holding them together tightly. "Surprise."

Her sarcastic tone made him smile and reach for her shaking hands. He entwined their fingers and squeezed gently. She squeezed back, then looked at the judge across the table with a smile. "Hello."

The judge smiled back. "Hello, let the record state that we are recording this meeting, and Miss Martin has just arrived. Miss Martin, please state your name, your relationship to the defendant, as well as your relationship to the officer sitting beside you."

Maryanne smiled her fake smile, and it made the nerves in his stomach wreak havoc. He was afraid she would lie or say something else that could ruin his career. He squeezed her hand and caught her eye.

"Truth. Tell them everything." He hoped that was enough to save his job.

This situation was much bigger than the Halloween pot brownies. He didn't disclose their relationship at the arrest, and there could be serious consequences because of it.

She tipped her chin up and turned her face away from him.

"Honestly, Gunner, when have I not told the truth? My name is Maryanne Martin. The defendant is my ex-boyfriend, and the officer beside me is a childhood friend and the father of my baby."

She placed the hand he wasn't holding on her stomach.

The judge blinked and the defending attorney grinned that sly, smarmy smile. "Congratulations to you both. We have some questions regarding your relationship—"

She shook her head with a frown. "I'm sorry, but how is that relevant to the case?"

The prosecuting attorney sighed. "Mr. Williams did not notify us of the conflict of interest. It's possible that his relationship with you clouded his judgment and led to profiling the defendant, which led to the arrest. If that's what happened, it's possible that your testimonies will be thrown out."

The defending attorney smiled. "Or the entire case can be thrown out."

Gunner's veins filled with icy dread, and Maryanne's eyes widened, and she started to tremble.

"No, you can't throw out the case. You can't let him go. If you did, he would—he would—"

She sucked in a breath, and Gunner pulled his hand out of hers to push her head down between her knees.

He began to rub circles on her back. "Breathe, M. It's going to be okay. They'll do the right thing, don't worry."

He frowned at the attorneys, who glanced at each other and then at the judge.

The judge sighed and rubbed his forehead. "Ma'am, we're going to ask questions, but we truly want to know so justice will be served. For now, don't worry about the consequences. Just answer the questions, alright?"

Maryanne slowly sat up and straightened her sweater before playing with the hem. She breathed in slowly, and Gunner moved his hand off her back, only to have her reach out and grab his hand like a life raft, holding on tight for dear life.

One of the lawyers asked, "When did you and Mr. Williams begin seeing each other?"

"October."

"And when did you first see the defendant in Texas?"

"Halloween."

They asked her questions about their relationship, when she saw Barry in town—never—and about the day of the arrest when she'd interviewed Chester.

After half an hour, the judge turned to him. "Thank you, Mr. Williams. We're going to question Ms. Martin about her relationship with the defendant, but you are free to go. However, please stay near town for the rest of the week. We may have further questions and might need you to come back in. In the meantime, please take in the sights and enjoy our little slice of Colorado. We will continue keeping your sheriff apprised of the case and if your failure to disclose the relationship will lead to the arrest being dismissed."

Gunner stood, his stomach in turmoil over the breach of protocol, and reached out to shake their hands. He slid his hand to Maryanne's shoulder and squeezed it gently, before stepping into the hall.

The Sheriff Gets His Girl

He stepped away from the door and called the sheriff. "Hello?"

"Ray, it's Gunner. Why didn't you tell me about failing to disclose the relationship to these Colorado lawyers before I left?"

Ray chuckled from the other end. "Walk into a shit pile, did ya?"

Gunner raked his hand through his hair and turned at the end of the hall. "Yes, I did. How could I forget to have told them like that?"

"Take it easy, son. It's not that big a deal."

"Yes, it is, Ray. They're talking about throwing out both Maryanne's and my testimonies, *and* the entire arrest itself for conflict of interest."

Silence came through the phone before Ray cleared his throat. "Look, you did your job and did it damn well. If anything gets thrown out, he'll still end up back in prison. You know how those drug dealers are."

Gunner growled. "Yeah, but what if he comes after Maryanne? Ray, I—" His throat closed up, and he cleared it.

Ray sighed. "Yes, well, we won't let it come to that either. But you know... it would help protect her if you got married."

Gunner groaned. "Not this again, Ray. I told you, I'm not going to marry her just because of the baby."

"I know, but hear me out. If you're married, then the relationship doesn't have to be disclosed in any future issues. It would be a known thing. Plus, Joey ran a few polls on social media to see how people are feeling about you now that it's been a few weeks since that crap fest of a debate."

"I don't care about the election anymore, Ray." Gunner wasn't even nervous about what Joey had found out. He was more concerned with how Maryanne was doing in the office.

"You're losing by four percent."

He was nothing but annoyed to be talking about this now. It was like Maryanne consumed him, thoughts, feelings, everything.

Ray continued barreling through. "A separate poll said that if you were married, twelve percent would then change their vote to you. They like the idea of a family man."

Gunner frowned. He didn't want to get married just to win the election, but the idea of marrying Maryanne did help settle his nerves. He felt his shoulders lower, some of the tension releasing at the thought of her beside him permanently.

Could he convince her? If what Kendall had said on New Year's was a sign, she was open to the idea. She'd said she dreamed of being a mom, but did she want more kids or just the one? Did she want him long term or—

"Gunner? Did you hear me?"

"I heard you. I'll think about it."

A snort sounded through the phone. "You don't have a lot of time to think here, boy. Decide before you come home. The election is at the end of next week, and it might help the case too."

Gunner sat on the chair outside the chamber door and leaned his elbow on the chair arm to stretch his legs out. A beep sounded on his phone, and he glanced at it. "Hey Ray, I gotta let you go. Mom is calling."

They said goodbye, and then he switched over. "Mom? What's up?"

"Did you make it safely to Colorado?" His mom sounded like she was putting up dishes, which made him smile.

"Yeah, Mom, I made it."

"Oh good, I just got off the phone with Margarita, and she said that Maryanne is on her way up there too. Not sure what part of Colorado other than the Denver area, but she's supposed to be hanging out with friends for some reunion. Maybe you can find her and take her out on a fancy date. I worry about her being in that big city in her condition."

He chuckled. "Actually, I've already found her, Mom. I'll fill you in later, but don't worry. I'll take good care of her."

"Oh, I wish you two would get married already. It's obvious you love her."

His heart froze in his chest, ice spreading through his arms. He wheezed a breath.

"I—I... Mom, leave it alone. We'll work it out or we won't, and it'll be exactly how it's supposed to be."

After a beat of silence, Ava said, "Well, that's mighty wise of ya. My little boy is growing up, becoming sheriff and seeing that he can't control everything. Now to just work on your ability to see the grey areas."

He raked a hand down his face. "What do you mean?"

"Not everything's black and white, Gunner. Didn't you see that from the debates? Maryanne stuck up for you, but she lied. Not a big deal, but that you let her? That's the grey area and a big deal for you. There's hope for you yet. She's good for you, Gunner, makes you relax and think of the big picture instead of the rules, so put a ring on her finger as soon as you're back."

Gunner frowned, unsure of how his mom always knew everything. Few knew that part of her debate speech was a lie.

"We'll see, Mom. I'll talk to you later. Love you."

They hung up but Gunner didn't have long to think about the irony of the sheriff, his mom, grey areas, and lying before Maryanne came through the door, followed by the clerk.

"We'll call you with the schedule for tomorrow." The clerk gave a friendly smile to them both before shutting the door to the office.

Maryanne looked pale, but her jaw was firm and lifted defiantly as she met his eyes. He stood and crossed his arms.

"So... why didn't you tell me you were coming up here?"

Oh, hell no. She held up a shaky hand and cocked her hip. She was not some prisoner or a grounded teenager, so he couldn't just tell her where she could and could not go. If he was going to treat her like a teenager, she was going to act like one. She stomped her foot and waved her hands as she whisper-yelled at him.

"What the hell, Gunner? You're seriously trying to tell me where I can and cannot go?"

She squared up to him, crossing her arms and mirroring his stance.

"I'm protecting you, Maryanne, and the baby. What happens if you came up here and got in an accident or were mugged or something? You were in a wreck barely five months ago. You don't need to tempt fate like that with another opportunity."

"I'm not tempting fate." She rubbed her temples and stomped down the hall. It occurred to her that she probably looked crazy, and she hoped no one came through the doors to see them arguing.

"I had to come up here, and you know what? I was looking forward to it. A few days where I can eat what I want, do what I want, go where I want, without you dictating my every fucking move."

"I'm not dictating, I'm protecting. It's my job."

"I'm not a job. I'm your—your—hell, Gunner, I don't even know what we are. Oh sure, we're having a baby, but it's like those 50s sitcoms. You know what we are? Roommates. We're roommates who are having a baby and have incredible sex. Only difference between us and those fucking shows is we sleep in the same bed, and I own my own business. Other than that? We're fucking roommates."

He stepped forward and wrapped his arms around her, and the scent of his cedar and pine cologne hit her nostrils. She was a sucker for that cologne. And with him pressing so close...

God, she was already wet and aching. If she were honest with herself, she had been since she'd seen him sitting in that office.

He growled, and it made the hair on the back of her neck stand up. "The hell we're roommates. I told you in December. You're mine."

She snorted, tipping her chin up to glare daggers at him. "For now. Once this baby is born, you'll leave."

"For now. For forever."

His mouth met hers roughly, hungrily, like a starving man, and it melted her heart. She didn't want him to leave, and she didn't want to be just roommates.

They'd finally gotten to a good spot right before he left. She was afraid this trip would set them back, but the only way forward was to talk. Talk it out, then talk more, talk about deeper stuff.

Her body ached for him, but her heart needed to know the man behind the uniform.

Chapter Forty-Two

Gunner's heart raced as he kissed her. It was true, she was his, but he needed to make it official. Not for the election, but because she belonged with him, and he wanted the entire world to know she was his.

He smiled and pulled her slowly back, his mind racing with plans to make it permanent, and he cupped her soft face in his rough hands.

"God, I've missed you."

Her hands crept along his back, sending shivers up his spine. "It's only been -four hours, Gunner."

"I know, it's too long. Let's never go that long apart again, okay? We're so much more than roommates, M. Let me show you. Let me prove it to you."

When she relaxed in his arms, he kissed the top of her head and pulled back with a smile.

He was happy that she was now relaxed in his arms, exactly where he wanted her to be. He helped her shrug into her red jacket, grabbed her free hand and walked with her through the hall.

The Sheriff Gets His Girl

"Where are we going?" Her voice was still wobbly, making him frown.

"Have you eaten lunch?"

She shook her head. "No, I just missed lunch with my flight. I had a big breakfast, though."

"Which you threw up?" His brow arched as he met her eyes.

She brightened. "Actually, no. I think the iron infusions are working. I'm still queasy but not throwing up every single meal. Besides, my friend, Wendy, has a plate waiting for me at her Bed and Breakfast in Golden."

He glanced at her. "Is that where you're staying?"

She nodded as they walked down the hall.

He squeezed her hand. "If you'll come with me to my hotel, I'll grab my stuff, and we'll go down to Golden. I can stay with you there?"

He pushed open the door and tucked up his collar as the icy wind hit them, then he turned his body to block the wind from her.

"Sure." Her voice was soft and uncertain. Pulling out his keys, he remote started his truck as they walked down the steps, then slipped an arm around her waist as they navigated the parking lot.

This was right, having her next to him. He was dreading this trip all day yesterday but now, he was excited at the idea of staying with her in a hotel in a new town. Maybe they could be tourists and go on a proper date while they waited for the lawyers to decide if they needed to come back.

When he opened the door for her, he quickly walked around and hopped in himself.

Turning to her, he grabbed her hand. "Are you sure it's alright for me to stay with you? Not gonna lie. I didn't sleep well without you last night."

A slow smile spread across her face. He wasn't sure if the sun came out or if it was just her smile that made the day seem brighter. She settled back against the seat, her posture more relaxed.

"I didn't sleep well either, so yes. You'll get to meet Wendy, too. We're supposed to go out for karaoke later. Do you want to go with us?"

He grinned. "I'd love to. You know I love to sing."

He plugged the address for his hotel into the GPS, then began driving. As he pulled onto the highway, he kept his voice even and without inflection.

"So you didn't tell me you were coming up here. In fact, you specifically said you were just going back and forth from the bakery. What changed?"

She sighed and looked out the passenger window, turning from him. He reached over and grabbed her hand, linking their fingers. He didn't want her to pull away. They'd had enough of that to last awhile. She didn't look back at him, but did squeeze his fingers.

"I lied. Last month I got a letter about needing to testify against Barry. When you said you were going out of town, it seemed perfect timing. I didn't want to worry you about traveling because you were already asking all the time where I was, when I was going to be home. And honestly, I just wanted to get this over with so we can start fresh with the baby without it hanging over our heads."

"That makes sense." He knew he'd been over the top on keeping up with her whereabouts for a while. And to be honest, he still was. Syncing their phone calendars had definitely helped.

She'd lied, but he couldn't be mad about that, since he'd liked too. He'd told her he was going to an annual training.

It had made him feel uneasy the entire drive up. Time to come clean and get it out in the open.

"I got an email. Normally, they keep the arresting officer apprised of the case, but except for that one request to come up here to testify, they went through the sheriff."

A soft chuckle ran through the cab of the truck, scratching the itch that was constantly beneath his skin when he wasn't around her.

"So you didn't have training this week and lied to me? I'm not sure if I want to be proud of you for relenting on those high morals of yours or upset that you lied to me."

His shoulders haunched as he turned through traffic. "I'm sorry I lied. I didn't want to worry you either, but how about neither of us lie to the other ever again. Deal?"

She finally looked at him, a soft smile on her face. "Deal."

Something released in his chest. This was what he wanted, this truth between them. In the spirit of honesty, he could admit to himself that he wanted more. He wanted to talk to her about everything and nothing. He wanted her to tell him every little thing about her day, and vice versa.

Well, that started now. "How'd it go with the lawyers today? You seemed nervous."

She glanced back out the window. "Yeah, I was and still am. What if they decide I was an accessory, Gunner? I'm scared."

"You did nothing wrong, Maryanne."

It broke his heart to see her so stressed and anxious. He wanted her—no, he needed her to be happy. How could he fix this?

"Barry was funneling drugs through my bakery here, Gunner. It may have taken me a long time to find any sort of proof. And when I did, I ran away. They could charge me with not turning over the evidence or letting someone know about it."

She was right, but it was highly unlikely. Maybe he could talk to the lawyers about keeping her out of trouble.

He tried to reassure her. "And I didn't disclose our relationship. That could get me kicked off the force completely or get the case thrown out. Ray doubts it and said they'll want bigger fish than you or me."

"Jade said something similar when I went and asked her about it. She helped me make a plan, but seeing you there and having all those questions kind of threw me off my game. I'm hoping they ignore the two of us and focus on the thumb drive I gave them."

"What kind of stuff is on it? How much evidence do you have?"

"Honestly, I'm not sure. There are some spreadsheets and all my financial information about the shop. It doesn't make sense to me but maybe it'll help them keep Barry behind bars or catch those bigger fish."

They turned into the hotel and Gunner left the truck running while she waited for him to grab his stuff. When they were routed to Golden and back on the road, he offered Maryanne a bag of trail mix.

"Need a snack, some peanuts for our peanut? Speaking of, is flying safe for the baby?"

He waved the snack bag, making her chuckle. The sound went straight to his cock, making his dick twitch. It was like his cock had ears and was tuned to the Maryanne radio station.

"Flying is fine until the third trimester." She took a handful and started to chew.

"Well, cancel your return flight. You can drive back with me."

She arched an eyebrow at him, making him grin. He loved to see her get an attitude with him when he tried to tell her what to do.

"Is that an order or are you asking?"

He snorted. "I'm just saying, it'll be cheaper to cancel your flight. And if we've both agreed that we sleep better with each other..."

He trailed off and glanced pointedly at her, wiggling his eyebrows. A smile hovered on her lips, toying with him and making him want to kiss her.

"Fine." She pulled out her phone and typed on it.

He asked about her favorite places in the area, and they made plans to check a few out tomorrow. She talked about her friends, her culinary school, and her shop, her voice wistful and bitter.

When they pulled into the Bed and Breakfast, Gunner whistled. The place was enormous.

"Damn, this place isn't a Bed and Breakfast. It's a mansion."

"Basically, yeah. You can see why Wendy was so excited to get the job here. She's the cook and photographer. I'll introduce you, but first, we should check in."

They walked to the front desk and spoke to the attendant, who confirmed that Maryanne's bags were already in her room.

Gunner took the keys from the attendant. "I'm going to take my bag up. Will you order me something to eat, and I'll meet you in the dining room?"

She nodded, so he headed up the stairs. It reminded him of a French chalet, with dark wooden accents, cream and grey furniture, and walls decorated with majestic mountain scenes.

Their room was much the same, with a blue king bed,

grey walls with some kind of pattern wallpaper on it and an en suite bathroom. A two-person shower took up one wall, with double sinks across from it.

He sat on the chair by the balcony door and called Jade. It was as he suspected. Maryanne hadn't told Jade about her fears of being arrested for withholding information.

Jade was going to call the prosecutor, and see if she could verify that Maryanne was safe, since she was cooperating now. He also asked for information on what exactly could happen to him for his failure to disclose the relationship with Maryanne.

His stomach was still in knots over the unknown consequences, but he knew being with Maryanne would help settle the nerves.

Walking back downstairs, he glanced around the dining room. Several tables were laid with rolled napkins and cream tablecloths. A family and a few couples were already dining, their voices soft in the large room, but no Maryanne.

He walked to the swinging door on the opposite side of the room and looked into the circular window.

His body seemed to relax when he caught sight of her in the modern kitchen. With stainless steel and grey floors, it was very clinical, the exact opposite of Maryanne's colorful bakery.

She was like a bright splash of color on a plain background as she stood at the work table in the middle of the room.

He pushed open the door, and she glanced at him with a smile. She was kneading dough while a curly haired woman stirred something in a pot on the stove, her hair barely contained by the ball cap and ponytail holder.

He breathed deeply, the savory aromas reminding him

of home. "Damn, that smells good. Don't think I realized how hungry I am. Think I can get some of that?"

The curly haired woman turned with a polite smile, but her eyes widened as she raked her gaze over him from boots to hair. He arched an eyebrow when she met his eyes, making her cheeks pinken.

Maryanne grinned and waved a dough covered hand at him. "Wendy, this is Gunner. Gunner, this is Wendy."

"Damn, girl. This is your baby daddy? Do they make any more like him in Texas?"

Maryanne and Wendy laughed as Gunner grinned and put his thumbs through his belt loops. He winked at Maryanne. "I've got four brothers, so yep. There's a lot more where I come from."

"Maybe I'll come visit after all." She laughed again, then turned to the two plates on the counter. "I went to high school with Maryanne down in Fort Hood. I've heard a lot about you, Gunner. Nice to finally meet you."

He winked at Maryanne, who blushed so prettily he wanted to kiss both her cheeks and savor it. "Oh really? Good things, I hope."

Wendy poured the stew into bowls and set them on a tray with the plates. "Verdict is still out on that, but you treat Maryanne like a queen, and I'll let you live."

He laughed, then stepped forward and took the tray. "Fair enough. Here, I can carry that. Who's it for?"

"Oh, this is yours and Maryanne's," Wendy said. "She ate the last of the bread while waiting for you, so she's restocking my stash."

Maryanne chuckled and dropped balls into the baking sheet.

He turned to the door of the dining room and glanced over his shoulder with a grin. "Not sure I can wait for you to finish whatever you're kneading, M. You better come along, or I might eat yours too. It smells so good."

He pushed through the door, Maryanne's laugh sent a shot of joy to his heart as it followed him into the dining room. God, what that woman did to him...

Now to plan what he was going to do to her tonight. He sat down the tray and began to set the table.

Chapter Forty-Three

Maryanne watched him walk out the door until Wendy cleared her throat. "Well, this story just got even more interesting."

Maryanne frowned as she washed the dough off her hands and avoided her friend's piercing gaze. "I told you it was long and complicated."

"No wonder you're knocked up. He's a hunk, and you're clearly in love with him."

"What? No." Maryanne fidgeted with the towel as she dried her hands.

Wendy snorted. "Yeah, you totally are. You can't lie to me, M. We've been best friends since high school, and it's no wonder." Wendy's voice trailed off as she glanced toward the door. Maryanne didn't want to talk about it anymore.

There was no point in admitting she loved him because it wouldn't do any good. For now, she just wanted to enjoy this little forced vacation with her friend and Gunner. First food, then karaoke. She pushed through the swinging door.

When she sat down for dinner, Gunner was half done with his own. Before she picked up her fork, she nodded to his plate. "Do you want me to go get another serving?"

He chuckled, the sound shooting straight through her heart. His phone dinged, and when he glanced at it, a smile spread across his face.

She clenched her teeth as jealousy raced through her. Who had put that look on his face?

"Good news, M. I talked to Jade when I went upstairs. She's just spoken with the prosecutor, and they're going to formally type up a letter acknowledging your immunity in the case. So when you talk to them, you'll all sign and notarize the letter. Then you can tell them everything without being afraid."

Her mouth fell open as she dropped her spoon into the bowl. "What? Seriously?" He'd listened to her. Not just listened, but made it all better. Tears pooled in her eyes. "I didn't know they could do that, or that they would."

He smiled that satisfied, smug grin of his, making her heart flutter. "This is where you say, 'thank you, Gunner. After we finish this food, let's go upstairs and I'll thank you properly.'"

He wiggled his eyebrows suggestively, making her burst out with laughter. The other diners looked at them but Maryanne didn't care.

She raised a brow and winked. "Thank you, Gunner. After we finish this food, let's go upstairs, and I'll thank you properly."

He sucked in a breath and his eyes deepened into that predatory look she loved. He'd not expected her to follow along.

She tilted her head. "Unless you'd rather talk about

boring stuff, like moving into the house, money, and all that grown up crap?"

He blinked, seeming to shake off whatever naughty thoughts he'd been having. "We can talk about that while we eat, I suppose. We're all set to move into the house next weekend. When we get back, I'll help finish packing the apartment."

She took a bite and hummed as the flavors burst on her tongue.

He continued. "And money? What do you want to know?"

She swallowed her soup. "Well, you bought the house and the car, but is that too much? The realtor got the down payment I sent, right?"

"She did, yes. We're ready for closing, but with this trip, I didn't want you to be alone in a new place by yourself, trying to unpack everything. So I already have the keys, and we're good to go, sellers are done with their part. We just need to go sign."

She looked down at her plate, fidgeting with the napkin. "Gunner, this is... well, I'm frustrated because you keep making these decisions without talking to me about them. I didn't know the house wasn't closing, and now I didn't know that it's ready. So excuse me if I don't sound all that enthusiastic. Congratulations on your first house, Gunner."

She waved a hand and sat back in her chair, crossing her arms.

He hesitated and grimaced. "Kind of like how we didn't tell each other we were both coming up here. I get it, Maryanne. Our communication sucks, but I'm willing to work on it, be real and honest from here on out. Are you?"

She scowled, waving her hand wide. "Are you fucking

serious? I've been in this from the beginning, chasing you for years."

He leaned forward and grabbed her hand. "But we haven't talked, M, and that's gonna change. So about the house—it's yours. I put it in your name, so you need to go sign for the paperwork, and then it's done."

Adrenaline pumped through her veins, and she rolled her shoulders to shake out the tension. "And will I be responsible for the monthly payment? How much will that be?"

He shook his head, frowning as he sat back in his seat. "No, that's on me. With your down payment and mine, we only owe a hundred thousand on the house. The monthly payments are going to be fourteen hundred, but I'm paying that as well as the taxes. Not you."

"You're paying for the house, my car. What, do you want to pay for the baby too? Because the bills are already coming in for the doctor's appointments, and my insurance is shit."

Her stomach churned as she fidgeted with her glass. Picking up her spoon, she finished the last of her soup and avoided his gaze.

He put an elbow on the table and leaned toward her. "Yes, I should pay for the doctor's appointments. Just give me the bills when they come in."

She ate the last slice of bread. "It'd be much easier if we just got married, Gunner. Then I could get on your insurance, and we wouldn't have all this back and forth about the bills of who's doing what."

His eyes flashed the darkest green she'd ever seen them, and he clenched his fists in his lap and jerked back. "We can't get married for the insurance, Maryanne. Absolutely not."

Her heart broke. That's not the reaction she wanted. She'd been hoping that he'd be more open to the idea, but she didn't want to give up yet. She tightened her jaw and tilted her head.

"What about for the election? I overheard some ladies at the Diner the other day. They said they'd vote for you if we were married. Who knows how many people feel the same way? It could be the difference between winning and losing the election."

When he crossed his arms, she knew she'd lost him.

"Maryanne, we are not getting married to win the election. Yes, I want to win, but marriage should be more than convenience of insurance or to win a stupid election. Are you done eating?"

She nodded so he stood up, holding out his hand. "Well, come on. We have plans upstairs, remember?"

She shook her head, refusing his hand. "No."

Had she ever told him no before? She was always chasing him, it seemed. But her heart couldn't handle sleeping with him right now, after he'd just shot her down so effectively. She was too raw, too vulnerable.

He didn't wait for an explanation, though. She could practically hear his teeth grinding together as he clenched his jaw. Then he turned on his heel and walked out of the room and up the stairs.

She laid her head in her hand as someone slid into the newly vacated seat. Glancing up, she saw that the rest of the dining room had emptied, so it was just her and Wendy.

"What was that all about?" Wendy jerked a thumb to the door Gunner had disappeared through.

"Well, I think I proposed, and I think he turned me down."

Wendy just blinked owlishly, so Maryanne sucked in a breath and replayed the conversation.

When she was done, Wendy was tapping her foot impatiently. "That jerk, just like a guy to think of sex first. But to be fair, you proposed a marriage of convenience based on insurance and the election. I love you, Maryanne, but if you proposed to me like that, I'd turn you down too."

Maryanne laughed, and Wendy nodded her head. "See? I'm right, but there's nothing for it but to belt out some tunes and sing at the top of our lungs with the rest of the girls from culinary school. It's exactly what you need to take your mind off it right now."

She helped Wendy bus their table, then grabbed her purse from the kitchen where she'd left it earlier. When they arrived at the karaoke bar, three of their other friends were there already, Mindy, Erica, and Vani. She pasted on a smile and hugged the girls as they caught up.

Wendy brought her a drink, whispering into her ear, "It's a virgin. Don't worry."

The current song ended and Mindy and Erica hopped up to take their turn on the machine.

An hour later, Maryanne's heart was light. She had almost forgotten the fight with Gunner. The girls were great at taking her mind off things and letting her just laugh and have harmless fun. Wendy was the only one she'd kept in touch with in the past few years, but she had missed this group.

She refused to be sad, though, determined to make it a fun night. Taking her turn on the machine, she started singing Beyonce's *If I Were a Boy*.

She'd barely gotten through the first verse when she saw a familiar figure in the back of the room, sitting at a table by himself. How had he followed her there?

The Sheriff Gets His Girl

Once again, she sang to Gunner. Staring through the dimness, unable to see his eyes, but knowing he was watching her. The shivers up her spine told her so.

When the song was over, she went back to her table amid the clapping of the others in the bar.

Someone else got up and sang, but she kept glancing to her right and catching Gunner looking at her. When that song finished, Gunner stood up and walked to the stage.

Wendy nudged her in the side. "Is that Gunner?"

Maryanne could only nod as the other girls asked who Gunner was.

Wendy shrugged. "He's... um, M?"

"He's my... boyfriend. We had a fight earlier."

She didn't want to get into the baby daddy explanation right now, not when he was taking the microphone in that firm hand of his.

"Evening, folks, this song goes out to a very special lady tonight."

His deep voice made her core quake. Why had she turned down the sex earlier? Oh yeah, she was hurt.

"Damn, even his voice is sexy." Vani said as he started singing Alicia Keys' *No One*.

He stared at her the whole time, never taking his eyes off her and making her breathe heavily at the truth behind his words. He always wanted to know where she was, but they'd not talked about forever. It was all about the baby and surviving the moment.

By the end of the song, the girls were practically drooling and fanning themselves, but Gunner didn't step down from the stage.

"I hope y'all don't mind my singing, because I've got one more song. This one I'll need help with, though. M?"

The lights from the stage eliminated all shadows from

his face. His eyes flashed with uncertainty before he smiled, trying to cover it up.

She stood up slowly and climbed the stage to stand at the other microphone. Alex and Sierra's *Little Do You Know* started up, making Maryanne jerk in surprise. He'd remembered talking about this song with her a few weeks back.

She sang the beginning, pouring all her hurt, fear, and pain into it, staring into his eyes the entire time. When it was his turn to sing, the emotions that poured out of him ran over her body in waves, making her tear up.

He offered his hand again, and this time she took it as they started singing together. He slowly pulled her closer until they were almost chest to chest, singing into their microphones with all they had.

She didn't realize tears were rolling down her cheeks until the song ended, and he reached his other hand up to wipe them away. Leaning down to kiss her, the crowd started hooting and hollering at them, but it barely registered as his lips touched hers, anchoring her to him.

Sagging against him, he wrapped his other hand around her and deepened the kiss, the microphone in his hand pressing into her back. She chuckled and pulled back.

"Is that a microphone in your pocket, or are you just happy to see me?"

He burst into laughter before setting his microphone into the stand and walking off the stage with her, hand in hand. She couldn't stop the grin that spread across her face. Her heart was floating on clouds.

No, they hadn't actually settled anything, but somehow singing with him had opened up the lines of communication once again. They'd be able to work through this, whatever it was.

She introduced him to the rest of her friends, who

fawned over him. It annoyed her when Mindy put her hand on his forearm.

But he stepped away and wrapped his arms around Maryanne from behind, continuing the conversation over her shoulder as they both faced the group. She felt like the luckiest girl in the world as they chatted.

Chapter Forty-Four

Gunner was wound tight the next day when they went back to the courthouse but not because of the case. Walking hand in hand, they stood in front of the judge and attorneys.

The judge cleared his throat. "We'll keep this brief. Your testimonies are important to the case, but it is unclear if either of them will be thrown out. We are also unclear if the case itself will be thrown out because of the conflict of interest. Ms. Martin, we'd like to ask you some follow-up questions about the information you gave us. Mr. Williams, you may wait in the hall."

Gunner kissed her on the cheek and walked out of the office. He was too nervous to sit, though. Even with the judge holding his future in his hands, that wasn't the biggest part of today. For once, his career was not the goal here.

He was sweating already as he paced the hallway. He pulled out his phone to check on the plan with Wendy, because he wanted this week to be the best, most relaxing vacation of Maryanne's life. Didn't matter what brought them here, he wanted to make it special because she was special.

When the door opened and she stepped out, her posture wasn't as stiff as when they'd arrived. She bounced over to him at the end of the hall.

"It went well?"

She beamed. "Yes! They're going to file a restraining order based on my information, just in case it all gets thrown out, but they didn't seem to think it would be. I'll come back tomorrow for that paperwork. What do you want to do today?"

"I want you to show me some of your favorite places. Where do you want to go first?"

"Mr. Williams, we're ready for you now," the clerk said through the door. Gunner sighed as Maryanne rolled her eyes and plopped onto the chair in the hallway.

"I'll make a plan for us while you're in there. I have so much to show you," she said. He took a deep breath and went back inside.

When he came out an hour later, she jumped up and slipped her phone into her pocket. She rattled off a rough plan while she waltzed down the hall, and he hung back slightly to both stare at her ass and type the plan to Wendy.

When she turned, he slipped his phone into his back pocket and pushed the front door open for her. Then they went sightseeing in Denver before back to Golden before evening traffic picked up.

While they were eating at a little Indian restaurant, she poked fun at him for not being able to handle the spice. But he convinced her to order mild because the acid of the spice might upset the baby. It was fun to learn to compromise like this.

Then they went for a walk along the creek trail that ran through downtown Golden.

The trees were still frozen with snow on them, but the path itself was clear, the concrete wet. The water was mostly frozen over the creek but it still flowed in the middle, the sound washing over them and just continuing her relaxed state as she hummed.

It made him feel good, to see her so happy and carefree again. His nerves were completely shot though at the thought of what he was about to do. He bounced from foot to foot as they walked slowly.

"How'd you sleep last night? You seem to have endless energy today," he asked.

Gunner tucked her hand into the crook of his arm as they walked. He didn't want to hold her hand because then she'd realize how sweaty his palms were, soaking through his gloves.

"I seem to sleep really well when you wrap me up like you do."

"You twitch a lot, so I wasn't sure if holding your legs down with mine helps. But I guess so?"

She nodded, chatting about their preferred type of mattress, soft or hard. It didn't matter what the topic, he loved hearing her voice and learning more about her.

In the next lull of conversation, he rubbed his neck. "Did you have any dreams last night?"

She glanced around at the creek and the trees. "I had a dream about some moose."

He barked out a nervous laugh, causing a bird to fly off and surprising him almost to jump out of the way. This wasn't going to get any easier, so he sucked in a deep breath.

"Well, I've been dreaming about you lately."

"Me?"

Her squeak of surprise was cute, but when she turned those big, beautiful brown eyes on him, he was lost. It was like when he'd saved her at the pool when they were kids. Those eyes had captivated him ever since.

The weak winter sun peaked through the trees, putting a halo around her red beanie covered head. Hair framed her face, and he reached up and pushed it behind her shoulder. They'd stopped on the path under the bridge just like Wendy had advised him to do.

He cleared his throat, pushing past the knot that threatened to close it up. "I've been dreaming of a life with you, M."

She blinked in surprise, then frowned. The sight made his heart skip a beat. "You have me, G. We're living together and moving into the house, aren't we?"

He released the breath he'd been holding and he took her hands in his. "I mean, I want you in my life permanently, Maryanne."

Her brow lifted, skepticism etched on every feature of her face as she pulled away slightly. "Even after all the problems I've caused? The surprises and messing up your plans?"

He nodded, needing to feel her skin. He peeled off his gloves, then removed hers, dropping them all to the concrete sidewalk.

"Yes, I want that spice, that unpredictability in my life. I've lived years with routines, plans, and structure, and I've needed that, true. But I think I need you more."

She tilted her head. "Is this about what we talked about at dinner yesterday?"

He grinned and dropped onto one knee, making her gasp, her right hand rushing up to her chest. The concrete path might be clear but it was still cold and wet, immediately soaking through his jeans.

"Damn straight it is. Will you marry me, M? Will you make a life with me? Stand by my side whether I'm sheriff or not, make more babies, and feed me all the bear claws I can eat?"

She chuckled, tears rolling down her cheeks as he slid a ring on her finger. She gasped, jerking it out of his hand to stare at it. "Gunner! When did you—"

"I actually picked it up a few days ago before I even got into Denver. I stopped for lunch halfway here, and the jewelry store was across the street. I kept staring at it, and all I could think as I ate was that I had slept horribly the night before... because you weren't in my arms. And I wanted to make sure I never went another night without you."

"You'd planned on proposing this whole time?" Her jaw dropped, and she shook her head. "Why didn't you say anything yesterday? I thought I'd made you mad."

He nodded, still on one knee, and took her hand back in his, kissing it.

"Mad that you wanted to get married for all the wrong reasons. And maybe because I wanted to propose to you, not have you propose to me."

He grinned slyly and winked, making her laugh. The sound shot straight to his cock, making him ache from more than the cold. "So is that a yes? Do you want to get married? I can be a hard ass sometimes, so you'll need to be patient with me."

She leaned down and kissed him softly. When she stood up, that mischievous grin made that dimple appear and his heart flipped.

"Yeah, and I'm a bitch sometimes. We go together like peanut butter and jelly."

"You stick with me, and I'll get all gooey on you?"

She threw back her head and laughed, the sound spreading like wildfire through his veins and heating him from the inside out. Standing, he brushed the wet spot on his jeans as she admired her ring. It wasn't big and bulky, but the opposite. The band was flat, with the stones barely raised in a pattern of sparkly diamonds.

He shifted on his feet. "Do you like it? I didn't want one with a rock that stuck out. I figured that'd get in the way of baking and might scratch the baby."

Her smile shone brighter than the sun as she threw her arms around his neck. Her cinnamon scent enveloped him as he breathed deep, soaking her joy into his soul.

"I love it. It's perfect. Who knew you were so sweet?"

He silently vowed to show her sweet every day, to be romantic and keep that happy smile on her face for the rest of their lives.

"So it's a yes?" He nuzzled the space underneath her ear, and she shivered in his arms before pulling back to peer into his eyes.

The light reflected off hers, shining as bright as the ring on her finger.

"Yes, Gunner, I'll marry you."

He couldn't wait any longer. His lips crashed into hers, his tongue sweeping inside to taste her sweet nectar.

When they broke apart, footsteps echoed on the path, making them look up. Wendy was grinning ear to ear as she held her camera.

He watched the recognition sweep across Maryanne's face, and it brought him so much joy to see her light up. Wendy pulled Maryanne into a hug.

"Oh my God, that was the sweetest thing."

Gunner reached out and shook her hand. "Thanks for

the assist. You were right, Wendy. This was the perfect spot for it."

Maryanne grinned as she realized Wendy had caught the whole thing on camera. The girls poured over the camera, looking at the shots as he stood, staring at his future wife and sliding his gloves back on.

"So when's the big day? I suppose I'll have to drive to Texas for it, huh?" Wendy slid her camera strap around her neck.

He watched Maryanne pale and rub her forehead. "Damn, I'll have to plan a wedding now. That's going to be so much time and effort. Ugh."

He broke into their little girl talk. "How about this weekend?"

Both heads swiveled to him, big eyes staring at him with twin expressions of both horror and interest.

"What?" Maryanne croaked out.

"Why don't we get married this weekend? The Bed and Breakfast is gorgeous, Wendy can take pictures, and didn't you say last night they're trying to break into the wedding market? They can practice on us."

Wendy squealed, and Maryanne opened and closed her mouth, unable to speak.

"Wendy, how long does it take to get a marriage license here?"

She blinked owlishly. "A few days maybe."

"Excellent. M, do you want to wait until after the baby's born for the wedding?"

She snorted. "Definitely not." She bit her nail, and he handed her gloves to her. She frowned as she put them back on and said, "I think this weekend is fine, but there's so much to do. And what about our family?"

The Sheriff Gets His Girl

He shook his head and shrugged. "What about them? I say we just elope and go home married."

She put her hands on her hips and squared up to him. "Gunner, we talked about this. You can't just keep making all these decisions."

He grinned and tipped her chin up with a finger. He loved it when she got all sassy. "Do you want to invite your family and make it a big, fancy thing?"

She shook her head, melting into his arms as he wrapped them around her. "No, but we can't leave them out."

"I bet we can appease if we tell our moms they can plan a reception or something down there."

Wendy interrupted. "So no big, fancy wedding?"

He squeezed Maryanne closer, smelling her cinnamon shampoo while the warmth from her seeped into every bone in his body.

She laughed in his arms. "As high maintenance as I am daily, the idea of planning a wedding was already giving me an anxiety attack. We had enough of that with crap with Cindy's, right, G?"

She pulled out of his arms, making him feel cold and bereft again.

He snorted. "Yeah, no THC in anything, please. I don't care if it *is* legal here."

Maryanne laughed and hooked her hand through the crook of his elbow to walk back along the path.

Wendy walked on the other side of her. "So what are the top things you want in a wedding? Let's start there."

Maryanne leaned her head on his arm while they walked. "I want a bouquet and a dress. That's all I care about. Think we can find those, like, tomorrow?"

"Oh yeah. I got you. I'll make it happen." Wendy bounced along beside them.

He wanted the details so he could call his mom. "Where do you want to get married, and when?"

"Right here, next to the creek where you proposed."

Her smile warmed his heart, driving the cold away. He reveled because he had made her so happy. Could he do that every day?

She turned back to Wendy. "I need limited options. Give me like three or four things to choose from for each. I don't want to be overwhelmed with choices. Oh, and can I use your kitchen for the wedding cake?"

Wendy grinned. "Hell, yeah, you can! I've been craving your cakes for two years, ever since you left!"

"I'll help. I love helping you bake." He wrapped an arm around her shoulder, both to draw her closer and to keep her now shivering body warm. They'd been outside for almost an hour now.

Maryanne snuggled him as they stepped up to the parking lot. They made plans on the way back to the Bed and Breakfast. They'd apply for the marriage license that afternoon, then tomorrow the girls would go dress shopping.

Chapter Forty-Five

A knock sounded on their door. Maryanne turned her head over and glanced at the clock. Nine-thirty! How had she slept so late?

She smiled slowly, thinking of how they'd celebrated their engagement last night. They'd had sex on just about every surface in their little room, plus the bathroom and even the balcony, which had been colder than expected.

The knock sounded again, and a groan sounded beside her.

"What?" Gunner's deep voice ground out, sending a shot of awareness through her body.

She opened her eyes again and glanced at him. He was facing her, his arm curled under the pillow, his eyes still closed. The sheet barely covered his hips, and one of his legs was out of it but holding down her own underneath.

Wendy called out from the other side of the door. "Hey, Maryanne, I have a full-serve breakfast here. Do you want me to leave it out here or bring it in?"

Maryanne raised the sheet to cover her chest. "Um, you can bring it in."

Wendy unlocked the door and propped it open with a foot, bent to pick up the tray she'd set on the floor, and then walked inside to the small table beside the door to the balcony.

Maryanne giggled when Wendy glanced at them, blushed, and then nervously started chattering away.

"Good morning, y'all. We just finished the breakfast rush, and I wanted to bring the love birds breakfast in bed. Also, we have a dress appointment in an hour. Gunner, you'll have to come with us to find a tux too. Then we'll eat lunch and head to the flower shop at two-thirty. I have to be back here by four to start dinner. So hop up, sleepyheads!"

Gunner lifted his head, making Wendy freeze on her way back to the door. She glanced from Maryanne to Gunner and back again, the blush creeping higher on her chest, before rushing out the door.

Maryanne turned onto her side to face Gunner, laughing softly as he blinked his eyes open.

"What happened?" His growl made her want him even more.

Even though her clit was sore, her pussy craved him again. She hooked a leg over his hips and ran her hand down his bare chest.

"It's time to wake up and go shopping. Are you hungry? That bacon smells delicious."

She slid over him to straddle him, rocking her hips into his. He hissed, grabbing her hips and holding her off his morning wood.

"M, I gotta pee."

She laughed and rolled off him, swinging her hips as she

walked to the breakfast tray. She felt his eyes on her naked ass as he got up to go to the bathroom.

She sat at the little bistro style table, crossed her leg at the knee, and perched on the edge of the chair as she made her plate.

When Gunner came out, he stalked toward her. He stood next to the table and reached for a scone.

She deliberately ignored his naked form right next to her... until his cock started to get hard again, that is.

She bit into the bacon biscuit she'd made and gave him the side eye. Damn, but he was sexy everywhere. His thighs were like tree trunks, the kind she wanted to climb and never get down.

When he palmed his cock and stroked it slowly, she nearly choked on her food. She met his gaze through her eyelashes.

"How much time do you need to get ready this morning?"

His eyes roved over her face down to her breasts before turning deep forest green. That predatory look sharpened his features, making the five o'clock shadow stand out on his jaw as he stroked slowly.

She ate the last bite of her biscuit, then drank her juice as she stood, a drop or two dribbling down because she was too busy looking at him to pay attention.

"I'll need about fifteen minutes for make-up and ten for hair. Do you want to take a shower with me?"

Reaching for the napkin, she slid it over her chin and down to her breasts. But his hand shot out, stopping her as he gripped her wrist lightly. He leaned forward and licked the trail of juice from the tip of her nipple up to nearly her collarbone.

She moaned. The sound seemed to release the beast

within him, because he reached around to her ass and lifted her against him. She wrapped her legs around his waist as he carried her into the bathroom. His lips traced an invisible trail up her jaw to her ear lobe.

Stopping by the shower door, he growled, nipping under her ear. "Start the water."

She reached over and turned it on, causing her breasts to pull away from his. He leaned down and sucked one into his mouth.

The gentleness of last night was gone. This man was on a mission, and her body shook in anticipation as their lips met in a fiercely raw need of pure desire.

"I can't wait, M."

He pushed her against the wall of the bathroom, hiking her legs up and pushing into her. She gasped, wrapped her arms around his shoulders and gripped his hair.

"God, yes, Gunner."

They were fast and furious, her back hitting the wall and his pelvis hitting just the right spot on her clit. Soon they both exploded, and she clawed his back as she moaned.

He settled his head in the crook of her neck while they caught their breath. Then he carried her, still joined, into the now warm shower.

An hour and fifteen minutes later, they walked into the dress shop. Two women looked up from the front desk with identical practiced smiles.

Wendy stepped forward. "Hello, we have appointments for ten-thirty? I spoke to someone earlier. I'm Wendy, and this is Maryanne and Gunner, the bride and groom."

Maryanne looked around, gripping Gunner's hand in hers, already overwhelmed with all the dresses lining the wall.

"Ah, yes. I'm Margaret, and the bride will be with me

while the groom will be with Jessica. Sir, if you'll follow her to the tuxedo side of the store, she'll get you fitted in no time."

Gunner leaned over and kissed her on the cheek. "I can't wait to see you in your wedding dress. Or to peel it off you."

He nipped her ear, then waltzed away through a side door, her eyes following him and wishing he could stay with her.

"Now, what style of dress are you looking for?"

Maryanne looked around and shrugged.

"Honestly, I hate making choices like this. My sister got married a few months ago in a mermaid type dress. I'm curvy, as you can see, but it's going to be an outdoor ceremony, and I want something different from my sister's."

Wendy looped an arm through hers and tilted her chin up as they followed the woman all the way to the back. A separate room had several couches and mirrors lining the wall, with several changing rooms along a side wall.

The woman waved Maryanne to the largest changing room. "I've pulled half a dozen dresses from the conversation I had with Wendy this morning. Just let me remove the mermaid dress, then you can start trying them on."

Wendy turned to smile at Maryanne, patting her hand. "Don't worry. I told them exactly what we needed, but I didn't know about Cindy's wedding. That's so exciting!"

"Yeah, that wedding was something else, but it took her *hours* to find a dress. Please tell me we won't have to go through that today?"

Wendy's freckles stood out on her face as she flipped her wild hair over her shoulder.

"Won't know if you don't go try them on, will we? Let's

see what we're working with. Hurry, I don't know if I can wait much longer. This is so exciting."

Wendy was right. The fourth dress she tried on fit like a glove and made her sigh in relief. When she stepped into the lounge area, Wendy's eyes bugged out and her mouth formed a silent *O*.

Maryanne walked to the little raised platform, satisfied that she could walk with the loose skirt. The top was lace, long-sleeved, and formed a deep v in the front and back. It fell at the waist, at just the right spot near her hips.

She raised a leg, liking that she could move in it. Raising up on her tiptoes to simulate heels, she frowned.

"Ma'am, how fast can we have this hemmed?"

"We can have it ready by the end of the day if need be."

Maryanne smiled, catching her own eyes in the reflection. She was hopeful and excited. "Wendy, take some pictures so I can text them to Mom and Cindy."

He hadn't said he loved her, but getting married was a big sign that he wanted to stay with her, right? She nodded softly to herself, then posed for the picture and asked about shoes and accessories.

She texted the pictures, then texted Gunner that they'd found one and would be out in a few minutes.

Half an hour later, they met Gunner at the front of the store where he sat on a chair scrolling on his phone. When he looked up, he smiled, making her heart flip.

"I kind of expected you to wear it out the store."

Maryanne laughed and kissed him on the cheek.

Wendy nodded with a grin. "Gunner, it's gorgeous! You're going to be amazed, with the snow and the creek—oh, it's going to just take your breath away!"

He wrapped an arm around Maryanne's waist and

smiled. "Don't need all that to take my breath away. Maryanne already does that with every smile."

Maryanne's heart hitched, and the women seemed to melt at his words as he led her to the front door.

Maryanne dug in her heels. "Wait, we have to pay—"

He pushed open the door. "I've already taken care of it."

Maryanne did a double take, then wondered why she was surprised. Gunner always tried to handle these things.

Wendy brought up the rear with a sigh. "Aw, that's the sweetest thing. Maryanne, I'm definitely going to visit you guys. Maybe even be there when the baby's born."

"I would love that, Wendy. You'll have to stay in the new house with us. We have four bedrooms upstairs."

They talked about the new house as they walked to a lunch spot Wendy wanted to take them to.

When they got back to their room that night, Maryanne's feet hurt. She hadn't expected to walk so much while here.

It was barely three-thirty—it hadn't taken nearly as long at the flower shop as the dress shop—and she desperately needed a nap.

"I'm going to go start on dinner. I'll see you two love birds later." Wendy practically bounced into the dining room.

Gunner wound an arm around her waist as they went up the stairs. "Come on. Let's take a little nap before dinner."

"Is that our new code word? Because I don't have the energy for another round right now. We didn't exactly get a lot of sleep last night." She yawned.

He chuckled. "I meant a literal nap, M. Peanut is tiring you out."

They might need to improve their communication, but

he was already melting her heart constantly with sweet words like that.

Gunner stretched when his phone dinged. Maryanne was still napping, her pajama tank top twisted around her chest already and one meaty thigh on top of the covers. He tugged the blanket over her as he reached for his phone and got up. He walked to the bathroom, but paused in the doorway as he processed the email. The marriage license was approved, and they could pick it up before noon tomorrow or they'd have to wait until Monday.

He glanced over at Maryanne, brushed the hair out of her eyes, and felt his heart skip a beat because soon she'd be his.

He went downstairs to talk to Wendy about the plan, then he called Andy.

"Hey, man. How's your trip going? Congratulations on the engagement."

Gunner scratched his chin as he stood on the front porch of the Bed and Breakfast. "It's going well. Wish y'all could all be here, but we'll celebrate back home."

"No worries, man. Cindy can't take off work since she's so new, but you better believe the reception here will be huge."

"That's okay with me, but I have a problem I need your help with." Gunner explained what he needed, and of course, Andy could hook him up, even from Texas.

When he went back upstairs, Maryanne was just coming out of the bathroom.

Frowning, he rushed to her side. "Did you get sick? Are you alright?" She smiled sleepily.

"I'm fine, and I haven't been sick since being here, so that's progress." She yawned.

"Do you want me to bring up a tray for dinner, and we can go to bed early?"

She shrugged as she snuggled into the wing-back chair in the corner and wrapped a throw blanket around herself. "That's fine."

He knelt by the chair and pushed the hair out of her face. "Do you want to get married tomorrow afternoon or on Monday?"

Her eyes jerked awake, widening as she blinked several times before replying. "Geez, what a way to wake a girl up." She chuckled and wiped her eyes.

"I also heard from the lawyers while you were asleep. They're done with us for now, so we can go home anytime. If we get married tomorrow, stay here for the wedding night, then hit the road Sunday morning, we'd roll into Crimson Creek Monday night."

She nodded. "Yeah, that's fine with me. I'll text Zarrel and update him, but we might need to spend three days on the road. The baby books say to watch swelling ankles when traveling."

His heart skidded to a stop. "Do we need to call the doctor first?"

She shook her head. "No, I cleared the trip with her, so she knows. She even gave me some iron pills, just in case I got sick again. We'll be fine, G."

Gunner smiled as her eyes relaxed around the edges. "We'll take it day by day and see how it goes, alright?"

That applied to their relationship too. They were finally in a good place and learning how to communicate, but he still worried about her.

She needed to rest up and relax, take care of that baby,

and be happy. Hopefully, he could keep her happy the rest of their lives.

The next day when he stood on the creek near the spot where he'd proposed, he found that the cold didn't bother him at all. In fact, he was burning up. His palms were sweaty, and the tux felt too tight.

He pulled at the collar; even though he'd gotten a size too big at the neck, it still felt like it was choking him.

One girl from karaoke night started playing soft music on her phone. Another one held her phone up, recording everything in Zoom. She walked up to him and flashed the phone around so he could see the little tiles. There was his mom and dad, his brothers, Cindy and Andy, Margarita, and even Zarrel, Kendall, and some others from poker night.

He waved. "Hi, Mom!"

"Oh, sweetie, we are so excited. I'm sorry none of us could come up there. It would have been fine if we—"

"Ava, let it go. They need to do this on their own, and it's foal season." His dad reached for his mom's hand and squeezed.

"Don't worry. We are already planning the reception here, remember, Ava?" Margarita piped up as she wiped her eyes.

He hoped they were all okay with this and happy for them, not just putting on a brave face. But he couldn't worry about them right now, because the music changed. The woman holding the phone stepped behind him, standing at his shoulder and holding the phone up for everyone to see Maryanne walking up the path. Wendy walked just in front of her, snapping pictures of him and Maryanne and swinging back and forth.

But it was all just peripheral movement. His eyes had

zeroed in on Maryanne. Her lacy dress was gorgeous, making her perky tits practically spill out of the v-neck. The baby bump wasn't even visible, with the way the dress fell around her ample hips. It swayed as she walked, making his hands itch to grip her waist.

Her hair was pulled up in an elaborate half up-do, with most of it spilling over her shoulder, the pink highlights matching the flowers in her bouquet. It seemed like the sun shone just on her, lighting the path as this angel walked toward him to steal his heart forever.

But that wasn't quite right, because he'd given his heart to her long ago. Maybe even as far back as that first kiss, the one that had scared him into running the other direction.

He'd finally come full circle, running back into her arms, and it was exactly where he wanted to be forever.

She reached his side and turned to face him. With Wendy on one side taking pictures, the woman playing music stopped and switched to video mode.

There wasn't a preacher or traditional vows, and they'd gone over the plan with Wendy earlier. Instead, Gunner cleared his throat, his hands sweaty and his heart pounding.

"Maryanne, I've known you my whole life but it's only in the past few months that I see what a treasure you are. You balance me in ways I didn't even know I needed. I can be myself with you, but you also make me into a better version of myself. Someone who's not so linear, who can stop and dance or laugh—God, how you make me laugh. I can't imagine marrying anyone else, Maryanne. I'm so blessed to call you mine forever."

She sucked in a breath as a tear rolled down her cheek, somehow not leaving any make-up trails at all.

"Gunner, you were my first kiss, and I'm happy that now you'll be my last too. I chased you, threw myself at you, over and over until you finally caved. You know how persistent I am, what it's like to live with my cranky self, and yet you're still here. I'm amazed that you want to spend the rest of our lives together, as it's all I've ever wanted."

It was his turn to suck in a breath. Did she mean it? They'd never mentioned love, but wasn't that what he was feeling? It was more intense than anything he'd ever felt before. He snapped himself out of it because he had to finish the vows.

"Maryanne, I will always honor you, protect you, serve you, care for you, and provide for you. I will be faithful and true because honestly, you're the only woman for me."

She smiled a watery smile and squeezed his hand.

"Gunner, I will love you, honor you, challenge you, bake for you, and be always by your side, no matter what, until the day I die. I will be yours and only yours. I always have and always will."

They paused, but his throat was closing with emotion. She'd mentioned love, so did that mean she loved him? He couldn't say anything else, and without a preacher, he didn't know how to end the ceremony.

He cleared his throat and looked at Wendy and back to Maryanne. "So—are we married?"

Maryanne chuckled, and it sent a hungry wave of desire and joy through him. He pulled her roughly against him, her gasp silenced when he kissed her deeply.

He poured his heart and soul into that kiss, telling her he loved her with his mouth. The hunger built, threatening to overtake him as she sunk warm and pliant into his arms.

The cheers from the video call had her breaking the kiss and looking around. Spying the woman holding the tablet, Maryanne's face lit up in surprise.

He bent down to nuzzle under her ear. "I arranged a

video call for anyone back home who wanted to watch. Surprise."

She gasped, pulling back to stare at him with wide eyes. Then she grinned and threw her arms around his shoulders.

He sucked in a breath when her breasts pressed against his chest. He wrapped his arms around her and breathed in that cinnamon scent that made him horny and comforted at the same time.

"Want to say hi to our parents, Mrs. Williams?" he growled in her ear, loving the sound of her new name on his lips.

She was his now, forever. His heart felt like it was going to burst out of his chest in excitement as they pulled apart and walked to her friends.

The smile on her face was worth it all, and for once, he just relaxed and enjoyed the moment and his wife.

Chapter Forty-Six

Maryanne waved to her friends when they piled into their vehicles at the Bed and Breakfast.

Wendy turned and hugged her. "I'm so excited for you, Maryanne. It was a beautiful day, and it's the perfect start to the rest of your lives together. I've packed up the rest of your wedding cake, and sent up some snacks to your room. Don't feel you need to leave tomorrow if you don't want to. I'd love y'all to spend another day or two in town."

Maryanne squeezed her neck and pulled back with a smile.

"We'll see how it goes tonight. I might wear him out so much that we end up sleeping all day tomorrow."

They laughed, and Maryanne caught Gunner's eyes, his brow raised. He was leaning against the outside wall, arms crossed and waiting for her.

When she was close, he swung her into his arms, bridal style and making her squeal and laugh. Wendy held open the door as he carried her over the threshold.

"Thanks for everything, Wendy. See you tomorrow." His

clipped tones made a shiver race up her spine, but he grinned down at Maryanne and winked.

She laughed again and wrapped her arms around his neck as he took the stairs carefully up to their room. He kicked the door shut behind them and stood her next to the bed. Gently, he cupped her face and kissed her, their tongues dueling slowly. She tried to pull him closer, but he broke the kiss with a chuckle.

"No, M. Let me show you how I feel tonight." Her core was already pounding, waiting and ready for him, but he slowly slid a finger along the v cleavage of her dress.

"Do you know how much I love you in v-necked tops? This dress is perfect, and I'm never going to forget the way you looked in it today."

He eased the dress off her shoulders, her heart racing at his words and soft touch. It was loose enough that it fell to the ground, leaving her in new underwear and thigh highs.

He stepped back, his gaze flirting down her body and making her nipples harden. His jaw clenched when he saw them, and he pounced, wrapping her in his arms.

Maryanne gasped as his mouth crashed to hers. He slid his hands down, pulling her thigh highs off before slowly pushing her onto the side of the bed. He knelt at her feet, pulling off her shoes and the stockings. When he lifted her foot and kissed the instep, she felt her pussy throb and her heart melt.

This man surprised her every day. She never knew which side of Gunner she would get, and she loved all of them. The next kiss was on the inside of her ankle and made her heart skip a beat. Then he worked his way up to the back of her knee.

She was gripping the sides of the bed as he placed her raised leg over his shoulder and ran his thumbs up the inside of her thighs. A wave of need rolled over her as he met her eyes, his dark hazel gaze making her breath hitch in her throat.

Keeping eye contact, he bent his head and licked up to her clit.

"Fuck." She gasped, her back arching as she laid down and tried to draw him closer with her heels on his back.

He slowly grinned, that predatory glaze falling over his eyes, before he sucked her into his mouth. She couldn't stop the bucking of her hips as he brought her swiftly to the edge and then backed off.

She whimpered. She'd been so close, but now he just licked slowly and leisurely, barely paying her any attention at all.

Wrapping her leg around his neck just made his hands grip her thighs and spread her wider. When she was spread as wide as she could go, he leaned back and blew softly on her overheated core.

Her legs shook from wanting him, needing him to give her—

"More," she demanded. His eyes flashed as he dove for her clit and sucked on it hard.

The unexpectedness of it caused her to spasm, crying out as she came all over his face. He didn't stop until she begged,

"Gunner, enough. God, Gunner!"

Only then did he lean back, his smile like the Cheshire cat as he stood, grabbing under her thighs and lifting her. She wrapped her legs around him, anticipation rising.

He spread her wide and slid home as he pinned her against the bed, making her gasp as sensation after sensation swept over her.

The softness of the bedspread at her back. The heat

radiating between them. The hard cock that fit perfectly inside and made her feel complete, like the last missing puzzle piece had now found its rightful place in the world.

"Look at me, M."

His growl set off a spasm deep inside her, making her clench on him as she met his eyes.

Without breaking eye contact, he slid out, then in again, hooking her knees onto his arms. Slowly at first, but soon he lost as much control as she had, slamming harder and harder into her, making the bed scrape the floor as it moved.

She held onto his biceps as they flexed. His eyes spoke to her as she clenched on him with every thrust. They said he needed her, that he'd always need her.

"You're mine, M. *My* wife. Mine. Mine. Mine."

He repeated the word with every thrust until it was a choir of angels echoing through her head.

She gasped, thrilling at his tone, the words, the permanency and safety in them. He plunged as deep as he could go and grunted. He broke eye contact, ducked his head, and sucked at the base of her neck where it met her shoulder.

The kiss made her clench on his cock, and he stilled and swelled inside. He filled her, and it set off an answer within herself as she came, milking him with a groan.

"I love you," she whispered into the growing dimness.

Her heart was racing so fast she wasn't sure how loud she said it. But part of her heart cracked when he just looked at her and blinked, that stoic expression not showing his emotions.

"You're my everything, M." His voice was soft, his kiss sweet and slow, a balm to her fragile heart. It wasn't the big L word, but it was a start. Right?

Two days later, Maryanne leaned her head against the window of his truck as they drove home from Amarillo. Their wedding night had been mind blowing. He'd practically worshiped every inch of her body.

They'd started driving home late Sunday morning, waving a tearful Wendy goodbye, and had stopped in Amarillo for the night. The honeymoon suite had been pretty gaudy, with a heart-shaped bed and a jacuzzi tub right in the room.

Gunner had been horrified, but she'd thought it was hilarious. He'd stopped complaining when they'd taken the bubble bath together. She smiled at the thought as her mind drifted in the half sleep state, the monotony of the road lulling her to sleep.

They'd talked of everything and nothing on the drive too.

Well, when they weren't singing together. It was quickly becoming one of her favorite things to do with him.

They'd both watched her ankles for swelling and had taken several breaks. Gunner had set a timer to stop every two hours, and they walked around wherever they were, shopping along small-towns and even swinging by a big car graveyard on the side of the road.

When they pulled into Crimson Creek, she rubbed her eyes and looked around.

"We're at the new house? I thought we were going to my apartment?"

She caught his smile through the street lamp out front before he hopped out and came around to open her door.

"Nope, I have a surprise first."

He took her hand and led her up the front porch.

When he unlocked the front door and turned on the light, he bent and scooped her into his arms, making her squeal.

"It's tradition to carry the bride over the threshold, right?"

She relaxed and wrapped her arms around his neck. But when she looked around as he stepped inside, she gasped.

"That's my couch! My—my entire living room is here! What—how—"

He kicked the door shut and walked down the hall to the master bedroom.

"Everyone wanted to do something for us since they didn't get to attend the wedding. Parker said it only took a few hours to get it all moved in after church yesterday. Mom said that we should start our marriage in the house we're going to raise our babies in."

Her stomach flipped. "Babies, as in plural?"

He grinned and nodded, making her heart melt. That meant he was for real about their marriage. He really did want to make it work long term, and she felt the worry lessen that he would divorce her and walk out.

He pushed open the master bedroom door with his boot.

"Turn on the light."

She did and squealed, patting his chest for him to put her down. Her bedroom furniture was here, but so was a little bassinet, rocking chair, and changing table in the corner.

When her feet were on the floor, she ran over to them. They were green and white plaid, the same shade as his eyes.

"Gunner, this is..." Tears spilled down her cheeks.

"Do you like it?"

The uncertainty in his voice about ripped her heart. She spun to face him, then threw herself into his arms.

"Gunner, it's the sweetest thing anyone's ever—no, that's not right. It's the sweetest thing you've done since surprising me at Christmas. It's perfect."

"Holly helped with the colors. She said you had a bunch of stuff saved on Amazon, so I snooped to figure out what you wanted."

Good Lord, if she didn't love him before, there was no way she could have held off now. She squeezed him tighter, love bubbling up inside her.

"Gunner... I love you, you know that? You're the best man I've ever met. I can't believe you did all this..."

Her voice trailed off as she met his lips, searching for the love she craved from him.

She didn't want to give him time to say it back because she was still half-afraid he didn't, that he would cast her aside. She pushed the thoughts away and wrapped her arms around his neck.

Chapter Forty-Seven

Maryanne went into work the next day floating on cloud nine. She was married, expecting a baby, and life was finally falling into place. After work, she brought her nephews and niece over to her new house to help her unpack. Cindy and Andy met them at her house around six-thirty.

"Oh my God, I can't believe you got married without me," Cindy cried, throwing her into a tight hug.

Maryanne laughed. "Well, I saw all the stress your wedding put you through. I knew I didn't want to do *that*, so we just eloped."

"Kinda wish we would've done that." Andy arched a brow as he walked past them into the dining room. Cindy slapped him on the bicep as she followed him, laughing as he spun her into his arms for a quick kiss.

Maryanne called the kids, who stomped down the stairs to take a seat at the dining table. She'd piled up a big thing of pasta, French bread, and salads in the center of the table.

She checked her phone to text Gunner before she sat down to eat with her family.

Are you coming home for dinner? I have the kids, and Cindy and Andy just got here for pasta.

It was loud as the kids talked about school. She asked Cindy about work, then Andy about his. Owen and Mandy fought over the last piece of bread until Andy slid his piece over to her.

Maryanne smiled as Mandy turned up her little nose at Owen and bit into her piece. Owen just rolled his eyes and ate his.

This was what she wanted with Gunner, a loud, boisterous table filled with kids, laughter, and talking.

An hour later, Andy kissed Cindy on the cheek as she started to round up the kids. Maryanne frowned as he waved and went out the front door.

"Where's he going?"

Cindy looked at her like she was losing her mind.

"It's Tuesday poker night, remember?"

Maryanne felt the vise around her heart ease as it clicked in her mind. That's probably why Gunner hadn't made it home yet. He was probably catching up at work before going straight to poker night.

"Hey, Cin, can you text Andy and tell him to have Gunner text me when he gets there?"

Cindy nodded as she rounded up the four kids to head out. After waving them off, Maryanne cleaned up the kitchen and dining room, made Gunner a plate, covered it in clear wrap, and placed it on the kitchen island.

Then she took a shower and crawled into bed, alone again. She sighed, angry and hurt that they were barely home for a day and their communication had already broken down. She bit her nail as she thought of how to fix it.

Her phone dinged with a message from Gunner, and the pressure eased in her chest.

I missed you today.
At poker night, but will be home soon.

> *We've been back in town one day, and we're already back to not communicating.*

I know, and I'm sorry, M.
Maybe we should start checking up on each other while at work.
Then we can steal a few minutes together.

> *Something has to give, G.*
> *You stop by the bakery at 6am, and I'll bring you lunch this week.*

Can't go wrong with food.
It's a date.

She smiled, the knot in her stomach easing. It wouldn't fix the problem, but it was a start. She put the phone down and went to sleep with a smile.

The rest of the week was exhausting for Gunner since the election was on Friday. One night, he crawled into bed behind her and just wrapped his arms around her. She was gone in the early morning before he woke, and asleep when he came home.

He texted more throughout the day and stopped by the bakery at six every morning to steal kisses and hear her voice.

Then when she got off work at two, she brought him lunch and hung out at his desk in the police station. It was good between them, easier than it had been, but he could tell she was frustrated by his long hours. She hadn't said she loved him again, but he couldn't bring himself to admit his feelings, either.

Thursday when he got home, he saw a big envelope on the dining table labeled *Peanut: Do Not Open* in big letters across it. Maryanne was singing in their bedroom, so he followed the sounds and stood in the doorway, watching her putting away laundry while dancing.

Her eyes landed on him and she paused mid-note, her hand pausing in the air as a wide grin spread across her face.

"Gunner, you're home early tonight. I—did you see the envelope?"

She bit her lip and twisted her hands. He stalked toward her, wrapping her into his arms with a sigh. She melted into his arms, her body loosening as he held her. He raised a hand to the back of her head and nuzzled her neck.

"God, I've missed you this week. Why do we have jobs? Let's both quit and stay at home all day every day, okay?"

She laughed and squeezed his neck. "I missed you too. Long hours suck, but after spending so much time with you in Colorado, it makes me want to spend more time with you now, ya know?"

He breathed in the scent of cinnamon and nodded, her hair wild around him. "Definitely agree. That's why I wanted to come home before you fell asleep tonight."

"Yeah, I'd prefer going to sleep together. But about that envelope. Before you find out from someone else, you should know that I went to the doctor this week."

He stiffened and pulled back, frowning down at her.

"Without me? Shit." Guilt raked down his spine. Why had he let the election and missed work swamp him this week? It was the first week of their marriage, and he'd already missed another doctor's appointment.

She arched a brow and grabbed the stack of t-shirts from the bed, walking to the dresser to put them up. "It was on the shared phone calendar, but we haven't really been together long enough this week to talk about it."

He raked a hand down his face and fell back on the bed, kicking off his boots.

"This fucking election is a nightmare, M. There have been people coming out of the woodworks, talking about my platform and changes they want. Then there were the kids that were finally caught vandalizing."

He slid his hands to cradle his head with a sigh.

She nodded, putting up the rest of the laundry. "I thought it seemed rather busy when I took you lunch yesterday and today. What are you going to do with the kids?"

He caught her by the waist and wrapped his arms around her, burying his head in her slightly rounded stomach. He kissed the baby bump and breathed in deeply of her cinnamon scent, the tension between his shoulders releasing.

"We're still trying to figure out what—if anything—we can charge the teen vandals with. There's a lot of paperwork for that, on top of the election crap."

He nuzzled her stomach. "I would have made time for the doctor's appointment, M, if I'd realized. You and Peanut are my priority, not the election or the job."

His heart stopped as he realized just how true that statement was. He cleared his throat and continued, not letting himself think about the emotions. "So, how did it go? Did she say it was all fine and no complications from the road trip?"

She smiled softly, barely tilting her lips and drawing his gaze. He wanted to kiss her, hold her, and never let her go, but the emotions made his chest tight.

"Well, the doctor took new pictures. That's what's in the envelope, along with the gender."

He lifted his head to look at her, tipping her chin up so he could see her face.

"Do you know if it's a boy or girl?" He held his breath, only releasing it when she shook her head.

"No, our parents are having the wedding reception shower on Saturday, so I figured we could all find out then. Does that work for you? Do you even want to know before the baby's born?"

His entire body ran cold while his lungs worked overtime, and he kissed her softly. When he felt like he could breathe, he nodded. "Yeah, I do. I like to be prepared, remember?"

She grinned, making that dimple pop out and drive him wild.

"Yeah, me too. So we're going to eat, do the gender reveal, then open presents, alright?"

He kissed her cheek and eased her onto the bed. "Do you have plans tomorrow? I'm thinking of playing hookie at work. Tomorrow is the election, so everyone will go to the polls and vote. We can hole up here in the house and just catch up from the missed week. I've gone into Maryanne withdraw and need my fix."

He nuzzled her neck and found the ticklish spot, making her laugh. She ran her hands on his biceps, and he pressed his hips into hers, pulling back to see her gorgeous face.

"Let me text Zarrel and see if he can handle the bakery

by himself tomorrow, then we can hide from the world and just relax to take your mind off the election."

He growled. "I can think of something that will take my mind off it."

She chuckled, the sound easing the tightness in his chest. He leaned down and kissed his way down her neck, his hands running under her shirt.

On Saturday, Maryanne was at the bakery for the lunch rush, relaxed and happy from her day off with Gunner the day before, when Holly came running in. "Gunner made it! The election results are in, and he's the new sheriff!"

Maryanne's body went hot and cold at the same time. She smiled and tears made her eyes burn, so happy that he'd achieved his dream, but in the back of her mind she wondered if she'd see even less of him now that he had more responsibility at work.

Before she could respond, her mom came in, shaking off the rain and setting her umbrella against the wall. "There you are, Maryanne. I need your new house key to decorate."

Maryanne blinked. "Decorate? What are you decorating?"

"For your baby shower, of course. And your bridal shower, then your house-warming party. And now a celebratory election party too, remember? We talked about this last weekend while you were driving back home? Ava and I planned the party?"

Maryanne sighed and slid into a booth seat. The thought of socializing drove her heart rate up, and her head started to hurt. She rubbed her temples and nodded.

"Yeah, okay. There's a spare key under the welcome mat."

"Alright, I'll go get it cleaned up before everyone comes over."

Her mom bounced back over to the door as Maryanne called after her, "There's no need to clean. I've got it all settled, all boxes gone, and the whole place is spotless. It's not like I've had anything else to do this week, after all. What time is the party? When do I need to be there?"

Her mom opened her umbrella and the door.

"Five o'clock. We're serving dinner, but since the guys are invited too, it's finger foods, pizza, and beer. Be there by four, okay?"

Maryanne nodded and waved as she left. Guess they weren't doing the grill idea anymore, which was less work all around and fine with her.

Zarrel came out of the back, wiping his hands on his apron. He took one look at her tired face, then spun on his heel and went into the back again.

"Um, did you forget about the party?" Holly asked softly.

Maryanne met her eyes, frowning with a sigh. "No, I just don't know that I'm ready to socialize with a lot of people tonight. I'm just tired. Is that a pregnancy phase?"

Zarrel returned with a cup of peppermint tea and her extra bottle of CBD from her office before walking away. She'd gotten in the habit of checking the label, which made her smile every time she thought about the whiskey cake.

She dropped some under her tongue, then sipped her tea while they talked pregnancy. She'd been feeling exhausted since she'd been getting the iron shots. She hadn't been sick, but was still nauseous all the time.

Zarrel came back with some scones for the both of them. "This party tonight is going to be amazing."

Maryanne yawned. "Yeah, it's going to be great."

Holly arched a brow. "Maryanne, why don't you come over to the studio and let me give you a massage for a while? And you can nap in my apartment, since your mom is at your house. Will that help relax you before the party?"

Maryanne chuckled. "Yeah, but you might need to give me a massage after the party too. A baby, wedding, and election shower? That's going to be a lot of people and stuff going on."

"You can do it." Holly patted her hand on the table.

Zarrel wiped down the other tables.

"Go on and get that massage, M. You definitely need it. You've been looking pretty tired since coming back from Colorado. I think you've hit the stage where you need to nap all the time."

Holly and Maryanne looked at each other and burst into laughter as they slid out of the booth.

She passed her now empty tea back to Zarrel, then followed Holly to the door. She pulled up her hoodie, but the awning that spanned their stretch of four buildings kept most of the rain off her. It had been much too long since she'd had a massage.

Chapter Forty-Eight

Gunner smiled as someone else slapped him on the back. He saw movement out the window and could barely make out two figures leaving the bakery through the rain. He watched them walk to the yoga studio before shaking the hands of the guy congratulating him.

"You did it, my boy!" Ray beamed. The man actually beamed, with a smile Gunner had never seen before. It looked like the man had gotten younger just in the past hour since they'd gotten the results.

The rest of the station was buzzing with activity as everyone came in to shake hands with both Ray and Gunner. There was no sign or mention of Willowby.

Gunner pulled out his phone, wanting to find Maryanne. She was the only one he wanted to share this moment with, but his gut twisted when he saw unread messages from her.

OMG Congratulations, G!
I'm so proud of you, and can't wait to celebrate with you. xoxo

The Sheriff Gets His Girl

I'm so relieved, to both have it over with and to have won.
Are you at work?

> *Yeah, I'm at work. I need to see you.*
> *You're the only one I want to celebrate with.*
> *Are you at work too or can you swing by over here for a second?*

Half an hour later, she still hadn't texted back, so Gunner checked in with Zarrel. He glanced up from the text and caught Ray as he walked past.

"Hey Ray, I need to slip out and find Maryanne. I'll be right back."

Gunner slid on his jacket and walked down the street to the yoga studio, pushing open the door and making the bell ding.

Holly came down the stairs, a grin on her face. "Gunner, congratulations on the election. That's fantastic."

"Thanks, Holly. Is Maryanne here?"

"Yeah, we just finished her massage, and she's probably asleep by now. But you're free to go up and check on her. She's been so tired this week."

She stepped off the stairs and Gunner walked up.

He pushed open the door with the massage sign on it. The lights were off, pale light coming through the window.

Maryanne was lying face down on the massage table, a sheet covering her. He walked silently over, bent down, and saw her eyes closed, her snore audible now that he was so close.

His phone buzzed, and he checked his text to see Ray needing him back at the station.

He replied, then switched to camera mode, knelt down, and took a selfie of him and Maryanne's sleeping face. After sending the picture to her phone, he followed up with a text.

Wanted to celebrate with you but couldn't bring myself to wake you. Hope your nap is as wonderful as you are. See you later.

A few hours later, when the office had slowed to just a trickle of people and the sky had cleared, Gunner opened his phone to text Maryanne, seeing a message from earlier.

I thought I was dreaming when I smelled your aftershave during that nap. lol

You were too cute to wake.

He grinned, then checked the rest of his messages because the poker night group text had blown up.

Frowning, Gunner re-read that last message. Shit, he'd forgotten about the party at his house. He sighed because all he really wanted was to lock themselves in their bedroom and hold her.

Yesterday's day off was wonderful. They'd cooked breakfast, showered together, watched a movie, napped, and played strip poker, which had led to some rousing sex.

He turned to tell Ray he needed to head out when his phone rang.

"Hello?"

Landry sounded almost as tired as Gunner felt. "Gunner? Where are you, man? Mom is freaking out because you're not here yet."

Gunner rubbed his forehead and put on his jacket. "I'm at work. Where else?"

"Well, get your ass to your house right now. The party starts at five, bro."

Landry hung up as Gunner glanced at the wall clock.

How was it already four-thirty? The day had gone way too fast. He grabbed his keys and stopped by Ray's office. He felt dizzy as he realized that it'd be his office within the next week.

Holy shit. He was the sheriff.

All the tension left his body, leaving him breathless because he'd be able to provide for his family better. They'd be proud of him, and he could make this town a place he was proud to raise his kids in.

Kids. Maryanne. He popped his head into the office. "I have to head out. Apparently there's a baby shower at my house."

Ray waved for him to go, the smile still on his face and kind of creeping Gunner out. "Go on and enjoy your family time. We'll sit down on Monday and work out the details of the transition."

Gunner waved to Joey as he left. When he turned into his neighborhood, he cursed. Cars lined the street, many parked the wrong way, and his fingers itched to write them a ticket. The house was at the end of the road, with a field immediately behind it.

Diagonally about a hundred yards up was the city's public pool where he'd saved Maryanne so long ago. The parking lot there was full too.

He parked behind his mom's truck in the driveway, his bumper crossing the sidewalk and barely in the street. In the back of his head, his conscious reminded him it was illegal to block the sidewalk. He sighed and brushed it off as he walked up to the front door. Several people were hanging out on the front porch.

"Congratulations, Gunner!" "Way to go, man!" "I knew it'd be you."

He shook their hands, barely registering who they were

as he walked inside. Maryanne was smiling, directing people to grab a plate and eat.

Extra tables had been set up against the dining room wall. Her dining table from the apartment was loaded with food, and his stomach growled as the smell of pizza and cheese hit his nostrils.

But he couldn't take his eyes off Maryanne. He felt such a sense of guilt in leaving work for a week for the Colorado trip, which is why he'd tried to make up for it with extra hours this week.

He frowned, his stomach in knots, because he couldn't keep doing that to Maryanne. He didn't want his kid growing up without him home. He would *not* be an absent dad or a deadbeat husband.

Maryanne didn't look energized or excited about this party. She was wearing her fake smile. He saw the tension around her eyes, and her posture was stiff like when she was at the lawyer's in Colorado.

She was talking to some woman from church as he walked up and wrapped her in his arms. She squeaked, cutting off her conversation as she wrapped her arms around him. He felt the tension drain out of both their bodies as the hum of voices floated around them.

He kissed her forehead, then released her to turn to the table of food. It was easier to mingle and talk to people when Maryanne was near.

After he'd finished eating, he kept one hand on her at all times, keeping her practically stuck to his side all evening. He didn't know if she realized it or not, but it made him happy to hold her hand as they sat on the couch talking to their friends and family.

"All right, is everyone done eating?" Landry called out.

Gunner groaned. "Who put him in charge?"

The poker guys laughed as his mom raised her hand. "I did. Now, do you want to do the gender reveal or not?"

The entire house seemed to yell out, "Yes!"

Landry grinned as he walked to the kitchen. Both he and Zarrel came out carrying a large sheet cake. They walked to the living room and set it on the coffee table in front of Maryanne and Gunner.

Maryanne had tears in her bright brown eyes, but was already eagerly leaning forward to look at the cake.

"Zarrel, did you make this? It's gorgeous."

Zarrel practically beamed. "Yeah, I wanted nothing but the best for my boss. But you know, you're more than a boss. You're my family, my sister, my friend. Thank you for welcoming me, M. I'm so happy for you guys."

Maryanne's mom smacked Zarrel on the arm and frowned. "You knew the gender all afternoon? Why didn't you say something? You know I've been trying to find out for days, ever since she went to the doc this week."

Gunner felt a stab of guilt. He didn't even know about the doc appointment. How was he supposed to be a decent dad and go to all the soccer games and things if he couldn't even keep track of her doctor's appointments?

Zarrel shrugged with a grin. "I wasn't gonna ruin this. No way."

Maryanne reached for the cake cutter, then handed it to him. "Together?"

Gunner nodded, and he wrapped his hand around hers. He held her shaking hand and leaned forward to kiss her deeply, sweeping his tongue inside to the whoops of their friends.

When he felt like he needed to take her right there or burst, he slowly broke the kiss and leaned back. Their hands still intertwined, they smiled at each other.

Her voice was soft beneath the chatter around them. "Do you want a boy or girl? I didn't even ask."

"Doesn't matter. You're what matters." He kissed the tip of her nose, and the women around them collectively said *aw* while the men snickered. Gunner grinned as Maryanne's dimple popped out.

They both turned to look at the cake as they cut into it. They pulled the piece back to reveal—

"It's a girl!" His mom screamed so loud he nearly dropped the cake cutter as he jumped. His dad's eyes shone with tears.

Margarita grinned. "I told you!"

He glanced at Maryanne, her jaw was slack as she blinked, staring at the cake.

He took a finger and turned her chin to look at him. "We're going to have a girl?"

She nodded as a smile spread on her face. "A girl!"

She threw her arms around his neck and launched herself into his arms. He really did drop the cake cutter then.

It clattered to the floor as he wrapped his arms around her and pulled back onto the chaise lounge, dragging her onto his lap, legs to the side. He placed a hand on her back and nuzzled her hair as she laid her head on his shoulder and cried.

Everyone came up to congratulate them as Zarrel and Landry plated up the cake for people, and Holly cleaned the cake off the floor. Maryanne's tears finally slowed down, but he didn't let her off his lap. It was less overwhelming to have her so close. Fucking hell, they were going to have a *girl*, a precocious, sassy little black-haired angel like Maryanne.

When everyone had a piece of cake and the leftover sheet was returned to the dining room table, Landry clapped his hands. "All right, now we're going to hear the couple tell their love story, and then they'll open presents. After presents, there will be a memory type question-and-answer session. Whoever answers the most questions about their love story will win the prize: a fifty-dollar gift card to Maryanne's Half Baked."

Fuck Landry and his stupid games. What was with him? Where did he come up with these things?

Maryanne blushed as she looked at him, making his heart stutter. "Do you want to tell it or do you want me to?"

"You can. I just want to stare at your beautiful face while you talk."

He kissed her cheek, making the crowd *aw* again and the guys groan. Maryanne giggled, though, so it was totally worth the cheesiness. She turned to the crowd and told them about their first kiss back in high school.

Then she told them about their second kiss at Holly and Kendall's when they went to raid the bake sale goods and an abridged version of Halloween and how he saved her from her evil ex-boyfriend.

She had the crowd captivated.

Hell, he was captivated and had been since he'd first seen her struggling at the pool. When she finished the story of him proposing by the creek and their wedding there a few days later, several of the ladies were openly crying.

Lola crossed her arms and leaned against the living room wall. "When did you know that he was the one?"

Maryanne turned and met his gaze. Her eyes pierced his soul with the love that shone brighter than the lights.

"That first kiss in high school knocked my socks off. I was more than tipsy and when that kiss made me pass out... he got me home somehow. And I didn't get in trouble with 'Buela either, so I don't know how he did it. I knew then that he could do anything and would take care of me and be a gentleman the entire time."

Gunner's heart pounded in his chest as her words registered through his mind.

"What about you, Gunner? When did you know she was the one?" Landry asked over the chatter of voices.

The noise died down as everyone waited with bated breath for him to reply. For once, the words flowed out without the knot of anxiety choking him up.

"When I was twelve, we were at the city pool. I was playing rough, dunking my brothers, when I felt my entire body grow freezing cold. It felt like someone walked over my grave, so I swam to the edge and pulled myself up. I told my brothers I had to go to the bathroom."

He swallowed as Maryanne's eyes went soft and wide. She remembered that day as much as he did.

"As I walked along the edge of the pool, I saw this little dark-haired imp struggling to get her head up long enough to take a breath. She was right under the lifeguard, who couldn't see her. I jumped in and hauled her to the side. When she'd spit out all the water she swallowed and looked up at me with those big brown eyes... I was a goner. I just didn't realize it until last fall."

There was a beat of silence until everyone started talking at once, awing and sniffling. But Gunner didn't see or hear them. He didn't break eye contact with Maryanne, not even as tears poured out her eyes. He leaned forward and slowly ran his lips over hers in soft, little kisses.

He didn't want to stop, but Parker ruined the fun when he called out, "Get a room!"

Gunner pulled back and scowled. "I would but y'all won't leave my house."

The crowd laughed and Landry said, "Okay, okay. Let's

open presents, shall we? The sooner we do presents, the sooner we can leave these newlyweds to their fate."

Gunner kept her on his lap as presents were handed over. He loved to see her face light up as she opened each one, sometimes crying, sometimes laughing. When her laugh lit up her face and captivated him, he swore the lights in the house grew brighter and chased away all the shadows.

Chapter Forty-Nine

After presents, they played silly games for another few hours, much like Andy's bachelor party. The older crowd left by nine, and their friends kept the drinks and laughter going. Gunner started to loosen up and have fun, more so than he would have if it was just the guys.

When all the beers were gone and everyone but Maryanne was thoroughly tipsy, Landry stumbled to his bag and pulled out some guns.

Gunner blinked, rubbed his eyes, and looked again. "Are those... paintball guns?"

Landry's grin made his stomach drop. Whatever he had planned, it was gonna be wild.

"Yesh, I gots permission to set up some hay bales in the field next door. I alsho set up obst—obstuckles earlier. Who wants to play? Less team up." Landry had all the guys' undivided attention.

Lola crossed her arms as she glared at Kendall, which made Gunner chuckle. Maryanne came in with a glass of water and handed it to him. He drank, not realizing until he tipped his head back just how dizzy he was. How many drinks had they had? He'd lost count.

Gunner set his now empty glass on the coffee table and grabbed Maryanne's hand, pulling her back onto his lap. He nuzzled her ear, making her squirm and his cock jump like a trained dog. He certainly felt like a dog. A horn dog.

She pushed on his chest with a giggle as he hit a sensitive spot. "Stop. We're going to go play."

"But we can just let them go play and lock the door, then we'll have the house to ourselves. I've missed you this week, M. Come on, would you rather play with those drunkards or with me, your loving husband who has naughty plans for you?"

He breathed in her cinnamon scent, feeling relaxed and happy for the first time since they came back into town.

She laughed, snuggling into his chest. "Y'all go ahead. We'll be out soon."

Landry and Parker drunkenly led the pack outside, waving paintball guns and slurring the rules of the game.

Gunner kissed her, his heart racing as he held her. "This was the best day. First the election, and now I'm holding the most beautiful woman in the world."

She laughed, the sound radiating joy through his body and making him warm and tingly. "You're drunk, G. Haven't seen this side of you since Halloween."

He groaned. "God, let's not talk about *that* right now."

She laughed again and winked at him, her dimple popping out and making him bend his head and kiss it.

He couldn't resist her. This woman had stolen his heart. Hell, his entire mind, body, and soul. Not a minute passed that he didn't think of her. His lips kissed a trail to hers. He wanted to tell her he loved her; had he done that before? He couldn't remember, but knew he hadn't at the wedding.

Damn it, his throat closed up again, so he just broke the kiss and stood. The room spun around and for a minute his heart raced, because he could have sworn he had two Maryanne's. God, that would have been a fun time. He shook his head.

Get your head in the game, Williams.

She patted his chest, and he slung an arm around her shoulders. "Come on, G. Let's go check on the game and make sure no one has passed out in the field."

"Is this what being responsible parents feels like?" He chuckled, and they walked out the front door.

The group was all talking at once, reviewing the game and almost to their front door when a vehicle pulled up in the drive. Everyone stopped as Joey stepped out and walked toward them.

Gunner frowned, some of his buzz floating away at the sight of the deputy in uniform. "Hey, Joey. What's up?"

Had something happened at the station? Did he need backup and couldn't reach Gunner on the phone? Gunner released Maryanne's shoulder and felt his pants pockets. He'd left his phone in the house.

"No, man. I, uh—well, this is awkward. We got a call for noise disturbance out here." Joey rubbed the back of his neck as he shifted on his feet. Silence rang out before nearly everyone started laughing.

Gunner didn't. What did this mean, for the new sheriff to get the cops called for an out-of-control party?

"We're sorry for the noise, Joey." Maryanne placed a hand on Gunner's chest and snuggled into his side. It made the vise around his heart ease a little, the worry lessen.

Maybe she could help. It might all turn into a shit show, but she did somehow make things better in the end.

Parker held up Landry as they stumbled up the stairs. "We're all about to leave and go home. Don't worry."

"Do you want some cake while you're here?" Maryanne waved to the door.

Joey glanced around, shoved his hands in his pockets as he shifted on his feet.

Holly trailed after Parker and Landry. "There's some pizza and pasta too."

Joey shrugged, and they all went inside. Holly and Lola got Joey some food as Parker helped Landry pack up all their gear. Landry fell on the floor, making Parker laugh and stumble into the wall.

Maryanne snorted. "Well, looks like the spare rooms upstairs will get some use after all. I have some blankets, but there are no beds up there. Or y'all can take the couch."

Parker shoved Landry onto the couch, and his head lolled to one side as he glanced blearily around the room. "You look like you've lost your blankie. Just sleep it off, Landry."

Zarrel, Nick, Kendall, and the others gathered up their things as Lola and Holly came back from the kitchen.

Gunner frowned. "Who's sober and driving?"

Lola raised her hand as Holly paled and shook her head. He forgot that Holly didn't drive.

Lola frowned. "I can only fit four of y'all in my truck."

Holly shrugged. "I can stay here. It's fine. Get the guys home."

They all crowded out the door, Joey following them as he finished a bottle of water. He turned to Gunner as he stood at the door.

"Sorry about the call, Gunner. I didn't know it was you when I came out. Do you want me to take anyone home?"

Joey looked unsure of what to do, but Gunner just shook his head.

"It's fine, man. This will hopefully be the one and only time that I get called out on a noise complaint. But if you want to take home some of these drunkards, be my guest." Gunner chuckled, which made Joey seem to relax. Joey smiled and his shoulders fell as he ushered a few more people out the door.

In the past, Gunner would've gotten more uptight about an incident like this. Maybe it was the booze, maybe it was Maryanne, or a combination of it all, but other than general embarrassment, he wasn't too worried about the noise complaint.

When he turned back, Maryanne was passing around blankets to Holly and Parker, who both decided to sleep in the living room—one taking the new recliner and the other taking the other half of the L shaped couch. Landry was already snoring on the chaise.

Gunner sighed, then grabbed Landry's cowboy boots and pulled them off, tossing them toward the door as Maryanne covered him with a blanket.

She went around the dining room and kitchen, turning off the lights and grabbing a bowl of blueberries before meeting him in their bedroom. He closed the door behind them as she chuckled, walking to the bedside table to set down the fruit.

"What's so funny?"

She glanced over her shoulder, that teasing look in her eye driving him wild with need. "Landry on the couch. Taking care of him is good practice for us as parents."

Gunner chuckled, kicking off his own boots and following her to the side of the bed. He eased her sweater up and over, tossing it aside. God, her tits were magnificent in that black lace bra, but he wanted her naked.

When he ran his hands in her leggings, he groaned. "Shit, Maryanne. Why are you always going commando? Do you know how that drives me wild?"

She chuckled, her hand raking through his hair as she looked down at him. Once more, he worshipped her on his knees, his queen, his wife. His cock twitched as he slid her pants slowly down her legs, and kissed her ankles, then the backs of her knees.

"Lay down, M. Let me love you."

Her heart raced at his words. He still hadn't said he loved her, but he *was* using the word more often. She wanted to tease him though, so instead of doing as he asked, she grabbed some blueberries. She looked at Gunner kneeling in front of her and slowly pushed the ripe fruit to her lips, sucking it inside.

She moaned as the flavor burst on her tongue, and the sound made him jerk into motion. He stood, but instead of kissing her, he reached behind her and grabbed a handful of blueberries. He tugged her down to the bed.

"Come on, M. I want to feast on you, so lay down."

Her eyes widened at the order as he released her wrist. His voice rasped over her, sending shivers up her spine. This time, she listened and laid back on the bed, automatically spreading her legs as he crawled between them.

When he was on his knees, he pushed hers wider and placed blueberries in the dip of her collarbone, between her breasts, and in her belly button.

Then he took one and placed it between his lips, leaned forward, and kissed her with only their lips touching.

She sucked in the blueberry, tasting the tartness and smelling his pine and cedar musk. The sensations were heady, making her light-headed with anticipation.

Then he slowly ate the berries off her, nipping and sucking, gripping her hips to keep her steady when she started to squirm. When he had eaten them all, he pushed her legs apart and grinned up at her.

"I love to see you like this, like the only dessert buffet I'll never get enough of."

His words brought a tear to her eye and set off butterflies in her stomach. But before she could process, he had that wicked mouth on her pussy, licking and sucking until she was writhing and panting.

The pressure built until she screamed, spasming around his fingers as his lapping slowed. When he finally pulled back, he kissed his way down her thigh to her ankles, then up the other leg.

She was squirming by the time he slid home, then she was clawing her way to the finish line, barely beating him there. She fell asleep still wrapped around him.

Chapter Fifty

April

"Where are we going?" Maryanne climbed into his truck. She was so tired from the long morning rush at the bakery; it was always busy on payday weekends.

Things had changed since the election, though. They'd coordinated their days off so they could be together, just relaxing at home. They'd also kept up the visiting each other at work throughout the week, and Gunner spent at least an hour with her every day.

Sometimes that was at the bakery helping her. Sometimes it was in the evening, when he'd come home from a tough day at work and just want to snuggle with her on the couch while they watched tv.

Today, he'd texted her that they had a date after she got off work. He just smiled, the light bouncing off his jaw as he drove out of town. She ignored the urge to slide closer to him and run her fingers over his scruffy chin.

She turned to the window and leaned her head against it. The spring sun felt good on her face.

"We're just going to go relax for a bit. The stress of the past few days can't be good for the baby." He reached over and turned up the music on the radio, then switched to the CD she'd made him for Christmas.

The rumble of the truck lulled her as she set her hand on her baby bump. She hadn't gained a pound until she hit five months, then she'd ballooned up steadily. Week by week, she'd seen the scale go up and her belly go out. When he finally pulled to a stop, she jerked awake.

"There's my Sleeping Beauty. Feel better after your nap?"

He smiled as he turned off the truck and unbuckled. She groaned and stretched before slowly getting out of the truck and joining him. He grabbed a duffel bag from the back, then placed a hand on the small of her back to lead her through the overgrown field.

She knew this was his parents' land; she'd been here before, back in high school. She glanced to her right and saw the roof of the barn where they'd had their first kiss.

She felt herself blush as she remembered him pressing her against the barn wall. That kiss had been the primary ingredient of all her hopes and dreams.

They turned away from it as he led her towards a copse of trees. The sun shone down through the barren branches, the late spring not yet starting new life. They walked for perhaps another fifty feet when they came to a very large pond, almost twice the size of a football field.

She gasped. "Has this always been here?"

He chuckled as he led her towards a small flat space off the path they'd been following. A rowboat was tethered nearby, bobbing slowly in the gentle spring breeze.

He opened the duffel bag and pulled out a throw blanket. Spreading it out, he motioned for her to sit. She laid down instead, sighing as the sun shone down on her face. She laid her hands on her swelling stomach and turned onto her side.

He pulled out a light sweater and rolled it up, sliding it gently under her head, then he looked at her. She couldn't see his expression with the sun behind him, but she felt his fingertips softly trace her cheek.

She sighed, feeling the tension in her shoulders ease. He might not have told her he loved her yet, but it was little things like this that spoke more than words.

"You can go back to sleep now. I'm going to go fishing, but I'll be right here. The bag has snacks and dinner, so let me know when you get hungry, and we can have our picnic date."

He took two steps, then turned back, dropped to his knees and kissed her on the forehead.

She watched him get a fishing pole and a small tackle box out of the boat, then stroll a few yards away and sit on the bank. She saw his biceps pop under the t-shirt. She shivered, telling herself it was from the chill breeze, but knowing it wasn't. She closed her eyes as she drifted off again, thinking of him kissing her awake like a real Sleeping Beauty.

"Maryanne, wake up, little girl."

Gunner's voice echoed through her dreams. She felt his scruff scrape the side of her neck, making her press her legs together more as she stretched herself awake.

He was laying behind her, propped up on one elbow, and she turned onto her back to stare up at him.

"How long was I asleep?" Her voice was groggy and

low, and the sun hung in the trees, blocking most of the rays.

"Just over an hour. I caught a few fish, but then I got bored, so I came to join you." He lowered his head and kissed her lightly. His hand was resting on her stomach, and as she turned her head to deepen the kiss, her belly jumped.

Gunner jerked back and glanced down, his eyes wide and jaw slack. Maryanne giggled and glanced down, watching the baby roll over inside.

"What the hell was that?" Gunner whispered.

"Why are you whispering?" she whispered back, rubbing her lower stomach as his hand hovered above.

"I don't know. Was that the baby? Is that normal?" God, he was adorable with that bewildered look on his face.

"Yeah, I believe so. Holly said it's the greatest feeling, and I felt it a few days ago but thought it was just indigestion."

They watched, her t-shirt stretched tight over her belly with an arrow pointing to it and the words *Bun in My Oven*. When nothing else happened, she twisted, pulling up her knees to take the pressure off her back.

Gunner sat up and walked to the truck. He came back with a small cooler and sat it beside her. Pulling out the sandwiches and lemonade, he helped her sit up and handed one over.

When she bit into it, she groaned. "God, this is the best sandwich I've ever eaten."

"I figured we'd have peanut butter and jelly and talk baby names."

Her heart leapt as she smiled a sneaky grin. "I have thoughts. How about Merlina?"

Gunner choked on his lemonade, which made her laugh. When he could finally talk and she'd caught her breath, he gasped, "What the hell, M? Is she gonna be a mermaid or a wizard? Absolutely not."

Maryanne laughed again, joy spreading across her body as they debated names, flirting and teasing as the names got even more outrageous from there. When they'd finished eating, she tossed her trash back into the cooler and looked around with a frown.

"Um, Gunner? Peanut is pressing on my bladder pretty bad. Do you have any toilet paper or—"

"Oh, yeah." He reached into the cooler and pulled out a few napkins. He helped her stand, then walked with her to a nearby tree. As he inspected the spot for snakes and poison ivy, she grinned. She wouldn't needle him about it, as he was being very sweet and protective. When he nodded and stepped away a few feet, she turned to the tree and glanced back at him.

"Gunner, I can't go with you so close. Go away. Go back to the truck or something."

This was so weird. Not the peeing outside in the wild, but being this close to him. You'd think after months of living together that they'd be able to pee in the same vicinity, but she absolutely could not wrap her head around it right now.

When she'd finished, she went to the truck where he waited with hand sanitizer. He rubbed it into her hands, gently massaging her fingers and palms.

"When did you learn to pay attention to little details like this?" She genuinely wanted to know because what she remembered of him from when they were kids... he'd always been a big picture guy.

He paused, holding her hands and refusing to make eye contact. Then he tucked her hand into the crook of his arm and walked her back to the blanket. He'd packed up their food and all his fishing equipment. Laying down, he patted his shoulder, so she laid down and used him as a pillow.

"Gunner?" She glanced up at him, but his eyes were closed and his breathing was even. Maybe he wanted to go back to sleep, but she was wide awake.

"What do you know about why Chase is in prison?" His voice was low and gravelly. She froze, then started tracing circles with her hand on his chest.

"I wasn't in town when it happened. I was back home at Fort Hood for the school year. There was a wreck, wasn't there?"

She felt him nod, and his body tensed up. She slung a leg over his, and he sighed, wrapping his arms around her and holding her tight.

"It was a normal weekend during my senior year. About this time of year, actually... right after Spring Break. Chase was bored. He'd been bored most of school."

Maryanne snorted, thinking back on those days. "Well, yeah, he's a genius. If I was as smart as him, I'd have been bored too. When we were kids, and I wrangled Parker and Landry into cutting up around town, Chase always turned us down because he was too busy reading a book or doing some kind of experiment. Eventually, we stopped asking him."

Gunner shifted under her, then hugged her tighter, so she continued tracing circles on his shirt.

"He *is* a genius. If he would have moved up a grade or gone to a smarter school... Hell, if he would've home-schooled and advanced as fast as he wanted... but that's not what happened. He was bored, and he'd been running around with the wrong crowd for about six months. He'd gotten more and more annoying as time went on. I was a senior and wanted to just graduate and get out of there."

The guilt in his voice made her chest ache, and she kissed his shoulder. "No one blames you for that."

"I know. But that night... he'd swiped some alcohol from the bunkhouse. I could smell it on his breath, but he wasn't drunk. He wasn't slurring or stumbling or anything. I thought maybe he'd just spilled it or something and hadn't actually drank any."

The crickets sang as the sun sunk lower in the sky, and birds swooped across the pond in the trees.

"He took the truck that all us boys shared and went to town. Mom and Dad were already asleep, and I just wanted him to get out of my space and leave me alone. He'd asked me to take him to town, but I knew he'd be meeting up with that crowd that kept getting him in trouble at school, and I wanted nothing to do with them. He—he wrecked on the way there. A family was on their way home from Dallas. A little girl died, and another was ejected. She broke a few bones in her leg, but other than a limp and permanent road rash, she's okay now."

"And they charged him with vehicular manslaughter?"

Gunner squeezed her again, and she leaned up on one elbow to look at him. His jaw was clenched, his eyes closed.

Her heart broke as a tear rolled down the corner of his eye and into his hair. She kissed his cheek, tasting the tear and trying to soak up his heartache. It hurt her to see him hurt.

"Yeah," he breathed. "He got fifteen years. Fifteen fucking years, all because I didn't listen to him or drive him into town. I should have, and I didn't."

"It's not your fault, Gunner. *He* chose to drink and drive."

Gunner sighed. "They found alcohol in his system, not much but any amount of underage drinking is bad."

Silence settled on them as the sun went down, and she waited. She'd waited for him for over a decade, and she'd wait now for him to talk.

"He's supposed to get out next year."

"That's good, right?"

Gunner shifted and opened his eyes. The emeralds shone brightly in the fading light as he frowned.

"I'm not sure. He refuses to see me, and when he calls, he'll talk to Hunter and Landry and Mom. But not me."

She leaned forward and kissed him softly before pressing her forehead to his. "I'll be right there with you when he's released. We'll throw him a welcome home party."

Gunner smiled as she pulled away, his voice proud. "Did you know he's gotten his bachelor's degree while in there?"

Maryanne sighed as some of the pain in her heart released. "Really? That's amazing. What's his plan once he's released?"

Gunner shook his head as he set his hands on his bent knees and looked across the pond. "Not sure. It's in accounting, and he helped the prison somehow. I don't know what he wants to do when he gets out, but he's as smart as ever. I just—I hope it hasn't broken him beyond repair."

Maryanne rubbed his back and leaned her head on his bicep.

"Zarrel is pretty well adjusted. I'm sure Chase will be fine, after a while. It's like separating from the military, I hear. From talking with Zarrel, anyway. It takes a few months to a few years, then you'll know whether he goes back in or adjusts to regular civilian life."

Gunner sighed, then kissed her forehead. "Come on, M. Let's get home before the bugs eat us alive."

He helped her to her feet, then packed up the blanket.

They walked hand in hand back to the truck as the sun set behind them. Her heart hurt for his pain—why had he kept it in for so long? They'd become closer over the past few months. Even through the pain in her heart, she still smiled because he finally was opening up to her.

Chapter Fifty-One

July

Maryanne laughed, and the sight made Gunner's heart lurch. For a few months, she'd seemed so emotional. She'd cry over nothing, then clam up and not tell him how to fix it. It'd been rough until she'd started seeing Tasha for counseling. His mom had said it was just normal pregnancy hormones, but he didn't really think so.

He walked through the crowd, keeping Maryanne in his sights as much as possible as he monitored the festivities. Every Fourth of July the town put on a big parade in the early afternoon.

Then they'd gather in the park for vendors, games, and fun before a concert in the gazebo at seven and fireworks at nine. Maryanne had set up a booth of baked goods. Ivy, the high school girl, ferried more from the bakery—where Zarrel was baking as needed—and the booth.

He'd pulled the girl aside and made sure that she was giving Maryanne a bathroom break every hour on the hour.

He passed by a booth set up as a psychic and stopped as Landry stumbled out, his face ashen and pale as a ghost. Gunner ignored the flow of people around him as he caught Landry's arm.

"You okay there, bro?" Gunner frowned, looking into the booth.

"She—how did she know that? She's not really a psychic. She's just the school counselor."

Landry threw himself out of Gunner's grasp and tore through the crowd, for once not waving and smiling and stopping to chat with everyone and their grandmother.

Gunner turned as Tasha pulled back the curtain and stood in the doorway.

She was certainly dressed like a fortune teller, complete with jingly, brightly colored skirt, heavy eye liner, and a lot of scarves, one even around her head. Without the glasses, she looked completely different, unrecognizable except she tried to adjust her glasses before remembering they weren't there.

When Landry dropped from view, she spun her gaze onto Gunner.

"Do you want your fortune told, Sheriff?" She'd adjusted her voice to have a thick, fake accent.

Gunner shook his head. "No, I'm good. Thanks, though. Holler if anyone gives you trouble."

"Um, Gunner? One quick tip, if I may?" Her normal voice poked through and her spine straightened as her gaze shot toward Maryanne's booth.

He turned back to her and stepped off the path closer to the entrance of her brightly colored tent, a smile on his face as he teased. "Is it free or will I owe you for this tip?"

She scrunched up her nose as she winced. Glancing

away toward Maryanne before looking back at him, she lifted her chin.

"You might want to come clean to your wife about how much you love her. That's all. Tip's free, but come see me if you want to talk about *why* you haven't told her you love her before now."

With that truth bomb, she flounced back into her tent and played some kind of music to draw in the crowd. What did she mean, he hadn't told her he loved her? Surely he had.

Pressure built in his chest as he walked back along the gravel laid path, smiling vacantly at people as he thought. He spied his mom and dad at the dunking booth. His mom was rooting for some kid to throw a good one. She glanced at his dad, who winked at her.

They told each other they loved each other every day. He knew they didn't end a phone call without saying it, and even said it every time one left the house or went into the field. That was part of marriage. So why hadn't he told Maryanne already?

He'd known for months that he loved her, would do anything to protect her.

A slow smile curled his lips up as an idea came to him. He caught sight of Cindy and Andy at a booth, their kids playing some kind of dart balloon game, and he stopped to make a plan.

A few hours later, his nerves were completely shot as he led Maryanne through the crowd to the side of the gazebo. Cindy, Andy, and their kids were all together with their camping chairs. Cody, the oldest nephew, hopped up and gave his seat to Maryanne.

"Thank you, Cody. I swear this baby is not happy with me today. She's going to be a soccer star just like you."

Cody grinned as James, her other nephew, grabbed the cooler and slid it over.

"Here, Auntie M. Put your feet up on this."

Gunner smiled, his heart speeding a rapid beat, and he hoped they had little gentlemen like these boys someday.

But first, he needed to ease Maryanne's fears and tell her he loved her, and it was going to be tonight. It was the perfect time for it.

He kissed her forehead. "It's show time!"

She smiled at him, her eyes tired but happy as he turned to step up to the open air gazebo's microphone. His brothers were warming up inside, but his microphone was right in the middle of the doorway opening. It was hot, muggy, and he'd sweat so much, his uniform was completely soaked.

He tapped the microphone as he looked at his watch. It was exactly seven o'clock. Two more hours, and he'd make his grand gesture in front of the whole town.

"All right, all you party people. Let's get this shindig started with some good ole *Born in the USA*."

Many people hopped to their feet as they began to sing, but he was glad Maryanne remained seated. He watched her wiggle in her seat for the next hour and a half, drinking water and playing with her nephews and niece when she wasn't watching him and singing along from her seat.

When he sang Katy Perry's *Firework*, she grinned, and that dimple popped out in the dim fairy lights in the trees.

He motioned for her to come up there with him, and she lumbered to her feet and joined him. She held his hand, and they sang until the chorus when she let go and threw up her hands, dancing with her belly sticking out in her red and white tank top, her blue pleated skirt waving around her ankles.

She slowed, a grin on her face as she belted out the song with him, sharing his microphone and staring into his eyes.

She amazed him. So full of life, joy, and love. Yes, that was love shining in her eyes, and he hoped she could see it in his too. Just a few more minutes and he'd make the announcement for fireworks and tell her and everyone in town how much he loved her.

When the song was over, she held her belly and kissed Gunner on the cheek. "I'm going to the bathroom. I'll be right back."

She smiled and waved to the masses, who were demanding an encore. He held her hand as she stepped down the few steps. "Alright, but hurry back. I want you to be here for the last song before the fireworks."

She nodded and wove through the crowd, smiling at people as she passed.

On the edge of the crowd, Holly joined her. "Oh, Maryanne, that was so fun. What a beautiful moment between you two. Do y'all sing together a lot at home?"

Maryanne nodded and smiled. Things had been weird between her and Holly since she'd started showing. Now that her belly was so big, it was sometimes awkward to talk with her. Her friend would sometimes clam up and just look away. The flash of pain in her eyes told Maryanne she was thinking of her lost little baby. And the thought of losing her own Peanut always made her choke up and cry.

"Yeah, when we're doing the dishes or laundry, we'll sing together. Sometimes we have a karaoke battle at home."

They discussed music genres until they were halfway to

the bathroom. The baby kicked hard as her stomach roiled. Maryanne's steps faltered, then a sharp pain shot through her lower back. She gasped for air, the sharp pain spreading across her back.

Holly frowned, fluttering around her. "You okay? Are you going into labor?"

When the wave eased and Maryanne could keep walking, she sighed.

"Doubtful. I'm not due for another two weeks. I met with the doctor a few days ago. She said I was thinning but not dilating. She also said the Braxton Hicks contractions I've been having the past few days are normal too. Peanut has been doing somersaults in there all day long. She's settled down while I was sitting, listening to Gunner, but dancing on stage was probably not the best idea."

Maryanne laughed again as she continued walking to the porta potties at the far end of the park near the parking lot. Her back was constantly hurting now. She hadn't been able to get in a comfortable position all day, the pain just escalating to a roaring ache that wouldn't leave her alone.

"Well, you better tell me if they are real contractions. Kendall is right over there and can check."

Holly looped her arm through Maryanne's. Maryanne winced as another wave washed over her. "Yeah, that wouldn't be weird at all. He's your brother, and I see him all the time. I don't want him looking at my lady bits."

Holly laughed, and Maryanne rubbed her belly as they reached the porta potties.

"Do you want me to hold your phone?"

Maryanne laughed. "How'd you know?"

Holly rolled her eyes. "You told me last year that you only make that mistake once."

Maryanne winced as she handed over her little purse.

Her skirt didn't have pockets, and she was trying to get used to carrying a purse because babies came with a lot of stuff.

Slipping inside, she took care of business and came back out. Holly was holding up hand sanitizer.

While she cleaned her hands, Holly went inside. A shadow came around the side, catching Maryanne's eye.

When she turned to see who it was, her body froze as the blood drained from her body. Her hands automatically circled her stomach to protect her baby, shaking as she curled her body away from him.

"Barry," she gasped, her feet rooted in place as a wave of pain washed over her body from the inside out. She couldn't move even if she tried. Her body was stiffening, making her cry out.

"Well, hello there, Mary. Are you enjoying the holiday?"

His beard was scraggly now, not groomed impeccably like at Halloween. His messy bun was pulled nearly out, like he'd forgotten it was up and had tried to run his hands through it.

His black t-shirt was stained, and his skinny jeans had holes in them, and not deliberate, stylish holes either.

She breathed and clenched her teeth. "You look like shit, Barry. What are you doing here?"

He rocked on his feet, his hands behind his back as he smiled that slow grin that sent shivers up her spine. She used to think those were shivers of desire. Now she knew it was fear because he was creepy as fuck.

Holly opened the door to the porta potty, saying as she stepped out, "Who are you talking to, M? Oh, hello."

Barry leapt away and pulled his hand from behind his back, leveling a gun at Maryanne. Holly cried out as Maryanne turned her body away from him again, hugging her belly.

Sweat shone on Barry's dirty forehead. "Don't move. Who are you? Shit, it doesn't matter. Mary, come on, and whoever you are, you'll have to come with us too."

Maryanne's blood ran cold and adrenaline began to pump through her veins as he walked closer. She stepped back, but he waved the gun down to her stomach.

"Nah, huh, huh. None of that now, Mary. We have unfinished business, and we're going to pull that little baby daddy of yours into it too. Come on. What's your name, sugar?"

Holly slid closer to Maryanne and grabbed her hand, squeezing it hard enough to take Maryanne's mind off the pain in her back spreading through her stomach.

"Hol—Holly. Who are you?"

"This is Barry," Maryanne hissed. Holly's hand shook with recognition of the name.

Barry worked his way to flank them, pressing the gun into Maryanne's back and pushing them forward into the parking lot.

"Where are we going?" Holly asked, her voice raised in fright or to catch someone's attention, Maryanne didn't know.

But Barry wasn't stupid.

He barked out, "Hush. Keep it down, or I'll be forced to use this thing too soon, and that's not my plan. Remember that barn from Halloween, Mary? That's where we're going. Out in the middle of nowhere."

She absolutely couldn't let him hurt the baby or Holly, but the pain shooting through her body was making it difficult to think through options.

Chapter Fifty-Two

They arrived at a black BMW that had seen better days. Scratched up and missing a taillight. Maryanne remembered Gunner saying that that's why he'd pulled him over back in December.

Maryanne taunted him, kicking the car. "Still haven't gotten that taillight fixed, Barry? That's not like you."

He'd always been so proud of his car, washing it weekly and making sure they always drove it and not her Mustang. Kicking it was almost as satisfying as kicking him. She watched his face grow darker with rage.

On second thought, maybe it wasn't a good idea to make him mad. He rushed her, pushing her against the side of the car with the butt of the gun pressing under her chin. She gasped as it scraped the skin.

He growled, "Shut up. I've been in jail because of you, Mary. It's your fault the whole thing toppled down, and you're gonna pay. Now, get in and drive." He stepped back and waved her to the driver's seat.

She raised a brow, knowing it would infuriate him further. "Yeah, I'm not going anywhere with you."

"Yes, you are. Unless you want me to shoot you right here? Then pick off a few of the townsfolk when they come to see what the noise is?"

Just then fireworks began to shoot off, catching them off guard. Barry jumped, then waved the gun at her face before she could take advantage of it.

"Or maybe this will work. They won't come running during the show, will they? They'll just think it's another firework going off."

The grin on his face caused her breath to hitch and sweat to bead on her lip. "I can't drive, dip shit. I'm too big."

He frowned, then waved at Holly. "You drive then. And I'll keep the gun on Mary."

Maryanne looked at Holly, who had lost all blood in her face. Her ashen skin was pale as a ghost.

Maryanne stepped in front of Holly. "No, she can't drive. You'll have to man up and drive yourself."

The dig did not go unnoticed. Barry sneered, then twisted Maryanne's arm behind her back and pushed her around to the passenger side.

"Open the door and fucking get in the car, Mary. Holly, is it? I don't believe you can't drive, not in this hick town in the middle of no where. You're driving. *Now.*"

Holly stumbled around to the driver's side and threw open the door as Maryanne opened the passenger side. She slid into the passenger seat, and Barry pressed up behind her.

His body touching hers made her want to throw up, and she breathed deeply and slowly. Then she nearly gagged as she smelled his cheap cologne.

"Holly, start the car and roll down the windows. Quick, I'm going to be sick."

Maryanne groaned, rubbing her stomach as she tried to squeeze herself away from him.

Holly pushed the button to start it, then turned on the air and rolled down the windows. She fiddled with the seat, moving it forward and adjusting the mirrors.

"For crying out loud, put it in reverse and go already," Barry yelled in the small space, making both Maryanne and Holly jump. "You know the barn I'm talking about?"

Holly nodded as she slowly backed up and crept through the parking lot. When they finally got on the highway, she still kept the car at miles per hour. The further they went from town, the higher Maryanne's anxiety climbed.

Barry began to rant and just as they pulled up to the barn, Holly hit a bump and squealed. Maryanne's anxiety spiked, and she turned slightly and threw up all over Barry's legs and shirt.

Holly slammed on the brakes and put it in park as Barry started yelling. "Holy fuck! You little bitch. You did that on purpose."

He threw open his door and pulled Maryanne out by an arm. She fell on the ground, and Holly cried out, jumping out of the car and rushing around to her side.

Holly helped her sit up. "Maryanne, are you okay?"

Maryanne saw spots as her vision swam. Looking down at her skirt twisted up around her knees, she pulled on Holly's arm to bring her closer.

She whispered, "Holly, my water broke."

Holly gasped, and fear raced up her spine as Barry paced beside them, screaming for them to get up and get in the barn.

Landry caught Gunner's eye as they finished their song. He tapped his watch, and Gunner glanced at his own. It was nine o'clock. Nerves raced through his veins, making him bounce at the microphone.

Glancing at her seat, he saw it was still empty. She hadn't come back from the bathroom yet. He saw Cindy shrug as she was looking around.

So much for his grand speech, but maybe he could still salvage this. "Cindy, can you record this?"

At her nod, he cleared his throat.

"All right, our last song of the night is gonna be *America the Beautiful*. But before we start, I just want to say that I'm damn glad to be here tonight. Not just in the USA celebrating our freedom, but I'm glad to be here with my wife, whom I love more than life itself."

He took a deep breath as the crowd murmured.

"We're going to sing *America the Beautiful*, but to me, nothing is more beautiful than my wife. She's the peanut butter to my jelly, the banana to my pudding, and the cookies to my milk. She makes life worth living. She's the fun balance to my serious nature and definitely makes me a better man. Not sure where she's at right now, but hopefully she hears this and joins me as we watch the fireworks right after this song."

Landry led them into the song, and he sang, scanning the crowd. When the last note of the song died down, Andy with Mandy in his arms ran around the edge of the crowd toward them.

Frowning, he felt his stomach bottom out. The man didn't run in public because of his prosthetic leg, and for him to run with his daughter? Something was up.

He hopped down from the stage and met him at the chairs where Cindy had her boys. Andy breathed deeply and set Mandy down, who jumped over to Owen and grabbed his hand as the fireworks began. The kids pointed at the sky as they popped overhead.

But Andy grabbed Gunner tight on the shoulder and said over the noise, "He's got Maryanne and Holly."

Gunner felt his face flush as his blood rushed to his head. Fire ran through his veins now, as his stomach flipped.

"Who? I thought they went to the bathroom."

Andy nodded, waving at his brothers to come down from the stage. "I don't know who it was. He had dark hair in a man bun, a dark t-shirt, and ripped jeans. But he had them at gunpoint and forced them into the parking lot."

"What? Why didn't you—"

"I had Mandy!" Andy shouted, squaring up to Gunner and pushing him in the chest.

Gunner stepped back and ran a hand over his face as his brothers crowded around. Cindy waved her phone, having hovered behind Andy.

"I texted Kendall. He's on his way. Gunner, who would do this?"

Gunner's vision swam as he lost feeling in his legs. Landry caught him under one arm and Andy caught the other. Hauling him up, he locked his knees and opened and closed his mouth. His entire body went numb as he jumped into action.

He pulled up his phone and looked at the tracking app. "Her phone is—is on our land. At Mom and Dad's?"

He showed it to Andy, who frowned before his eyes widened.

Landry looked over his shoulder. "That's the barn."

Kendall and Nick came up, and Andy filled them in.

Gunner reached for his hip radio and called Joey and Garrett and the two other deputies as he strode to the back of the crowd and the parking lot. The rest of the guys followed him, even Zarrel meeting up with them, and they murmured together behind him.

"Come in, all deputies. Come in, all deputies."

The radio crackled when Joey replied. "Go ahead, Sheriff."

His throat threatened to close, and he shook himself as he spoke into the radio. "Maryanne and Holly have been kidnapped by a—"

"A black BMW," Andy cut in.

Gunner felt his legs threaten to give out again because there wasn't any doubt in his mind now. He cleared his throat and grabbed onto hood of his SUV.

"It's her ex, Barry," he gasped into the radio, his hand shaking.

Garrett's voice came through the other end. "What? That guy in the BMW that we busted back in December?"

"The one that was sent to Colorado?" Joey asked.

"Wait, isn't that where you went in February and eloped?" Zarrel asked.

Gunner raised his hands and barked into the radio. "Quiet. Barry, whose real name is Bruce, is Maryanne's ex-boyfriend. He was here trying to expand a drug ring, which we busted. I don't know why he's out of jail, but we know he's armed and holding them at gunpoint at the Williams' sale barn."

Andy looked at Kendall and scowled. "He made Holly drive."

Silence reigned as they processed that. Everyone knew Holly wouldn't drive willingly. Gunner felt the fear rise in his throat and checked the app again.

"I'll explain on the way. We have to go. Now."

He threw open the door to his truck and started it, his mind not even registering that he had more guys in this SUV than he had seatbelts for. Another vehicle pulled out behind them as Andy's phone rang, and he answered it.

Gunner reached for the radio as he drove.

"Maryanne's phone is showing at the sale barn at Mom and Dad's. Everyone in this truck is deputized. We have to protect the girls. Joey, go back to the station and find out why this guy's out of jail. Garrett, I need you and the other two newbies to make sure all these people get home without a problem."

Gunner felt like he couldn't get enough air in his lungs, as his chest was caving in.

Kendall held his phone up from the backseat, and Landry spoke from the other line. "We're right behind you, bro. What's the plan?"

Gunner gripped the steering wheel, his knuckles turning white.

"The rest of us are going to grab whatever firearms we can find and meet at Mom and Dad's house in fifteen minutes. Then we're going to surround the barn."

"Gunner, it takes fifteen minutes to get out of town. We need time to run home and grab our guns." Nick, the former Marine and fellow poker buddy, said through the phone.

Gunner shook his head.

"No, fifteen minutes is all you get. Get out to Mom and Dad's. If you're late, make sure you turn off your headlights as you go out there. We don't want to tip them off. Stop at the bottom of the hill, about a half mile out. Then walk or run the rest of the way. Do not go anywhere alone. If you make it to the house and no one's there, wait for someone to join you. Does everyone understand?"

Cindy's voice rang out through Andy's phone. "Gunner, are they—"

"Going to be fine. I won't let anything happen to her, Cindy. Take the kids to Andy's aunt and uncle, then find your mom and go to the station with Joey. I'll be updating him on the radio."

He exited town and picked up speed, quickly breaking the speed limit to his parents' house.

A bunch of big ex-military guys peeling down Main Street while fireworks went off overhead probably didn't send the best message, but frankly, he didn't give a fuck. He'd do anything, break every law he needed to, to keep Maryanne safe.

Chapter Fifty-Three

Gunner left his mom and dad's house and hopped back into his truck to drive to the barn. He tossed a pair of his dad's gloves at Zarrel in the passenger seat.

"Zarrel, you're gonna have to stay with me the whole time. You're a felon, and I've knowingly armed you. If anything happens, I need you to not get caught up in it."

Zarrel snorted as he leaned forward in anticipation.

"I'll gladly go back to prison if I get to kill the little motherfucker who touched Maryanne. But if you don't feel comfortable arming me, that's alright. I'm pretty good with my fists."

Gunner shook his head, and his conscience didn't even argue with him. He needed all the manpower he could get. "Don't care at the moment, Zarrel. I just need Maryanne to be safe."

"And Holly," Kendall growled from the back seat.

Gunner nodded as he threw his truck into park and turned off the engine. He didn't close the door when he hopped out before he started jogging up the road.

Andy, Kendall, and Zarrel got out of the truck as Landry, Hunter, Nick, and Parker got out of the vehicle behind him. He heard guns click as safeties were checked before footsteps shuffled over the grass. It was eerily quiet, with only the cicadas chirping in the light breeze.

When he caught sight of the barn, he slowed to a walk, careful of his footsteps making noise in the darkness. He crept up behind the car and texted Joey the license plate number as the other guys came up behind him.

He motioned for three to go left and three to go right. Then motioned for Zarrel to stay flanking him.

The others crouched away, stepping silently in the grass to either side of the barn. They'd cover the other exits, but he and Zarrel bee-lined it for the swinging, open door to the barn. It banged against the wall in the wind, each sound making his heart jump.

He timed it so that he slipped inside in between gusts and immediately slid along the wall to the left. Zarrel followed, a dark shadow in the dim interior.

He let his eyes adjust to the lack of moonlight, but he heard voices in the middle of the sale barn floor. It was just hay storage this time of year; the ranch hands had barely filled up the left side. In front of him was an open space but a light shone from in front of the hay.

As he crept closer along the side of the hay, he saw figures crouched on the other side of a lantern. A low moan sounded through the building, sending a shiver of dread up his spine.

He recognized that moan, although it wasn't from pleasure. It was from pain. The bastard had already hurt Maryanne. His vision saw red, and he would have jumped up and raced to her side if it weren't for Zarrel wrapping his meaty arm around his chest and holding him still.

"Listen," he whispered in his ear.

Gunner stilled, and as he breathed, another voice rose.

"I don't fucking care," Barry said. "We're going to call your little baby daddy and get him out here. Then when he gets here, you'll all die a fiery death."

Maryanne gasped and ground out, "How are you going to start the fire, Barry? Your plan is flawed. You don't even know how to light a fireplace, or have you forgotten that I was always the one who did that?"

Gunner smiled. Atta girl! She was goading him. Not the wisest choice, but it kept Barry talking.

Zarrel released him and pointed to the hay, whispering, "I'm going up."

Gunner nodded. Now that he could hear Maryanne, he didn't care where Zarrel went. She was alive, and she was going to stay that way.

He crept along the edge of the hay and tucked his head around the corner. Grinding his teeth, he saw that Maryanne was leaning up against the hay, the lantern to her left.

Holly was holding Maryanne in her arms, his girl leaning back into Holly, hands on her stomach as it rolled.

Maryanne gripped Holly's knees, one on either side of her. Barry was pacing back and forth in front, waving a gun toward them as he murmured.

Gunner didn't have a clear shot. But maybe if he could draw him away... He reached into his pocket and pulled out a coin. Tossing it hard, it landed on the other side of the barn to his right.

The sound rang out over Barry's muttering, making him spin. "What's that?"

Maryanne grunted. "Prolly some rats. You know how

these old barns are. Oh hey, why don't you go join them, considering you're a rat too."

Barry swung back and pointed the gun at her. Gunner's veins ran cold, and he couldn't feel his feet. Shit. That hadn't worked.

"Shut up, bitch. I don't know how old barns are. I'm a city boy, remember? And I was living just fine with cash to spare until you ruined it. Ruined it!" Barry screamed, hand shaking in the light.

Maryanne gasped as she gripped Holly's knees so hard Holly winced. "Where'd the cash come from, Barry?"

"Where else? Juan Dog finally trusted me enough to let me open up the Dallas operation. I was head boss down here, and you fucking ruined it."

The waving gun made Gunner's stomach drop, so he grabbed another coin and threw it. When Barry looked over, he threw another, then another.

The next one had him stepping away from the girls and toward Gunner. Just a few more feet, and then he'd be clear... When Barry had stepped forward five or six feet, Gunner saw Zarrel in his peripheral vision. Zarrel leapt from the hay just as Gunner rushed his knees.

The three of them stumbled and tumbled to the ground. A loud bang echoed through the room as Gunner felt a sharp, searing pain in his leg. He jerked in pain, his own gun flew out of his hand and disappeared into the chaos of flailing limbs. Zarrel pinned Barry down with surprising strength.

Panicked yells and shouts filled the air as doors burst open, but Gunner's sole focus was on retrieving the gun from Barry's grasp, twisting it away from the girls. He lunged for it, ignoring the throbbing pain in his leg, and successfully wrestled it away from creepy Barry.

Zarrel wrestled Barry's other wrist under his knee and started punching him in the face. Gunner slammed Barry's gun hand to the concrete, making the man grunt.

Again and again he slammed it, almost in time with Zarrel's punches to the face.

Three hits and the gun finally went slack in Barry's hand. Zarrel punched him a fourth time, before Gunner pulled out his cuffs and slapped them onto the wrist.

He grabbed Zarrel by the collar to stop him from punching him a fifth time, growling, "Turn him over. The cuffs!"

Zarrel raised up and slammed Barry into the ground face first. Barry grunted as his hands were pulled behind him, and Gunner snapped the cuff on his other wrist.

Zarrel rolled over, flopping onto the ground as he sucked in a deep breath. Gunner turned Barry around and looked at the man's bloody face. His heart raced with adrenaline, but one thing was repeated in his mind until he couldn't ignore the call of it.

He reared back and punched Barry. Damn, that felt good. Cuffed or not, the bastard deserved it.

"That's for kidnapping," he ground out before throwing another punch.

"That's for attempted murder."

Three. "That's for fucking with my wife."

Four. "That's for threatening my baby."

He threw a fifth one before he heard Maryanne moan behind him, pulling him back from the red haze that clouded his vision.

"Maryanne," he gasped, throwing the now unconscious man to the ground and stumbling over to her.

Fire shot through his thigh, making him stumble the last

few feet to her side. Kendall knelt in front of her, her skirt shoved up.

Gunner's mind couldn't process what was happening until Kendall said, "Holy shit. Okay, Maryanne, you're crowning. You have to push. Someone call the ambulance!"

"Fuck. The baby's coming? Now?" Gunner screeched.

Yes, that sound actually came out of his mouth. He glanced around as Landry leaned over the unconscious Barry, pressing his shirt to the man's stomach, and Parker pulled out his phone to call.

Zarrel sat, elbows on his knees, as he breathed deeply.

Glancing up, he met Gunner's wide eyes. "It's alright, man. You can do this. She can, and so can you. Come on, get your head in the game."

Gunner nodded absently, then turned to Maryanne. Holly was in the coaching position they'd practiced at Lamaze class.

Maryanne's eyes were closed. Sweat coated her skin, plastering her black hair to her forehead. He pushed it out of her face and ran his hand down her arm to where she gripped Holly's knees. He laid his hand on hers and opened and closed his mouth.

What did he say? How did he help?

Kendall put his hand on her bare stomach, her tank top was pulled up, showing her belly but still covering her breasts. "All right, now push. Come on, Maryanne."

Her skirt was around her waist, covering her below, but when Gunner glanced down and saw the head, he felt his legs give out. Thank God he was on his knees or he would have fallen over.

Zarrel grabbed him from behind and propped him up. "Easy now." Zarrel's deep voice echoed in the darkness as Maryanne sagged back into Holly.

"Good job, Maryanne. A few more, and she'll be here. Take a breather until the next contraction, while I check her positioning." Kendall rubbed his hand along her stomach, feeling the placement.

Maryanne's eyes popped open as she looked around wildly. "Who—who's here?"

Gunner caught her eyes and pushed the hair from her forehead.

"Look at me, M. It's okay, I'm here. Holly and Kendall, Zarrel and Andy. Nick, Landry, and Parker have Barry, so don't worry about him. Just focus on me and the baby, M. That's it, breathe, just like we rehearsed."

She moaned, her face twisting in pain that made his own body ache with the need to take it away.

"Here's another one," Kendall said. "Now push."

Maryanne pushed three more times but wasn't making progress. Her lips pinched, panting, as her hands trembled on Holly's legs.

Glancing over his shoulder, Gunner yelled, "Parker? How far out is the ambulance?"

"Five minutes, Gunner!"

He turned back to Maryanne. She was so beautiful and strong. "You can do this, M. You're a wonderful mom, and she can't wait to meet you. You're almost there," he crooned softly.

She met his gaze as tears started falling from her big brown eyes.

"Gunner, it hurts. It hurts so fucking baa—" She cut off on a scream as she started to push again.

Kendall shouted over her, "Gunner, pull back on her thigh. Zarrel, come around and pull back on her other one. Come on, Maryanne. This is it, breathe and bear down."

Zarrel scrambled around, and they both pulled her thighs back toward her hips as she screamed louder. The sound of sirens mingled with her screams as her stomach flexed. Kendall caught the baby, tucking her to his stomach before she slipped to the floor.

Gunner watched as he rolled her into the bottom of his shirt, then glanced back at Maryanne.

Her eyes were closed, her face was pale. "Maryanne? You did it, sweetheart. You did it. She's here."

His voice was soft, echoing the wonder that spread through his limbs. He pushed the hair out of her face again as she opened her eyes and blinked away tears. Her wild gaze looked down and saw their baby girl. Kendall held her, using the edge of his shirt to clean out her nose and mouth.

A cry rang out over the sound of sirens, and it was so beautiful, it brought tears to his eyes.

Maryanne sobbed at the sound, and Kendall leaned forward to place the baby on Maryanne's chest. Gunner folded up the edge of her tank top to cover the baby as two more t-shirts fell onto Kendall's shoulders.

Gunner glanced back to see that Nick, Parker, and Hunter had all taken their shirts off and offered them for clean-up while still keeping an eye on Barry instead of Maryanne's spread thighs.

Andy was standing near Holly and Zarrel by Maryanne's shoulder, his phone out to presumably take pictures, although his ashen face showed that he'd never attended a birth before.

The paramedics came in as Kendall said, "Alright, Maryanne. One more push, and we'll get the after birth. Do you feel that contraction coming? Are you ready?"

Maryanne glanced at their baby, wrapping one arm

around her and reaching for Gunner's hand with the other. She squeezed as she yelled, bearing down and pushing the rest out. The paramedics crouched around, and Kendall ordered them to bring different things.

Chapter Fifty-Four

Maryanne finally relaxed, letting go of his hand as he kissed her forehead. "God, Maryanne. You're so strong, and brave and amazing. I'm so proud of you. You brought our baby girl into this world, and she's perfect. Look at her!"

Tears still streamed down her cheeks as she looked at their baby. The cries became louder, and Holly pointed. "Look, she's rooting already. That means she's hungry. Do you want to try feeding her?"

Maryanne nodded, then slipped her breast out of her tank top. Maryanne turned the baby's head, and she latched on, making Maryanne gasp.

"Is it okay? Does it hurt?" Gunner was in awe that she could provide for the baby like that.

Maryanne giggled, the sound shooting straight through his heart to his soul and telling him she was going to be okay. His legs gave out, and he sat down on his butt, hard. He might have bruised his tail bone, but his entire body seemed to go numb as he started to shake.

"God, Maryanne. If Barry had—"

"He didn't."

"I almost lost you." Fury set in at the realization that she could've been taken from him for good.

She glanced over at Gunner and took his hand, anchoring him like a lifeline. "But you found me, just like I knew you would. And this time, he's going to jail for life. I don't care what I have to do, who I have to talk to, or how many testimonies I have to give."

"Oh yeah, he's definitely going to jail."

Zarrel cleared his throat as Joey came in. "Um, Gunner, Joey's here. What do you want to tell him?"

Gunner shook his head and glanced over his shoulder. "Fuck. Okay, tell him I'll be right there. Say nothing else though, because I have to do something first."

Zarrel lumbered to his feet and walked over to the officer, a paramedic, and the rest of the guys who stood around Barry.

Looking back at Maryanne, he sucked in a breath. It had to be now.

"Maryanne, I fucking love you."

Crap. That wasn't how he wanted to say it, but he got her attention. Her head swiveled to him, her eyes bulging out in the light, her mouth forming a silent *O*.

The dam had broken, and the words flowed out.

"I've loved you all my life. I loved you when I saved you at the pool. I loved you when I kissed you in this barn back in high school. I loved you in Kendall's pantry when you sassed me. I loved you on Halloween. I even loved you through the whiskey cake incident. I loved when you stood up for me at the debates. I loved seeing you light up in Colorado at our wedding. I love seeing your face first thing in the morning."

The Sheriff Gets His Girl

He paused for a breath and wiped a tear from her cheek with a shaky hand.

"I love your bear claws, your hair changes, and your quirky style. I love that you wear lipstick every fucking day because it makes me want to smudge it with my dick. I love how talented you are, how compassionate and caring, and I'm so fucking proud of you for bringing our baby girl into this world. No one else can do what you do, M. You're the only one who has my heart, mind, body, and soul. It's always been yours, even if I haven't said it."

Tears were pouring out of her eyes now, mingling with the sweat as her lips trembled. Paramedics swarmed as they slid a board under her to lift her onto the gurney. She reached out for his hand as they raised her up, her eyes wide in panic until she was settled.

She met his eyes, her smile wide and wobbly with emotions. "I love you too. I always have and always will. Maybe we can tell each other that, though? Maybe every day?"

He grinned as he stood, leaning over the gurney and kissing her deeply. The paramedic cleared his throat, and Gunner pulled away. "You got it, little mama. I'm going to touch base with Joey, but I'll ride to the hospital with you, okay? Let them hook you up and check her over."

Maryanne grabbed his arm as he started to pull away. "Wait, what are we going to name her?"

Gunner turned and reached out a finger to trace along his daughter's pink cheek. She was still sucking away, making him smile. "Looks like she has my appetite, huh? How about Constance? Because my love for you is as constant as the stars above?"

Maryanne smiled a watery smile and nodded. "Constance Star Williams. Connie for short."

He grinned and glanced back at his daughter. He grazed her tiny hand, and she wrapped hers around his finger. It wasn't a figure of speech. He knew this baby girl would have him wrapped around her finger physically, emotionally, and mentally her entire life.

His heart burst with love as he whispered, "Welcome to the family, Connie."

A lone tear fell down his cheek, and he leaned back to wipe it off. Maryanne chuckled at his macho tough guy act as the paramedics wheeled her out of the barn to the ambulance.

He limped over to Joey, hovering near Barry who was also cuffed to a gurney. "Joey, I didn't read him his rights. Did you?"

Joey nodded with a frown. "Yeah, that's what Zarrel said. I took care of it, not that it matters. They say it's not looking good."

Gunner frowned. "What do you mean?"

"He has severe head trauma, plus a gunshot wound to the stomach. They're suspecting internal bleeding, and his head is already swelling, so they're thinking brain trauma too. It'll take a while to see if he pulls through. You'll need to make a statement. Everyone here will need to."

Gunner nodded, meeting Zarrel's eye. "Alright, can you bring the paperwork to the hospital? I'm going to ride in the ambulance with Maryanne."

"Sure thing, boss." Joey turned back to Gunner's brothers and friends to take their statements.

"Um, Joey, can you make sure they get Barry Bruce loaded up? Double check those cuffs and make sure they do a drug test."

Gunner nodded as the second paramedic team started to wheel him out. Joey turned on his heel to follow.

When the barn was empty of everyone except Holly and the guys he'd brought with him, Gunner turned to them and stared into their eyes one by one.

Except for Holly, who was just staring at Landry's bare chest, even though several of the guys were now shirtless.

He shrugged, then said quietly, "In your statements, make sure you say that Zarrel was near the door and ran straight to Maryanne. He was not involved with the shooting or wrestling Barry Bruce to the ground. Got it?"

Everyone nodded, eyes flicking from Gunner to Zarrel and back again.

"I'll not forget this, guys. I—If anything had happened to them..." He cleared his throat and straightened his back. "I won't forget this. Thank you."

Several of the guys shifted on their feet, but Kendall nodded at Gunner. "When you get in the ambulance, have them look at that gunshot wound you got there."

Gunner looked down, surprised to see his jeans darkened, wet and sticky. No wonder he was limping and his leg ached.

Gunner nodded, turning to Zarrel. "Walk with me to the ambulance?"

The two walked off as the group talked quietly behind them, Zarrel throwing an arm under Gunner's shoulder to help him walk. Gunner sucked in a breath as Zarrel asked quietly, "Do you think I shot him in the stomach?"

Gunner shook his head. "Not really sure. It could have been me since my gun was fired. Or even his own gun that went off."

"I keep getting in trouble around here. First the cake, and now this. If you want me to go back to Dallas, just say the word, Gunner. I respect you enough to do it, if you think it's best."

They stopped at the end of the ambulance. The doors open, he could see Maryanne inside, the baby now sucking on the other side. Smiling, he turned to Zarrel.

"Nah, that would be terrible. I wouldn't be able to keep you out of trouble if you did that. Besides, baby Connie needs her godfather to stay in town."

Zarrel's big brown eyes bulged as his jaw went slack. "Seriously?"

Gunner grinned and leaned forward to hug him.

"Yep, will you take my truck and make sure everyone gets back home safely? The gun you had should only have my prints on it, since you wore the gloves. Don't worry, Zarrel. It'll all work out."

He handed over his keys and slapped Zarrel on the back, then hauled himself up into the ambulance.

Chapter Fifty-Five

Two days sleeping in a hospital chair had left Gunner with a serious crick in his neck. He stretched as Connie cried in the corner bassinet.

He limped to her, picking her up and cradling her to his chest. Maryanne didn't even stir as he slipped onto the bed beside her, opened her hospital gown, and settled their baby girl on her chest.

He smiled, his little champ chowing down and cutting off her soft cries. The motion caused Maryanne to twitch, then her head lolled to the side as she pulled her arm up to hold Connie.

His heart was so full of love and peace. After the chaos of the past few days, he was ready to be discharged and go home.

The door opened, and Joey's head popped inside. Gunner waved him away, then slid off the bed, propping pillows around them. Maryanne opened her eyes as the bed moved, adjusting Connie as he kissed her forehead.

When he stepped into the hallway, Joey frowned as he

rubbed his forehead. The man deserved a raise, with how he'd stepped up the past few days around the station.

"What's up?"

Joey rubbed his forehead and started spewing out issues with paperwork, updates on Barry Bruce's medical status, and what the Colorado force was saying.

"There's an issue with the paperwork that I need your help on. Also, I finally found out that he was released early because of a plea deal, not because the case was thrown out. He ratted out some big drug lord that he worked for in exchange for an early release."

Gunner shoved his hands in his pockets and rocked back on his heels as Kendall joined them. "That's what Maryanne said he was going on about. Some guy named Juan Dog?"

Joey nodded as they discussed the case in Colorado.

Gunner crossed his arms and shifted his weight to his uninjured leg. "Why didn't I get any updates on his status?"

Joey shoved his hands in his pockets. "They were sending the fucking emails to Ray, but he hasn't touched shit since the week after the election. And when they'd call, dispatch told them to hold and they'd get you, but they didn't want to talk to you. They wanted to talk to Ray. I don't think they understood that you are sheriff now, and he retired. Pretty sure I made a few enemies from chewing out those people on the phone."

Gunner sighed as Kendall joined them in the hallway. "I appreciate you, Joey. Is there an update on Barry Bruce?"

The pressure on his chest increased when Kendall nodded. "Swelling on the brain isn't going down, and he hasn't regained consciousness. It's a waiting game at this point."

Joey swore under his breath, then ran his fingers

through his hair. He paced as he started ranting on all the procedures that needed to be done with both Colorado and Texas.

Gunner chuckled, causing Joey to halt mid-sentence and mid-step, his leg raised in the air as he stared at Gunner with wide eyes. Two years ago, he was just like Joey, sticking to every rule and high-strung over every detail. Joey wasn't used to this relaxed side of him, the side that laughed with hands in pockets.

It was a different reaction than Ray would've had too, but this was the type of sheriff Gunner wanted to be. Although it wasn't off to a great start, he wanted to lead with wisdom, laughter, and peace.

"It's not funny, Gunner," Joey scowled.

Gunner nodded and pulled out his phone. "I know, I wasn't laughing about that. Just kind of hit me how different this year is from last year. Give me an hour to get someone to come and sit with Maryanne. Then I'll come by the station for a while before they discharge her, alright?"

Joey sighed in relief and nodded before turning to walk back down the hall.

Kendall tipped his head. "You look like shit. Have you even showered since coming to the hospital?"

Gunner shrugged, shifting to stand on his good leg.

Kendall noticed, arching his brow. "How's the leg?"

"Good. Got the bullet dug out. They're still running it through the lab to see if it was Barry's gun or one of our own that misfired in the shuffle."

Gunner hoped it was Barry's because he wanted the man to go away for life. He squared his jaw as he thought of all the things he needed to do for the next few hours at work. "Do you know when they'll be discharged?"

Kendall looked at his watch. He'd had the overnight

shift and was about to get off work. "I'll put in the order before I leave but they won't release her and do all the paperwork until after lunch."

Gunner nodded. "Okay, I'm going to run to work and get some stuff sorted out with the case. Then I'll come back to take them home. Let me know if anything changes."

He texted his mother-in-law but as Kendall walked off, he turned to say, "And take a shower before you come back, you hobo."

Gunner chuckled as he came back into the hospital room, the sound drawing Maryanne's eyes. His were soft, shining in the dim light from the machines.

"Good morning, sweetheart." He leaned down to kiss her forehead again.

She sighed wistfully. "We'll get to go home today, right?"

Her own bed was calling her name, and her hands itched to bake something. Even when she'd been on bed rest after the wreck in December, she'd not sat in the bed for two days straight.

He nodded with a smile that sent shivers up her spine. "Yeah, this afternoon. I've called your mom to come sit with you for a while because I need to run into work, okay? Will you be all right for a few hours?"

She nodded, knowing he wouldn't leave her side unless he had to. Barry had caused so many problems, and Gunner was her hero to sort through all of them.

Holly pushed open the door with her hip, looking over the top of an enormous basket that she struggled not to drop.

Gunner hopped to her side, taking it from her arms. Then he set it on the corner of the counter.

Maryanne smiled as Gunner rubbed the back of his neck, his head tilted and mouth frowning.

Holly laughed softly at his confusion. "It's a diaper cake. You unroll them before you use them."

"Oh." He scratched his head, and Holly and Maryanne looked at each other before bursting into laughter.

It startled Connie, making her jump and cry. Maryanne switched sides, soothing her and rocking until she latched onto the other boob. Gunner's eyes stroked her skin; she could feel his stare as she slowly covered up the first breast. She caught his predatory gaze through her lashes.

He stalked to the bed and leaned down, devouring her mouth.

She moaned when he broke the kiss, then he kissed Connie before whispering, "I'm going to head out now, if that's alright? Holly will you stay with her until Margarita comes?"

Holly nodded, moving out of the way as Gunner turned and left.

"Whew, that was hot." Holly fanned her face and making Maryanne chuckle as she laid her head back against the pillow.

A week later, Maryanne talked to Zarrel on her tablet as he worked at the bakery. Her mom had been covering the two days a week that Zarrel took off, but today wasn't one of those days.

They had two birthday parties this weekend that needed a set of cupcakes and a birthday cake. She was explaining the order when the front door bell rang.

"Zarrel, I gotta go. Someone's here. I'll check back in later."

She hung up, walking to the front door to look through the peep hole before opening it. Holly, Lola, Cindy, and half a dozen other girls stood on her door step.

"What's this?" Maryanne stepped aside to let them in.

They placed platters and casseroles on her dining table as Cindy hugged her.

"It's the church meal train. We have casseroles to freeze. I convinced everyone to drop off at the church yesterday so we could bring them all by at once. Is that okay?"

Maryanne grinned. "Yeah, that's fine. How was girl's yoga night this week?"

They talked about it, then about the showdown at the barn. It was the talk of the town, but most had respected her need for privacy this week.

She hadn't had many visitors until now, but when they asked, she told the story of how Gunner had leapt onto her evil ex-boyfriend and tackled him. Gunner had told her of the plan to keep Zarrel out of it, and she agreed.

It melted her heart to know that Gunner was okay with doing the right thing, even if it wasn't legal. He'd grown a lot over the past year. Hell, so had she, since she was now a mother.

Just then, Connie started to cry. Holly jumped up and ran into her bedroom. Holly had been the only one who'd come over every single day since they'd been released from the hospital. The awkwardness between them was gone, and now Holly was officially the godmother and took her role seriously.

Holly was still seeing Tasha for grief counseling, though. She came back out with the baby, crooning to her as the other ladies peered over her shoulder.

The door burst open, and Gunner slammed the door

The Sheriff Gets His Girl

behind him. He'd taken two steps inside before he realized they had company.

The thunderous expression on his face dropped, and he smiled his polite smile as he nodded at everyone. Maryanne stood and walked to him, wrapping her arms around his waist. His stiff posture seemed to relax as he bent and wrapped her into a hug.

"You okay?"

He nodded as he breathed into her neck. With a shaky breath, he looked around. "Holly, we'll be right back. I need to steal my wife for a minute."

Cindy grinned and Lola winked as the group talked over the baby. Holly didn't even look up at them.

He led her into the kitchen, where he grabbed a bottle of water and chugged half of it. When he wiped his mouth, he leaned against the counter and met her eyes.

"Yeah, so Barry died."

Maryanne gasped, her hands shooting up to her mouth. She couldn't believe he was gone. She'd been having nightmares about the gun, him raving and pacing.

"The bullet to the stomach came from my gun. Ballistics came back today, and the bullet that went through my leg was from his gun. But with the death, I'm being placed on leave while the state investigates."

She walked to him and wrapped her arms around his waist. He squeezed her, and they breathed together, arms wrapped around each other, and she soaked up the cedar and pine, both processing what this meant for their future. They'd talked about the various outcomes that could happen over the past week of being home.

"How long will it take for the investigation to wrap up?"

"Not sure. Could be a few days or a few weeks."

Drawing strength from each other, relying on each

other, was a skill they were still working on. It was getting a little easier each day.

She leaned back and smiled up at him.

"Well, this is a blessing, then. We don't have to worry about Barry anymore, and now you get to be home with Connie and I for a while. So yay?"

Her words had the desired effect because Gunner smiled, some of the tension around his mouth releasing. She knew the guilt Gunner would have over Barry's death, regardless of who was responsible or that he deserved it. He already struggled with the guilt over his brother, Chase.

"Let go of what you can't control, G. We're both safe with a wonderful daughter, and I love you for being our hero. You did what you had to do, and it's going to be okay. We'll count you being home as a stay-cation."

He shuddered a breath, tucking his head into her neck as he said, "I know, I love you too. The next few weeks are going to be hard, though."

She snuggled into his chest. "Alright, so a hard stay-cation, but that's okay too. It's not like we've done anything the easy way. Why start now?"

She winked at him when she leaned back, which made his shoulders fall as he smiled.

Leaning up on tiptoes, she pecked his lips, teasing him and drawing him out. From the living room, they heard the group of women coo over something Connie did.

Maryanne broke the kiss, grinning and catching his eyes. They weren't as haunted as they'd been when he walked in. Now they twinkled in the light as he wrapped his arm around her waist and turned to talk to their guests with a smile on his face.

Side by side, they faced their future together.

Next in the Crimson Creek Series

vinci-books.com/songwriter-gets-his-girl

**One dream of motherhood, one chance at stardom—
when the music stops, who will be left standing?**

Widowed Holly' ready for motherhood—no man required. But when handyman Landry offers a more tempting solution, friendship ignites into passion. When fame calls him away, will he choose his dreams or the family he's always wanted?

Turn the page for a free preview…

The Songwriter Gets His Girl: Prologue

I'd say it's the perfect day, but it fades to gray without your face. In the sunlight, can't you see? It's not the same without you here with me.
undefined.

Five years ago

"Who knew Tennessee was so beautiful?" Landry Williams glanced out the window of his childhood best friend's truck. The trees were turning colors, and the sun reflected oranges and reds as it began to set. There was a nip in the air that didn't happen in Texas this early in fall, and he was damn glad to get out of the state.

"Getting sentimental in your old age?" Andy smirked, making Landry laugh.

"Twenty-four is hardly old, but if it was, what does that make you, Grandpa?"

Andy chuckled and shook his head, making Landry grin. Andy may have been a few years than him, but the two had been best friends while growing up. He was one of the few who'd left Crimson Creek that Landry kept in contact with.

"So, what made you decide to come up for the weekend?" Andy pulled away from the Nashville traffic and onto the road leading north to Fort Campbell.

"Parker has a rare weekend off from soccer at his university. His roommate, Mike, is from Nashville, so they flew up to go to some party with Mike's parents. They're apparently big names in the music business."

"You didn't want to go with them to the party?"

Landry turned from the window and grinned at Andy. "It's been almost a year since you've been home. I'd rather catch up with you. Besides, Pops would've killed me if I was this close to your base and didn't come see you. What have you been doing?"

Andy laughed. "How's your grandpa doing after losing your grandma?"

Landry shrugged and looked back out the window. "He's ok, mostly. He hasn't been alone at the shop since and is feeling smothered by Mom. He practically pushed me out the door, said he could handle all the jobs by himself this weekend."

Landry loved working with his grandpa as the town's handyman and general contractor. They stayed busy, and Landry had been working since high school to take over the business. His grandparents had semi-retired a few years ago, but his grandpa had thrown himself back into it after his grandma passed.

"I'm sorry I missed her funeral."

Landry shrugged off the tightness in his chest. "You

were deployed, dude. Don't worry about it. I hear you got a promotion too. How's that going?"

Andy talked about his last deployment and his promotion, then asked about news from their hometown.

Landry snorted. "As if your Aunt Suzie doesn't keep you updated on all the latest gossip."

But like any loyal friend, he launched into the latest drama at the church, whose family was moving out, who had moved in, and what school friends were married now.

"So, what's the plan for the weekend? What kind of trouble are we gonna cause?"

Andy turned off the highway and into Clarksville. "Pool party tonight with my Army buddies. Remember Kendall, the guy from basic training years ago? It's his house. Tomorrow, we're going fishin' and campin' at Land Between the Lakes."

He parked the truck, and they hopped out. The little house was in a small neighborhood, and vehicles already lined the street.

They walked up the sidewalk to the front porch just as the door flew open. The last of the sun's rays landed on a gorgeous, petite blond, her hair spilling in waves around her shoulders.

Her thin green sweater hung off one shoulder, her top the same forest green as her eyes. She glanced at them as she walked out the door.

Landry was mesmerized by the flecks of gold in her eyes that shone in the light, glimpses into heaven that he couldn't quite grab but wanted to reach for.

She blew a bubble with her gum and popped it right as she passed him on the stairs, her pink lips causing his cock to twitch. He turned to watch her bounce down the stairs and to a little white car.

Her hips were distracting in those skintight blue jeans. So much so that he stumbled on the stairs, his arms flinging out and catching Andy.

Andy grunted. "What the hell, man?"

"My bad. Got distracted." Landry hadn't even turned to look at Andy; he was still watching the woman get into her car and drive away.

Andy chuckled. "Yeah, I see that, but she's off limits. That's Kendall's sister."

The door opened again, drawing his attention. A tall blond shook Andy's hand, his green eyes warm and smiling.

"Andy, you made it. Perfect timing, man. Come on in. A few guys from my platoon are here. Did you invite yours?"

"You know it. This is Landry, a childhood friend. He's up visiting for the weekend. Landry, this is Kendall."

Landry stepped up to shake the man's hand. "It's nice to finally meet you. Thanks for letting me crash your party."

"Hey, the more the merrier. You just missed my sister, but the rest of the guests are inside. I'll show you around, and you can tell me about Andy and Crimson Creek. Is the town really that great?"

Landry was led inside as they talked. Music played softly on a karaoke machine in the corner. He lost track of the names of those he met and how many snacks he ate. An hour later, he was slightly tipsy when the bubble gum angel from earlier returned.

He tracked her as she drifted across the floor to her brother, who stood making cocktails at the wet bar. Landry guzzled the last of his drink and walked over for a refill, eager to meet her.

"I don't care, Holly. He's not welcome, and you shouldn't be drinking." Kendall's frown could rival Andy's scowl, and Landry wondered if they taught that expression to every Army recruit.

"Kendall, I'm twenty-one. I can drink if I want to, just like everything else. It's my life, remember? Not yours." Her voice was soft and lilting, like honey draping across his tongue and making his mouth water.

"I'm just looking out for you, you know this. It's what big brothers are for."

"Well, back off a little and let me be me. First order of business? A drink."

Landry slid his drink across the bar's countertop. "I'd like one too, while you're at it. Hello, Miss. You must be Kendall's sister?"

He held out a hand to shake and barely heard Kendall growl. Her eyes narrowed, her lips tipping on one side in a mischievous smirk.

"Well, hello to yourself. Name's Holly, but you're the only one here who will talk to me tonight. He's warned every other person away."

Their hands met, and Landry felt his tremble, not from her grip but from the electricity that ran down his arm at the contact.

He cleared his throat. "Landry. I'm a friend of Andy's from Texas, which might be why Kendall didn't warn me away. I'm not a military guy like all these fine gents."

Holly grabbed their drinks and handed his over before looping her arm in his and dragging him away from the bar and Kendall's murderous gaze. "Excellent, I'm about fed up with military guys. Tell me, Landry, what do you do if you're not military?"

"I co-own a handyman business with my grandfather. If he didn't need me so much, I would've joined the military, but it hasn't worked out that way."

She led him to the front porch where a swing sat empty in the corner. He sat and took a long drink of his beer, his mouth parched in her presence.

She pulled a leg up and turned to face him, her back to the arm of the swing, and set it to rocking softly with her other leg.

"That's very admirable of you, to stick around for him. What's he like?"

Landry opened up like never before, perhaps from the alcohol or perhaps she just had that effect on him. He didn't even talk with his mom so freely. He talked about losing his grandma last year and how his grandfather's health had declined steadily, how he'd wanted to go off to college and had a full ride music scholarship but had given it up.

"So if you could do anything in the world, what would you do?" Her eyes glowed in the soft porch lights. He could happily get lost in those eyes every day of his life.

His heart raced at the thought. Maybe she was the one. Maybe she would complete him and make life worth living, the way his grandma had made life worth living for his grandpa.

He took a drink to settle his nerves. "I'd make music that brings happiness to others. I like to make people laugh and see them have a good time. My brothers and I play on weekends at the local bar, and it's so fun. They aren't there to see us, of course, but we make them smile and help them relax after a hard week. So it's worth it to me. I don't want to play at a bar forever, but I... well, it's fun."

She tilted her head to the side. "Fun is good. My brother loses sight of that, but it helps balance all the bad that's happened."

"I'd hate to think anything bad happened to you."

Her blush made his pants a little tighter, and that coy

glance away slayed him. Her voice was soft, floating on the breeze and barely discernible.

"You're sweet, but life isn't all sunshine and rainbows."

The sadness in her eyes speared his heart, making him nearly gasp from the suddenness of it. He wanted nothing more than to see her laugh and smile and be happy. He finished his drink, then turned to face her more.

"So, what happened?"

She shook her head and glanced to the parking lot. "Mom had cancer and my aunt died in a house fire right after I graduated high school. That was when I moved in with Kendall, and he isn't the easiest to live with."

"Yeah, he seems pretty protective, but I imagine I'd be the same way if I had a sister."

She rolled her eyes. "Yeah, but I started dating an Army guy while he was deployed. Then my boyfriend deployed right before Kendall came home. But now Eric's back, and Kendall's not happy about it."

She looked out at the driveway, as if she were waiting for someone.

He frowned and looked down, picking at the label on his beer bottle. "Are you still dating him?"

She sighed and sank against the back of the swing. "I don't even know anymore. He went to the field last week, and right before he left, we had a big fight about Kendall and the meaning of family. We broke up, but he texted me earlier about how he needed to talk to me. I didn't answer."

She took a sip of her drink, and the crickets sang to them in the cool night. His heart jumped to hear she was single, but she was clearly still hung up on this other guy. He couldn't stand to see her so sad. The sadness that hung around her ate at him, driving his need to fix it, to cheer her up and change the subject.

"So I hear this is supposed to be a pool party? Is that music I hear in the backyard?"

She brightened and nodded. "Yep, pool's out back. Did you bring a swimsuit? You can borrow one of Kendall's if not."

"I brought one. It's in Andy's truck." They walked to the truck, talking about everything and nothing at once. By the time she led him to the bathroom to change, he knew her favorite food, drink, color, and preferred music. And best of all, she was smiling and laughing again.

When he shut the bathroom door and changed, he realized it hurt to be away from her. He wanted to spend the entire night with her, just talking and seeing how her mind worked.

Well, to be honest he wanted to fuck her, but that was just part of it. A knock sounded on the door.

Her face lit up when he opened it, then her mouth formed an O as her gaze drifted over his arms and across his pecs. He wasn't ripped like a bodybuilder, but being a handyman kept him in good shape. Of course, he flexed a little as he reached for the towel on the shelf by the door.

She shook her head, then sucked in a breath, pushing her breasts against the thin fabric of her hot pink bikini, visible in the see-through swim cover she wore. She'd reapplied her lipstick, and his swim trunks were not doing a good job of keeping his erection down. She popped another bubble, the pink rivaling her lipstick and swimsuit.

"Ready?" Was it just him or was her voice breathier, higher? Was that what she'd sound like when he fucked her? God, he hoped so.

He nodded, and she spun on her bare heel and led the way out the back door. The party was in full swing now, with a few dozen people lounging or swimming in the pool.

Some guy did a cannonball right as they walked past, splashing them both. Holly squealed and Landry laughed, ushering her to the end of the pool and a quieter corner of the back yard.

His hand tingled where it settled on the small of her back.

She waved to the side of the house. "Pool or hot tub?"

It was well lit, but only a few people were in the hot tub, hidden from the rowdier guys in the pool.

"Hot tub." He wasn't sure he could survive the heat combined with her next to him, but he didn't want the guys in the pool staring at her in the bikini. The urge to keep her from prying eyes and all to himself was too strong.

He climbed into the hot tub, quickly sinking down to hide his erection. She took off her swimsuit cover, and he sucked in a quick breath. She was lean and toned but not really curvy. He immediately wanted to pick her up and feel her wrap her legs around him. She was small enough to balance easily.

A tall, dark-haired soldier came up behind her. Before Landry could open his mouth to warn her or jump out of the hot tub, the man had wrapped his arm around her waist from behind. She gasped and turned around.

She squealed a laugh as he picked her up and spun her in circles before setting her down. Her bikini-clad body smashed against the man, still in most of his uniform, and he leaned down to kiss her. Landry's breath whooshed out like someone had punched him in the gut.

She pushed against him and broke the kiss. Landry gripped the edge of the hot tub, ready to leap out and punch him if he didn't let her go.

"What the hell, Eric?"

The man grabbed her hands and pleaded with her.

"Look, I'm sorry about last weekend. This was the hardest week of my life. The deployment wasn't even as bad as this week, because then I could still talk to you. But this week without you? Knowing you were mad and disappointed in me? Holly, I can't be without you again. Please forgive me."

She sighed, and he kissed her again. Landry felt like he was going to be sick. His fists clenched and sweat broke out on his forehead. What the hell was going on?

When they ended the kiss, the man hugged her tight. "Damn, that was a long week in the field. I came straight here."

"I can tell." Her laughter rang softly through the night, the voices of the others in the hot tub drowned out by her joy. "You didn't even shower, Eric."

"No time. I can always just jump in the pool." The man's lopsided grin was sickening because Landry knew that look. It was the same look his dad gave his mom and his grandpa had given his grandma.

His head spun as he looked at Holly, because she was giving the man the same love-sick look. Shit. Of course, she was taken. They might have been broken up, but her face said it all. She loved him.

And that guy was the luckiest son of a bitch at the party. She was gorgeous, sweet, kind, and sassy.

Landry's eyes landed on Kendall when he stormed outside and glanced around. Catching sight of Holly, he hustled across the yard, dodging people as he strode through with a scowl. But before he reached them, the soldier dropped to one knee. Landry and Kendall both froze, jaws dropped in surprise.

She pulled away with a gasp, but he kept hold of her hand.

"Holly, you're the reason I get up every morning and

why I try to be the best man I can be. You're my future, my joy, my entire world. I can't stand to be apart from you, not talk to you before going to bed. Will you marry me?"

Holly started jumping up and down, pulling his eyes. Landry's body reacted with a jerk and tucked away the memory to analyze later.

But right now, his heart was being drug through the fire, hardening him as once again he was left on the outside of happiness. Throughout high school, he'd been the third wheel, the geeky band nerd little brother.

After high school, he'd learned the business, taken handyman certification classes, and watched as friend after friend found their special person and got married. He'd slipped into a pattern of one-night stands and girlfriends who only lasted a few weeks before they realized he would never move out of his hometown or get a different job.

This gorgeous woman had given him hope. But it was a pipe dream meant for everyone else but him.

The man slipped a ring onto her finger and then swept her up into a hug. The whole crowd cheered. Except for Kendall, who strode forward, a fake smile on his face as he held out his hand to shake his soon to be brother-in-law.

The Songwriter Gets His Girl: Chapter One

I'd say it's the perfect day, blue skies and golden rays, but it's missing something sweet, since you're not here next to me.

April, 2 years ago

Leaning her head against the passenger side window of Kendall's car, Holly stared at the man on the ladder fixing the Diner's sign. It was spring in Crimson Creek, Texas, and the trees on Main Street were blooming beautiful lilac-colored flowers, but inside Holly was still cold and frozen.

She'd felt like that since August when her entire world fell apart. Her mind shied away from that night, and she focused on regulating her breathing like the therapist said as Kendall parked on the street and cut the engine.

"Come on, sis. Let's get some lunch. I don't have groceries, but we can eat before getting you moved in. Then I can get groceries later."

"Still living on military grub?" Even her voice sounded hollow to her own ears. Catching sight of her reflection in the window before she opened her door, she sighed at the bags under her eyes and the wan, lost expression on her face.

They reached the sidewalk, and Holly frowned as she pulled her sweater around her. The man on the ladder seemed familiar somehow. He was a typical small-town hunk with his dirty work boots, faded jeans, and a green Henley. He was beefy too, rather than tall and lanky like her brother. Covered in a fine layer of dust, he used his cordless power drill to fix something behind the sign.

As they walked closer, he glanced down. A smile broke out on his face, and she stumbled to a halt. It was the guy from the pool party, from when she'd gotten engaged to Eric years ago.

He stepped down the ladder, his movements hurried and causing his foot to miss a rung. She gasped and stepped aside as he fell the last two feet, wincing as he landed wrong.

"Whoa, you ok, Landry?" Kendall reached out a hand to grab the man by the shoulder so he wouldn't fall all the way to the ground.

His name was Landry. She'd forgotten that, in the excitement of the engagement.

Landry grimaced, putting pressure on his foot with a hiss. "Yep, just fine. Probably sprained it, but nothing an ice pack won't fix. I see you convinced her to move to town after all."

He nodded at Holly, his hazel eyes bright in the spring sun. His light hair was almost brown, with natural blond streaks any girl would kill for. She nervously touched the end of her long braid, now dyed silver. Her hair used to be more blond than his.

Kendall nodded, clapping Landry on the back. "Come inside with us and prop that ankle up. We'll get some ice on it. If you're hungry, then by the time we're done eating, you'll probably be ok to get back to work."

"Aye aye, Doc." Landry winked at her brother, who just rolled his eyes and moved the ladder out of the way on the sidewalk, laying it on its side.

Holly blinked, unsure of this side of her brother. Admittedly, they hadn't seen a lot of each other in the three years since she'd married Eric, but with his death last August, Kendall had been... nicer wasn't the right word. Deferential?

Three years ago, there's no way that Kendall would've invited anyone to eat with them. He'd always tried to keep her away from guys, which was why he and Eric hadn't gotten along very well.

She took a deep, shuttered breath as Landry hobbled closer.

"Hello again." She nodded her head and held her hand out, but the man didn't stop to shake her hand. Instead, he wrapped her in a warm hug.

She froze in his arms, her hands automatically going to his waist. Her heart stopped, her breathing stopped. Everything froze.

There hadn't been anyone to hug for a while now. Her in-laws were cruel, and all her friends had sort of just stopped coming around, not knowing how to be around her when she was so broken. This was... nice. She swallowed hard as her eyes teared up.

"I'm sorry about your husband and baby." His voice was low, raspy from emotion that only came from someone who'd experienced significant loss and was still dealing with it. It choked her up, a knot forming in her throat as she blinked back tears.

The hug lasted longer than it should have, but she didn't mind for once. It was the warmest she'd felt in months, like she was protected and nothing could hurt her again while she was in the safety of his arms.

God, she was a mess. She sucked in a ragged breath, breathing in the comforting smell of leather and mint, and whispered, "Thank you."

He chuckled awkwardly and pulled away to look down at her, his hazel eyes bright in the spring sunshine. "Sorry, I'm a hugger. And we've already met, so it's not as awkward as hugging a stranger, right?"

His grin was infectious. She didn't even realize she was smiling softly back at him until Kendall froze, looking at her with surprise. Then she caught sight of her reflection in the windows of the Diner. She shook her head, surprised by the normalcy of her smile.

Landry continued. "Don't think that your brother is the only friendly face you have in town. Anytime he's at work and you need something, just call me. You hungry? I can introduce you to everyone in the Diner."

She nodded, swallowing hard and wrapping her sweater around her again as they walked the last few feet to the Diner's door. Kendall opened it, and she stepped inside. With red and white checkered floors and red booths along the wall, it was a classic all-American place that smelled of fried food and home. A counter with bar seating right led to the kitchen. It was country cute and reminded her of her aunt with its homeliness.

She'd grown up in Dallas and then had moved to military bases with Kendall and then Eric. This small-town thing was going to be an adventure, and Kendall said she needed it. God knew she needed something to get her out of the hell loop she'd been in with Eric's parents.

She walked to the booth where Kendall now sat and slid in next to him, but he frowned. "No, you sit over there with Landry, so he can prop his foot up. I've already asked Dot to bring him a pack of ice."

Holly sighed and stood to take the opposite bench, the red leather smooth under her black yoga pants.

"Thanks for this, Kendall, but you know I'm fine, right? Nothing to worry about, although I'm not one to turn down a meal." Landry chuckled as the waitress brought a bag of ice.

"You must be the Doc's sister. It's nice to meet you, honey, and really hope you like living here. You need anything at all, just pop your pretty head in here and holler, okay?" The woman's smile was genuine, surprising Holly.

Landry laughed as he took the bag of ice and slid in beside her. "I just told her the same thing outside."

Holly just nodded back at the waitress and picked up her menu, hugging the wall and putting as much space between her and Landry as possible. His body heat was still radiating toward her like some kind of furnace.

Maybe he was a lava god or something. Except he kind of looked like the actor in that new King Arthur movie that had just come out. Maybe a Viking, but with shorter hair, his hair cropped close on the sides but longer on top. Not quite the military hair cut she was used to, but long enough to run fingers through.

"You ready to order?" the waitress asked.

Holly glanced up, shaken out of her musings to see Kendall frowning, his brow wrinkled in worry. Landry was smiling patiently, his eyes seeing too much.

They must have already ordered, and she'd missed it, lost in thought again. She turned the menu over.

"Just a loaded baked potato is fine, no bacon. Thanks."

They handed the menus over, and Kendall turned to Landry. "She's a vegetarian. Don't know how, since we grew up in Texas eating lots of barbecue."

Landry grinned and met her eyes, his mischievous and making her lean away. He was too full of joy, his face ready to burst into laughter at any moment. It must be exhausting to be that happy.

"Really? That's kind of cool, but don't you miss it? Come on, what was your favorite meat?"

She shrugged. "Don't miss it, no."

Kendall jumped in, raising his brow at her. "She used to love when I'd smoke ribs and pulled pork, but when she moved in with me after high school, she decided it was vegetarian for her. I thought it was just another little rebellion at being uprooted, but I guess I was wrong."

Holly smirked and crossed her arms. "Let me get out my phone to video that. I need it on record."

Landry laughed, the sound somehow making her feel lighter. He pulled Kendall into a conversation about the different things he'd done around town, since Kendall had only been living here about a year. They were apparently in a weekly poker game at Landry's house.

That was good because her brother had been lost after he'd retired from the Army. He hadn't been happy at the big city hospital but coming to this little town of Crimson Creek had been good for him. He seemed less stressed and more rested.

When a lull in conversation came, Holly interrupted. "Are you still doing handyman stuff, Landry?"

His eyes met hers in surprise. "You remembered?" He

cleared his throat and glanced away as pink tinged his cheeks. "Um, yeah, I own the company, now that my grandpa passed away too."

She laid a hand on his arm, feeling sparks up her arm and jerking it back. "I'm sorry for your loss. What happened?"

Landry shrugged, his eyes sad as he fiddled with the straw in his water. "Broken heart. He hung around for a few years after grandma passed, but never got his energy and drive back. Ended up having a heart attack, which took him fast."

She swallowed hard and focused on breathing evenly. Before she could reply, the waitress arrived with their food.

"Here ya go, folks. Doc was telling me last week you were a yoga instructor. Are you going to open up a yoga studio? We sure could use it. There's nothing here. No gym, no workout space, nothing. Only way people are active is if they play in the softball league or go to the city pool."

Holly's eyebrows rose in surprise. "I hadn't thought about it, to be honest, but I suppose I could."

Landry swallowed a drink of his water before saying, "There's a few places on Main Street that could easily be remodeled into a yoga studio. I'm more than happy to help you look at them and decide, analyze the renovation budget, and all that."

"That'd be great, since I wouldn't even know where to start."

The waitress nodded. "Oh, you're in good hands. Landry's the best handyman in town."

Landry laughed. "I'm the *only* one in town."

The little brunette grinned, placing her hand on his shoulder and making Holly's stomach drop. She didn't know what this feeling was, but she didn't like the waitress touching him. "Doesn't make it any less true."

Landry waggled his eyebrows. "Make sure you tell my brothers I'm the best when they come in next."

She laughed before seeing if they needed anything else and leaving them to eat their lunch.

Grab your copy…
vinci-books.com/songwriter-gets-his-girl

About the Author

Jane Poller always wanted to write romance. After years of back and forth, she finally took the plunge and never looked back. She still teaches online and homeschools her teenagers full-time. But with a commercial pilot and Army veteran for a hubby, she has a lot of free time in between his trips to write whatever stories the characters demand of her. She lives in Texas in a small town on four acres with her family of four, plus their two dogs. When she's not doing all the family things, she's reading in the hammock by the pond, writing in the treehouse, quilting and crafting, or arguing with her characters who refuse to do what she wants.

Acknowledgments

I'd like to acknowledge my editors, beta readers, and ARC readers. Your support knows no bounds. Thanks to the girls at Critique Match and those in the Romance Writers Workshops—y'all light me up. Thanks to my Clitiques too, for keeping it real. Thanks for your encouragement when I needed it most!

www.ingramcontent.com/pod-product-compliance
Ingram Content Group UK Ltd.
Pitfield, Milton Keynes, MK11 3LW, UK
UKHW040122190326
469155UK00004B/1304